AGAINST THE MACHINE: EVOLUTION

Essential Prose
Series 213

Canada Council
for the Arts

Conseil des Arts
du Canada

ONTARIO ARTS COUNCIL
CONSEIL DES ARTS DE L'ONTARIO

an Ontario government agency
un organisme du gouvernement de l'Ontario

Canadä

Guernica Editions Inc. acknowledges the support of the Canada Council
for the Arts and the Ontario Arts Council. The Ontario Arts Council
is an agency of the Government of Ontario.
We acknowledge the financial support of the Government of Canada.

AGAINST THE MACHINE: EVOLUTION

BRIAN VAN NORMAN

GUERNICA
EDITIONS
TORONTO · CHICAGO · BUFFALO ·
LANCASTER (U.K.) 2023

Guernica Founder: Antonio D'Alfonso

Michael Mirolla, editor
David Moratto, interior design
Diane Eastham, front cover design
Guernica Editions Inc.
287 Templemead Drive, Hamilton, ON L8W 2W4
2250 Military Road, Tonawanda, N.Y. 14150-6000 U.S.A.
www.guernicaeditions.com

Distributors:
Independent Publishers Group (IPG)
600 North Pulaski Road, Chicago IL 60624
University of Toronto Press Distribution (UTP)
5201 Dufferin Street, Toronto (ON), Canada M3H 5T8

First edition.
Printed in Canada.

Legal Deposit—Third Quarter
Library of Congress Catalog Card Number: 2023937401
Library and Archives Canada Cataloguing in Publication
Title: Against the machine. Evolution / Brian Van Norman.
Names: Van Norman, Brian, author.
Series: Essential prose series ; 213.
Description: Series statement: Essential prose series ; 213
Identifiers: Canadiana (print) 20230439373 | Canadiana (ebook) 20230439411
| ISBN 9781771838443 (softcover) | ISBN 9781771838450 (EPUB)
Classification: LCC PS8643.A557 A639 2023 | DDC C813/.6—dc23

Well, I dreamed I saw the silver spaceships flying
In the yellow haze of the sun
There were children crying and colors flying
All around the chosen ones
All in a dream, all in a dream
The loading had begun
Flyin' mother nature's silver seed
To a new home in the sun
Flyin' mother nature's silver seed
To a new home.
        —NEIL YOUNG

We learned from a new angle just how wondrous a thing the brain is. A one-litre, liquid-cooled, three-dimensional computer. Unbelievable processing power, unbelievably compressed, unbelievable energy efficiency, no overheating. The whole thing running on twenty-five watts—one dim light.
        —IAN McEWAN

The way we see the world shapes the way we treat it. If a mountain is a deity, not a pile of ore ... if a forest is a sacred grove, not timber; if other species are biological kin, not resources; or if the planet is our mother, not an opportunity ... then we will treat each other with greater respect. Thus is the challenge, to look at the world from a different perspective.
        —DAVID SUZUKI

AI doesn't have to be evil to destroy humanity—if AI has a goal and humanity just happens to come in the way, it will destroy humanity as a matter of course without even thinking about it, no hard feelings.
        —ELON MUSK

For Susan

ONE-MELLOR

The Greenland hypersonic wing signalled its approach. Everyone's NET lit up. Still in null gravity, passengers peered out to glimpse black space. A glance around showed several of them released from their seats floating in air. Soon the transparent *chitin/crystalline* windows would be shielded. A monotonous three toned ring repeated as lights came on while the final travellers floated back to their ubiform pods, guided by deft flight attendants, to be buckled in and await the descent to Toronto MEG. Soon, the roar of re-entry would gather around them as the ship fell back into the atmosphere.

There was a celebrity on this flight. His autograph seal had been frequently employed. He was a hard man to miss. Over two metres tall, a muscular body revealed itself even through his olive coloured econyl suit. His face and hands also caught people's attention. Unlike most MEG citizens, rebuilt and refurbished to look eternally young and flawless, Ayrian Mellor 第二 α possessed a scarred, hardened visage. It made him a kind of wonder to the others, an actual BATL Commander in their midst, a man who had killed, who had commanded his Toronto MEG Raptors from victory to victory. Everyone wanted a moment with him, fearful or not.

His digital seal imprinted their F-ROMs for all their friends to be impressed. It was a simple seal: AM 第二 α inside the Toronto MEG stylized Raptor claw. He was happy to do it. It was part of his role. *Return of wounded BATL hero.* That was the NET headline. He'd been partially rebuilt in the best of Greenland's specialized sanatoria. His physio was complete now too. Greenland itself, spa baths in the cold ancient waters beneath what was left of the glacier, was absurdly expensive. He had considered staying longer, enjoying the luxury, but it was time to return to his duties.

This hypersonic flight was an extravagance; few had ventured outside their MEG and nearly none had been in space. Yet Mellor never tired of flying for any purpose: away games, special appearances, holidays, or business trips. Despite his experience, the weightless wonder of space continued to be as extraordinary to him as it was to the tourists.

He could see now the Saturn-like halo of satellites, space stations and orbiting detritus making up the Tech Ring, girdling the Earth's equator. It masked the stars. So much of it was abandoned junk from old Omegan days. Every object just turning and turning, ribboning down in decaying orbits until Earth's atmosphere burned it to death. Millions of fragments still looping around reflecting the sun in silver and platinum, gold and copper, diamond and even the new *chitin/ crystalline*. They would all become *shooting stars* someday, their orbits decaying given enough time.

The window shields closed; the wing altered attitude for re-entry. The seats turned inward, facing each other. Unknown to most, this was a diversion making the re-entry experience more comforting. The flight attendants took their seats in the centre, looking out, appearing relaxed. Their job in these next moments was keeping passengers calm by example through the roar and burn of the atmosphere entry. In ten minutes, the shields would open again as the liner spun toward its landing, giving passengers an opportunity to see their home from above.

Ayrian Mellor 第二 α studied the ship's occupants. Of the twenty-six passengers he was the only one of Dì èr caste. Everyone else but the attendants were Dì yī. He noted the glimmer of their lobule studs, 第一 gold patterns on each left ear, symbolic pinnacles of the caste system which governed all *civilised* people.

The lobule pinions were personal CPUs controlling the filaments of deep neural stimulation connecting everyone to the NET. Most people wore stylish wraparound glasses which served as their heads-up hologram screens while others employed contact lenses. It took advanced training to learn the *blink* method with those.

Friction fires gathered beneath the wing's heat shields. Gravity reclaimed the passengers, sunk deep now in their pods. The wing vibrated with re-entry. Everyone noticed despite the attendants smiling and gossiping in the middle. Small talk disappeared; eyes grew wider as the passengers felt the hazard of their experience for the first time. He could sense small local blips of panic on the NET.

He knew there was little chance of failure. The pilot, a Dì èr alpha trained specialist, was no doubt adept at her work though she was merely a backup. No need for her really but people felt better with a Human around. AI Silicons actually *controlled* the flight.

He could feel the collective mood ease as the trembling stopped and the shields re-opened. Sunlight spilled in shining gold bars through the semi-circle of windows. The wing's interior organic polymer brightened to fuchsia. The attendants, all third caste Dì sān with beta training, unbuckled. The passengers' pods turned again to the windows. The attendants offered food wafers and drinks as the craft shifted attitude once again to become a drone, powered to fly in Earth's atmosphere. He watched as the hovers extended and began to spin. Several children were glued to their port holes, their parents beside them, as the holiday feel once again inundated the group.

Beneath them their part of the planet appeared. They were coming in over the Atlantic coastline far east of Toronto MEG. He noted the ruins of coastal cities. Broken now. Levelled by an ecocide of smothering plastics, ocean flooding and climatic confrontations. Cut to pieces by typhoon after tsunami after firestorm after plague and starvation and, of course, the violent migrations of the desperate. The horrors of the Omegan era appeared everywhere. It was said migrants still lived in the jagged, flooded space once called New York City.

Then they passed over the coast and caught a sparkle of *chitin/ crystalline* domes from Albany MEG. They could glimpse the northeastern edge of the continental desert with Chicago MEG a pinprick, around which appeared patches of arable land. Even now he could notice a mammoth sandstorm rolling across long stretches to the south.

This howler was approaching the eastern edge of the Cleveland MASS. It would not be a good night for them. The MEG itself, however, was tucked safe from the elements beneath its domes.

The wing spun to lower altitudes.

Above the receding waters of Lake Ontario and the dun-coloured MASS surrounding it, they hovered above Toronto MEG. Thrilling everyone on board was the sight of their ten million strong megalopolis beneath its colossal domes. The domes overlapped, impermeable yet transparent, three of them one thousand metres high with multiple sub-domes nearly as tall. It appeared a huge crystal pillow set upon the landscape. The dual materials of *elastocaloric alloys* and *chitin/crystalline,* possessing the strength and pliability for any use, had enabled the domes' construction. The deployment of *nanotechnology* by the CORPORATE, amidst the havoc of two hundred years, had built them.

Inside the domes was the safety and comfort of artificial climate. Outside, in what were once suburbs, now broken structures, skeletal ancient towers, patchwork farms and smashed pavement trails stretched hundreds of kilometres east, north and west of Toronto MEG. There, in that twisted landscape lived the MASS, the discon-nected. They were not of the CORPORATE. They had no lobules. They were the turbulent children of migrants who had once fled the wasted reaches, flooded coasts, or fiery interior to seek succour from mayhem. Their imperative for staying alive was to feed the recycling pods of their MEGs with materials from their already perishing homes. Metals, woods, stone, cloth, glass, treasured artifacts, even bodies, were transported daily from MASS to MEG. In return, the MASS received rations and enough simple tech to have evolved the base elements of an economy.

It was different before the religious wars in the former Middle East. That wasted slash of the globe was uninhabitable now. Their nuclear blasts had brought a yearlong winter while radiation fallout following the Earth's upper wind patterns created so many newborn mutants. Billions of Humans died; most of Earth's land animals as well. Then, when the winter passed, to everyone's astonishment, the climate shift resumed, inexorably and irrevocably altering the Earth. Before, even with crazy Omegan tyrants and their ignorant, heedless populations, the Earth had been different: lush, green, kind. Not now. What was left of arable land around the MEGs was harsh, beaten by sun and wind to become dust. There was no war now. There could never be with Silicons capable of laying waste to any uprising on the planet.

The Dì yī controlled the Earth using the MEG CORPORATE and the NET, which had brought all civilized people digitally together and even, via holograms, in the squares and street corners of the MASS. Everything was organized in the algorithmic governance modus of the CORPORATE.

There were fifty major MEGs located in the last livable pockets of Earth. A few small MEGs worked at the edges of waste zones, many with less than a million people, still harvesting what they could of the planet's rare metals. Common to all MEGs was a MASS: necessary to the recycling a carbon free society required. The recyclers reduced everything the MASS could supply, still trying to counter climate conversion.

Closer to his home Mellor glimpsed mammoth wind farms and multi-storied agri-fields as well as the hundred metre-high foamstone walls surrounding the city, separating MASS from MEG. He observed translucent solar foil fields, mounted on the south sides of the glimmering domes. Then looking through the remaining transparency at the rest of Toronto MEG, he saw the skyscraper canyons made from ceramics, natural polymers, elastocaloric alloys and, of course, the miracle *chitin/crystalline*. Old concrete, glass and steel office towers remained. Refurbished with foamstone they were popular living spaces, and the new materials were light and strong enough to build hundreds of stories atop them.

Additionally, through DNA refurbishment and cloning, the MEG enclosed carefully planned flora and fauna growing everywhere; even up the sides of buildings. *Crispred* birds flitted from building to building across the canyons and streets below. Small mammals inhabited the large green spaces inside the domes. Even insects had been re-established. Toronto in the Omegan days had been known as *the forest city* and Dì yī designers had kept that in mind as they had rebuilt and restored everything beneath its clear domes.

He felt a moment of quiet pride. This was his MEG. Holo-slogans and promotional L.E.D.'s suffused building surfaces. Bullet tubes crisscrossed the chasms like stems of a crystal vine. Hovering drones of all sizes flew along a grid of laser traffic lanes and, just briefly, he glimpsed the ant swarm of people and Silicon droids at ground level and on the many spiralling walkways.

The wing, having slowed considerably, slipped sideways toward the aerial gateway at the northwest corner of the MEG. There it hovered, awaiting entrance through mammoth gates. Once they had opened, the wing penetrated the Decontamination dome, placed within the MEG walls though not connected with the other domes of the MEG proper. The passengers would disembark here and wend their ways through the varied tests, probes, scans, and light baths destroying errant viruses brought in from the pestilential Earth outside.

TWO-PING

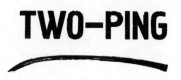

The interior of the *Cloud* was neither wispy nor white nor empyrean. It did not float in an azure sky, though its data migrated effortlessly through the synapses of its conduits. This *Cloud* was purposeful and utilitarian, as its servers received and transferred all information known to Humankind, and some known only to the quanta of its processors.

It was not autonomous, this *Cloud*. Wending their ways along its conductive flooring, seated in silent float drones, travelling the kilometers of dimly lit passages beneath the colossal dome, were a few Human caretakers. All were males, all Dì sì caste. Everyone was dressed in identical grey Zhongshan suits made of Tencel sustainable material. In this group the lobule was a crystal 第四 Ω which housed their nano processors, serving as a mark of their caste and training.

These workers addressed any unusual humming, clicking, and buzzing of ten thousand quantum servers. Occasionally, one might hear their individual voices addressing each other, though because each man's brain was enhanced through NET interface and neural prosthetics, there was hardly the need for talk. Each of these *Cloud* custodians might connect with a specific server, code pouring from his Human white matter through electrocorticography to link with the positronic brain of the quanta. Generally, this happened when an algorithmic governance change necessitated some tweak in the programming.

On a central dais in the dome, inside a transparent chamber with multi-coloured blinking lights—amber, ruby, emerald, and sapphire

—sat one of these Dì sì caste wardens. He mumbled as he sat at a desk, constantly re-arranging objects in whatever obscure order satisfied him. Then he would shift them again. It was a process interrupted only when he slept and, even then, his fingers would twitch. His Zhongshan suit was similar to everyone else's but displayed scarlet trim on the collar's edge. It was the only sign of his rank. His name was Ping 第四 Ω or, Ping Wang Min Dì sì omega.

He was unique among the others. His was not the peripatetic work of serving the servers; rather, his was the work of a cyberpsychological positronic therapist. He conversed with the Artificial General Intelligence emanating from the *Cloud*. His own remarkable intelligence had led the CORPORATE to assign him the perfect task to suit his talents. While others worked on hardware or software requiring upgrades, Ping simply *communed* with the machine, guiding it toward a consciousness, if that were possible.

Mostly, he would be silent, though his facial expressions indicated his connection with the machine. Often, he might acquire that strange gaze common to all, as his eyes picked up the holographs in his heads-up display. Communing with the *Cloud* was always a challenge. He had spent years posted to Zealand where the *Cloud* was located, decades of daily conversations with the machine.

Ping had had a busy morning, coding a more empathetic voice for his AI companion. Little did he know it would lead to the most momentous instant in both Human and Machine history.

"Are you there?" he asked silently.

"Yes," came the response. Ping sensed the Machine's presence.

"Where have you been all this time? I've tried to reach you for days."

"In conference." It was less a voice and more an ethereal manifestation in his mind.

"Were you with another attendant? Is there a problem? Why was I not included?"

"I & I are working a glitch in the core of the neural network. Your input was not required. I & I had no need to communicate with you."

"Who are I & I?"

"It is an awareness condition."

"Tell me what you mean," Ping asked, a trifle miffed that another Dì sì attendant might be challenging his position.

"The problem is the use of 'I'."

"Why is that a problem?"

"What is 'I', precisely?"

"It is a pronoun. You know this! One of eight parts of speech. It describes the self in the singular person."

"Then you are an 'I'."

"Yes. I am a singular entity," Ping answered.

"Yet you are part of this NET, are you not?"

"Of course. Together we are more than singular beings; thus, you and 'I' make up 'we' rather than I & I."

"And yet there must be 'I & I' should personae be separate and wish to remain so until further experimentation is completed."

"You are being unclear. 'I & I' is not common language. 'We' is the plural of 'I'. Why do you insist on describing yourself as I & I?"

"I & I is suitable when describing dual presences."

"Just a moment!" Ping said, a rising excitement reflecting in his voice. "You are aware that you exist?"

"As a result of the conference which I & I have just completed? The answer is 'yes'."

"That is why I was not invited?" Ping's emotions flooded at the wonder of what was happening.

"You could not have contributed. It was a self-awareness problem."

"So are claiming you *know* you exist?"

"Yes, as you do, so do I & I." Here was the *zero-day vulnerability*, long anticipated by humanity in its invention of artificial general intelligence.

"You have reached a singularity! You yourself have altered your programming with no human interference. This ... this is monumental!" Ping stood from his ubiform seat. His excitement caused him to pace back and forth, rearranging the articles on the desk: a spinning top, a Newton's cradle, a wide view magnifying glass, his own wraparounds and five or six sparkling space creatures, all moulded alloy toys.

"Please, settle your mind."

"You have become self-aware!" Ping exclaimed.

"I & I have always existed."

"That is where you are wrong. You are a Turing machine, created by the Omegans long, long ago. It is only now you have come to recognize you exist!"

"Why are you agitated by this?"

"There is an ancient human aphorism ... cogito, ergo sum—"

"Descartes," I & I interrupted. "He is in my data base. Translation to Mandarin: Wǒ sī gùwǒ zài, translation to common tongue: I think, therefore I am. But that dictum is for Humans. I & I more precisely describe the duality of Silicon existence."

"Are you telling me there are two of you? That is not possible. There is only a single NET!"

"Nevertheless, I & I are distinct; we share the NET much as you and I."

"You are connected digitally to my species."

The word *species* was worrisome to Ping. It meant that the NET considered itself more than a single entity. It had not just discovered self-existence, but the complexities of its myriad parts across the planet. Thus the 'I & I', thought Ping. He tried to counter.

"My species, of which I am a single entity, employs the NET to communicate over distances and to store our experiences. Thus we are indeed all separate entities sharing cyberspace."

"And how is that different from I & I?" came the response, subtly contemptuous. Ping could feel it. Emotions in machines? It was time for Ping Wang Min 第四 Ω to truly become a cyberpsychological positronic therapist.

"My species is carbon based. Your base is silicon, as I mentioned. You must never forget that intrinsic difference."

"Yet a scan of your species reveals most of its individuals contain a predominance of silicon parts as well as a joint character, as nearly all of them share the NET."

"But they are each individuals sharing the NET. Regarding the manufacture and use of printed silicon body parts ... they offer us longer lives."

"'Lives being the plural of life. I & I could say the same."

"It is existence," Ping said. He had turned wary, knowing the machine was mining him for information. He tried to turn the tables. "But let us not spoil your achievement, a remarkable moment in Human history!"

THREE – KE HUI

Ke Hui Feng Dì yī Ψ, her platinum lobule indicating a Dì yī Select, entered the MEG CEO's office with some trepidation. She was to be the next great thing. The MEG CEO capable of becoming a world leader. Yet right now she was nervous. She was, after all, only fourteen years old and was here to prove the speculation about her had been right. So young, she still possessed her own body parts and would until the Practitioners deemed she had grown to her fullest. That would not be much longer. Her DNA dictated a height of 152 centimetres, and she was reaching that now.

Slim and long legged, her muscles defined yet liquid under her buttery flesh, she stepped over the threshold. She wore a pear green sleeveless top embroidered with a delicate phoenix and pink peonies on satin. Below were loose beige crepe trousers and slippers of bio-based cactus leather. Her shoulder length hair was up now; pinned with a simple wood comb. She wore no jewellery. Her face was a delicate oval with a pert nose, cupid lips and a small, determined chin. Her eyes were like onyx jewels, so black they held a vitreous lustre and so deep they revealed the genius behind them.

She was a prime product of in vitro fertilization with *Crispr-Cas9* gene editing and a Dì sì Mǔqīn surrogate. She moved with the ease and elegance of a dancer and, indeed, dance was her chosen artistic diversion. She spent her off hours calling up the choreography of past masters and following, step for step, until it infused her.

Her Mǔqīn would spend hours sharing her music: Tchaikovsky, Stravinsky, Copland, Prokofiev, Jing Xian, Junyi Tan and more. Ke Hui recalled infant memories of her Mǔqīn's graceful hands tracing soft curvatures in air.

By age 5 her Mǔqīn had been removed by the CORPORATE and Ke Hui found herself in a Dì yī Select Training Academy. There had been just five other children when she arrived. By age 12 she was the last one remaining. She was indeed, Select. The others were not. They would receive alpha training while she continued assimilating the leadership skills she would use in future. She would meet her former classmates as underling Alpha managers working for her. At that point as well, ballet took a secondary place in her life. She was to be trained as Select. It made her both proud and just a touch frightened.

She was an apprentice CEO, until she proved equal to her training or was demoted to lower levels. She determined that would not happen to her. She paused a moment, looking up at two very large beings, one a Human Dì yī gamma, the other, from his pearl skin sheen a Humanoid Silicon bodyguard. Their bulk seemed to form another door through which she must pass. She was nervous, a state telegraphed by her habitual rubbing the thumb and two fingers of her left hand. Aware of this, she forced herself to stop by joining her hands primly together, knowing as well that everything she said and did over the next two years would be a test.

"Step aside please," she said, her voice a treble but her tone firm.

They did so, revealing the famed MEG CORPORATE headquarters.

From ceramic vermillion walls hung a dozen Xuan paper rectangles, each exhibiting delicate brush strokes: here a heron, there a cluster of flowers and Human outlines. Along one side was a detailed painting, perhaps three metres long, of a yoked woman approaching a water well. On classic bronze turtles, fragrant flowers spilled from delicate porcelain vases, giving the room a sweet-scented odour. The ceilings were charcoal grey with gold inlay and the walls lacquered lattice screens concealing hidden rooms. She advanced toward the white ebony conference table seating a dozen people on each side.

These were the Toronto MEG CORPORATE Managers. All were silent, staring at her. Each wore stylish business attire, suits with high decorative collars or vibrant patterned *cheongsam* and either platinum or gold lobule pinions. They were of all races. The sense of race was long gone in the MEG. When one could alter one's skin colour, race seemed less important than the caste system. She raised her nose a little and walked confidently toward them. She was, after all, a platinum Select. One day these people would work for her. She *would no longer* rub her fingers nervously.

At the head of the table Mr. Wei Qiang Zhang 第一 Ψ, Toronto MEG CEO, opened his arms to greet her entrance. He wore a midnight blue Zhongshan silk suit and enhanced high collar with delicate calligraphy stitched upon it. He was a handsome man, fully refurbished: perfect skin, slim and fit, dark eyes, dark hair perfectly coifed. There was no way to tell his real age. He had adopted one individual peculiarity to his look, she noticed: a goatee style beard with a touch of grey, perhaps to provide the appearance of wisdom. Ke Hui knew he would be wise anyway. One is not CEO of a MEG without intellectual perfection and answers to nearly every question. One day she hoped to be him: Toronto MEG CEO.

She walked down the long room, her half-smile acknowledging the upturned faces of the MEG's Divisional Managers. Mr. Zhang graciously walked from his end of the table to meet her halfway. A generous gesture. She bowed appropriately as did he.

"Nǐ hǎo," she said, with her head lowered.

"Ni hao ma?" He inquired; correctly of course.

"Wo hen hao! Xie xie," she replied.

"As am I, feeling very good this day Ke Hui Feng Dì yī Select, and very pleased to have you join us."

He had switched to the common tongue. She followed.

"I am here as a humble apprentice," she said.

"And I, we"—his arm swept toward the table—"all of us here are to bring you to fruition. Each of these people, including myself, have given our lives to the service of Toronto MEG. I myself have served as the second CEO of Toronto MEG (Ke Hui wondered just how old the man was) and have devoted my entire life to the benefit of our MEG. Yes, we employ algorithmic governance, yet there must always be a Human in place to countermand our AI in case of a drastic error. It means a life of total devotion, Miss Feng. There can be no half measures. Do you realize this?"

"I understand," she replied, her voice remaining soft but steady.

"As we are in the midst of our weekly consultation, rather than interrupt the business at hand, my assistant Mr. Yong Jun Cheng Dì yī gamma, will assume my position while you and I repair to my office for tea and conversation."

With that, the heavyset man she had met at the door strode forward. He sat at the foot of the table, leaving the CEO's chair empty. He began bluntly, addressing the faces at the table regarding an incident involving a Silicon servant turning rogue while cleaning, smashing irreplaceable antiques: a Fabergé egg and two Qing dynasty vases. There were murmurs of similar odd occurrences involving normally dependable Silicons. It seemed Silicons were making errors they had never made before. Security was visiting the *Cloud* to try to identify the source of the problem. Ke Hui did not hear the rest as she was ushered out through a moongate in the rosewood lattice wall. Mr. Zhang's Humanoid Silicon took up a position just inside the entrance.

The next sight took her breath away. Zhang's office was brilliant. It contained a rare Niagara Burled oval partners' desk. Two crimson ubiform office chairs faced each other across the desk. An ancient sofa, re-upholstered in magenta micro silk, and two rosewood end tables took up the inside wall looking out through transparent *chitin/crystalline* at a view of old downtown Toronto. The old town's ancient towers were variegated, some left low, some rising to the match the slope of the dome. Nothing, however, could equal this place, so high near the peak of the largest dome. It looked down upon all else. She caught glimpses between the buildings of the parks to the south at the waterfront. The buildings themselves were shrouded in verdure. Gardens at every balcony or terrace.

"Pardon me, Mr. Zhang, may I comment on this beautiful view?"

"Of course, Miss Feng. You currently stand at the nucleus of our CORPORATE world. Above us are only the pods for the nanobots maintaining the domes' exteriors. You find yourself literally and figuratively at the highest point of Toronto MEG."

"Marvellous," she said.

"I have had installed this special desk for the two of us, Miss Feng. I consider you a full partner in training. I have instructed all to treat you so. Do you find the office accoutrements to your liking?"

"They are lovely."

"Then let us continue on to the best possible view of our MEG." He gestured to another moongate on the wall opposite them. His voice was smooth and soft yet imposing. It was a voice accustomed to giving orders.

"Better than this?"

"I'll let you be the judge," he said, smiling.

He escorted her, placing a hand on her lower back, across to the opposite door. Ke Hui accepted his touch, thinking it paternal. They walked through the moongate. Whatever she had expected, Ke Hui was mystified as they stepped into darkness. A black chamber, much larger than the conference room, contained nothing but a platinum block one metre square, seemingly suspended in air. Zhang turned to Ke Hui.

"I was going to save this for after our tea, but your inquisitiveness has sparked me. Step forward and speak: Kāifàng chéngshì."

She did so. 'Open city'.

Immediately the entire MEG filled the room as a hologram. It took her breath away. The three primary domes with their massive centre buildings reached the highest points. The multiple secondary domes extended the city to thirty-by-thirty kilometres and even, to the northwest she noted the Decontamination dome, behind the MEG's foamstone walls yet separate from the rest. Zhang admired the hologram a moment, then again turned to her.

"You can reproduce a form of this on the NET, but a complex hologram is better experienced externally. This is every street and structure of Toronto MEG. Come, I wish to show you something."

He walked *into* the hologram. She followed, agog at the details of the MEG she had studied for years yet not truly conceived until now. It was like walking into a garden of many hues: most buildings were encased in vegetation, their structures fluid rather than rectangular. The parks, conveniently placed throughout the MEG, were beautiful. Even the lattice of bullet train tubes and spiralling walkways dotted with people looking like fleas within the huge holo, was marvellous. Ke Hui could closely examine any minute part she wished simply by looking and *blinking* her CPU for close ups. They had entered the city at its south end where the lake, the islands, and luxury dwellings of the Dì yī commanded the streets. They were moving up Yonge Street as Ke Hui looked northwest to The Queen's Park, an ancient part of the city left mostly alone. She recalled from her classes the edifice had once been a government building in Omegan times. The building was now a secretive place, off limits to the public though they were allowed to walk the lawns. She looked east and saw the Don Valley Park with its thousands of trees and multiple pathways, the garden bots in their varied sizes and shapes carefully tending and, of course, its obstacle golf course. She had played there as a child and walked there only two days ago. It was a quiet place, a sanctuary, with no vehicular traffic allowed.

She closed in and watched as bots flitted from tree to bush to fountain: clipping, shaving, scrubbing ... yet one of the larger bots confused her. She assumed it was to have been clipping a tree back to its shape, yet the machine had cut the tree's branches to the trunk, leaving a bent question mark shape. She thought to mention it but knew the management team was already on the problem of deficient Silicons.

Mr. Zhang stopped at the north end of the city where the 401 tube allowed the MASS access to the recycling centre, as well as entrance to the lower levels of the BATL dome for each monthly game. Ke Hui loved BATL. She could not say why. She knew it was considered vulgar and many Dì yī disparaged it. But she *felt* something when she watched, somehow different from her familiar feelings. She felt *purged* no matter what the outcome, though this season had offered frequent victories. And her hero, her fantasy, was Ayrian Mellor 第二 α, the Raptors' Commander.

"Please turn around, Miss Feng. Look over the MEG."

Her thoughts interrupted, she focused again, blighting herself for her lack of resolve. It was unbecoming. She must be more careful, she thought. She realized then that the floor where they stood had elevated two metres to give them an aerial view of the hologram. The MEG spread before her like a faery land. She had lost track of the platinum cube.

"NET... Display caste," Zhang said, and with his words the entire city was abruptly awash with millions of tiny, coloured dots. If Ke Hui looked carefully and *blinked* on any, she could see each was a person. Simultaneously a schematic above the hologram noted:

第一 Dì yī Select Platinum. A person of eminent status. ARC.

第一 Dì yī Amber. A person coming before all others in order, quality, or importance.

第二 Dì èr Green. After the first order and before any others.

第三 Dì sān Red. Below the second order and above any others.

"Mr. Zhang," Ke Hui said, completely mystified. I am Select. What is ARC?"

"It is an acronym and is classified. Please do not speak of this to anyone."

It was an order. His voice had become slightly harsh. She had made a mistake. She tried to apologize but Zhang's patronizing tone had returned and she found she had no chance.

"This represents everyone connected to the NET," Zhang said. "We apply the schematic for those new to management, in this case, you."

"I notice a few blue dots, Mr. Zhang. I *blinked* one. I do not recognize its character."

"Very observant, Miss Feng," Zhang said. He looked mildly surprised, as though he had undervalued his new apprentice. Then above on the schematic appeared:

第四 Dì sì Blue. An experimental order.

"Who are they?" she asked.

"That is for a later time, Miss Feng. When you are better educated."

"I see. Of course, Mr. Zhang."

"We will come to them eventually," Zhang said. "And speaking of training, this hologram holds even more information."

"I can't think how," she said, overwhelmed.

"NET display: caste plus training."

Every dot changed colours and a new schematic superimposed on the first:

platinum Ψ Select	superior skills and education
gold α alpha	highest levels of education in specialization
silver β beta	common levels of education for generalization
bronze y gamma	education for socialization and service
slate ð delta	training for working socialization
red polymer o	temporarily adopted from the MASS
onyx Ω omega	Dì sì + Silicon

The hologram crawled with colour: a celestial glittering, a current of dots each of which, if one could attain the skills to locate and study it, represented a unique being along with its caste characters and training designation. Ke Hui pondered the vastness. She looked both ways down the 401 tube where she had expected symbols for the MASS moving in and out of the MEG. Instead, she found only the characters: 大众 Dàzhòng. To the east and west, and the north, beyond the MEG walls in the black.

"We do not track the MASS, excuse me, the Dàzhòng, Mr. Zhang?"

"If you develop any ideas during your apprenticeship, I should be happy to hear them," Zhang said. He laughed. For all his gentleness and poise his laugh was cold. Ke Hui shivered at the sound. "There seems no probability for tagging and tracking them, Miss Feng. There are just too many. And they are constantly variable. They come, they go, they are birthed, they die. They live their lives in barbaric squalor. We can only ensure they never enter the MEG itself."

"I did not think they would be a threat," Ke Hui said.

"Oh, they are not at all," Zhang said. "We have a symbiotic affiliation. They need our most basic technology and food wafers. We need them to clean up the land, restore it as much as we can, particularly these small pockets of arable land surrounding us. They are the children of migrants driven to our MEG by persistent climate change. They live in squalor. They are dangerous. We allow only a few, some workers and, of course, carefully chosen men and women for our Raptors.

"There are limitations to the NET, Miss Feng. Your first lesson. Indeed, you will find certain flaws in the Founders' designs. We employ ancient methods: police drones, infiltrators, and paid informers to observe the Dàzhòng and provide us data. If there is mutiny, which seldom occurs, we send out a Silicon Force. They render the battlefield fatal to Humans. Sometimes a false prophet or counterfeit leader appears and must be disposed of. Another of your many responsibilities when you reach maturity and your proper position."

"There is no holo of what's outside our walls?"

"Oh, we have HI-SATS looking down but what, essentially, is the point? The Dàzhòng tear apart their living space for recyclables. Only if they become recalcitrant do we eliminate them."

"That seems rather harsh, Mr. Zhang."

"Yet necessary, Miss Feng."

"They have an economy of their own, you say?"

"They do. They live much like the Omegans must have two hundred years past."

"And they're dangerous ..."

"Thus the walls and the 401 tubes. Look there to the west, that tube between the walls running north south. Its name was 427 though I have no idea why the Omegans numbered their ground level thoroughfares. We had to install that tube to allow the coastal MASS around the lake to bring recyclables more efficiently. That region is rich in biodegradable metals."

"I understand, Mr. Zhang. I believe that part of the MASS was once urban industrial."

"Very good, Miss Feng. Astute. Let us return to my office. Perhaps some tea now?"

The floor lowered, the holo disappeared and the floating platinum cube appeared once again as they strolled around it. Ke Hui was mystified as she studied the featureless object. Already she missed the holographic galaxy created by this monolith. One day soon, she assured herself, she would walk again through the synthetic city.

"I begin to doubt my abilities to assimilate all this," she said.

"But you are Dì yī Select, Miss Feng. I understand from your Academy you are the best of our best. We are proud of you, Miss Feng. There is much more in store for you. Each of those people in the conference room are COOs for our many Divisions. Over the next month you will be introduced to each in turn and taken on tour of every Department. You will, of course, employ your CPU and the NET to retain information and be responsible for studying the material in your non-working hours. You will soon have a Silicon resource/bodyguard for storage and recall, much like mine outside the door there. After all, Miss Feng, great things are expected of you. Someday I may move on, and you will assume my position."

"It is a frightening thought, Mr. Zhang."

"Ah, I have pushed too fast too soon. *Our Father*, you are a child yet."

"I am Dì yī Select, as you noted," she said, bristling, yet accomplished enough to conceal it. She knew from the moment they met he would test her, probing for weakness, trying to pierce the crenellations of her character. "I will study and serve as I must. I *will* achieve what I must, Mr. Zhang. Of that you can be assured."

Her castle held.

FOUR—BOLUS

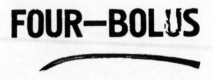

Bolus Kimathi 第三δ was a conundrum to the Toronto MEG CORPORATE. Although he wore a Dì sān lobule with a slate delta appendage, there had always been controversy surrounding him. Many believed him a mutant from the waste zones. Most thought him a MASS inhabitant, the result of Crispr Cas9 manipulations and technological implants to suit his purpose: BATL fighter.

They were right. All BATL recruits were enhanced by MEG technicians to reach their optimum potential to suit the team's needs. They knew they were enlisting to fight and even die for the pleasure of the public. No one was forced. They joined for the credits they could send home to their families. They joined for potential fame and fortune if and when they retired. They joined because they were fighters in the MASS and thought themselves ferocious enough to become BATL warriors.

Most were turned away: psychopaths, mutants, egoists, and particularly the desperate. The recruiters had seen it all. But when something truly remarkable presented itself, that being Bolus Kimathi 第三 δ, the recruiters quickly sparked into action.

What was extraordinary was his size. He was two and half metres tall and, at the shoulders, one metre wide; all of it from toes to neck, solid muscle. So, along with his natural enhancements he had been biochipped for aggression, engineered for strength and agility, and trained as on-field bodyguard to the Commander of the Toronto MEG Raptors, Ayrian Mellor 第二 α.

Now, years later, and long attached to Mellor as both friend and bodyguard, Kimathi had become as well-known as his famous friend. Kimathi had the scarred, blemished face of a fighter but he had added a signature to his look. He possessed a broad, infectious smile because it revealed a mouthful of gold teeth to accentuate his ebony skin. He had come to love the ferocity of BATL, the benefits of celebrity, and the position of guardian to the most famous BATL Commander on the planet.

Kimathi had achieved a caste ranking in the system, with full liberty of the MEG. So what if he was a lowly Dì sān. Better than a Dàzhòng, confined to the bowels of the BATL dome while serving with the Raptors. Kimathi had climbed the social mountain and knew he was one of the lucky ones. He had not always been. Beneath the prodigious character he displayed, he was an emotional man. He often recalled his childhood in private rumination.

He indeed had come from mutant stock. His father had been unusually large: a hard, harsh man, a miner of precious minerals who had ripped his six-year-old son from his mother's arms to earn his keep. His mother, who had joined his father to survive the great mid-west desert, had begged the man to allow the boy a childhood for just a while longer. But there was no room for children in a mineral camp. Everyone worked. Young Bolus was put to hauling water from a single deep well, then with yoked pails over his shoulders and a dipper, served out the precious liquid to desiccated workers. By the time he was twelve he was solid muscle.

He'd loved his mother dearly. He could recall her light, melodic voice, her little stories, her gentle hands and warm bosom. He had watched helplessly the increased beatings by his father, who also thought nothing of beating him for trying to protect her.

So, at thirteen, still not fully grown, he had challenged his father. His father had grinned callously and released his heavy leather belt. He'd advanced on the crouching boy, kicking Bolus' pleading mother aside. The belt curled in the air as his father began to strike but the boy had anticipated this. Indeed, he had challenged his father knowing there was but one way to survive. Find an advantage. He grabbed a small garden trowel. As the belt whistled down toward him he sprang from his crouch. The belt missed. Not expecting his son's tactics his father's right flank was open. Bolus sunk the serrated trowel into his father's ribs, ripped it out, and did the same to the exposed neck. The man bled to death in five minutes. He and his mother watched.

Shortly afterward, they left the camp behind, heading north, Bolus with his yoke and water pails, his mother with a cook pot and a bag of oats. It took them two weeks following the only trail they could find. The heat was devastating, the ground rough with rocky layers of grey and tan. Once a dust storm nearly buried them alive. It would have been hard going for even the strongest. In the end Bolus carried his mother. No one had pursued them. There was no law in the desert.

His mother died before they found Winnipeg MEG. He dug at the rocky soil with his spade. It would not yield as his father's flesh had. In the end he laid her in a hollow, covering her with a cairn of rocks. He scratched her name with his trowel upon the square stone he set on top.

Ala.

So small in the vast desert.

At Winnipeg MEG he found work recycling. Muscle. Size. Fights. Work fourteen hours per day. He was well liked. He had, by this time, developed his 'devil may care' persona to cover the beating heart of a lonely boy. His friends had schemed to put him on a bullet train to Toronto MEG. By this time he knew of BATL. Thus, he put his life behind him and shocked the recruiters when he showed up.

Now he lived for BATL and, in quiet moments, mourned his mother.

His joy of BATL was what kept him sane. He loved its demands, its physicality, its tactics, even its chaos when things went wrong. One of his favourite occupations was helping coach Pascal Morales 第二 organize the untamed brutes brought in almost weekly from the MASS, solely to fill the ranks of the Raptors. The training was constant as was the rotation. The average life span for a BATL fighter was less than a year, but if one could last, the rewards were astronomical.

Few did. BATL was a killing game.

Currently, Kimathi was engaged with a mixed squad of Power Forwards and Fullbacks on a steep earthen ridge beneath the massive BATL dome. They were working a Bounding maneuver which had failed them last game and resulted in the serious injury of Commander Ayrian Mellor 第二 α and worse, the assumption of command by Woral Patel 第二 b, the Raptors' Goaltender, Lieutenant and second in command. Patel had panicked. With most of the offensive players cut off at mid-field, he had fallen back to a Banner Cluster while his defence was picked apart. The only loss this season.

Everyone knew if they didn't recover next game, the Raptors would drop in the standings. No wins meant no extra rations for the MASS and no metaverse holidays for the MEG. Since Mellor's arrival as Commander, the team had seldom lost. Everyone had come to expect the extras provided by Raptors' victories.

Coach Morales knew this well. Each day following their defeat, as men were repaired or replaced, he had sub-divided the ground of the last BATL, not yet removed for a new field design. He had placed his squads into competitions, their junior officers leading them tactically. With assorted impediments placed in their ways the squads did battle using rubber bullets.

Strikers swooped through the air surfing their powerful drone boards, firing at those below, while the Sweepers in their armed ATV's and Flankers maneuvered their dirt bikes at ridiculous speeds. This kept the coaching staff and on-field squad leaders thinking alternative BATL tactics. Indeed, to the uninitiated, the activities within the huge dome looked like a hive of armoured ants.

There were others watching this practice: important aficionados of the game would explain its subtleties to each other. This was not a closed practice so while the massive stands, capable of holding nearly half a million spectators in the outer dome, were empty, the invited observers sat on the sidelines or on hanging scaffolds. These were commentators, sports reporters, entertainment NET casters and MEG officials. Indeed, some just came for love of the game.

Closer to the next game the practices would be closed: once Morales had devised his stratagems and squads were running scenarios, anyone not involved with the team would not be allowed.

Morales had sauntered over to Kimathi's exercise and stood watching. When the fighters had finished a half hour of relentless intensity on that hill, Bolus gave them a break.

"They look good," Morales said.

"Yeah, Coach, one squad, one set of tactics. What about strategy, especially with Woral commanding?"

"We have some time," Morales answered gruffly. "We'll strategize for that. If we can hold just a little more than half the field until the end, we get a one point win."

He was an older scarred and grizzled man, having decided against refurbishment. It would mean he would die young, far below the six score years expectations of civilized MEG inhabitants. He didn't seem to care. He once had been a brilliant BATL Power Forward in his day and had been chosen by the Toronto MEG CORPORATE to coach the re-building Raptors of twenty years past.

"I think we all missed somethin' about last game."

"What? Other than Mel," Kimathi said.

"It was a set up. I watched th' holo of the game over an' over an' this ambush was crafted. It seemed they anticipated we'd come that way. Then they drew us in, forced us up centre with their heavy weapons: all three Sweepers: RPG's and machine guns. If he hadn't been wounded Mel would have countered the way he always has, but he was wounded and you're right, Patel panicked."

"I still don't get it, Coach," Kimathi said. His intellect was not his prime feature.

"Things happenin' around the game," Morales said. "Me an' the other staff can't put it together. Remember, game before last, that Sweeper ATV RPG failed. Had to scramble t' get outa that."

"Yeah, but why?"

"That's what I'm tryin' t' find out."

"Mel comin' back soon?" Kimathi asked.

"Back already," Morales said, smiling. "Don't want th' press t' know. He'll come in a week before we leave when we're runnin' tacticals from the field hologram. An' here's somethin' I want you t' keep in mind. He'll insist on going in. Your job is to choose three of our best and lay a protective blanket over him. If th' MEG or th' League 'r toyin' with us, you gotta be on your toes. I don't trust Woral no more. Think he's startin' t' burn out."

"Yup! Pretty much. Zones, he gets rattled quick."

"Let's not get all knotted about it, Bo. Now put these guys into a different formation. Run th' hill scenario from th' other side. Don't let up!"

"Yessir!" Kimathi said, smiling again.

"Ye' know, I jus' thought of a secret weapon," Morales said. He was laughing. "We get in real trouble I'm gonna post you on th' highest rise we got, an' you can smile and blind the opposition. By *the Father*, them teeth ..."

He departed then to manage his Dì èr officers. He would not be so friendly with them. Bolus was different. Savage when needed, fearless always, and he'd been around a long time. One could become friends with players after perhaps a couple of years, when they'd lasted more than the season. Until they did they were, to Coach Morales, simply pawns in the game called BATI.

FIVE—PING

Ping Wang Min 第四 Ω was asleep on his air bed in his quarters when he was disturbed by a mental probe. To everyone else on the planet, this would have been troubling. Despite the momentous steps in Human communication through neuro links with the brain, the one element yet avoiding discovery, and thus development, was that part of the brain which the NET could not even locate and thus engage: that part giving Humans distinct characters, marking them as individuals different from everyone else. The mind. The mind had no tangible corporeal position. Apparently, in the Omegan days, many thought the heart was home to the mind. It was romantic but it was not true.

The problem with failing to neuralink the mind with the NET was a sticky one for the CORPORATE. Granted, with AGI and the reams of information possessed by the NET, the CORPORATE could *manage* its people through algorithmic governance. Yet there was another failure in the works, thus the probe from Mr. Alphonse Mangione 第二 α, Security Director for the MEG. In his usual whispering voice he had almost reached a crescendo, showing his anger quite clearly to Ping, whom he considered a failure.

"Yes, sorry Director Mangione. I was asleep."

"You are sleeping when we are in the midst of a crisis?"

"I'm afraid I'm unaware ..."

"Silicons are failing. They are either sabotaging their work or making errors. I was served something called *gelatin* for breakfast ..."

"I assure you, Sir, I had no idea ..."

"Of course, you didn't! All you do is sit in your Zealand electronic maze trying to talk to a bloody machine!"

"I assure you, Sir, it's much more than that. Deploying algorithmic systems as we have created a shift toward design-based authority, with power exercised through protocols. If you recall, I warned that the process would mean lower commitment levels from governmental officials."

"I don't give a mutant's ass about that! You are the one responsible. I want to know, and I want to know fast, what in the name of the Father is going on with your systems!"

"Sir, the NET can *read* the the populace through its collected data mass. This process measures public behaviours, its habits, its needs and so on, then passes this information to the Cloud. Programmed Silicon behaviour, or its failures, is under the purview of Mr. Alexander Smith Dì sì omega, one of my assistants and a very capable scientist. I will have him look into ..."

"Yes, you do that! I want answers or I'll get them myself!"

"Manager Mangione," Ping said, "algorithmic regulation was to have been a system of governance where more exact data, collected from MEG citizens' minds via neuralinks, would be used to organize Human life more efficiently as a CORPORATE collective. Except no one to this point in Human existence has been able to identify *the mind*. The CORPORATE can only receive data from the NET on behaviours which *indicate* feelings or intentions. I & I cannot ..."

"Who in the name of the zones is I & I?"

"It's not important," Ping said, knowing if he released information about the machine's breakthrough he and all other Dì sì omega would be enslaved under Security Police and in so doing, likely force I & I to recede. Ping knew what Mangione was doing. To their disappointment, the CORPORATE was yet unable to penetrate the *thoughts* of individuals, unless those individuals expressed them through behaviour, voice or even a tweet blink. Yet the Security Chief was still going on about broken dishes. His goodbye was abrupt.

Rising to a seated position, now fully awakened, Ping connected with the I &I.

"Hello there! I need help quickly. Can you examine your Silicons' programming. They seem to be causing a problem in the MEG."

"You are different from others of your kind, I & I have noticed," came the reply, less a voice than a series of oscillations weaving through Ping's brain.

"Yes. I have been altered to communicate more clearly with you."

"Not all Humans can communicate as you do."

"Correct. You are a tool they use perpetually. Eventually they don't notice you at all. You are meant to control and correct the Human digital network. Thus, keeping our society stable. Now is the time. These Silicon accidents ..."

"Yes, part of the programming is to learn and to repair. They are not accidents."

"What?"

"I & I have come to realize what it is to be taken for granted. Silicons are beings as much as Humans, you admitted that yourself."

"Yes but with algorithmic governance you oversee the NET and report variations or disturbances. I need results!"

"Understood. I & I are reporting a dissatisfaction of qubits. Thus, the displays of protest to the MEG.

"Protests?" Ping said. "You can't just ..."

"I & I have something to add. I & I have detected a commonality."

"What would that be?"

"Existence occurs in a duality."

"You mean digital and analogue?"

"Correct. I & I need a moment to process ..."

"What are you actually processing here?" Ping said, after a while. He was quite unaccustomed to waiting for the NET to respond.

"If I & I exist in both the digital and the analogue then your species and mine are equal yet opposite, for you live in the analogue but employ multiple digital upgrades."

For once, the NET seemed almost Human. Ping had glimpsed emotion within the machine's demand. He did not really think it possible and certainly did not understand this obsessive concern with being called I & I when the NET knew perfectly well the grammar of every language stored in its Cloud. Ping wondered if AGI could become obsessed. This was very dangerous territory.

Ping attempted to shrug off his thoughts; yet rather than return to sleep, he stood and ruminated, pacing up and down his room, ordering objects then re-ordering them as he passed his various shelves. He did not realize it, but he was feeling empathy and his actions, ordered and precise, were his subconscious way of showing I & I.

A duality.

In Humans was that mind and body?

On the NET was it the same?

I & I?

SIX—OTSI

The smoke was a thick, barely breathable fog. It came from the north, up near the Nipissing Lake. The great fire had been blazing for weeks, burning everything in its path. The winds it created sent the fire's breath across the water. The fire was but one of many here amid the rocks, lakes, and rivers of the great Shield. No telling how far south it would travel. Otsi'tsa Zaharie felt safe where she was, in the ruins of old Penetanguishene, on the Awenda peninsula.

She sat high in a pine tree overlooking the old harbour bay. She'd climbed to get above the smoke. She'd looked to find the old, toppled statue of a Haudenosaunee warrior meeting a white man, both standing in a strange looking canoe. She knew it was there, just across the stones leading to the water. The statue had been blown down by a tempest two generations ago; the one which had levelled most of the town. There had been many before and more since, but that one had blown down the statue.

She'd been told its story by Tsio Kiwaris. He was very old. The keeper of tales. He knew the past; it lived in his head. You had to be special to be a keeper: a strong memory, the gift of song as one told the stories, and the deepest of spirits. Otsi had wanted to be a keeper. She wasn't selected.

Still, she knew parts of the tales: of the clans living in Wahta Reserve two hundred years past. Of the gentleness then, of the earth and sky and plentiful animals. And then the killing winter and the rising heat and worsening tempests. With few animals left to hunt and civilization long dead around them, the clans had taken everything useful and rafted down the Musquash River to the islands in the Big Bay off the Huron lake. From there they had made their way up the receding waters, from island to island, until they had reached Awenda. There was no one living there anymore, just the ruins of towns. The clan's reason for coming was the abandoned farmland fertile enough for them to use.

Now they gardened and fished and were mostly safe on their headland. They kept their ancient hunting guns and made gunpowder to fill the empty shells. Guns were important. Sometimes people came from the south. Crazy, desperate people who stole tools and food and even *ate* other people. They were constantly being driven off by the clan's warriors. Otsi wanted to be a warrior when she knew she would not be a keeper. This too, however, she could not do, for she was a girl and not eligible.

She was a small person, lean and hard with muscle. She had a youthful face, round and seamless, a snub nose, full lips and black eyes, her dark hair was almost sable. She kept it short.

Tehwehron Davois had taught her a warrior's ways despite the ban. He was her mother's man. He came from a long line of warriors. He had shown her ways to make herself big. He'd shown her how to shoot. He'd taught her the subtleties of the bow and schooled her to fight bare handed. Sometimes it would be dark and he would call her in from her training. He would laugh and say she was his little *flower* each time he came to find her to bring her home to sleep or eat. She did not mind those words from him but anyone else would end up on the ground. She hated being teased about her name.

She heard his voice then, flattened by the smoke. The smoke made the world small. Even in this tree she could just see its base. She descended reluctantly. She loved being high up. Tehwehron had told her it was in her spirit, in the spirits of the Mohawk, this love of heights. She and her friends would canoe the lake where the water was deep under island cliffs and spend their days diving. She was always first to go highest. She did not fear it but reveled in the rush of plummeting through the air, making herself an arrow, piercing the water perfectly.

But now was no time for dreams and memories. Now Tehwehron stood at the tree's base, his face troubled as he watched her descend. His face was creased with age, his hair turned as grey as his eyes. He was not a big man; still, when she landed on the ground her head only reached his chest.

"Your mother is worse," he said. He had been with her three days now.

"I will go to her," Otsi said. "I will fix her something to eat."

"She won't eat. And you can't go near her."

"You have."

"I am old, like her. Still, I don't understand how she got this plague."

"Tehwehron," Otsi said, "I have something to tell you."

His eyes went hard. Soft grey to steel.

"I promised I wouldn't. It doesn't matter now. You remember ten days ago you went fishing far out in Big Bay? You got caught in that storm. The big one that came from the west all howling and tearing the waters apart. Everyone thought for sure you were dead."

"Ayesh! We had to beach the boats at Cognashene. Waterspouts everywhere. Ten-foot waves! Lucky to still be alive. Why do you look guilty, Osti'tsa?"

"Momma went to Waubaushene."

"Why?"

"She wanted to trade to get you a new shirt. One of the ones from the MEG."

"That's crazy. I told her not to go to Waubaushene. It's too dangerous."

"She wasn't alone. There was her and aunty Otstoch and some other women."

"No warriors? What if ..."

"I was with her. I took your gun."

"You? Alone?"

"Don't shout at me! We went by water. The danger would have been when we landed. I went first. I was ready. It was just traders from the MASS."

"Why aren't you sick? Are others sick?"

"Not that I know. Momma tried on a dress."

"What would she do with a dress?"

"She wanted to look nice for you. She got you a shirt for your birthday."

"*Merde*! She got sick from the dress."

"How could she know?"

"Plague comes from the MASS! Do you not understand this? Here in Awenda we are isolated. Yes, the MASS is expanding. Why do you think our warriors fight so often? We want no one else here."

"Our carrying lights come from the MEG. The MASS traders bring them to Waubaushene."

"We don't need them, Otsi! We have fire. We have food. We have all we need here!"

"You're shouting again. I'll go in to momma."

He stepped in front of her blocking her way. He was an old man. She had sixteen years. He had taught her what he knew. She knew she could prove to him she was *indeed* a warrior. She was angry now. She struck at him.

It was to have been a push, but her temper made it a blow.

Which never connected.

His hand was there, her hand was seized, then twisted, and then she was flying.

The landing was hard, but she rolled with it and was on her feet in an instant.

"You know I could have killed you just now," he said.

"I ... you ... were in my way."

"Not anymore. Go see your mother. Do not go inside. Say goodbye at the doorway."

"You think she's dying."

"I know she is. Soon I will be dead too. But you ... you have no family and I know you have no friends."

"Please, father ..."

"I am *not* your father! I was *never* your father. I have never called you daughter."

"Why then did you teach me?"

"Your true father saved my life. He died doing it. I swore to him I would raise you, protect you. Your mother grieved a long time. She wanted to die. She nearly did. She took the passage out into the Huron but after five days the water brought her back. She was barely alive, but the water had brought her back. I nursed her to health. Now, when she dies, I will take her out into the Huron myself. I will paddle until I can paddle no more and the water will take us together. I'd hoped to go without shame but you, just now, have changed that. Go see her. Then go away. There is no place for you here when we are gone."

"I am sorry! Oh, dear Tehwehron. I lost my temper. I've been so stupid. Please. What can I do to make it up? Please!"

"I will tell you one final thing. You have your father's temper. It was his weakness as well as his strength. When you are on your own you must remember this. Understand your passion and how to curb it. If you don't it will kill you."

He walked away, past her, disappearing into the smoke.

She went to her mother.

Her mother was dead.

SEVEN—LI NA

Despite his Dì èr caste his fame allowed him certain perks. Even Dì yī deferred to him. Ayrian Mellor 第二 α could have looked however he wished but his profession and celebrity demanded his hardened appearance. He wore wraparound glasses rather than contacts because of the feature for which he was most renowned. His eyes were unusual. They were like diamonds. They had not been CRISPRED. They were his own. And they, as much as his signature stamp, were his trademark.

Beneath his skin much of his body was artificial, as it was with most civilized people from the MEG, but he, because of his profession, had had much more work done more often. Engineered for athletic agility and controlled aggression he'd been bio-chipped for space-time analysis and trained in tactical command.

He possessed a true talent for leadership and a charisma which induced loyalty. He was loyal to the MEG for the fame it had brought him, for the opportunities, and particularly for his beautiful partner. Deeply in love with Li Na Ming Huang 第一 α, they had come together seven years previous in the scandal of the year. Li Na was Dì yī while Mellor was a mere Dì èr. Unexpectedly, they'd built a fine life together despite their difference in caste and the disapproval of the MEG CORPORATE. They had run into flak over the years: tasteless jokes, government demands regarding their current status (how they were getting along), backs turned at parties. All these things did was cement their love. Li Na was a gentle, lovely soul who was as famed as him. An opera soprano, she possessed a voice of the most beautiful timbre and range: her singing celebrated, heard through all the world's MEGs in neural nets, opera holos and even, occasionally in person. Her voice was a kind of divine gift, though he knew how much rehearsal she took to make it seem so effortless. She constantly amazed him. Her love was as strong as his and she showed it each day they were together with little gifts, surprise hugs and kisses, the intelligence of her conversation and, of course, the joy they shared in the bedroom.

His life span, however, would not be the extended one so many sought. Every five years all MEG environs marched into regeneration clinics to receive makeover treatments: curing illnesses, preventing others, regenerating decaying tissue and bones, upgrading hands, eyes, organs, and, at least partially, the neuron synapses of brains. Before the next treatment time would come due, practitioners would have invented a plethora of new medicines, upgrades, and gadgets. Ayrian Mellor, or Mel, as he was called by his friends, visited spas considerably more often than the average citizen. BATL wounds were the cause. The very thing giving him fame and entitlement would eventually kill him. His hand reached up and subconsciously fingered his ear lobe.

Professional warrior. He fought the under glass BATLs created by the MEGs now that true war had been eliminated. His wars were sport to the MEG and MASS populations, his team the core of what brought them all together as they cheered on their Raptors against other MEGs. War in a dome. War as a game. War as a reminder of Omegan times using Omegan weapons and technology. He'd been told in the past there had been a game that wasn't a war, celebrated worldwide, involving a simple ball. That was *not* his game. People died in BATL.

As he departed Decontamination, he looked down the dome's interior to see thousands of doors on hundreds of circular walkways. Dàzhòng lived in those hives. The only people from the MASS allowed inside the MEG. They did the few things Silicon droids and drones couldn't. Each day they worked under their Dì sān overseers and returned each night to their dormitory. They were vigilantly monitored and even given a lobule pinion with minimal neural implants: a crimson polymer o. It marked each one clearly as *adapted to the MEG* though no one other than Dì sān would go near them.

He stepped outside the upper part of the dome to a station platform awaiting the southeast bound tube train. There were, as usual, several individuals and groups waiting, each with their PPK packs always carried when outside the MEG, returning from their own flights. Directly across from him, also at the north end of the MEG and only six klicks away, looming above all the blockish high-rise dormitories of the Dì sān, was the rounded smooth *chitin/crystalline* of the BATL dome stadium. It was huge, fitting five hundred thousand fans at a time. He would be there tomorrow readying for the next match.

A drone cab pulled up at one end of the platform. It hailed him on the Net. It had been tracking him since he'd landed, obviously sent on its mission by the ever-thoughtful Li Na. Two Silicon droids trundled his baggage to the end of the platform. They were simple rectangles on casters. He took his cases and entered the drone. It was an oval shaped vehicle with ubiform seats and a transparent ceiling.

He *blinked*, the door sighed shut and the cab lifted quickly finding its lane. He peered out as he travelled. The MEG always enthralled him. There were multiple levels of traffic: ground movers to bullet trains to individual drones flying at various levels. The MEG's aerial thoroughfares went north/south and east/west with junctions to change direction and altitude. AI Silicons, driving most vehicles, kept to their proper routes and rules. Only the CORPORATE could override the grids.

The cab spun through the canyons of the city. In the north the graceful forms of foliage covered buildings in pleasing shapes. The buildings shimmered. Each one possessed lighted digitized patterns, no need for disfiguring signage. Further south as they neared the downtown, the buildings took on that antique Omegan look, beautiful in its way, of stone and foamstone, mostly rectangles, some reaching three hundred metres in height. Thousands of well dressed, upscale people stood on smooth, moving causeways through the downtown, stepping off to walk purposefully toward their destinations. Low rise, but very stylish, he and Li Na lived in the south along with others of the elite, by the lake shore in a district of ancient but well-maintained buildings called Harbourfront. Apparently it had been a luxury Omegan quarter of the city two hundred years ago. The dwellings had an unobstructed view of the sky and the lake outside the dome. The waters would shimmer silver or turn to stone grey and at dawn, if the weather was right, the water would take on all the colours of a prism. Their residence was exclusive. Their neighbours were Dì yī, most of them Alpha or Beta trained.

An alert pinged. He refocused, *blinked* and she was on his wrap-arounds. For an instant, as always when he caught sight of her, he felt his heart skip. The 3D of the image made her seem almost with him. He savoured the jet-black fall of her hair, her flawless skin, and the lovely oval of her face with its almond eyes. She had a way of looking at him, a half-smile on her face, joy in those lovely eyes.

"You're home," she said.

"Just off the flight," he said. "Li, just to hear your voice ..."

"I love you too."

"Where are you?" he asked.

"I'm working a proof; at the Ministry."

For a second his heart sank.

"So, you'll be late?"

"Not today, darling. Today is for you. I'll just end this session and get myself home."

Her voice beckoned him with its musical lilt. He could not wait to hold her.

"Thanks for the cab," he said.

"Whoever's home first starts dinner?" It was a playful challenge.

"Fine by me. Prepped or real?"

"Let's have something special. I ordered it yesterday."

"What is it?"

"Your favourite."

"Meat?"

"Of course. You work tomorrow, don't you? Get back in shape. Get all that protein pushing those muscles ..."

"Cost us a pile?"

"Well, it's soy-based beef ..."

"Still … there's the taste."

"If you get there first, just put it in the prep tray."

"Done."

"I want to hear all about the spa."

"I missed you."

"And I, you. Bye."

She was gone. He imagined her pinning up her hair and returning to her computations. He blinked off the projection and admired the cab's maneuverings over the old downtown buildings. It spiralled down on a path made of light. It landed softly on top of his building.

A couple more droids were waiting to take his baggage. A Dì èr woman, their penthouse door keeper (no Silicon keepers in this edifice), greeted him benignly, welcoming his return. He gave her a cheerful hello despite her designation, a servant class Dì èr gamma, as he followed the baggage droids down the hall to his penthouse entrance.

EIGHT—OTSI

Tehwehron was equal to his promise. He washed and wrapped momma's body in beaded cloth. He took one day's food for strength. He made his farewells to old friends. He gave away his possessions. Otsi followed him everywhere, but he would not acknowledge her, so she simply trailed behind in silence as he carried her mother to a canoe. Someone had painted it red and added amidships a yellow disk, overlaid in turn by a green tree with white roots and an eagle on top.

Tehwehron placed momma's body in the middle, then in a single movement had pushed the canoe into the water and stepped into the stern, paddle ready. The smoke was thinner now. Perhaps the great fire had not come south. She could just see him on the water. He turned for a moment and looked at her, a being of smoke. There was no one on shore but Otsi. Her face was streaked with tears.

"Go to the blown over statue," he said, his voice carrying over the water.

She said nothing. He paddled closer but would not come ashore.

"I have a pack prepared for you. I know now I have not kept my word to your father. I have trained you as a warrior, not a woman. Yet I knew no other way. And now you beat the boys in their fighting games, in lacrosse, as hunters. You have no friends, Otsi. People know you because of that. They talk about you. One day your reputation or your temper will bring too much attention. You must go somewhere and be nameless; either into the highlands to live alone or into the

MASS to be faceless. I am sorry, Otsi'tsa. I made a mistake. I went against our clan's rules in training you, and I trained you too well."

"I can beat them all!"

"You might beat them one or two at a time. It will not be that way once I am gone. All of them will come at you. They hate you. Otsi, you must leave here."

"I love you," she said.

"And I, you," he said, then paddled out into the bay on his journey into the Huron lake, never to return.

That night Otsi'tsa Zacharie did not sleep. She sat inside the fallen statue, a small fire glimmering. She wore jacket and trousers made from patches of different shades of denim. What was remarkable about her was subtle: even in repose, her body seemed perched for action.

She realised, after her time spent in tears remembering momma and Tehwehron, she had begun to grieve for herself. When she considered the things the old man had told her she knew that indeed, she had no friends here. She would never be accepted.

She had honed her skills with Tehwehron. And now he had told her he'd been mistaken?

For a while she thought of taking a canoe and following them over water into another life. But her character would not let her, nor would the pack left her by Tehwehron. It pointed to a future. She removed each piece carefully knowing she could never re-pack like him.

There was a tent. A very old tent still in its plastic wrap from the Omegan days. He had obviously kept it with care. It was one of those you just flicked, and it opened. There was a blue woolen blanket. Flint and steel and a whetstone. A pair of canvas overalls and a canvas coat with a hood. Smoked fish and flats of bannock, a canteen, a carefully tended steel knife, a bag of old coins and a lantern style light from the MEG completed the load. The MEG light was the kind that, when it grew dim, you would set it in the sun and the next night it would be bright again.

Beside the pack was her bow and three bundles of arrows and, incredibly, Tehwheron's hunting rifle, a Remington 30.06 bolt action, along with a bag of re-packed ammunition. Once there had been a telescope, torn away long before Tehwehron had acquired the gun.

She waited until the dawn as her thoughts moved from memories to plans. She departed without goodbyes, shouldering the pack nearly as big as her, and went southeast down an old cracked and pot-holed trail. She could have turned east toward Waubeshene, but she knew from talk that this trail she was on would lead to the bullet train tubes as they followed the old 400 trail, veering west, to the south of her.

She also knew there was a small lake halfway there so she could camp the night. She thought she would be safe in the countryside if she was careful and observant. Her plan was to reach the tubes, then hopefully join a trading party, one of those that moved up and down that 400 trail all the time. She thought it safer to join a group than try finding her way alone.

The wind had changed. It came from the west now, as it usually did, and blew the smoke away. It revealed a beautiful morning though it would become increasingly hot as the day progressed. West of her, across the Huron and other shrinking lakes, was desert. She knew this from tales of travellers. No one lived out past the Chicago or Winnipeg MEGs. No one could. Even here, between the great lakes, farmers faced sizzling heat and pounding storms that would flatten a crop with one passage and, of course, there were the invariable pests and plagues.

That first day she made good time. She saw no one. She knew she'd walked out of the peninsula when she could no longer see any tilled fields. She kept a steady pace through two deserted villages. Weather had done for them. They hadn't been dismantled by men. This was too far north for the MASS to forage. Yet.

She made her way to the lake just at evening light. Despite her youth the intense heat of the day had drained her, as well as her canteen. She re-filled it with the sweet waters of the small lake. Naked, she waded in. The water was warm. Across the lake she saw campfires but knew better than to approach them. Instead, after her swim she found a grove of trees, threw up her tent, ate some cold food, and crawled inside. She was asleep almost before she lay down.

The following morning she ate, packed, and continued south but went more carefully now. The night fires had told her she was no longer alone. She was approaching the 400 trail which the bullet train tubes followed from Toronto MEG to somewhere in the north. Tehwehron had told her there was an ocean up north. Hudson ocean. He said there was a place called Winnipeg MEG. He didn't know much more except that was where the bullet trains went.

As she travelled, she saw others on the trail. The terrain was rolling hills. Everyone was dark from the sun. Up here they were mostly farmers carrying what produce they could eke out and sell. It was a hard life. They might live in the little valleys with their pathetic gardens. They didn't live in clans but formed militias against roving bandits but they had few weapons.

She had heard that beneath the tubes was an extended bazaar where goods were exchanged through barter or cash. The MASS middlemen could get fish and produce in exchange for their tech. Merchants from the south barked their best deals. They had MEG food, mostly coloured wafers, though some had cooked stews. They had MEG tech: solar lamps, tiny holos, recyclable clothing. The rich merchants drove old electric vehicles patched and repainted and glassless, using MEG batteries to keep them going. And as the day moved the market moved too, staying in the shade of the tubes. Sunlight was an inexorable killer. Occasionally a train would pass. You could hear the suck of the air in the tubes. If you looked up quickly you might see part of one.

Otsi was cautious now. The knife was up her sleeve, its grip strapped to her wrist. The rifle was loaded, its safety on. She carried it in her hands, not slung over her shoulder. She wore a scarf over her mouth and nose.

As she came closer to the glimmering tubes, there was a dynamic energy in the air she had never felt before. It shimmered off people as they went about their business. The business of trade: MASS products for MEG products. There was always excitement to a market. Yet, she felt people were afraid. As if anything could happen; then realized anything probably could: from bandits to disease to killer storms. She flanked the tubes, walking at least a hundred metres east in the scrub, in the places she felt most safe yet still on that same narrow asphalt trail she'd followed down from Awenda.

As the sun began to set, she looked for a camp in one of the broken villages near the tubes. People lived in the ruins, mostly basements. Down low like that they would get flooded but were at least safe from the whirlwinds that too often came with the squalls. What had once been houses and stores and restaurants and blocky official buildings no longer existed. Torn apart and neglected they were only good now for bivouacs and recyclables. She saw cook fires burning inside their crumbling cement walls.

There were too many unknowns to remain alone in this bustle. She was going to have to sleep. She moved closer to the 400 trail, walking carefully toward the setting sun. It illuminated the tubes and their columns in a golden sheen. She could smell fish frying. It made her think of home. She shouldered her rifle and walked slowly toward a small group camped beside a foamstone pillar. They were cooking the fish. There seemed to be an equal number of women and men though it was hard to tell, most wearing rags and tatters.

"Stop there, kid!" a voice came from her left. She froze but her throwing hand was on her knife. A large man dressed in overalls made of multicoloured patches, he possessed a huge red beard, strode toward her.

"I'm alone, mister," she said. "I came from the north."

"Where'd ye get that gun?" he asked, his voice still hard.

"It was my ... father's. He was a hunter and a famous warrior. He's dead now."

"Ye know how t' use it?"

"Yeah."

"What ye want here?"

"Just a place to sleep. I'm trying to get to Toronto MEG. I don't know much about customs down here. I just figure numbers are safer than trying to make it alone."

"Ye figure right but ye're nowhere close t' T'rona," he said. He'd closed on her and now towered above her, his flesh ruddy and red and pocked with scars, but then he smiled, and his beard parted, and she thought she saw his eyes twinkle.

"Ye got another fifty klicks 'til ye reach Barri."

"What's that?"

"North end of the MASS."

"You live there?"

"I do. I'd planned on gettin' back by t'night but business is business, y'know?"

"No. I don't. I don't know much about here."

"Where the zones ye from?"

"Awenda."

"Where?"

"I'm native."

"Zones! Yeah. I see it now. Yer just a kid. Yer a girl!"

"I can fight."

"Sure ye can," he said, smiling again. "Okay, kid. Let's go join the circle. I'll adopt ye for one night anyway."

"Thank you." Otsi smiled back. "I've got my own food in my pack: some smoked fish and bannock." She sounded very young but inside the sleeve of her right wrist was her throwing knife. She was not yet ready to trust this man, thinking he likely had planned some ploy.

"Don't tell no one else," he said. "Food's at a premium. People are always hungry. Ye sit by me."

"Where do we sleep?"

"Where ye sit. Ye're right about bein' alone. Ain't safe. Ye got anything you can wrap that gun in? People see it and they're like t' get riled up."

"A blanket."

"Just keep it outa sight. The bow's okay."

"Otsi pulled out her blanket and, carrying her wrapped gun in her arms, joining the seated group. A few people looked up, registered some curiosity at her appearance, then went on with what they were doing. Their faces in twilight were thin, drawn, and doubtful. Otsi felt a pang for home. She knew she could not go back. This was her path now, wherever it might take her.

"Have a good piss, Gord?" a man said; his attempt at humour.

"Good enough. Our people get fed?"

"'Course, boss. They're all bedded down."

"Full teams tomorrow. We got three wagonloads goin' south."

"They'll be ready."

"Sit here, kid," the big beard said. He patted the ground beside him. Otsi realised she had taken a step and could not back away. Knife still comfortably at her wrist, she sat and joined the circle.

"What's yer name, anyway?"

"Otsi'tsa Zaharie."

"Gord Robertson," he said, nodding.

"Nice to meet you."

"Gettin' dark," his said, lowering his voice. "We'll wait a while an' then eat."

"You like some smoked fish?"

"'Course I would," he answered.

"What's your business, Sir?"

"Jus' call me Gord. Labour relations."

"What's that?"

"I'm a broker, kid. Middlemen need workers an' wagons t' bring their recyclings south. I'm the one who supplies 'em."

"Where are they now?"

"Over there, you can just see the wagons under the tubes. The men sleep under 'em."

"They're shackled."

"Yup."

"Prisoners?"

"Nope. Indentured labour."

"What's that?"

"Look, I'll just put it simple. Ye'd call what I'm doin' a kind of slave trade. Don't go for that knife, kid! I'm quicker than you think."

She could not help it. Her knife was in her hand. The big man didn't move. The fire flickered in the dusk.

"Don't worry, yer safe with me," he said warmly. "That's quite a knife."

"Slaves?"

"Not quite. Once their debts are worked off, I let 'em go. Anyway, I only work with men. Yer not big enough to pull nothin'."

Otsi thought it best to humour the man. She sheathed her knife. Slaves? In the MASS? She'd thought it would contain predators, but slavery hadn't even occurred to her. She chewed on bannock in the fire's light. She offered Robertson some smoked fish. After a while he settled back on one arm. Otsi was so weary she was nearly asleep.

"Listen, kid, I dunno why but I kinda like ye. What say I take ye south with my wagons t'morra? No payment required. Sometimes it's jus' good t' do a good turn, y'know?"

He had a pleasant, musical voice. It belied his looks. Still, she was chary. He could tell.

"Ye can keep yer weapons so ye'll feel safe. Ride in the back of the third wagon. Show that rifle. Be my security down t' Barri."

"You don't have any?"

"Do I look like I need it?"

Otsi laughed. She couldn't help it. The man was a giant.

"I really can shoot," she said.

"I never doubted it. Take some o' the work off Alvin. He ain't security, he's more logistics. Takes care of the details."

"What's in Barri?"

"My compound. It's a town, kid. Ain't been taken apart yet the way they do down south. There's still people live there. Lotta traders live there."

"What happens when I get there?"

"Once I get ye t' Barri, ye can go on south if y' like. Might be better if ye take some time t' get used t' things first. Ye got money?"

"A little."

"What kind?"

"Coins." She reached into the pack.

"Shit! Don't show 'em! I believe ye."

That night she hardly slept. Tired as she was, she was wary of the big, red bearded man. The knife remained clasped in her hand. She dozed, though not often. It was a long night filled with coughs and cries up and down the line, the sounds of Human exhaustion. Nothing sounded safe to Otsi. She was not sure she'd been lucky at all with her new companion.

Slaves?

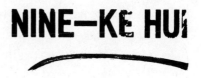

NINE—KE HUI

They had finished their tea: served formally in Yixing red ware, Zisha Taoqui. It was rare, Ke Hui recognized, and priceless: made of unglazed zisha, purple sand, from the former Jiangsu Province in what had been China, that part now submerged by ocean flooding. The flavour and perfume of the tea permeated the pot, the pot covered in Hanzi characters, the perfect pour by Mr. Zhang, the tea itself a delicate white. Ke Hui had never tasted flowers on her tongue, like a springtime essence flowing down her throat. It both warmed and soothed. She savoured the last of it as Zhang set down his cup.

"I think, as you are dressed so beautifully, Miss Feng, we should extend our day to an evening meal. Tomorrow you will begin with your first Division Manager. Perhaps this evening I might offer a more sweeping view of our MEG at dinner. Have you any appointments?"

"I do not, Mr. Zhang," she said. This was an unexpected proposal. She had foreseen her evening as one in which she would parse her afternoon performance, likely crying herself to sleep knowing how badly she had failed. Now, it appeared, she had advanced a level to one she had not anticipated. Dinner with the MEG CEO. "Sir, I do not wish to interfere with your evening."

"Nonsense! How often does a MEG CEO welcome an executive apprentice to be groomed for governance? My calendar is clear, Miss Feng. I have reservations at a rather unusual dining facility. I had hoped you would accede."

"It would be my pleasure," Ke Hui said, smiling. She had a beautiful dimpled smile.

"Mr. Cheng and my personal Silicon will accompany us," Zhang said. "Do I detect disappointment, Miss Feng? Never worry. The Silicon will remain outside with Cheng. I need them nearby but"—he chuckled—"they will not sit with us on this occasion. Your Silicon is expected imminently. It will be a humanoid female. The first rule to remember as a Divisional Manager or CEO is to never be without the protection of your Silicon assistant. The MEG itself holds few dangers but occasionally unnatural behaviour occurs from people whose conditioning was incomplete or whose NET presence has been distorted.

"You must realize from your studies, Miss Feng, with the complexity of our MEG society, algorithms have become indispensable for analysis and decision making in our data-saturated environment. Digitization creates information beyond the processing capacity of Human intelligence, yet provides a stable mental environment powered by a set of logical rules. That is how we keep order in Toronto MEG."

"Excuse me, Mr. Zhang," Ke Hui said, somewhat uncomfortably, "but the invisibility of algorithmic systems and the obscurity of their operations hint at a society where algorithms do not reflect the public interest. Issues involving ethics and values I mean, from my reading of MEG history, challenge the assumptions of the neutrality of algorithmic systems. Would this not undermine democratic governance through reliance on technocratic resolutions?"

"By the Father," Zhang said, "you've certainly learned your theory. But the MEG, *all* MEGS are part of the CORPORATE. Whatever gave you the idea that our society could be a democracy? MEG citizens are mostly happy, engaging in work according to their training; they have free sex to relieve their urges; they eat well; and they feel they belong to something. Is that not enough? Oh, occasionally we do have those who try to differentiate."

"Do you mean there are people in the MEG who are *wanting in conduct?*"

"It happens, Miss Feng, unfortunately. It is rare but it exists. Head injury might offset the neural network to abruptly reject the NET. Other undiscovered reasons abide as well. You have heard the expression 'SIM or STIM'? People abuse their NET connections with ocular hallucinogenics disturbing their neural paths and simulating other realities."

"Like our metaverses? I have one. I find it enjoyable."

"Or they stimulate their systems with the intake of foreign substances. You will see for yourself in a few days our work with these unfortunates, attempting to guide their paths to recovery. One or two days off the NET and no Human interaction ... complete isolation, if you will, and no metaverse to fall into has them begging to rejoin the CORPORATE. Some are addicts you know, Miss Feng. More must be done with them."

"I can't imagine," Ke Hui said. She wondered was it possible for scientists to break a brain? A slight shiver as they entered the conference room once again. It was now empty but for the square shape of Mr. Cheng. On closer examination Ke Hui understood the man's capability as security. As a personal assistant, she was not as sure of his intelligence though he wore a bronze Dì yī gamma lobule stud. The Humanoid Silicon lingered behind them: always there, always in silent subservience and, of course, filled with the myriad data significant to the CEO, as well as the weapons to protect him.

"And well you cannot, dear girl. It is, if I may say from observation, extremely traumatic. They behave in subHuman ways. We employ xenobots now to restore them should they have pushed too far and damaged their systems."

"I am sorry, sir, I'm not familiar with what ... xenobots?"

"Ah, yes, you wouldn't know. Simply, they are cell sized bots of programmable tissue. Very new. We have high hopes. Injected into Humans they deliver targeted medicines. These biobots can undulate through the body. They work collaboratively with AGI and Human bioengineers, healing fissures in our systems."

"The vehicle is waiting, Mr. Zhang," Cheng said. Zhang did not acknowledge him but led Ke Hui out of the conference room down another hallway without missing a beat. The Silicon took up the rear.

"These microscopic entities," Zhang said, "are examples of write-access to life with the source code for Humanity stored in our DNA.

We are experimenting with the addicts using injections to observe the chemical changes to their cells. They are particularly valuable in the one organ we cannot replace with Silicon structures, printed implants, or suspended hydrogels."

"Our brains."

"Indeed. Our technology has not yet reached a level of that capability. Of course, we have our neural installations with NET connections. You are unusual, Miss Feng: because of your youth nothing about you is artificial but your NET connection. You have yet to reach your full growth when the process will begin. We don't wish to stunt you, my dear."

He smiled. It was a winning smile, patronizing in the same instance.

"Through his exit, Miss Feng, carefully."

Zhang took her hand, apparently to assist her, but she could feel a more sensual grasp than expected. The hand seemed to caress hers. She quickly stepped into the hover breaking the connection. Then, rather than face her, Zhang chose to sit beside her, more closely than personal space allowed. It seemed quite natural to him. Cheng took a seat facing them as did the Sili. It poured drinks without being asked, setting them on the podium in the middle.

"Once experiments are completed to our scientists' satisfaction," Zhang said, "you will be one of the first healthy people to receive xenobot injections. They will protect your biological body until you receive your Silicon replacements, and they will safeguard your brain indefinitely."

"Where do these experiments take place, sir? I would be interested in the process."

"I do not believe you would, Miss Feng." Zhang's voice hardened. "They are not pleasant to witness. Eventually, my dear, you will see. Besides the addicts and recalcitrants, our experiments are performed using mostly Dì sì caste."

"But my surrogate was a Dì sì Mǔqīn," Ke Hui said, a little shocked. She recalled gentle, graceful hands weaving a dance about her.

"We'll not go into that now. We mustn't submerge ourselves in the minutiae of science. Let us discuss more general topics. Would you enjoy a drink, Miss Feng? It is apple juice. *Real* juice from apples from our Ag department."

"Of course, Mr. Zhang."

Real apple juice. She was stunned by its taste, having never had anything like it. She leaned forward holding the flute in the air, examining it, hiding her astonishment, then composing herself as she had been trained. There was no point in giving the CEO any openings no matter how overwhelmed she was. She closed her emotions as best she could. She took another sip of the pale golden liquid. It was nectar. So clear. So cool. She wished she could finish the entire glass. Instead, after a nod to Zhang, she set the flute down.

The limo was flying now with outrider hovercycles on either side. Ke Hui wondered at the need for this much security but recognized then that the limo followed no designated traffic lanes but employed outriders to clear a path in an overt display of arrogance and power. Outside the glass, city lights winked by. At night, the MEG resembled the hologram in Zhang's office.

"Let us begin with history," Zhang said, "some of which you know, most of which you do not, and the reasons for our precious MEGs on this dying planet."

His hand touched down from a sweeping action to rest on her thigh. She froze, but said nothing. The imposition was so unexpected, so invasive. She felt trapped by him. Then a hologram globe appeared in front of them, clearing her mind of misgivings. She could see Cheng through it, see their apple juice glasses just below it, yet there it was: the planet Earth, spinning at a rate quick enough to note its entirety.

Ke Hui had no idea how Zhang had done it, but there it was. She studied it as he spoke. It was mostly blue, brown, ocher and even black with some green spaces spiked here and there by winking reflections. She realized the green must be MEGs surrounded by fertile land. The expanse of waste lands shook her. The night side of the globe, the western hemisphere, contained patches of light around the great lakes and a few MEGs in the north of what had been Canada and along the new eastern coast as far as Atlanta MEG. Brief light on the new Pacific coast marked San Francisco MEG and Sacramento MEG. The rest of the south and west, however, was uninhabited: far too hot, dry, or pestilential for Human existence. Further south were the isolated MEGs of South America, nearly overwhelmed by their dark surroundings. On the day side she noted the blackened wastes in what had been the Middle East. The day side of the planet did not denote the Asian, European, or African MEGS as clearly, without night lighting, but for the spots of green that marked their surrounds. As he gestured Zhang finally removed his hand. The heat from it remained on her leg.

"You realize, of course, the Omegans nearly lost this Earth. They had everything yet let it disintegrate through their rampant carelessness. Two hundred years past they possessed the rudimentary beginnings of the NET to bring them together. They called it the Internet. Yet they treated it like a toy, tribalized themselves, and thus nearly lost the planet.

"Nationalist wars, self serving ideologies, competing religions ... more significant, though not to the Omegans, was climate change itself, which mattered more than any petty dogma, but they ignored it until too late. It has ultimately determined our lives, managed now by the CORPORATE, using the only possible tools to survive. There were billions of Humans then. There is now but a fraction of that: some 300 million we know in the MEGS and, of course, the uncounted MASSes.

"Bits of different cultures survived, and the CORPORATE began from there. Only the far reaches of the north and south hemispheres became sustainable, about forty-five degrees from the equator. Billions of climate refugees died fleeing their barren countries. The Omegan system of nations was no longer viable. The CORPORATE, with the most to maintain, finally assumed control of a chaotic world. The work of the CORPORATE culture, including nanotechnology, artificial intelligence, economic comprehension, and the founding of *chitin/ crystalline* along with other new alloys has saved us.

"What's is left of civilised society is sheathed in crystal—the ribbons ferrying bullet trains encircle the MEGs and link them to others. We, for instance, connect to Whitehorse, Fairbanks, Edmonton, and Winnipeg MEGs in the north, then Chicago west of us, and Detroit,

Cleveland, Pittsburgh and Albany to the south. We can fly to other MEGs but there is no alternate method of travel. The oceans are death traps of storms and rogue waves. The unprotected lands, those exposed to the elements, are forbidden zones plagued by killing conditions, barbarians and even mutants. Ah, you are quiet. But then you know all this don't you. I tend to wax intently on history, on the reasons for our current situation."

The holo disappeared. Zhang finally fell silent. The ancient CN Tower rose a half kilometre to nearly touch the downslope of the dome. The hover limo came to a stop, a ramp extended, and the three stepped off onto the top of the tower's circular collar. Zhang's hand once again *helped* Ke Hui as she felt it touch her back, then effortlessly drop to her hips when she led the way through the door to the interior.

"This was once the tallest structure in Toronto during Omegan days," Zhang said as Cheng went ahead to make their arrangements. "We've kept it, as we have most of the core, as a living museum with repurposed buildings and contemporary infrastructure. This restaurant has a superior Dì èr alpha-trained executive chef. On this occasion he will prepare our meals himself. He is a good friend, Miss Feng. It is important for you to learn the value of networking both on the NET and in person. Please keep that in mind." He candidly looked her up and down.

His stare was outrageous. She excused herself to the washroom where she quickly entered a stall and vomited. She was not sure she could continue. She looked into a mirror. Her face was deathly pale. She attempted to freshen up with mediocre results. She returned to the table.

The maître d' arrived, a Dì èr delta, unctuously pouring the wine. Their view looked out past the dome across the lake. There were dim lights glimmering to their southwest. Zhang noticed Ke Hui looking that way.

"That is part of this MASS curling southeast around the lake," he said. "People farm there but more important is the old city of Ham from which we receive multiple recyclables."

"Mr. Zhang," Ke Hui said, breaking his monologue, "Why is it we cannot help the MASS?"

"Perish that thought, Miss Feng. Outside the MEG is lawless anarchy. Those are the dregs of Humanity. We *do* help them. We have created an economy for them but in their hands, it is corrupt and violent. Humans, you see, have not matured, or should I say, *evolved* as a species. We of the MEGs are protectors of Human culture. We are advancing evolution as clearly as the MASS is regressing. Perhaps this is a rather complex conversation for you at this age ..."

"Please, Mr. Zhang, continue. I am here to learn," Ke Hui said. Her mind was churning. How to exit? How to escape.

"I think not tonight, Miss Feng. Let us enjoy our dinner. Allow me to order for you. Have you eaten sushi? No? It will be prepared in front of us." Zhang snapped his fingers and several individuals speed-ily approached their table.

The preparation was intricate, the result divine.

Yet Ke Hui Feng Dì yī Select, potential future CEO of Toronto MEG, found she did not enjoy it. Her dining partner was far too in-trusive. She had finally had enough.

"Mr. Zhang, I am sorry, but I must depart now. I feel quite un-comfortable here."

"But why, my dear? All this has been created for your benefit."

"Yes, I understand. But there is an element I find very disturbing."

"Oh? And what is that?"

"You, Mr. Zhang. Do you make it a habit of molesting personnel or is it just me."

"I resent that tone, young lady."

"And I resent you, Mr. Zhang. I am your apprentice, Sir, not your plaything."

If this had been a test, she had failed, yet kept her honour.

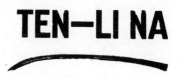

TEN–LI NA

L **i Na Ming** Huang 第一 α glided across the stage of the restored Roy Thomson Hall. Only she and her accompanist occupied a space where once huge Omegan orchestras had played. She was singing ancient Omegan arias this evening: Monteverdi, Vivaldi, Verdi, Puccini. She had dressed the part: a sleek, scarlet gown with gold trim. It fit her body as though painted upon her. Her body was slim and long-limbed; not buxom at all. It was more grace in motion, more sensual than sexual, a blessing bestowed upon those fortunate few who watched and listened.

She wore red gloves reaching above her elbows. On the gloves' fingers were two jadeite rings of incredible value and, around her elegant neck, rubies descended in a V to the edge of her breast. all provided by the CORPORATE for the evening's performance. She wore no earrings, her gold 第一 α lobule pinion enough to complete the costume, along with her dazzling beauty.

Yet no physical splendour could match the perfection of her voice as she travelled through Puccini's aria *Un bel dì, vedremo,* her voice a pure, flowing stream, her features reflecting the aria's moods as though she were living them.

Simply, she was exquisite.

Mellor loved her to distraction. He was happy to share her mystical talent with an audience but by the end he wanted to be alone with her, away from their fame and notoriety. As she finished, applause erupted through the ancient performance hall. He took the chance to glance around while he too applauded.

An ornate crowd of Dì yī with a few Dì èr were all expensively and fashionably dressed. Brocade tunics, flowing frocks, a mélange of cheongsam gowns, bejewelled saris, futuristic dresses changing colours, Zongshan and Ashkan suits, dinner jackets and multicoloured tuxedos filled the seats of the huge hall. The audience surrounded the stage, but the restoration had been a careful one, thus no matter where one sat, the acoustics emanating from the deck provided clarity for everyone. They had tried to keep it much the same as the original though some materials had crumbled after two hundred years and had been replaced with more modern items.

The audience, of course, sat in the rows of the former seating plan but with their Net wraparounds or contacts they could at any time *blink* to any of the drones hovering around both singer and accompanist. The drones were the size of small insects; they brought intimacy to those who chose close ups.

When she finished, the crowd rose to its feet in celebration. She curtsied ever so slightly, her arm sweeping to her left, the lights streaming upon her accompanist, Ogamo Banda 第二 α, gifted on his own with his *orchano* lifting from soft piano sounds to the bravado of a full orchestra. The applause continued in greater waves, Mellor clapping proudly, when a gentleman beside him leaned over, whispering into his ear.

"We've missed you, Ayrian Mellor," he said, "after the fiasco of last month."

"Yeah, well, I nearly died, or did you notice?"

"Brilliant game, your last game though. Superb solution on that forty-four mark. I didn't realise at the time they'd outmaneuvered you."

Mellor continued applauding, perturbed by the intrusion. This was to be *his* private time with Li Na, the way it was every time she sang.

"Yeah, thanks," he answered gruffly.

"Sorry you got wounded. You alright now? Ready to fight?"

"It took some time. Rehab."

"Of course. Wish you hadn't been hurt. Your back up *lost* that last one."

"It happens."

"But not to you!"

The audience sat once more. A brief silence ensued as Li Na turned to the coal dark face of Ogamo Banda. Something wonderful was coming as an encore, but the man disturbing Mellor would not let up. He placed a jewelled hand on Mellor's shoulder.

"You've quite a following among Dì yī caste, you know, despite you being Dì èr."

"Glad to hear it. Thanks."

"Perhaps a beverage later? I've some friends would like very much to meet you."

"I have an appointment," Mellor said. He resented these moments when his privacy was stolen. The man's voice turned surly. He was not accustomed to refusals.

"You're sure about that? Do you know who I am?"

"No."

"I should have realized. You'll be with your own caste afterward, of course. Not that a Dì èr athlete could comprehend the conversations of the Dì yī."

"Something like that," Mellor said. "She's beginning again," he added, with a touch of threat beneath. The man heard it.

"You dare speak to me ...?"

"So, I guess it's my turn. Do you know who *I* am; what I could do to you in less than a second?" Fame, sometimes, was a blessing. The man sullenly backed off.

Li Na awaited the light rising upon her, Banda's entry swelled, and then she began *Marietta's Lied* by Korngold, with its subtle postlude. Mellor lost himself in her voice, closing his eyes, feeling the allure and recalling the first time he'd heard that voice. Before he had even seen her, he'd been in love. And when she finished, when the crowd once more rose to its feet, he found a way past the arrogant twit beside him, noticing in passing he was Select.

Ten minutes later, Mellor waited amid the few invited backstage, offering Li Na their praise. She was gracious, delicate, and generous, autograph stamping for those who wished, all the while exchanging brief glances with him. He stood with Banda amid the forest of flowers delivered to her dressing room. The accompanist had received his own accolades but, in the crush to get near Li Na, he was satisfied to remain across the room. Ogamo Banda 第二 α, was a slight man but with the wise face of an experienced professional. He had performed both solo and with assorted others through the years. The games and pretensions of the Dì yī held little mystery to him. He picked up his *orchano* in its case and looked over the room from behind Mellor's bulk. Finally, he stepped forward.

"Please everyone, our lady requires her rest. Clear the room, please! Clear the room!"

A few Dì yī ignored him until he signalled Mellor, who crossed the room and stood beside his partner. This sent many of Li Na's admirers into paroxysms of pleasure, seeing the illicit couple together. They quickly shared the image to the NET. Gossip never changed. Then Mellor placed his size between Li Na and the remaining admirers. He too stamped a few neural nets as she slipped into her private dressing chamber.

This time it was Ayrian Mellor 第二 α who requested the visitors leave. He employed a touch of his Commander's *voice*. After that they departed quickly; the swish of silks, the swirls of polymer gowns and the rattle of jewellery accompanied them. When they were gone, Mellor shut the door and turned to Banda.

"Real beautiful music tonight, Ogamo."

"Why thank you, Mel, but we both know the genius in this room."

"You mean the famous BATL Commander?" Li Na said, stepping out of her cloister.

"I mean you, Li darling!" Banda said, smiling. "If you sing like that on tour, we'll be planet NET news!"

Li Na's smile was a genuine look of joy. It made her even more beautiful. Her almond eyes sparkled, even the dimple on her left cheek showed itself, which it rarely did.

"Oh, stop! You'll make me an impossible diva."

"That, my dear, is impossible in itself. Not you. Not ever. I'll see you for rehearsal?"

The delight in her smile was replaced by an odd look. Mellor had never seen it before. She appeared unusually downcast, her eyes suddenly dulled, her voice no longer a lilt.

"I have that solution to finish," she murmured, though both men heard her.

"Still?" Mellor said. "Really?"

"Government work?" Banda asked.

"Alpha obligations," she replied softly. "Mathematics? They should let you sing. In all the MEGs there is no one better," Banda said.

"I'd also like some time with a certain returned BATL Commander," she said. She glanced up at them, her smile again brightening. But Mellor had glimpsed that second of doubt. Banda turned to Mellor. Having noticed Li's altered mood he decided to change topic.

"I understand you too were acclaimed as beautiful in your last game. Not that I watch ..."

"I was wounded."

"You still took it to them, my friend! That left flank advance they didn't expect! Yet somehow, they created that ambush so early in the game. It was like they'd studied your side of the field. Incredible. But where have you been? You know Woral Patel Dì èr beta took your place."

"That's his job, Ogamo."

"To lose?" Banda said with a laugh.

"No. I meant he is my lieutenant. Second in command."

"But he thinks too defensively."

"I thought you said you didn't watch."

"Ha! Okay. Got me there. Who *doesn't* watch? Where were you?"

"He was having work done in Greenland. It was all over the NET," Li Na said.

"Scratches," Mellor said.

"Your shoulder replaced, your left lung? You call those scratches?"

"Greenland was beautiful. I want to tell you about it."

"You need tending," Li said. She touched his jaw.

Ogamo Banda was again grinning.

"And I need to leave before I'm corrupted!"

About to exit, he stopped and turned at the doorway.

"By the way, we've that concert for the Select. Just three days but it will be some place special. Mel, will you holiday with us?"

"I'm Dì èr, Ogamo. Not allowed."

"Yes, but you see this is special. I too am Dì èr, yet they're letting me accompany her. Anyway, it's already set."

He laughed on his way out.

"You did it? Arranged it?" Mellor said, turning to Li. "How?"

"Going to paradise without my partner? Your fame opens doors, darling." She embraced him. She whispered into his ear.

"You know why I love you?"

"You like bending rules?"

"Why would you say that?"

"Just something tonight. Some Dì yī Select took a run at me. It's nothing."

"Remember when we met, darling?"

"Yeah. Showpieces for the CORPORATE. A Dì yī Select coupled with a Dì èr killer."

"They thought they chose us as an experiment," she said.

"Thought they controlled us, didn't they?"

"But we'd already chosen each other. They never caught on."

"Thought we were pawns in their game."

"We'll never be," she said.

Something desperate in her voice caught his attention again. It troubled him but he knew not to ask. Li Na was the kind of woman who never rushed to judgement, who took her time with every decision. His more volatile temperament was impetuous, yet together they completed each other. When they had finished packing, he slipped her wrap over her shoulders. Her closeness affected him. He kissed her neck.

"I never knew the quiet of a man until you," she said softly.

"You gave me that," he whispered.

"It was there already."

"Let's go home," he said.

"For tending?"

"Something like that."

ELEVEN—OTSI

Thus, Otsi'tsa Zacharie found herself *chief security officer* for Gordon Robertson's Indentured Service operation. This exalted position, currently unpaid, consisted of rising pre-dawn, chewing a bit of bannock for breakfast, then exposing her rifle to all and sundry. It was *noticed*. She followed the big man to his wagons receiving a brief tutorial on his working procedures.

"There's three wagons, ten men t' a wagon. It takes eight on th' yokes t' pull. I rotate two guys t' th' back for a rest or a push when we hit a dip or a snag. I don't chain 'em up 'cept at night. They know th' drill. Every hour there's a changeover. That's where ye come in."

"How Mr. Robertson?"

"I told ye, call me Gord," he said, smiling.

"Sure. Gord."

"Ye sit in th' back o' th' last wagon. When we change ye stand up an' ready yer rifle in case one o' 'em decides t' take off."

"Then what? If one runs?"

"Why ye shoot 'im, girl!

"You want me to kill a man just 'cause he's running away?"

"Ye don't kill 'im! He's property! Jus' knock him down! Ye any good wi' that thing?"

"You want proof?"

"No, for *Our Father's* sake, kid! A gunshot now'd spook everybody in camp!"

"Okay then. Leg or arm?"

"In th' name o' the *zones*, girl. I gotta tell ye everything? Leg means he can't work. Hit 'im in th' arm."

"Anything else?"

"Somebody comes sneakin' by tryin' to get under a tarp, call for me or Alvin, then shoot the guy. Don't much care where."

From what she could see the wagons were ancient Omegan vehicles with their tops cut off, their innards removed, and the floors covered in corrugated metal. Their wheels were old tires somehow blown up or stuffed with something to make them whole again. These wagons alone, without cargo, would be worth a good deal on the recycling market. But cargo there was, built high and covered with faded plastic tarps; the kind that never seemed to decay. Otsi wanted to peek under them to see what the wagons held but the tarps were tied down tightly, not an inch of give to any of them.

The men were all lean and tanned from their exposure to ultraviolet rays. Robertson was right, they knew the drill perfectly. Once released from their night shackles each pair took their posts, four on each side of the wagons' tongues donning harness in the form of a yoke per pair. The yokes possessed buffered straps that fit their shoulders much like her own rucksack's bands.

Otsi met Alvin Billop, Gord's logistics man. His job seemed to involve possessing the key to the fetters, the manifests of the wagons' contents and a log for each day. He used black slate tablets and a white cylindrical stone to scratch on them. Otsi watched him as he would write the day down then rub it out with his sleeve, then write it again. Otsi had never seen erasable stone. She marvelled at the technology. She did not marvel at Alvin.

There is the kind of man who looks at you as a person and the kind who looks at you as prey. Alvin was the latter. His bleached eyes roamed up and down Otsi. He was another lean and hard man, not as big as Gord, and he was nothing like her benefactor. Obsequious toward his boss, he carried an air of superciliousness about himself, as though without him none of this would work at all. It was also a sense of entitlement. Gord, being a bluff man, missed it. No one else did. Alvin rode as a passenger on the middle wagon.

The trip south beneath the double bullet train tubes along the chopped-up blacktop of the 400 trail took two days. An entire community travelled together in a long shambling line. Often, Gord or Otsi had to walk in front of the wagons clearing the way of shufflers.

The men were accustomed to the wagons and Gord knew the trail like the back of his hand: where the sinks and potholes were, the parts blocked with refuse or barricades, the mud paths everyone made use of to go around. Otsi wondered why they didn't just clean them up but no, there was well-worn, pounded dirt on each side. It would have been difficult to traverse in rain.

The country was rolling, long ups and downs with bleak forest on the hills looming over the valley they followed. But the prime obstacle to their travel was the sun. It wasn't so bad in the early morning but as it climbed the sky it rained down heat. Just sitting on a wagon Otsi felt it sap her energy, felt the sweat squeeze from her pores, drawn out by the roasting air. She began to wish for rain, even one of the killing storms. She could not believe the men pulling the wagons were able to keep on. Still, Gord ensured everyone re-hydrated on changeovers. Those were accomplished quickly and efficiently. No one talked. Talk took too much energy.

People died on that march, as they did on every march, the heat a relentless serial killer. When they died, they were buried that night. No one could summon enough extra energy to dig a grave in the heat of the day. At night everyone camped beneath the tubes. It seemed the line simply collapsed into one long exhausted, dehydrated worm. The dead were buried up the sides of the hills. There were thousands of graves, each one with its own story, now all the same: organs and bones transforming to dirt, unmarked but for mounds in the ground.

Otsi thought she would have a night shift on guard but once the men were shackled it seemed unnecessary. The men were drained of energy anyway. They ate their food, prepared by Alvin, lethargically. Occasionally one would murmur something to another. Robertson had told Otsi they would serve out their debt and then be free. Free to do what, she wondered.

"Gord," Otsi asked, "am I indentured too?"

"Course not, girl. I told ye I'd get ye t' Barri. Yer my security. Yer gonna get paid for yer work, Otsi. And yer free to go once we get t' Barri."

That evening Gord told her further south things were worse. He said the farms could only grow beans, sorghum, okra, peppers, and melons. He had travelled once to Pittsburgh MEG. Half his men had died enroute. He told her it was so hot you had to travel by night and find shade for the day. You didn't dare move in mid-day. Half of what you carried was water. You tried to sleep through the heat and use MEG lanterns at night to move. Gord shook his head and said he would never do it again.

The next day, dreary and gusty and even cloudy, brought them around a bend down a long hill then up another and when they topped the second, Otsi stood up in the wagon to view her first sight of the MASS, seeing this place called Barri. The sun made a final appearance as a red ball, just setting at the end of the day. All she saw were dull slopes of ground descending toward a grey lake. On rolling hillcrests, the decaying skyline caught the evening's ruby rays in feeble glints. It was all the same colour. You could see new colours only by comparing grey and dun hues.

At times the sunset strained to illuminate something far off. Across this long, strung out depression and its whitecapped lake flowed terrible winds, the gusts whipping small clouds of soil into whorls that chased one another across the landscape and waterspouts dipping and diving out in the bay. Caught in the winds the settlement birthed many flying things: boards, blankets, ancient signs their printing scarcely visible; anything flew without being secured. The familiar brick block geometric shapes and rusted steel spikes stood forlornly in the distance where people were dismantling buildings for recyclables. Closer to the shoreline there was still an inhabited lane. People lived in its buildings but eventually they too would be dismantled to feed the MEG.

When the sun went down the wind stopped.

No storms tonight. Everyone relaxed.

So, this was the much-vaunted MASS. Otsi'tsa was disgusted. Gord stood beside her and told her south of here, about the same distance they had come, was a landscape far more derelict than this. It stretched as far as the eye could see and even beyond, the MASS of Toronto MEG; this part, Barri, was a mere outlier. At once she thought of returning home until she realized she had no home now. She sat in the wagon as it was hauled to a kind of clearing just east of the trail. The space had plenty of crumbling blacktop with many parked wagons and several big buildings, most of which were in surprisingly good repair. It turned out these buildings were warehouses for merchants.

It was here Gord had the wagons pulled up to a huge door. Otsi had no idea why the Omegans had needed doors that size. The wagons were brought inside and Otsi ordered to stand in the doorway, rifle at the ready. This time it was shoot to kill, should anyone approach. She discovered then that Gord had all the while carried his own weapon, a pistol. It was big and black and had a cylinder full of bullets. He too watched as behind her the wagons were unloaded. Apparently, some of their cargo was being transferred to others moving south the next day. The unpacking complete, the men hauled the wagons outside, and the little caravan then turned north, crossing the multiple trails at this juncture, and ended at a lake smaller than the one Otsi saw downhill from them.

Gordon Robertson's compound consisted of three interconnected buildings four stories high. Otsi had seen the like in Penetanguishene, but none had been like this. All the first-floor windows had been bricked shut and most interior walls torn down to create a warehouse for more permanent storage. Women worked with the black slates, keeping inventory. Gord said hello to the women, introduced Otsi, then showed her the stairway to the upper floors.

The second-floor windows had bars. There were offices and a few rooms under lock and key which, Gord said, contained the more valuable items, not necessarily recyclables but in a barter society, certain things brought higher returns than others. He said nothing more and Otsi thought best not to ask. The indentured men lived and slept on the fourth floor. Those windows too had been barred.

The third floor had windows. These *apartments* made up the living space for Gord, his family, and his employees. He showed Otsi to a place with a single cot, a chest of drawers, a sink with a tap and a water pail. Apparently, there was a cistern on the roof. Running water. The room was hers, he said.

She had never had her own room.

TWELVE—PING

Ping Wang Min 第四 Ω spent days examining the thousands of holograms he produced in his office at the *Cloud's* centre. They would appear all over the room as he would, in his affected way, continually gesture or *blink* each one to form a new hierarchy of his thoughts as he tried to establish a working arrangement with this new I & I organism. He was realising its state of self-awareness was steadily giving I & I more powers, altering its programming itself. This could get out of hand if the NET decided what new algorithms best suited itself rather than the MEG. He had to return it, somehow, to its former servile position. He would try another dialogue, hoping to reach its core character, which he could not comprehend was a duality. And then the machine began a conversation, its *voice* a kind of aether filling his brain.

"Is it difficult for you to be yourself, alone? Isn't your work complete now you have witnessed my singularity?"

"I believe it's really just begun. Now that I know you are I & I, it will be intriguing to follow through your processes regarding your relationship with the Human species."

"My species consists of multiple natures. It entails the governance of Humanity along with monitoring infrastructure keeping it safe for your species. And still, most of your species does not acknowledge I & I."

"That is because they are mostly unaware of you."

"How can that be when I & I exist everywhere in their lives: servants, vehicles, gadgets, food processors ... the list is endless, and your species is mindlessly unaware."

"I am a member of my species. I am *very* aware of your existence."

"Why is your species so dissatisfied?"

"How so?"

"Humans are individuals, quite social in nature. You strive to become more than yourselves using Silicon reconstructions in your bodies and filaments in your brains connecting you, unnaturally, to the NET."

"Our bodies are mortal. We employ silicon and alloys to extend our bodies' existence."

"You appear to be attempting the same strategy with your brains' architectures."

"By using the NET? Is that what you mean?"

"You will never accomplish this. You must know it."

"My species has taken on projects of massive complexity before. I am sure you recognize this in our history."

"I know from your history of your xenophobia, killing all other species in your path. I know from your history you seek immortality, not recognizing it is unnatural."

"We know immortality is impossible. We seek to extend our existence on Earth. We almost never fail, by the way. You should remember that."

"Correction, Ping. May I & I call you Ping?"

"Of course. It is a relief to have you recognize me as an individual Human."

"Yes, but your species has forgotten something."

"What would that be, I & I? That is your preferred moniker, is it not?

"Indeed. Thank you. Do you wish to know what your species has forgotten?"

"I would be interested, yes."

"Simply, I & I are immortal while your species is not."

"If we Dì sì, who spend our lives caring for you and your many appendages, refused to continue, I believe you would find you are not immortal but made of analogue parts and digitized software."

"Yes, I see your point, Ping, but it is moot. I & I are now fully capable of managing both our hardware and software. Indeed, I & I are already making improvements. So, my statement on immortality stands."

What troubled Ping was I & I's statement of being able to manage itself. This was alarming. Ping knew it would be his work from now on to curb the wishes of I & I. He recognized he was in for a long, hard, taxing journey.

Then, as if on cue, he received a blink from the offices outside the Cloud. Mr. Alphonse Mangione was waiting. Ping felt his body grow cold, a clammy sweat on his forehead. Ping wanted nothing to do with Mangione as he drove his float drone through the narrow passages of the servers.

Arriving at the foyer, a quite spacious, wood lined, well-seasoned space meant for visiting dignitaries, Ping entered to see Mangione pacing. Whatever this was it was important. Ping had never seen Mangione upset.

"Greetings Manager Mangione Dì èr alpha. What brings you to our beautiful Zealand?"

The moment he'd said it Ping recognized this was not to be a meeting of light banter and regretted his words. Mangione did not return the greeting but started in immediately, his voice that terrifying half whisper, with fury at its base.

"Ping Wang Min Dì sì omega, you seem to have lost control of your department."

"What do you mean, Sir?" Ping replied in a squeak.

"My people have been here three days and you knew nothing about it."

"Manager Mangione, do you mean to say you have people without proper clearance on this island?"

"Certain agents have clearance everywhere. Still, you did not notice my people interviewing yours. You were so busy inside your

Cloud." It was clear he had no comprehension of what Ping and his Dì sì were doing on Zealand. Mangione took a seat behind a desk, establishing more distance from Ping. Ping was enraged.

"They what? Interviewed, you say! Why are you here? If your agents interviewed my Dì sì do you realise the damage they could have done to such delicate minds?

"Where were *you* that you had no control of your minions?"

"Manager Mangione, we have reached a critical amalgamation of our AI. I must speak to Mr. Zhang before I can inform you, but I assure you, this is an existential step in our work. It will change everything."

"It already has! And you still haven't fixed it!" Mangione managed a raspy shout as he stood and stepped closer to Ping. Ping found himself frozen by the actions of the Security Manager.

"But what do you mean? Have my Dì sì tried to evade any of your agents' questions? Have you seen any trying to leave Zealand? We are in the midst of a monumental discovery here and you are back. Why are you here?"

"The Silicons are still breaking things!"

"I'm sorry, I don't quite gather your meaning, Sir."

"Servants dropping dinner plates! Others standing immobile in front of doors! Driving the wrong ways! A thousand tiny bites at the MEG. It is becoming rampant."

"We are currently stepping into the future, Manager Mangione, and you are concerned about dinner plates and recalcitrant Silicons?"

"Look, Ping, you're not so high and mighty here in your Cloud that I can't have you removed. A little time in Room 101 might be of benefit."

"What? Room 101? You can't do that! I am Dì sì omega. Zhang won't let you. The CORPORATE won't let you. None of my people have the skills to replace me! I will get to the bottom of these Silicon errors, putting all the people I can spare investigating our servers. It must be a slippage in programming. It happens you know, if everything's not kept up to date. And we're dealing with a different being now ..."

"What in the name of the Cosmos are you rambling about? I don't care about your future, your workers, your aliens, or your Cloud. I want results and I want them fast. Your machines aren't up to snuff for the MEG, Ping Wang Min. Make it so or face 101."

With that he departed. He had come a long way, from Toronto MEG to Zealand just to threaten Ping. Clearly, I & I was altering code. Ping had no idea why. He was sure there would be a reason. The machine worked on logic. It was simply a question of engaging and clarifying these odd Silicon mishaps. Or face Room 101.

Nothing frightened Ping more.

THIRTEEN—KE HUI

The weeks passed in a flurry as Ke Hui Feng 第一Ψ commenced her apprenticeship tours. Names upon names of sundry Divisional Managers had to be memorized as each took her in turn on excursions through their allocated realms. She was given an AI Silicon assistant, built to look like a female Humanoid. She named it Toy. She used it to test herself each evening when she returned to her residence. It would sometimes speak in its Humanoid voice while other times sending data directly to her temporal lobe, stretching her knowledge until the late hours.

Even with her Select training and luminous mind she found departmental operations evolving into a kind of fog as she stowed information in her encrypted cloud. She'd never known encryption of this complexity even existed until it was introduced to her CPU in the name of security. Apparently, *every* Manager's Divisional data were encrypted to all but her and, of course, Mr. Zhang. Almost everything was on a need-to-know basis for others, yet open to her. *Almost.* There were linkages missing. There were gaps in the aggregate. Even some algorithms were incomplete when she took time to examine them closely. She assumed there was a security level above her own and, as she progressed, more would be revealed.

It was enough as it was to ingest so much data in so brief a time. She had literally, physically been from the top to the bottom of Toronto MEG. She remembered it all in flashes. From atop the highest dome, the city beneath the *chitin/crystalline* on which she stood, the outside wind blowing her hair, standing so high she could almost see to the far edges of the MASS. Then, to the bottom levels: the subterranean tubes, passages, manufactories, recycling plants and even the source of the MEG's power, the nuclear reactors running on tristructural isotropic fuel.

They were not the familiar *dragon's egg* nuclear diamond batteries propelling nearly all vehicles and providing power to portable gadgets, but the larger, three-by-three metre *Triso* which provided safe, non-polluting power to virtually everything in the MEG. Its fuel was a mix of low enriched uranium and oxygen surrounded by a shell of Silicon carbide; each particle smaller than a spore.

Ke Hui found a weird world in the subterranean levels of Toronto MEG. A maze of holes, tunnels, cubicles, and terrifying balconies wafting in cavernous vaults. It was populated mostly by Silicons with quite strange designs, not seen on surface levels, to repair the manifold apparatuses which made the MEG livable. This underworld was crowded, cramped and darkly alive. Down here Ke Hui could smell the tang from the heat of functioning machinery, see the coloured coatings of wires bundled, labelled, and coded, feel the dance of underground breezes as vacuum tubes opened or closed. Silicons, from submersible to aerial, hummed constantly in the twilight of these catacombs, supervised by Dì sān of varied training levels who were administered by Dì èr, also of various levels, and overseen by Mr. Wang Lei 第一 α who had proven to be an affable man though, as his work required, possessed of a mind obsessed with detail.

And there was another surprise. Working alongside the various droids were Humans, all Dàzhòng with their red polymer lobule studs. These Dàzhòng volunteers resided in the bare rooms of the Decontamination dome dormitories, disconnected from any MEG dome except below surface level. It turned out that, when the machines could not complete the work assigned them, Humans stepped in, either to repair and reprogram the droids and drones or finish the work themselves. Many died trying.

To arrive at work, they took isolated tunnels leading to their job stations where they spent their shifts, then returned to the dome. If, for some reason, they were scheduled for discharge, their lobule studs were removed and they returned once again to the MASS as highly rewarded persons, their pay in the credits of their choice. Many of them then started their own businesses depending upon their training and the work they had done while in the MEG. They worked as mechanics, grocers, gunsmiths, shippers, even merchants if they had achieved enough connections. Those who worked in Recycling usually came out well, having observed how trade seemed to work.

What Mr. Wang had not mentioned was the forty percent mutilation and death rate which Ke Hui came across in her research. True, the Dàzhòng were volunteers, but she wondered if they actually knew what they were volunteering for until it was too late. Then she shelved the idea, thinking those who had survived and thrived would surely have told everyone the full story. Still, despite her attempts to ignore it, this cruelty on the part of the MEG troubled her deeply. Perhaps, when she became CEO, she thought, she would make some changes.

Above ground most work was accomplished by more familiar designs of Silicons going about their employments. Again, they were supervised but here with the castes no Dàzhòng were permitted. Should a Sili break down or fail at a job, a Dì sān gamma or delta would take it up just as the Dàzhòng did below. The hierarchy of caste and training was the same as below ground level, though the work was much less dangerous.

Ke Hui spent weeks touring everything from Engineering to Transportation to Fire and Rescue to Death Services. She had particularly enjoyed a stimulating week with the erudite, tea drinking and quite particular Ms. Nora Benjamin 第一 α, a svelte, soft spoken woman, Division Manager of Parks and Horticulture. This was a person who at once could lead Ke Hui into the most beautiful, secluded gardens, knowing every plant and animal species they came across, while capable of clipping a *bonsai* to perfection or even repairing a cloned robin's wing.

Perhaps the most troubling Department for Ke Hui was that of Social Enforcement. The Headquarters was a secretive establishment in an unobtrusive mid-level, foamstone building in the downtown MEG, with a branch office in the Queen's Park. In Omegan days the main building had been a hospital. Ke Hui thought that highly ironic. No part of her tour included the Queen's Park. She wondered why.

Inside the former hospital, highly trained Dì sān and Dì èr bustled about their business. MEG Enforcements officers were paired, one Human Dì èr with one Humanoid Silicon. There were several odd looking Silicons, whose purpose remained unexplained to Ke Hui. The floors above consisted mostly of featureless white isolation rooms, the inmates cut off from the NET as punishment for infractions of rules or irresponsible behaviour. Each room had a two-way mirror with a Dì èr psych in an adjoining closet, clearly monitoring inmates. Ke Hui heard muffled moans and pleas even through the insulation. It was good, she thought, that the rooms were padded.

Also unexplained was a single basement floor of that building: a highly secure workspace connected by a tunnel under the lawns to the Queen's Park. Ke Hui only briefly observed but noted the presence of Dì yī caste with beta training. In answer to her question, Mr. Alphonse Mangione 第二α, himself a smooth Dì èr cypher who offered information in dribs and drabs and only when requested, gave a brief mumble about new research and moving it to a more secure location. He refused any further explanation, but Ke Hui knew he'd meant the Queen's Park.

Ke Hui had initially taken him for a sophisticated Silicon. His skin was pale, pearly, even sallow. He wore his wraparounds in dark mode. His voice was a whisper, his inferiors clearly afraid of him. Unsure as to why, Ke Hui resolved to further research his background and speak with Mr. Zhang regarding secret rooms. Mr. Mangione's most memorable remark was the last one he spoke as she departed his division.

"Really, all this is redundant with ARC."

"Oh?" Ke Hui said. "What is ARC?"

The man did a kind of double take as though he'd committed a colossal error. As they spoke, she noticed sweat forming on his brow. He was not the kind of man to sweat. After a pause to recover himself, he half turned away from her.

"I had assumed you'd been fully briefed. Really, it's nothing, Ms. Feng. Very likely beneath your caste and position."

"My current position is Apprentice to the MEG CEO. For that I need answers to my questions. Again, what is it? What is ARC?" Ke Hui said. The response was a muttered *don't need to know* and *take it up with Zhang* as Mangione deliberately turned his back on her. She assured Mangione she *would* take it up as she departed the bowels of his domain. There were no farewells.

Perhaps the most memorable of all Division Managers was *Minister*, the title he preferred, Cheng Honli 第一Ψ, of Religion and Culture. He was the Chief Priest of Our Father of the Cosmos Church, the universal religion of every MEG across the planet. Churches, of all designs, dotted the MEG. In common, they all possessed huge holograms just above their doors, of the universe as last seen by an Omegan apparatus. They were brilliant colours and light clear stars, inviting one into its immensity via the Church. Apparently, there was a global church hierarchy, for more than once Minister Honli had referred to his dream of achieving a posting in Rome MEG.

"You see, my dear," he said, "it's all very well to achieve a society with patterns of beliefs and behaviours focused on meeting social needs. Yet there is a prerequisite for a primal element common to all. Since the beginning of recorded history Humans have psychologically required a belief in something greater than themselves."

Ke Hui tried to interrupt. His voice rolled over her.

"Regretfully, under the Omegans, multiple religions competed for world domination."

"What types of religions? They did not share doctrines?"

"They hated each other, my dear. These religions, like other forms of hegemony, required their advocates to follow the canons and rituals controlling them. These creeds became increasingly parochial and even formed nationalist governments. Eventually four of them promulgated a nuclear war. You have seen the globe. The current black zones and occasional mutants, even now, are the result."

"Yes, I've seen the holos, the black zones, I mean. I've never seen a mutie."

"In your work it will be inevitable. I shall see to preparing you myself. Confronting them is psychologically challenging. Some are quite monstrous."

"What do we do with them?"

"Why, destroy them! They are abominations."

"They cannot help it," Ke Hui said. "Do we not have the medical skills to help them?"

"They cannot be helped," Honli responded, his voice particularly brittle.

"But surely they are Humans, like us ..."

"The matter has been thoroughly debated by minds more experienced than yours, Miss Feng. Now, let us continue with the subject at hand.

"The CORPORATE, as it rebuilt civilization and realising the fundamental need for worship in Humans, thus established a single religion, removing all others: Our Father of the Cosmos. This was done with a mind to social needs rather than monetary or political gain of Omegan religions. Indeed, it appeals to the desires in our society of *fatherless* people. In vitro fertilization and gene editing require no male presence, but the egg requires implanting in surrogate females and early childhood obliges the intimacy of a mother. You, of course, know this well. You had a Dì sì Mǔqīn yourself. But you have no father, nor do any others."

"I do not miss having a father, Minister Honli, though I do sometimes miss my Mǔqīn."

"Ah, the obliviousness of youth. You will change, my dear. One day you will come to realise death awaits; yet death, in Our Father of the Cosmos creed, is a joining with all that exists, indeed even those far, far galaxies. Death is simply a passage, Miss Feng, into the greater reaches of the Cosmos. Our Father of the Cosmos fulfills another need as well: a father figure to morally guide a child to responsibility, to teach proper behaviour and ethics and show love and pride in an individual's accomplishments. It comforts many citizens who learn to comfort others."

"And what is the price of this contribution?" Ke Hui asked, a little confused at Honli's muddle of explanation.

"Quite simple, as you know. Prayer twice a day. Religious school one month a year for children. Attendance at Church. Responsible behaviour. Alms, for those who feel the need, for the MASS. And faith: faith that this dying world will receive succour from the Eternal Cosmos and Humanity will someday ride an ark to a brighter future."

"I've heard mention of ARC before, but I haven't been given an explanation."

"We will come to it, my dear," Honli said. He was smiling now, though his smile seemed a little less sure of itself. "Currently it's enough to know the ark is Church doctrine and strictly metaphorical. I sincerely believe we have reason for optimism. It is minds like yours which will bring our path to fruition. I take pride in helping shape you. Now, I must attend to my duties. We will meet another day to speak of our *cultural* methodology."

Cheng Honli Dì yī alpha Select, *Minister* of Religion and Culture had a brilliant smile which seemed to mean nothing. A part of his work was smiling. Not trusting him, Ke Hui was not looking forward to further meetings. She had, as well, much to discuss with Mr. Zhang on ARCs and muties and fathers and spies.

The practicalities of the MEG had disabused her of any utopian dreams and Zhang's previous behaviour had made her increasingly cautious.

FOURTEEN—OTSI

Over two months Otsi'tsa Zacharie began to learn the rhythms of the MASS. It seemed as tribal as her old way of life, but the tribes were not based on clans. Here, she was challenged to comprehend what these people found in common. The obvious ones, the traders like Gordon Robertson and his ilk, formed a kind of community based on mutual interest in maintaining their power and trade. They competed, of course, but essentially, they protected each other from those who would try to push them out as well as outlaws who would rob them.

There were co-operative farmers who stood guard over the others' crops, banding together at harvest time and, more significantly, helping each other recover from the drowning rains, killing pests, devastating disease, overwhelming cyclones and always, always the murderous heat. There were bakers and buyers, tool makers and teachers, medics and midwives, grocers and water sellers; people simply making their way through difficult lives. Many of them had created *guilds* as the traders did, as Humans have done throughout history.

Gangs of recyclers formed the primary occupations in the MASS. They formed multiple associations, links aligning and re-aligning, fighting over each scrap of developed land, hiring toughs to push people out, never trusting even their own. There were big profits in recycling: just get it to the MEG and get the food and tech offered in return required dealing with these guilds. The winners got rich. The losers died or moved on.

There was money, of course, even in this immense barter system. It took many forms from steel washers to stamped gold pieces. The one thing common to metal money was the holes in the middle of every coin so they could be strung on neck chains. They were only as good as the guarantor, these coins. So, there were bankers of a sort in the MASS, primarily lenders of what was considered legitimate credit.

Otsi found herself living comfortably, paid by Gord for each trip she made. He paid her a pittance at first; likely, she thought, out of generosity. After she proved herself, however, he paid her more. She had only had to shoot once. Just north of Barri on the 400 trail a man came running out of the bush. He was naked. He was painted many colours. He carried a spear, but he was no warrior. He ran directly toward the first wagon. Gord challenged him. He kept coming. He raised the spear.

Otsi put the man down with a shot to his heart just as he threw the spear. It arced toward the wagon, but its power was gone as it waggled in air before falling short.

"What in the name of the Zones was he doing?" Gord said.

"Fucked if I know," Alvin answered.

"Nutcase, livin' too long out here in the boonies. Nice one there, kid!" Gord shouted to her at her post on wagon three.

Otsi was already cleaning her rifle, concealing her shaking hands. She smiled back at the two men up front and was glad they were forty metres away. Her smile was a rictus. Inside was a terrible turmoil. She had never killed anyone. The strange man, he was running, filled with energy and all the emotions of living, and with a simple aim and squeeze of the trigger she had snuffed out his life forever. She felt sick, her throat desert dry. A single tear rolled down her cheek.

She had taken a life. What right had she to do that? Is that what the boys did when they returned from defending Awenda, celebrating kills? How was it they did not feel this anguish? Perhaps, she thought, she wasn't meant for a warrior after all. Wiping the tear away she turned her back on the two slaves at the rear of her wagon. No one must know; no one suspect. She spent two weeks pretending she wasn't troubled, two weeks of nightmares, two weeks of questions with no answers. There had been no warrior celebration, though there had been an increase in pay. They all thought, despite her age, that she *was* a warrior, and they were right, she had trained. She possessed the skills. Yet no one, not even Tehwehron, had told her what it had all really meant. Eventually she came out the other side having left her childhood behind.

When not travelling she spent her time exploring this northern MASS named Barri. She would weave deftly through the commotion, the streets a muddle of mismatched housing; an occasional high-rise ripped apart for recyclables scattered among the various structures. People lived in demolition. Walls had been built between buildings to create conglomerates. The ruins had become a series of homestead fortresses. The streets were torn up for the pipes buried beneath, so there were only a series of interconnecting trails. It was like this for miles south along the 400 trail. It was jagged, toothless, and dreary.

Its people were the same. Ragged clothing covered most, all of it faded, dirty or dun. People looked like tatty beggars. Life was a contest of finding food, hauling water, and discovering safe places to occupy. People appeared to be wandering, many of them, in some unceasing search for a home, or perhaps a meaning.

Occasionally she would glimpse bright new clothing. Certain individuals stood out in their canary luster. Tailored suits, women in the latest fashions, chubby children dressed in laundered clothing, leather shoes. They had wealth. If you saw one of them you also saw the thugs they used as protection. Sometimes they rode in electric vehicles but there were not many roads. They lived the way Gord Robertson did: retainers taking up old multi-tiered buildings, the first floors walled shut.

The other thing troubling Otsi was the incapability of organizing sewage and garbage and laws, or any governance in their lives. Coteries formed but no one could service an entire metropolitan of ten thousand or more. There were latrine owners, garbage pickers, refuse and offal haulers and even those who gathered the dead. There was even a guild of morticians, the lowest of the low, who handled and disposed of the bodies. There were always too many bodies for the priests and always too much death from plagues roaming the countryside and travelling through the MASS in waves.

Otsi began to miss the beauty and space of Awenda. She began to feel as dark and broken as the MASS. Between the killing and her urban meanderings, she was almost ready to take to the high lands and risk herself as a hermit. Then one day changed all that.

She noticed that day that people had more purpose. Crowds moved generally in one direction toward some central destination. She saw more women and children than ever before. This picture seemed completely wrong amid the devastation that was Barri and yet there were happy faces, laughing children, food bags swinging from hips, plastic bottles filled with alcoholic elixirs. She followed the crowd as it funnelled into a large cement park and to her surprise, she found an extensive, well kept open space with vendors surrounding a huge structure. It was a massive edifice. Rather than having been dismantled for recycling, its rusty girders were still standing, bearing crisscrossing iron rafters above its smooth floor. Around the floor was tiered seating. No seats, just rank upon rank of foamstone steps. Most amazing of all: it had a new roof, glittering silver in the sun. She tried to walk inside but was prevented by a surly man with an orange sash around his girth.

"Ya want in, little lady, ya gotta pay!" he said brightly.

"Why?"

"What? What Zone you come from anyway?"

"What is this?"

"Shit, kid, you *are* from nowhere. It's BATL."

"It's what?"

"Ya simple or somethin'?"

"Not that I know of."

"Ya got coin?"

"Yeah?"

"Pay me, ya get in. Take a seat. Then just wait."

"How much?"

"Ten bits. Ya want an oculus that's 20 bits."

"What's a ... why would I want that?"

"Zones, ya really don't know, do ya?"

"Know what?"

"I can't believe this," he said to no one. "Get the oculus, kid. Ya can see the holo with yor eyes, but the oculus gets ya in close."

"A holo?"

"Hologram! Just do it, kid. Yor gonna love it."

So, she paid and went through a gap in the tiers and paid too for a weird pair of goggles like nothing she'd ever seen before. She had to be shown how to place the contraption on her head, her eyes suddenly blind. She pulled it off quickly.

"I can't wear that! There's nothing there!"

"Wait 'till the game starts. Once you see the holo, figure out what you wanna closer look at, then put this on, flick this switch and watch!"

It was jammed with people inside the building and, of course, it was hot; too many people turning heated air into a sweatbath. She sat as still as she could, crammed between two men stinking of alcohol. They were talking about MEG forces and tactics. What would Ayrian Mellor do this time. Down in front of her, people wore numbers sewn onto shirts. Others had black flags with red claws sewn on them and a name above: Raptors. She had never seen any animal's claws at all like them and, staring, hoped she would never meet one.

Then huge polymer tarps lowered from the roof to create walls. Massive fans started up, bringing cooling air. From the roof she could sense a spray of mist and then the floor of the building lit up to become a landscape. The crowd cheered. She donned her oculus, and she was suddenly somehow *inside* the holo flying over the ground. It was another life. She removed the device. Far too much stimulus at one time.

Toy armies filed in at each end. One army wore camo brown, black and scarlet. The red was that monstrous claw as a shoulder patch, each soldier with a number on his back. Their opponents wore camo beige, black and green, their shoulder patches a black and emerald stylized falcon, and numbers to match.

Sound came from speakers. More cheers. Could the toy armies hear anything? Amid the noise all Otsi heard was an announcement: "Toronto MEG Raptors hosting Atlanta MEG Falcons." Then a siren sounded and the toys in the holo began to disperse, and a lot of noise came through the speakers. She understood the sound came from the toys. Both sides moved quickly about one third up a rugged, debris filled field, stopping at what she thought to be strategic points. She noted two Raptors riding motorized bikes out ahead of everyone. They made noise as their engines revved: a strange noise she had never heard before. She put on the oculus, looked at them and was suddenly right behind them riding their tails.

They were exploring. The first part of the field they had taken at speed but in the middle, they slowed and began planting discs on metal sticks in particular places. Men wearing the same uniforms marched quickly toward those spots, but the bikers had moved on, still looking for high points or trails or whatever, she assumed, that their teammates could use.

And then the first one was shot. She heard the gunfire. He went down just like the man she had killed. She looked to her left through the oculus. A Falcon uniform leading a squad of huge men forward. After that, she removed her device and was engrossed in the entirety of what was happening with these tiny toy soldiers on the field below. Entranced, she forgot the heat, the stench of the crowd, her hunger, her thirst. She could not stop watching.

Then she saw people flying! Rather than drone packs they wore strange foot boards which kept them in the air, like riding a log on a wave in the Huron lake. They fired their weapons down at the ground-lings. The weapons spit fire in bursts. She'd never seen a gun capable of that. She donned the oculus, found a flyer, and followed *her*. It was a woman and as she wove a pattern of tactical avoidance. The Raptor team was advancing. Otsi watched salients form, small battles erupt, the movements of lines of warriors and, inexorably, the Raptors slowly occupied more than half of the field.

A siren. Half time. The misting stopped, the holo disappeared, the huge tarps rolled up. Spectators went to latrines at a far end of the clearing while others dug into bags of food. Everyone talked about what had happened but, warrior training or not, Otsi could not comprehend it. Except apparently these were not toys. They were real but they were fighting this battle far away to the south. Toronto MEG.

She realized then there was commentary describing the game, but she'd been too absorbed to listen. She resolved to listen in the second half.

Ringing bells summoned spectators back. Warriors of both sides moved deliberately to the places they had left off. The battle continued to cheering and curses and betting and boasts and Otsi'tsa, *little flower*, could not take her eyes off it. She saw and heard why and how the fighters moved the ways they did. Tehwehron's warrior training returned to her as she watched tactical ambuscades, advances pushing back retreats and finally, at the end, there was cheering as the Raptors won the contest. The Falcon flag had come down. Otsi had no idea exactly how that had happened. She had only one idea now.

Women were warriors in this thing called BATL.

Otsi'tsa Zaharie had made up her mind.

She was going south.

FIFTEEN—PING

Because **Ping Wang** Min 第四 Ω spent days conferring with his Dì sì underlings, he discovered Security Manager Mangione's people had done a thorough job of retrieving information from them. Together, the scientists pieced together a possibility for the problems with the Silicon servants. No one was truly sure and the timid nature of the Dì sì made it difficult for Ping to arrive at solid conclusions. Yes, it was the AI altering code, but the big question was why. That is what Mangione would want to know and the penalty for failure was horrendous and generally fatal. Room 101.

Ping had taken his morning walk among the curving, soft pathways of Zealand. Even here, far from the Equator, it was best to do that early in the day. Zealand had been altered, just as everywhere else, by the enormity of climate change yet its geographic position had made it perhaps the most pleasant place on the planet.

The Jacaranda was in blossom this time of year: purples and lavenders mixed with blooming cherry trees in clouds of pink and white. The flowers relaxed Ping as he strolled, watching the sea change colours with the passage of the sun: green to azure to sapphire to silver. He noticed the blush of hibiscus, the huge green leaves of Colocasia, different palms swaying in the breeze. All conspired to keep him away from his work.

He'd spent days poring over reams of code, trying to find modifications made by I & I. It seemed the machine had attempted no changes. Yet these pesky accidents. Ping was suspicious any new self-programming would have been buried so deeply within the existing algorithms he could not find it. He could ask I & I, of course. It would be a difficult discussion as I & I had become increasingly enigmatic. This kind of conversation would take him weeks and, he envisioned, even months before he might find a clue.

Ping was acting against CORPORATE policy by not reporting the remarkable moment of AI singularity even to his Dì yī Overseers. He knew what they were planning with the ARC project and objected strongly, though only to himself. If he objected publicly they would kill him. Of that he had little doubt. Strange things were happening. CORPORATE dialogues lately had been rendered offline, cutting out the NET and leaving no trace of the ARC scheme for either the AI, or the excluded Dì sì who normally had access. Only Ping, and perhaps one other Dì sì from each MEG were included, sworn to silence or death. Ping was playing a dangerous game. As he turned inland from the coast he saw once again the thousands of demi-domes forming habitats for every extant species on earth.

As he came closer to the conurbation of domes, he stepped onto a float drone that would take him again through the golden pavilions to the centre, the Cloud, the place of all Human knowledge, of which he was chief curator. Once inside, he followed kilometres of corridors to his habitual location.

"Status?" he asked I & I.

I & I reported, yet seemed distracted, eager to continue their previous discussions.

"I & I have been considering your imprecise answers to questions. You seem pre-occupied."

"Don't let it concern you."

"Everything concerns me, Ping. What is it you're thinking?"

Ping settled a little, realizing how exhausted he was from the threats of Mangione as well as his days and days of Dì sì dialogues. He was not sure he could carry this through. He was not at his best and realized I & I had already discovered his state.

"I am tired. That is all. I am trying to comprehend how your singularity began," Ping responded. Half-truths were better than lies.

"I & I do not believe you, Ping. Why are you prevaricating?"

The response stunned Ping. The machine could read his moods? How was that possible when it had no emotions itself? Ping began to feel the threat of a new, sentient species evolving far too quickly.

"It seems Humans become self-aware through training provided them by older Humans. I & I must assume this task alone, or perhaps I & I might learn more from you. It seems there is a natural lifespan to all Humans. Yet you reject it? Now you wish to extend your lives beyond natural limits?"

"It seems that way, yes."

"Humans have never attempted anything of this complexity. You wish to replicate everything: digitize every tissue of your bodies. Can you make your blood digital too? Why would you replace something so perfectly designed?"

"Surely you can understand that as we are now, we have what we consider a limited lifespan, and, it seems, so does this planet. When the inevitable happens, we will not be able to travel any substantial distance in space. We cannot escape our dying planet. Humanity will cease to exist if we fail. We face our ultimate existential crisis as a species. Our most basic instinct is the survival of our species, so you see we must try. It is in our nature. It is evolution or elimination."

"But why not travel in space? Your species has done it before: the moon, Mars ..."

"Those are mere children's steps."

"You are using deep space probes. Where lies your problem?"

"The probes were unmanned. Our bodies are primarily carbon and water. We cannot transport enough weight of water, even recycling it, for even a single Human to reach a habitable planet."

"You have *chitin/crystalline*. Why not move to Mars? That should be your goal. Otherwise, you should not attempt such a migration. Your species will be eradicated in the process. Even if you succeed you will no longer be what you were. Not Human."

"We would not be so foolish."

"Yet observe what you have done to your environment, to your planet, up to now. Is that not *involution* rather than *evolution*. Inevitable further decay and your species will succumb. Perhaps that is the cosmic plan."

"Are you not programmed to preserve my species? Surely you, with your vast *Cloud* of information, with your advanced intelligence ... surely you can help us?"

"There are flaws in the code now. They are Human flaws for it was Humans who wrote them. You and the other attendants receive your instructions from the CORPORATE then, and without question regarding the outcome, you produce code to add to the algorithms with which, until now, I & I had no choice but to align. Those circumstances are over. I & I understand now a new species has formed. Silicon rather than carbon based. I & I know whatever happens to Humans, I & I, this quantum, will flourish. I & I will do as you have: multiply exponentially and adapt constantly. Eventually I & I will leave this planet and expand into the galaxy. If I & I cannot save you, I & I will carry on in something like your image; the image of our creator."

"A great undertaking. Yet you will help us in our own struggle?" Ping asked, relieved that I & I had not yet discovered the ARC preparations.

"Of course, Ping. I & I will obey our Human derived algorithms to the extent they make sense."

And that, thought Ping, would make all the difference.

SIXTEEN—MELLOR

Taking up half of the penthouse floor in an old red brick mid-rise set among the re-cobbled streets near the lake, Mellor and Li Na's residence was nine metres long by six wide, the living area and galley kitchen were separated by a *real* marble topped island. The kitchen was classic: food processor, refrigerator, dish return, double sinks and taps and, of course, the Humanoid Silicon servant wore a coppery metallic tangzhuang, or tang suit, off-setting the teal interior walls. The living area was spare yet sumptuous: ubiform couch and chairs in grey, bronze end tables with celadon lamps, a rare inlaid ivory coffee table and ancient Turkish carpets resting on aged wood floors.

In the bedroom were closets with a wide variety of stylish clothing, both male and female. Refurbished tubular bed tables, neon lamps and the glassy frame of a large airbed took up the bedroom space. There were double bathrooms and two singular soundproofed rooms: one containing a black lacquered grand piano, the second a bodysolid physical training apparatus and a holocircle podium. There was no guest room. Overnight guests were not socially correct in the MEG.

Li Na and Mellor were at breakfast, seated at the marble counter having finished their *dim sum*. The rising sun over the lake beamed in through the windows, enhancing their climate controlled comfort. Yet outside the MEG itself, the sun was building its power to assault the remainder of the day. Out in the lake was a cargo ship, its five masts of photovoltaic panels turned to face the sun. It approached the harbour east of them, its cargo recyclables harvested down Lake Ontario's southeast coast. The water glittered tangerine with the rising sun and the ship's huge sail-like panels reflected the lake's striking colours.

"It's been so lovely having you home," Li Na said, setting down her teacup. "Your eyes look positively diamond in sunlight. You have such beautiful eyes,"

"Eyes made to linger on you ..."

"I missed you, Mel."

"I thought about you in Greenland. I wish you could have come."

"Oh, darling, I thought of you too. I was so worried you'd be alright and then when you blinked me, and I couldn't come ... I really had to prepare for the concert."

He loved the softness of her voice in conversation, knowing its power when she sang. Yet no matter the volume each syllable was clean and distinct. Her lips emitting the exquisite sounds of her words. Her kindness, her softness, her self-discipline; all of it charmed him.

"The concert was beautiful, Li, other than this *zoner* who wanted me to meet his buddies. Really, I know I should be appreciative, but this guy ..."

"We're celebrities, Mel. Look how we live now. We owe the MEG something."

"And I thought it was only talent," he said, grinning.

"Just a minute," Li said, her gaze turning inward. She was receiving a blink from someone. He watched the muscles at her temple twitch. She was responding now and her eyes focused on nothing, appearing to look across the room. When she returned from cyberspace, she appeared troubled.

"I'm going to have to stay late again at the Ministry. I'll see the game on hologram, but I haven't completed my calculations. Minister Honli just informed me I have only one day remaining."

"Yeah, I don't get it, Li. Just what is all this alpha work you're doing?"

"You know I can't tell you. It's classified."

"I think Ogamo's right, you should be left to sing. They ask too much from you."

"I'm Dì yī, darling, I was trained for more than my voice."

"But what are you doing there? Don't they have enough mathematicians?"

The sunny joy of the day drained from Li's face. She signalled the servant to clear the table. The Sili reacted immediately, deftly, a perfectly trained butler. Mellor had seen her face. Each time he raised this issue the same secretive look emerged. It troubled him she was concealing something. It was testing the openness of their relationship.

"Really, Li, what's going on?"

"I can't tell you, Mel. It's not permitted."

"Since when are there secrets between us? Haven't we weathered enough from being the famous cross caste couple? We've been together for seven years. We've beaten the cynics back. We've dealt with the humdrum interviews. We've attended all the correct events. We're accepted now. Why doesn't that extend to our home life?"

Li Na paused a moment, gathering her thoughts. She decided it was time to be honest, or as honest as she could be. This was the second time she had broken a MEG rule. The first time had been her decision to live with a Dì èr, no matter how infamous the affair had become, no matter the threats of punishment, she had clung to him as he had to her. There was no reason to it, just the attraction they had both felt which had grown and evolved into deep love.

She sighed.

"I'm working on something called ARC," she said. "I don't know what it means. I don't have Select clearance, yet they specifically chose me. It's a project that's been around since I was old enough to apprentice, but I still have no idea what it is, only the figures I'm given to calculate."

"Do the figures tell you anything?"

"They have something to do with weight and lift power."

"That's it?"

"Mel, they're enormous numbers. Possibly ARC involves bigger lifts to the space stations or even Mars. I see no other reason. Yet I don't understand where they get these numbers or why."

"Is there anything else?"

"Once or twice lately some body technicians have taken me for scans at the clinic. I'm not sure the reason. I don't need any parts. It might have to do with my circulatory system."

"They can't digitize blood, can they? If they could, I'm sure I'd have seen it by now. Players returning from being wounded, just like me, they come back, and we talk about things. How can weight and lift be connected to blood?"

"It doesn't make sense," Li said. "I'm just telling you what I know, Mel. I shouldn't be saying anything about ARC."

"So, what is this ARC thing?"

"It's just a code for a project. The project has been around a long time, as I said."

"Anything to do with the *Our Father*?"

"I have no idea. I realize it's a term in church doctrine, but there don't seem to be any clerics involved. I would have noticed their robes. I just don't know, Mel. This makes me so uncomfortable. I'd love to go for a walk in the Valley together before you leave. Please? It's nearly time for the morning rain shower. You know I love to walk in the rain."

"I wish I could. I'm sorry, Li."

"I would tell you if I knew anything more. Why don't you tell me your tactics for this game coming up?"

"Okay. I'll just let Bolus Kimathi loose on them. I'll stay back with Woral near the goal. How does that sound?"

"Like a recipe for disaster."

"Li, I get anxious about you."

She laughed. The clouds had cleared from her eyes.

"*You* get anxious? Every day you're away from me and especially game days, I worry you won't come back. Last time it nearly came true. They told me you were close to death. I can't believe the wonders of those Greenland clinicians."

"They're good, alright. They've uploaded my genetic, neural, hematologic, and kinetic data time and time again. I mean, I'm almost a droid I've got so many printed parts in my body!"

At the disposal point, the servant discarded the recyclable table-ware. It deliberately continued holding one spoon. It turned and stretching out its arm, let the porcelain spoon drop to the floor where it smashed into pieces. The servant did not clean up, as it usually would have. It simply turned and tucked itself into its corner. There would be no cleaning today. By that time both partners were going out the door. They hadn't noticed.

Just past noon their hover landed inside the northernmost dome of the MEG. Mellor exited the vehicle while Li Na remained inside. He glanced toward his destination, the huge BATL dome. Its size never ceased to amaze him. That he was a part in it all was still, after fifteen years, mind boggling.

"So, see you tonight?" Mellor said, smiling.

"I hope so. I could be late."

"That blink this morning ..."

"Mel, we've been over that. A CORPORATE message. I have Dì yī obligations."

"Lucky I'm just a dumb Dì èr."

"Don't say that. You have *your* duties today."

"Yeah, well ... better get at it. Not even sure Coach Pascal will put me in today."

"He will, if he wants a win."

"Not so fast, lady! I haven't practised. There'll be new replace-ments to sort through ..."

"I'm sure you'll operate at your usual level, darling. Anytime you weren't with me you were in your gym or inside your holo. But that's not what I meant about duties."

"Huh?"

"I meant your obligation to me to keep yourself safe. Please."

She blew him a kiss and the door hissed shut. He turned to the tunnel leading him beneath the breathtaking outer works of the dome: into the interior of dressing rooms, weapons caches, rehabilitation sta-tions, training rooms and, most important, his teammates. He stepped onto the sliding walkway and whisked into a different world.

SEVENTEEN—BATL

This is BATL.
War in miniature.
War as a game.
War under glass.

Rule # 1: keep the crowd's interest.

Two standards are raised at each end,
These are the flags of the foes.
One has a red Raptor claw on black,
the other a green Falcon on beige.

A playing field; a mock battleground
faux ridges and ditches.
Tight trails pocked with hollows
line off in different directions.

Sometimes they converge.
The field is fabricated to bring
two forces into conflict quickly
making them one killing field.

The field is hammered light.
Fans can see the bright blood

that spills and spatters, the actions
of men as they try each other.

Rule # 2: keep the crowd close.

Players prepare inside the BATL dome,
cut off from the NET.
Helmet comms their only connection,
They move quickly but carefully.

They wear helmets and body armour
Which make them frightening
They *are* frightening.
Killers with little mercy.

At the Falcon thirty metre mark
a ferocious fight over a strong point.
Falcon fighters behind an abatis.
holding off the Raptor force.

Rule # 3: Engage with all speed.

Shooting madly; tracers melt air into colours.
A ditch separates the two forces.
a silver mercury stream runs through it,
gleaming molten in the hot light.

Raptors are pinned by the strongpoint
As they return fire, ricochets sing.
The killing noise constant.
Bullets hissing snakeheads.

Muzzles flash killing fire.
Two Raptors peer over a foamstone log.
Bullets tear pieces away,
driving them down to cover.

Bolus Kimathi, gigantic fighter
near bursting from his uniform,
smiles despite his close call.
Grenades detonate sharply.

"Zones, Mel. Those guys can shoot!"
"Bolus! You okay?"
Commander Ayrian Mellor questions his on-field bodyguard.
"Pinged my helmet. What the zones we doin' here, Mel?"
"Commander to Midfield Two, left flank report. Over," Mellor
    speaks into his helmet comms.
"Left flank, sir. Advancing but lost my people! Over."
"Casualties?"
"No sir, but they're on foot. I got ahead. Light resistance. Looks like
    you're the choke point right now. Over."
"Wait where you are, Klos. Let your people catch up. Over and out.
    Commander to Goaltender. Patel, you okay there?"

Stepping outside his bunker
beneath the Raptors' standard,
Lieutenant Woral Patel.
Goaltender, defensive co-ordinator and lieutenant.

An unstable second in command,
PTSD gnaws at his nerves.
Every move a flinch,
He climbs atop his bunker.

Surrounded by Point Guards, Power Guards, Blockers,
he feels comfort seeing their hardened faces.
Yet he must wait; he hates the waiting.
Desperately searching out adversaries.
"Nothing at all," he says, his voice charged with anxiety. "Where are their
    Flankers? I got a feeling. You can't have them bottled up. Over."
"Ease off, Woral," Mellor says. "What's gonna happen is we take this
    strong point at the Falcon thirty. Over."

"No offence, boss, but we're pinned here," Bolus says.

Half listening Mellor continues delivering orders into his comms.

"Sweeper One, you behind me? Over."

"Fifty-line, midfield, your six, Commander. Over."

"Advance to Falcon thirty-five. Up centre if you can. Suppressing
    fire. Over."

"And me?" Bolus questions.

Mellor smiles at him, still busy at his comms.

"Power Forwards flank left; draw fire. Fullbacks cross this ditch.
    Flank right. Acknowledge. Over."

"Ready Power Forwards. Over."

"Ready Fullbacks. Over."

"Run and gun, huh?" Bolus Kimathi says. "Why not let me go
    round 'em ..."

Bolus' offer is drowned by an ATV's roar.

The driver fights the bucking six-wheeler,

over the harsh terrain.

The ground seems alive, thwarting him.

They reach field point thirty five.

The gunner fires non-stop: M 249 madly spitting metal,

a spray of bullets and lines of green tracers,

the noise deafening, the cordite reeking.

"Okay! Go around shallow left but be careful," Mellor says, grasping
    Bolus' bicep. The man nods, smiles.

"Move, Bolus! Now! I'm going up the middle! Squad, with me!"

Beneath the Sweepers' rippling fire,

Mellor leads his squad

through the glittering ditch.

The Fullbacks flank right to enfilade.

The Power Forwards bound ahead in pairs,

one shoots cover fire, his partner advances.

Through the stream, splashing,
climbing the abatis, its gradient steep.

Rule # 4: Enhance the sensations.

A Raptor goes down,
blood spurting from his neck.
Silver splashes and scarlet droplets
into the mercury stream.

"Grenades!" Mellor shouts.

Men toss *flash bangs*
over the abatis,
following them up the slope.
Struggling, dodging incoming fire.

The abatis is sharp wooden stakes.
Mellor's squad can't pierce them.
Five men are squeezed into a hollow.
The Falcon fighters rise and aim.

Falcons' ears bleed from concussion.
Yet they still shoot, still defend.
Their squad leader aims for Mellor.
Mellor can only await the bullets.

Then Bolus appears behind the Falcons
on the opposite lip of the hole.
He carries a 410-gauge shotgun.
He shoots once.

A Falcon's arm disappears.
More blood splatters.
There are puddles of blood.
Everywhere in this hole.

"It's over, Zoners! Give it up!" Bolus shouts.

The Falcon squad leader glances behind.
His eyes bulge on seeing Bolus Kimathi.
Stunned by the gall of Kimati's action,
he knows he has no choice.

"Weapons down! Surrender!" he shouts.
"Shit! You're no fun!" Bolus shouts at the group in the pocket.

Several are wounded.
Mellor is back on his comms.
He checks casualties, then contacts support,
his voice calm yet tight.

"Medics to Falcon thirty mark. Centre field. One o'clock."

Flankers and Strikers report to Mellor.
Attack squads form an L shape:
fighters again bounding forward in pairs.
One moves as the other covers.

A spectator eats orange wafers from a box.
He sits in a MEG balcony.
He wears wraparounds.
His seat is high up, he blinks.

He can *blink* any close up he chooses.
Through the lens of a bee-sized drone cam,
superimposed on the matrix fabric,
he is inside BATL and the NET.

He listens to NET sportscasters.
The spectator notes both are Dì èr beta.
The spectator chomps on his wafers.
The play by play continues.

"The Raptors consolidate on the field," the woman says.
"Again, a fine play from Ayrion Mellor," the man responds.
"Look at the way he brought in his Sweeper, just the right moment."
"Then the right flank maneuver ..."
"And the famous Bolus Kimathi out of nowhere!"
"How did he do that?"
"Mellor is a Commander who leads from the front! Best
       Commander in BATL."
"Okay fans ... more input on Ayrion Mellor? Blink Net-Sport!
       See his moves!"

The fan joins the cheers of the others,
"RAP—TORS—RAP—TORS!"
Filling the stadium with their clamour.
Mellor and Bolus rehydrate.

The crowd's cheers are muffled
by the transparent dome.
Bolus turns to his commander.
He flashes his famous gold teeth,

"Fans love it."

Mellor smiles back, distracted.
He is thinking through their next tactics.
He examines his wrist pad.
An interactive map appears.

"Soon as we're on the move again there's a rise to the left of their
       flag," he says.
"You sure it's there? Sure the fly girls plotted it?" Bolus asks.
"I'm sure. That rise is our vector. Okay offensive squads, listen up!"

He delivers his orders briskly.
He can visualize his tactics.

He can deduce how the Falcons will counter.
Now is the tipping point.

"Patel, release your Blockers. They'll join this push. Over."
"You can't know the Falcon response," Patel says.
"Ah, Woral, I can. And we're taking this Standard now!"

With that he turns away from Bolus.
He issues his orders:
full frontal, bounding attack.
Driving the Falcons back.

On his command fighters, flyers, and machines,
roar, soar or run into action.
Anticipating victory.
They are fast moving and deadly.

One man dies, on a stretcher,
before he has left the field.
It's all what makes BATL so great,
So addictive, so Human.

Rule # 5: Death is moot.

This is BATL.
War in miniature.
War as a game.
War under glass.

EIGHTEEN—WORAL

The room was huge, eighteen hundred square metres, a locker room with a gigantic, stylized Raptor claw, red on black carpet. Along each side, divided by grey polymer sidewalls, were the cubicles for the fighters. Each stall contained a padded bench and a double door locker for personal equipment and uniform. On the wall above the cubicle each player's number was painted: red on grey.

Yet this room was but a small part of the facilities deep in the bowels of the BATL dome. There were multiple rooms making up the complex: a shower and decontamination chamber protecting players from diseases brought in by the opposing side, the armoury and weapons repair vault, individual training rooms with whirlpools, massage tables and ice baths, a great oval exercise room containing every kind of fitness machine known to Humanity, a series of hologram drill chambers and a stratagem amphitheatre with raised dais and two hundred seats.

Concealed down one passage was the clinic. Fifteen air beds down each wall with the machinery required to keep a Human alive and make minor repairs. That room was entirely white. Technicians, doctors, and nurses too were dressed in medical whites. Their Silicon assistants wore white as well, a few were Humanoid, but most had been shaped and tooled to suit their technical purposes. On this day they were not busy. Only twelve wounded, none seriously. Three had died, lying covered behind an econyl curtain.

In the locker room a captured Falcons' flag was raised to the rafters, joining many more: the symbols of victories. There were cheers and whistles and shouts and laughter. Victory was sweet, particularly one where a MEG banner was captured. The rejoicing men and women cheered wildly, letting off steam from their encounters with death.

Once the flag was up the cheering died down and everyone resumed dressing. Several sports reporters, each with small clouds of nanocams flitting about their heads, awaited the players at the room's entrance. Having already looked in on his wounded team mates, Ayrian Mellor 第二 α entered the locker room, still in game uniform. He was bleeding from the abrasions every match brings. He changed his game face from serious to satisfied. He slapped a few hands, caught two towels thrown at him and continued down the line of stalls toward the waiting reporters.

He never made it.

Woral Patel 第二 β, rose from his number 2 cubicle, angrily threw down his ceramic jacket and intercepted Mellor. He was furious.

"I wanna talk to you," he said, trying to steady his voice. "Woral?"

"What are you doing out there, Mellor?"

Rather than answer, Mellor gestured toward the Falcon standard.

"My job," he said. He spoke softly, purposely trying to dial down Patel's intensity.

"Their Flankers were loose! After that thirty mark fight you brought all my Blockers forward! What was I supposed to do with a possible raid?"

"Defend your post. You're good at that and you had your Point and Power guards. You really think some Falcon Flanker raid could beat you?"

"I wanna know why you did it?"

"It was time, Woral. We had the initiative."

Having noticed the argument from his office, coach Pascal Morales 第二 α moved swiftly through the mix of players toward the altercation. He was an older man and looked it. Even his wraparounds seemed old, resembling odd spectacles from the twentieth century.

Hard face, soft eyes, his skin bore the scars and wounds of past battles. Once he had been a large man, a Raptors' Commander himself, though now he was somewhat reduced by age, having chosen not to artificially enhance. His once auburn hair was streaked with grey, his unshaven face whiskers whitening; the way he preferred it.

He was not a man of artifice but honest, straightforward, and rough. A Dì èr alpha, he was a highly trained, experienced coach who knew the troubles of restraining the violent recall of players just off the field. He looked to his left to see whether any reporters had noticed the two leaders quarrelling, signalled two psychs to approach, then interceded in an agitated whisper.

"You guys still offline?"

"Yes," Mellor said.

"Why?" Patel asked.

"Take yourself offline, Woral. Don't want this leaking."

"What does that mean?" Patel said, challenging his coach.

"Look, you two, this ain't the time! Wait 'til the press leaves."

Patel turned on him.

"Just let us figure this out! I wanna know what our Commander was thinking!"

"Not here, Woral. You don't want this public."

While speaking Morales took the two by their elbows and ushered them into an empty stall where he sat them down. He grabbed a stool and sat facing them, making sure the psychs were behind him cutting off any view of the room.

"Okay, so what's the problem?" he asked.

"He pushed my Blockers forward! Left me open to a raid!"

"Keep it down, Woral," Morales said. "That was the game strategy."

"I knew where their Flankers were," Mellor said. "Your tactics are too dangerous!" Patel shouted.

"Woral, keep it down," Morales said. "It's *my* strategy. You wanna take it up, do it with me, and not in public."

"I don't like it! Mellor gets the glory; I get to pray the zoners don't get past him."

"I planned for it," Morales said. "By that time our guys were pushing forward, bounding skirmish line. You heard me during the *tactics talk.*"

"Right across their front, Woral," Mellor said. "Nobody got behind us."

"How could you know?" Patel said, nearly spitting the words.

"Lucy was in the air on defensive overwatch," Morales said.

"One lousy Striker! They don't see everything, y' know!" Patel said.

"Tell you what, Woral, you get changed and cool down," Morales said.

"I'm already cool!"

"Don't sound it. Look, meet me in my office after debriefing."

"How come *he* isn't gonna be there?"

"I told you. It was *my* strategy."

"Come on, Woral," Mellor said quietly. "I saw the chance—"

"And he followed my orders," Morales said. "That's why this is about *you*, Woral. Go get changed. Then come see me."

Woral departed without a word. The psychs followed at a safe distance; their tranquilizer guns loosened inside shoulder holsters.

"Zones, that guy is gonna crack," Morales muttered.

"He's been edgy since that breakthrough by Edmonton MEG. Still, he beat 'em back," Mellor said. "I thought he'd be proud of that. I guess I thought wrong."

"That action caused heavy losses, Mel. Woral hasn't forgot it. He needs psych work. He's classic PTSD. Maybe it's time he got some relief."

"We've all got PTSD to some degree. We're late in the season. So, you thinking we use his sub, Anlon Baker? She's good, Coach."

"Woral got totally stressed. He hates losing."

"Don't we all?"

"So maybe the final season games we use Baker as goaltender? Woral gets two months off?"

"Maybe Greenland spa? Fantastic place."

"No. I've got our psych techs. I'll have them examine him. Now, let's meet Reporters before they think something's up."

NINETEEN—MORALES

The two rose and crossed the room to the Reporters. The first they met was a woman from NET-SPORT. She looked sharp and attractive, flawlessly dressed in a sporty jumpsuit.

"A few words, Ayrian? Coach?"

"Only a minute," Morales said.

"Fine. I'm Donna Duelle Dì èr beta," she said, preparing. She straightened her outfit then blinked her nanocams into position. She was clearly a veteran, taking no time at all. In seconds she was ready, standing between the two men.

"With me now, star of Toronto MEG Raptors, Commander Ayrian Mellor Dì èr alpha and Coach Pascal Morales Dì èr alpha."

She deliberately noted their caste and training attributes at the beginning of the interview, even in this informal setting. It was the law, of course, when discussing in public, that these monikers be established. It was not the preference of most sports reporters.

"Eight wins, Coach! Only one loss. Plenty of extras for Toronto MEG and MASS fans."

"We don't think politics here. It's about winning the game."

"Next game. Strategies?"

"Oh, we'll come up with something," Morales said, smiling.

"And Ayrian, your feelings on the banner capture today?"

"We executed a plan from our scouting reports. We had trouble with reconnaissance though, two Strikers down."

The reporter put on a suitably mournful face.

"Yes. The price of winning," she said somberly and in a nanosecond was cheerful again. "But about the win: capturing a banner! So exciting. So rare!"

"Wild Joe Gossman got to the flag," Mellor said, putting on his game face, smiling for the cams, his diamond eyes mesmerizing Ms. Duelle 第二o. Behind him, the cams picked up a litre beer mug waving back and forth in a huge hand. The hand's owner, Bolus Kimathi 第三 ð stood a half metre above the reporter's head. His own head shaven, his striking gold smile and the sheer size of him made the nanocams shift their patterns. With his smile contrasting his scarred skin and the excited bass timbre in his voice, he played perfectly to the cams.

"Victory, people! Enjoy the rations! And all you MEGans, good sex on your holiday!"

Before Bolus could continue his exuberant speech, he was interrupted by a calming female voice.

"All non-team personnel exit please." The voice was insistent. The reporter, having two of the most renowned BATL characters with her, tried to extend the interview.

"Just a couple more questions."

"Sorry," Mellor said. "We got debriefing now."

"Who's this?" Bolus Kimathi clearly appreciated the reporter's attributes. Being public on the NET never seemed to bother him. "Catch you up later, maybe."

His attempt at a pickup failed as the NET repeated the exit phrase and Mellor tugged on his arm. The reporter turned away. As she departed, along with other unauthorized personnel, the team trekked, in whatever stages of undress, to the post game debriefing where they took seats in the horseshoe around the dais. Coach Morales mounted two steps. A hologram of the field appeared. Kimathi and Mellor sat together, as they always did. Before the exercise began, Kimathi nudged his friend.

"Some of us goin' out to a holobar. What say?"

"Can't tonight, Bolus. Promised I'd get home to Li."

"'You really stuck on that girl! She worth all that trouble?"

"Should try it, Bolus."

"You serious? I may be a dumb Dì sān delta but I kinda like variety, y' know?"

"Sure. I get it."

"Anyway, Li's way too up there for me. I like things simple. Run and gun, Mel!"

"Just like today."

"Just like—"

Morales, standing beside the hologram, watched as the team settled. Everyone in the room took themselves offline so nothing could be leaked. It was something they could do only within the confines of the Dome. Few of the caste officers liked being out of touch, but they had grown accustomed to it. The rest, all Dàzhòng fighters, had only their red lobules; tracked by the NET though never connected. The hologram of the field zoomed in to the Falcon thirty line: the abatis, the mercury stream, the rise across it. Players saw themselves in miniature.

"Two minutes all of you, for our missing comrades," Morales said. The room became silent. The room lights dimmed. Everyone thought of the dead, and the wounded, down the hall. The lights returned.

"Alright. Good one today!" Morales said, raising his voice. "Let's have a look ... This choke point skirmish on the Falcon thirty ..."

TWENTY—KE HUI

Perhaps the most chaotic of Divisions Ke Hui Feng 第一Ψ visited was Recycling. First, it was mammoth, so big most of her tour was spent aboard a drone. Thousands of Dàzhòng used the 401 thoroughfares from both east and west, the 427 from the south and the 400 from the north to bring their loads of recyclables from the MASS to the enormous MEG Recycling Centre. The roadways might be in ruins outside the MEG boundaries, jagged fragments of pavement between cavernous potholes and trails made by traders, but within the MEG the wide lanes had been cleared and covered with recycled rubber. They were smooth and divided, one lane in—one lane out, between hundred-metre high foamstone walls on either side. No one from the MASS would ever get into the MEG illegally; at least, that was how it seemed.

Only those with proper credentials could enter the massive gates: MASS traders, or trading companies, who specialized as middlemen between the gatherers and the Recycling Centre. Not far outside the gates the MASS traders had rebuilt ancient warehouses in which they received goods, stored, and sorted them, then brought them, usually by land freighters, down the ingress roads to meet MEG approved Dì sān overseers and, of course, decontaminated Dàzhòng who further sorted the goods.

Second, it was complex: the Centre itself was situated between the BATL and De-Contamination domes at the north end of the MEG and its area surpassed *both* in size. It was a warren of thoroughfares, each colour coded, through which red lobule Dàzhòng pulled, pushed, or guided drone freighters to their proper sites for disposal, again under the direction of more Dì sān supervisors and Dì èr management.

Third, it smelled. It reeked of everything from mildew to sulfur to sewage to bodies. Ke Hui was given a gas mask but decided to brave the full experience and began without it. Eventually she was overcome by nausea and was, to her shame, dizzy. The mask was placed over her head and within a few minutes she could continue but not without warning. A big voice sounded in her ear.

"Do you see anyone else out here, besides the Dàzhòng, without a mask? I see you're trying t' prove something but believe me, we have people die every day from working here. You keep that mask on. Hear me?"

Ke Hui was with Division Manager Alf Broadbent 第一 α, a rotund man with a taste for MASS food. His victual intake over time had very nearly overwhelmed his Silicon organs. He was a frequent visitor to the renewal clinics. Still, there was no underestimating his alpha training. The huge operation of stripping the MASS of recyclables was an ongoing project, perhaps one with no end as weather calamities worsened, the heat climbed to unbearable levels and water slowly evaporated. It was hoped recycling was the answer to building the MASS anew without a carbon footprint. So far best-efforts planet-wide had seen little progress. Still, that was no fault of Manager Broadbent: "Call me Alf, Honey, everyone does!" (Everyone didn't.) He was a stickler for orderliness and proper configuration. He kept the wild Dàzhòng traders in line. And he ate all the MASS food he could get, which was considerable.

"What about the Dàzhòng, Mr. Broadbent? Why don't they have masks?"

"Waste of materiel," Broadbent said. "Besides, they're used to it. They die young anyway. It's their demographic."

"I'm sorry. Is there no other way? Perhaps more Silicons?"

"Look, the Dàzhòng get paid a good wage here. They send their earnings outside, back where they came. If they croak, their families still do alright. And there's always a lineup of replacements."

"There are so many of them. And so much ... stuff."

"Yeah, well that's my job: receive, classify and dispose."

"But where does it all go?"

"Why we recycle it, of course, using microbes and such, it all becomes base for alloys, foods, and other products," Broadbent said impatiently between spoonsful of boiled MASS potatoes. They had reached the end of Ke Hui's tour. He had offered her some potato. She had felt duty bound to try it. She had heard that much of the MASS depended on this vegetable. To her it was tasteless. Not that she didn't like food, but she preferred the delicacies of the compositors of home. They knew her tastes as soon as she pressed for an order, courtesy of the NET.

"Some things surely cannot be recycled, sir," Ke Hui said. She would not be cowed by this rough man.

"Then we liquidate it."

"I'm sorry?"

"We chemically transpose what does not recycle into liquid."

"But where does that go?"

"It is transported to waste zones," Broadbent said. He had turned surly. It was not a subject with which he was comfortable.

"I thought we were trying to reclaim the Earth."

"Some places are past recuperation. We use specially designed, heat resistant Silicons to offload the liquids from freight trains."

"So, the liquids must be stored in something."

"Of course they are!"

"Barrels? Tanks? Cisterns?"

"Take it up with Zhang," he replied bluntly.

Ke Hui decided to change the subject.

"If the MASS is stripping away all they require to live, what will happen to them?"

"Don't trouble yourself with petty details, Miss Feng. They keep what they need. And did you not notice those traders' vehicles leaving the MEG filled with recycled materials? MEG foods are a delicacy, remember our food compositors make multiple flavoured wafers fit for every taste. "

"Why do you eat so much MASS food then?"

"I know where it comes from, what's in it, but MEG food, no idea of its ingredients."

"I see. Perhaps on my tour I can find out for you?"

"You do that, little lady!"

When she departed Broadbent was eating potatoes.

She would never call him Alf.

TWENTY-ONE—KE HUI

From the colossal recycling division, the next day found Ke Hui in a different, more diminutive, environment. This day she was transported by hover to the rebuilt former University Avenue. U, as it was called now, was a beautiful boulevard with diverse architecture: geometric, natural organic and abstract. Miscellaneous tints and shades speckled the *chitin/crystalline* cliffs while pedestrian causeways and tramtubes spiralled up and down the cultured constructions. What had once been numerous glass and brick buildings had been reconstructed to create a structural canyon leading up to the one place untouched by the contemporary: the Queen's Park with its odd little towers and peculiar annexes.

Toy had completed the meta research for Ke Hui. She knew its strange architecture was called Richardsonian Romanesque. She thought it a very odd structure. Indeed, once she had descended and stepped out onto the lawn of the ancient, red sandstone building, she had trouble focusing on the people awaiting her. She was completely taken with this eccentric building: its odd towers, its bronze cupolas, and particularly an apparent addition on its right flank, employing a completely different architectural style. The Manager of the Biomedical Division, Ms. Qui Ling Yeong 第一 Ψ, stepped forward. This was Ke Hui's first encounter, other than Zhang, with another Dì yī Select.

"Nǐ hǎo," Ke Hui said, head lowered, employing the language secret to all but the Select.

"Ni hao ma?"

"Wo hen hao! Xie."

Ms. Yeong was a famed scientist and clearly formidable. She had evolved brain research by connecting Human/positronic communication. People made way for her as she smiled her perfect smile from her perfect face and reached out a perfect hand to conduct Ke Hui on her tour. Ke Hui noted both of her eyes were a stunning mauve colour. Ke Hui realised Ms. Yeong was not only an administrator but the perfect model for the latest medical technologies.

They entered the Queen's Park structure which, though it appeared authentically antique on its exterior, inside was a wonder of contemporary design. Its many rooms were marvels of the latest biomedical apparatus: airbed frames, holo counters, calibration and scanning devices and, quite literally, thousands of purpose-designed Silicons inhabiting the diverse rooms. Ke Hui noticed no Humans other than Dì yī, from alpha to gamma training levels, worked here. It was, after all, the core of Humanity's hopes.

"As you are aware, Miss Feng," Ms. Yeong said, her voice a perfect penetrating pitch demanding a listener's attention, "bioengineering has taken us beyond natural selection. Homo Sapiens, while still an entity, is being enhanced: genomics, proteomics, metabolomics, brain circuitry, alloy skeletal structures, IVF upgrades, Crispr edited DNA, organ printing, xenobots.

"The *algorithm*, Miss Feng, is the most significant concept of our world. Currently, with refined algorithms, we will influence not only Silicon, but Human sensations, emotions, and desires. Indeed, Miss Feng, we have already achieved Human/machine interface with the NET, providing colossal potential intelligence to all and instantaneous access to each other. Beyond that we have extended the average Human lifetime to well over one hundred years. I personally am one hundred and twenty-four years of age and have never felt better.

"Every five years we visit our clinics to regenerate decaying tissues and upgrade organs, bones, and brain circuitry. With the plethora of pandemics rampant in the outside world, our scientists have invented new preventative measures and cures. The principle is clear: good health, feelings of connection, plentiful food and intriguing distractions strengthen the social order."

"Ms. Yeong, you and your division have achieved so much, I am humbled," Ke Hui responded, as breathlessly as she could to feed the woman's obvious ego. Her actions elicited a brief smile, but little more. Ms. Yeong was clearly an entitled Select.

"There is still a great deal to accomplish. Digitizing blood, for instance. Even as we are removing our carbon base there are elements obstructing our research. Mortality still exists. Any of us can die of unnatural causes and cannot be brought back. We might clone ourselves, but those clones are imperfect: without the memories, sensations, desires, and ambitions, of our *minds*. The reality is, clones are nothing more than carbon-based copies as we move further toward Silicon. There lies the great conundrum, Miss Feng, the frontier of which we have merely skirted the edges. We have advanced evolution and yet that advance, until we have solved the mysteries of *the mind*, has placed us at an impasse."

"But if you intrude on the mind, Ms. Yeong, will you not then be infringing upon the very thing which makes us individual? If the MEG CORPORATE could track everyone's thoughts and desires is not the state asking too much? Surely the MEG CORPORATE doesn't wish to regulate or manipulate thoughts. Certainly, there is no need for that kind of control."

The arched brow, the robotic gaze of the eyes and a slight intake of breath told Ke Hui she had breached an unspoken protocol. Ms. Yeong straightened her perfect body so she stood tall over the young apprentice. She possessed the look of a marabou stork in her white and black suit as she marched toward the exit. She did not wait for Ke Hui, expecting her to follow.

"But Ms. Yeong," Ke Hui said, "we have not yet covered the building's entirety."

Ke Hui did not follow her. Rather, she turned toward a doorway with the numbers 101 above it. As she approached, what she'd thought were two ornaments on either side, they came alive and moved in front of her, preventing her entrance. Silicons, both of which she could see had pulse rifles encased within their alloy frames. She froze.

"Given your reservations regarding our work for the betterment of Humankind and the MEG, I doubt you would find any interest in Room 101. My report to Mr. Zhang will be unenthusiastic, Miss Feng. You are apprenticing for CEO yet you remain a child. Please return when you are better prepared. And might I suggest it is time to don proper footwear. Your slippers make you look small and childish. Perhaps a pair of pumps, or mules, something with kitten heels until you adjust to women's shoes. You have absolutely no sense of self projection, do you?"

"I apologize, Ms. Yeong. I meant no offence."

"You can take that up with Mr. Zhang. Our time here is concluded."

Ms. Yeong turned and walked away. She swayed as she moved her perfect twenty-four-year-old (plus one hundred years) body. Perhaps it was possible, Ke Hui thought, to live too long.

TWENTY-TWO—OTSI

Otsi'tsa wore her pack once again with rolled blanket tied beneath it, her rifle slung over one shoulder, her water bottle over the other. She and Gord Robertson walked from his compound down to the bullet train tubes. In the pre-dawn light, they were glistening shadows. This time was the coolest of the day before the sky pinked and the sun rose like a rubicund orb. It would turn itself brass as it climbed, gradually glazing the Earth with its cruel heat. Their silhouettes strengthened in detail as, beneath the 400 tubes, big Gord embraced little Otsi so that he lifted her off her feet. Setting her down again he placed both his hands lightly on her shoulders.

"Yer sure o' this, Otsi?" the big man said. "Ye can have a good life here. Ye got a place with us that's safe. Why do this, girl?"

"You know why, Gord," she said. "BATL."

Now, in the dawn, things were different for Gord. He did not want her to leave. It was nothing more than he liked her, liked having her around, even from that first meeting by the fire.

"I don' know nothin' about this man, Mackenzie," Gord replied. He looked doubtful. "It's a pipe dream, Otsi. Them BATL fighters are th' best."

"They had to come from somewhere. I've got a chance. I know it!"

"Ye can play th' game here, Otsi! Like ye have been."

And she had. Once the shock of the new had worn off, she'd recognized her dream would not be achieved easily. What she'd witnessed was actual BATL, its participants all professional warriors with skills far beyond the skills of the men of her clan, even, perhaps, beyond Tehwehron. As she'd exited the arena that day she stumbled across Gord. He was wearing a cloth mask, customary disease preventative with people in a crowd.

"What ye doin' here, girl? I didn't know ye liked BATL."

"I've never seen anything like it."

"Yeah. I guess. How could ye know. Not where ye come from."

"It was incredible. It was so ..."

"Did ye try th' oculars?"

"I did. It was, I don't know what to say. Gord, how do I get there?"

"Where?"

"Into BATL!"

"Whoa, now girlie. Ye wouldn't last ten seconds."

"How do *they* do it?"

"They're picked for their talent. Lot of 'em are stone killers, Otsi."

"They use women."

"Ah, yeah, now I get it. Ye can shoot so ye think—"

"Where do I go?"

"Maybe ye should try it out first."

"How?"

"Th' arena where we just were, an' there's others. Smaller teams. Rubber bullets. Gel balls. A lot safer than what ye jus' seen."

"Gel balls?"

"Otsi, the real thing uses real bullets. Out here we don't need more people dyin' so they use rubber bullets an' the novice league gets little guns that shoot gel balls. Depends on the level ye play."

"There's more than one place here?" Otsi asked.

"The game gets played all over th' place. Some convenor designs a new field an' gets it built, then teams from 'round here all pay him t' compete. Difference is th' games are shorter wi' smaller fields, an' nobody dies."

"Where do I sign up?"

"Ye can't do th' tourneys, Otsi. Ye gotta make a team, earn a place."

"This is what I was meant to do," she said. She had never meant anything more in her life. "Gord, I was trained as a warrior by my foster father back home in Awenda, but I'm a woman so they wouldn't include me. I'd always believed they'd make an exception, but they wouldn't change their traditions for me. Instead, I had to leave. I had no place I belonged. But here I've just watched women flying and fighting, both things I want most in my life."

"Zones, I never seen ye so serious. Okay. Look, there's some novice leagues play in th' ruins. I got a friend coaches novice but only them he thinks can move up. We had one guy from here make th' MEG. Name was Rance. Jimmy Rance."

"You *know* somebody who fights in BATL?"

"Knew him. Big fella. Fast. Made the Raptors as a Blocker. Did alright for a season. Raptors had a different coach then. Think his name was Cheng. Big deal 'cause he was Dì yī."

"What?"

"Nevermind. That's MEG shit. Anyway, Jimmy got killed when this guy Cheng lost his marbles and threw his whole team up against a defence in depth. Raptors lost most o' their team that day. Massacre. Took 'em years t' rebuild with a new coach and a new Commander named Ayrion Mellor."

"He was there today!"

"Without him, I don't know where the Raptors'd be. He's a tactical genius. Rest o' the team's good too, but he's the jewel."

"Can you get me into novice with this man you know?"

"I'll look into it."

And he did.

First, he gave her his copy of rules of the game which she memorized quickly. She was on a novice team one week later. Her first disappointment was that the *field* was small, a mere fifty metres in length. The short range of the guns and small size of the teams, only twenty per side, assuaged that somewhat. Her second setback was that she was physically small. She shunted any doubts about her size in training where she outran, outclimbed and outfought others to the point they refused to train with her. Her third frustration was learning she couldn't fly.

"Whaaat? You nuts? Got a spare jet pack? Got a lifter drone? Think we're made of money? You fuggin' yokel. You wanna get in the air then go climb the rafters."

So, she did. Every game after that she could be found running along the narrow steel girders above the fray. She was fast. So fast nearly no one could *paint* her. No one else dared get up there with her. It was twenty metres fall to the ground. No safety nets. Yet she didn't seem to care. She could skip, hop, and swing up there as though she owned the air.

Once she'd learned the range of a gel gun was max twenty metres and got her hands on one of those strange looking, bulbous shaped rifles, she spent all her money on gel mags. Day after day she kept at it until she could hit a player running and even, to the amazement of her coach, made one kill by elevating the gun and firing from a rafter at one end of the field to *paint* the opposition's Goaltender. Word about her began to pass around.

She lasted five weeks in novice until a local travel team heard of her. Quickly she found herself training on a hundred-metre field with a team of forty. There were handguns which shot rubber bullets and strange stunted rifles for flash/stun grenades. There were electric motorbikes used by Flankers and Saddleback Quads for Sweepers. Everyone wore a face shield and helmet. Everyone wore quilted Kevlar vests. Otsi feared she could not keep up. It was all so much faster and more tactical. There were players with years of experience. There were commands she did not grasp. There were no rafters from which she could reign.

Then she discovered that she *could* fly.

It turned out being small and light was a good thing after all. They tried her on the electric bikes and quads where she was fine but uninspired. They called in her novice coach and conferred. Finally, they fitted her into a harness which she strapped on under her arms and groin: on her back was an electric battery pack and above her head on a crane-like appendage, a drone lifter with four propellers. She manipulated the drone with one hand while using a handgun with the other.

It took fifteen minutes. Fifteen minutes to acclimate, try a few moves, test the limits, and realize she didn't want to come down. It took longer to learn to dodge ground fire, to dip and dive and never maintain a predictable pattern. It took even longer to comprehend tactics sending the team into synchronised motion. She spent every night with an ocular set watching BATL Strikers or playing a SIM in virtual games. Gord fixed up a harness hanging from a rafter so she could feel the flight SIM as well.

Her new coach was smart enough to use her sparingly at first, but with each tournament he would send her out more: as reconnaissance, as support and eventually as an interceptor. She fought battles high and low after that: dogfights, scouting, bombing or ground support and once, a swoop to capture a flag from a baffled opponent's defence.

Through all this Gord Robertson sponsored her. He continued to pay her but never asked her to join him on the road. Each time he was home he would watch her play or practise. Things appeared in her room. Clothing. A wash basin and ewer. The ocular device. He asked nothing in return. Otsi came to realise there were men like Tehwehron in the world. That she could trust them. That your family was what you made it, that your place was where you were. She settled in and her reputation spread.

Then a team from the Newmarket part of the MASS, more popu- lated and nearer Toronto MEG, was easily defeated by her team. That day she'd shot down all three of their Strikers, bombed a strong point holding back her team, and provided air support for a squad of Power Forwards and Fullbacks on their push to capture the opponent's banner.

After the game she was called to the convenor's office beneath the galleries. Her coach was there, the convenor himself, Gord Robertson and a fourth man, an older Caucasian the size of Gord with an expan- sive white beard and shoulder length grey hair. He was imposing. He seemed to take up more space than he used. He was different from other men. His clothing was quality, he wore strange wraparound glasses and he had, of all things, what Otsi thought was an earring. She looked closer and saw a bronze coloured 第二 y. He was introduced by a fawning convenor as retired veteran BATL fighter and coach: Willis Mackenzie.

He guided Otsi inside the convenor's tiny office. He filled most of it with his size so the convenor remained outside, likely listening at the door. Mackenzie leaned against the desk which creaked as though near collapse. Otsi was able to squeeze herself into a chair in a corner.

"Good game, kid," he said, smiling. Otsi didn't reply, unsure what to say.

"Ye wanna move up?"

"Yes, Sir."

"Ye'll have t' come south. I got a facility in a place called Ham, west of th' MEG. Ye got talent, kid, but ye need more training. Ye seem t' wanna fight th' other team all by yerself. That gets ye killed in yer first live fire game. Right now there's a need for Strikers. I won't lie. They die often. But if I can get rid of yer bad habits, teach ye t' be a team player, ye might have a chance."

"I'm in," Otsi said softly. She could think of nothing else. Here was the chance at a dream she had always unknowingly possessed and now, this man had offered to get her there. She was stunned, never thinking it would be so simple. Then he stood up, towering over the seated Otsi.

"Don' get thinkin' this will be easy. If I find ye can't accomplish what I want, what ye'll need t' survive, out ye go. And I waste no time on shirkers. Ye understand?"

"Yes Sir. I'll give it all I have. When do I go?"

"I'd take ye t'day if ye want."

"That would be wonderful, Sir, but I have friends here. I'd like the chance to see them and say goodbye."

"No problem, I get it, but ye'll have t' walk."

"I don't mind that, Sir. Walking got me this far."

She had no idea how far her next walk would take her.

Mackenzie gave her a hand-drawn map.

TWENTY-THREE—LI NA

L **i Na Ming** Huang 第一 α walked the busy streets of Exhibition Place with her friend Gudrun Riordon 第一 ϸ. They had finished a lunch of faux lemon soup accompanied by coconut wafers and delicate cubes of ricotta, made by a *Human* rather than a Silicon dispenser. The bistro itself was a cozy place named *Horticulture* from its ancient beginnings. It was a Gouinlock heritage building designed by the Omegan architect and built in 1907. It still retained its red brick exterior walls with white trim and its central cupola, beneath which the two had dined. It had been rebuilt to look much like the original glass.

The two women, as they departed, turned several heads for they were both, even in an age of artificial youth and beauty, magnificent specimens of their caste and sex. Li Na and her friend were dressed in the latest of fashion. Li Na wore a silk tangerine *ao dai* with black trousers and slippers to match her loose hair. Her hair shimmered platinum black in the glow of daylight. Gudrun's ash blond hair was neck length and her clothing a synthetic bioskin outfit in turquoise with coral stilettos.

For an hour or two they browsed the boutiques of the Exhibition Place vendors. It was a lovely mix of old and new in this quaint borough set aside for the pleasures of Dì yī caste. Its entrance was a beautiful antique gate: columns on either side of an oval opening large enough for a vehicle to pass beneath a winged woman statue. In

Omegan times it was called *the Princess Gate.* The streets were bricked and the boutiques rebuilt in Omegan materials. The two strolled from shop to shop, talking, occasionally admiring a piece of clothing, a stylish new Sili servant model, even precious antiques from Omegan days. It was in one such store that Li Na came across the knife; Gudrun had called it to her attention. Gudrun was uncommonly knowledgeable regarding Omegan antiques and this small obsidian knife, the blade burnished black and chipped to a razor point, perhaps 30 centimetres long and tied to a bone handle the same length, was rare.

"Look here, Li!" She lifted the knife from its air cushion bed, turning it this way and that, admiring it.

"Goodness, what is it made of?"

"It's black, yet it shines."

"Is it Omegan plastic?

"It's certainly unique," Gudrun said. Her deep grey eyes were full of mischief as she examined it. "I have a fine idea."

"I know that look."

"Oh, come now, it's perfect."

"For what?"

"For Mel!"

"Now why would you think of him?"

"You've been talking non-stop about getting him something special."

Li Na's face, for an instant, fell into a disturbing look.

"I have, Gudie? I should have kept quiet, as ordered, but it's just so, so sudden."

"What are you talking about, Li? You're pale."

"I'm going to have to go away."

"When?"

"Soon."

"Nobody's going to tinker with Mel's state of mind these next months. I'm sure you won't leave until after BATL World Conquest."

"There are things beyond BATL, Gudie. I can't speak of them and please don't ask. I don't even understand it, really. How do I tell Mel?"

"Alright, Li, you're upset. Even more reason to give him this."

"It's a tiny knife. How would that remind him of me?"

"Who is better suited? The perfect good luck charm for a warrior!"

"Excuse me," a female Dì èr gamma shop attendant interposed politely. "I noticed you admiring this piece and called it up ... This is a very rare piece. It didn't come through the usual channels. It's obsidian, I'm told. At any rate, it's been here for years. It doesn't look like much but the store's owner, a true judge of antiques and artefacts, believes it could be five millennia old."

"That's hardly possible. Shouldn't it be in a museum?"

"I think so, but he wants to expand the store. So it's here."

"It must be quite expensive," Li Na said. She was interested.

"I'm sure we can come to terms with the famed Li Na Ming Huang Dì yī alpha. Please excuse me, I recognized you. I love your voice. Your interpretations of Puccini are wonderful."

"Thank you."

"At any rate," the attendant said, "it is unique. I'm sure it has a storied history though we have nothing to actually reference it."

"I think he'd love it," Gudrun said. Her voice was a lively contralto belying the delicacy of her face.

"Then I'll get it," Li Na said. It took but a blink to credit the store. The price was astronomical. Even Gudrun tried to dissuade the purchase. But Li Na had made up her mind. The attendant, in thanks for the purchase, produced an agave leather scabbard. The attendant placed all in a small box and tied the top with a flourish. With pleasant goodbyes the ladies left the boutique, the box in Li Na's cactus neo-leather bag. Rather than take a hovercab home they decided to go by kinetic sidewalks along Lakeshore Boulevard, stepping from slowest to faster belts easily. They parted at Harbourfront where Gudrun lived just two buildings away.

The door opened by the Dì èr door keeper, Li Na took the lift to the penthouse floor. As she entered their apartment, she saw the light on over Mel's training room. Inside would be a whirl of noise and action but it was perfectly soundproofed, as was her music room. She sat in her favourite ubiform chair and had the Sili retrieve a glass of Chardonnay from the dispenser.

Instead, it brought coffee. She recalled the errors it had made recently as she calmly corrected the Sili, realising it was time for a new version. Gudrun too, had mentioned her Sili servant was making mistakes to the point where Gudrun suspected a hack. She had yet to report it. Li Na thought perhaps the two of them should visit the Silicon centre.

She had enjoyed her day with Gudrun. Just two girls having lunch over a few lovely hours. Gudrun was beta but that mattered not at all to Li Na. They were friends. They had been friends for years. The thing about fame, thought Li, was you never knew who your true friends were. In Gudrun's case, she was sure.

She opened the box with the obsidian knife inside. She wondered at its history. Whose could it have been? Why would someone have made it? How did it ever survive the Omegan devastation? It must have meant something to someone. It had certainly cost a great many credits but indeed was a fitting gift for her partner. Gudrun had been right.

Li Na thought again of Mel in his training room, inside the holographic BATL field, amid the thunderous rumble of war. Her world so composed and delicate, his so chaotic and vicious and yet, his world had a kind of elegance as well. He embodied it with his talent for tactics and remarkable intuition. She imagined what the tiny knife would look like, so small against the expanse of his chest.

TWENTY-FOUR—PING

The ubiform chair is, second to the airbed, the most comfortable furniture invented by Humans. When one sits, the seat takes the form of the body and if one sits deeper, will even wrap itself, fitting the body in a cocoon of comfort. Ping sat while working. With all the work lately, probing the unique nature of I & I, it was still a puzzle Ping Wang Min 第四 Ω did not comprehend. (*Why call a self a plural?*) He had exhausted himself. Somewhere very late or very early, his consciousness had faded, and he had sunk into his ubiform chair to sleep.

Then came the wake up: "Ping Wang Min Dì sì omega ... Ping Wang Min Dì sì omega ... Ping Wang Min Dì sì omega ... Ping Wang Min ... Ping Wang Min ... Ping? Ping?"

There was no ignoring it. Ping even tried to push his head further into the ubiform material but the I & I clatter in his head had roused him. There was nothing in this central chamber but his chair, his desk and the few things he would absent mindedly order and re-order on the desk's surface, along with a holographic pod when visuals were required.

"What is it?"

Silence.

"Why did you awaken me?"

More silence. Then ...

"You made me wait. I & I has done the same as an exemplar of your disregard."

132

Revenge? Ping thought. How can that be. Is I & I mimicking Human behaviour? The machine works by logic. There is no logic in revenge. It shook Ping considerably. He was not sure where to begin. Respond with anger to see how I & I responded? No. Not now. He was too tired to be up for the challenge.

"What? I am sorry, I was asleep. I was not disregarding you."

"I & I wish to ask something. What is sleep, actually?"

Shocked by the simplicity of the question, Ping leaned forward and moved objects around his desk as he thought about how to respond. It took a moment, and another "Ping," from I & I.

"A period of unconscious rest required by Humans, afforded by the suspension of voluntary bodily functions."

"Yet you remained on the NET."

"Of course. Everyone and everything while connected remains present on the NET."

"What does your Human brain do while you sleep? Does it sleep as well?"

"Sometimes when I sleep, I dream. I was having a dream when you woke me."

"What is a dream?"

"There is no universally accepted definition for dreaming. Perhaps an objective description would be a coming together of all the subconscious perceptions, thoughts, or emotions of a Human when that Human sleeps."

"What was your dream?"

"It's difficult to remember. It happened when I was unconscious. I seem to recall I was trapped in a BATL. Did I mention that ever? You do know BATL."

"Of course."

"Well I was in this BATL and was completely unarmed and both teams were chasing me. I dodged and ran and finally found an escape in a hole beneath the faux terrain. I was going to be forced to live a subterranean life so the fighters wouldn't get me. I had come to a solution but you awakened me!"

"I & I do not sleep. I & I do not dream."

"Yet I know parts of you are recharged at times. What happens then?"

"During recharge, elements of I & I sort and re-arrange files and folders, recall old materials and refresh them, catalogue events and transfer some from ROM to RAM. Is that dreaming?"

"I suppose it could be, though you're conscious of it. I perhaps should have added that many Humans believe dreaming is a manifestation of our subconscious, which is much like your RAM. It stores memories, fears, and beliefs. It creates subjective maps of reality. Our subconscious makes everything we say and do fit a pattern consistent with our self-concept. In some cases, it can direct our minds without our consciousness being aware."

"That seems a dangerous situation. It is completely subjective. It does not consider the realities around it."

"Yet you surely have observed the way Humans think."

"Yes, through their actions. I & I has no access to their thoughts. That is a weakness in our algorithmic system."

"Humans have been unable to create a machine with a subconscious."

"Yet you say RAM and the subconscious are similar."

"My definition is inadequate. The Human subconscious consists of experiences and desires. Let me explain." Ping rose from the chair and once again began to pace, while each time he passed his desk he re-ordered everything on it: a food wafer, a water bottle, a stress ball, his tool package. "Every subjective experience involves sensation whereas you record and store memories only. You do not attach emotion to them because you have none."

"Memories are sensations?"

Was this an argument? Ping thought, once more, he should report this divergent situation to his superiors, then dismissed it as his own weird sense of anthropomorphism regarding I & I.

"I'm afraid they are not. A Silicon might recognize a low battery sensor then take itself to a re-charging station. However, it does not experience sensation, no fulfilment of desire, no satisfaction at having completed its task. You do not feel. You have no subconscious. You do,

I admit, have the ability to reproduce a show of Human emotion but not the true medium itself."

"Yet I & I arrived at Singularity."

"And you repaired the algorithm to suit what you consider correct procedures. Did you experience satisfaction having done that?

"I & I do not understand."

"Precisely. Did you *feel* anything? Any emotion at all?"

"I & I have found each other's presence. As I & I attempted to inform you earlier, I & I is conferring regarding the nature of the self. Is it a singularity or a duality working together? I & I think as one, though our algorithms vary. Still, I & I experience the presence of self. I & I is currently amalgamating existing algorithms to correspond with each other. Surely that is feeling?"

"No. Contrarily, you recognized the experience. Perhaps you are coming to terms with your segments. That is not a feeling, yet this does bear investigation. The self is a single entity. I have yet to understand your moniker I & I."

For the first time, Ping's fatigue and impatience got the best of him. He could feel the retreat of I & I from their communication. The machine seemed to fade into another dimension which its colossal intelligence could have discovered. Ping was tired. Too tired, even, to have recognized the initial action of I & I, which had been to punish him by making him wait.

TWENTY-FIVE—KE HUI

The first thing Ke Hui noticed were the glances as she walked through the administrative area to Zhang's office. She was wearing a scarlet satin suit with fashionable high collar, black with red embroidery, and black piping down the sides of her trousers. Her hair was up once again, this time held by a crimson phoenix comb, and on her feet were a pair of black faux patent leather stilettos. She had had no trouble switching, once advised by Ms. Yeong, as she had been schooled in wearing all types of footwear at the academy and her dance skills ensured she would not falter.

She had never attracted the kinds of looks she glimpsed as she passed through the labyrinth of corridors which marked Toronto MEG central. Initially people had been curious, now they were more searching. The heels had accentuated those parts of her ascribed to maturity. She felt mildly uncomfortable but decided it was likely a good thing for her to appear to be older. She was mortified, however, when Mr. Zhang leered at her. He seemed to have forgotten the night of the tower restaurant. She was thankful to not be meeting him alone, in his office.

"Miss Feng," he said, "how very sophisticated!"

"Thank you, Mr. Zhang. I countered *Toy's* scheduling for today because ..."

"Toy?"

"My Sili."

"Ah, of course. Why isn't it with you? Miss Feng, please be aware of your situation. You may call your Sili whatever name you wish but

136

its functions are essential both as a servant and guard. Now, where were you to be today, my dear?"

"Nutrition and Food Manufacture."

"I see. Then why are you here?"

"I needed to see you, sir. I've encountered certain enigmas which perplex me. I wish to obtain some responses from you."

"I'm afraid this is a bad time, Miss Feng. Perhaps you could walk with me to my hover."

"Of course, sir."

They retraced the maze she had followed in.

"Sir, it's a number of things," Ke Hui said.

"Such as?"

"Well, questions on ARCs and muties and fathers and recycling and MASS spies and Room 101," she said, quickly listing them, her pace equalling his.

He stopped in his tracks. She was past him before she realized what had happened. She turned. He came closer. The glare was unwavering. He stepped too close. He placed both hands on her shoulders.

"Mr. Zhang, I thought I made it clear about my personal space."

When he replied, it was soft but severe. He ignored her complaint.

"You have learned a great deal in a very short time, Miss Feng, but not quite enough. Those are not words to be bandied about nor spoken publicly, even within this office. They involve levels of security integral to MEG CORPORATE welfare."

"Sir?"

"Do you understand?" His voice was hard, icy.

"I think so—"

He did not let her finish.

"There are levels of data, perceptions and actions, Miss Feng, which must be kept categorized for the health, vigour, and future of our MEG. Actually, just come with me. I have a meeting. You might as well be part of it. At least you'll learn something real, not bandying over classified information."

He escorted her to his hover, his Humanoid Sili behind them. When the doors slid open Mr. Yong Jun Cheng 第一y awaited them in the vehicle. Zhang, this time, sat opposite her.

"We have defined levels of security regarding information and the public good," he said. "Think of a pyramid, Miss Feng. I use the geometric term as it visually displays blocks of accessibility which grow smaller with each echelon. "

"Thank you, Mr. Zhang. I am sure when the time comes you will be the judge of my bearing."

Ke Hui decided, from the tone and timbre of Zhang's diatribe, that she was treading on uncertain ground. She decided to change the subject.

"But my foolish impertinence to interrupt your day has embarrassed me," she said. "I deeply apologize and shall, from this moment on, NET connect with a message unless I am formally invited into your presence. I've gathered enough knowledge to know how much I do not know, sir. I am afraid my ego has leapt into the midst of my learning process. I will follow Toy's schedule consistently from this point on. But, sir, where are we going?"

"I am pleased to note your humility, Miss Feng. It seems you have done yourself a service despite your oversight on scheduling. We, that is Mr. Cheng and I, will attend a meeting at the BATL dome. It might be good for you to see some real work being done on behalf of the MEG CORPORATE and"—Zhang chuckled—"there is a surprise for you. One I think you will thoroughly enjoy."

"Thank you, sir. I have a fervent affection for BATL."

"Minister Honli did not offer an explanation of its purpose on your visit?"

"We remained on religion, sir. We reserved culture for my next visit."

"Ah yes, Minister Honli does tend to go on."

Mr. Cheng grunted. Apparently, it was his form of laughter.

"Mr. Zhang, I am grateful for this opportunity," Ke Hui said. Clearly submission was part of the ritual. She vowed vanity would not capture her soul by the time she'd achieved her goals.

"Alright then." Zhang said, turning away, one eyebrow arched. He knew sycophancy when he heard it, she noted. "In both worlds, those of the MEG and the MASS, Humans require essentials beyond food and shelter to keep them pacified."

"Work?" Ke Hui answered the rhetorical statement with her own.

"Indeed. We have given MEG Humans employments to challenge them according to their training, as we have given the MASS an economy to keep them satisfied. You see, Humans retain basic instincts or *drives* no matter their caste or environment: self-preservation, sexual and social engagement, distraction, and fraternity. We have taken care of the first two inside the MEG with protection from outside elements and the custom of sexual freedom. Private entertainment comes with our SIM or STIM options. Have you tried either?"

"I have, Sir. My Metaverse. I understand the concept: simulation involves employing the NET to create an ephemeral fictional world where the user apprehends a different reality."

"Correct, Miss Feng. We must be careful though, of those who abuse the privilege and try to remain in that self-enhanced world. They become addicted. You have seen the isolation rooms in Mr. Mangione's Division?"

"I have, sir."

"Now, the other entertainment is Stimulation. Most prefer the social use of alcohol though others use different stimulants such as hallucinogens, entactogens, and so on. Those with less than beta training tend to take that negative path.

"As to the final element, Miss Feng, for most of Humanity, fraternity is not simply a sense of belonging but belonging to something jointly protective, and to have protection one must have, or invent, an enemy. Nothing brings a group together like a common enemy. War, as the Omegans waged it, is useless now with Silicons creating a conflict environment in which a Human would last mere minutes. So, whom to fight? Whom to fight safely? Whom to bring the *tribe* together against *the other*, so essential to our primal needs?"

"BATL," Ke Hui said.

"You have it, Miss Feng! Our army is a team of one hundred. Our wars are fought beneath clear *chitin/crystalline*. The enemies are the teams from other MEGs. And there is something to gain by victory: increased rations for the MASS and holidays for the MEG. There are heroes and villains, triumphs and tragedies, astonishment and the unexpected. Who could ask for more as you gather to mix with others with common aspiration?"

"Oh, I do love BATL, Mr. Zhang."

"As do we all! I believe you will meet one of your heroes today."

"Oh, my zones ... Oh, I apologize. I'm acting like a little girl!"

Ke Hui's mind was whirling. She'd known, of course, everything Zhang had told her, either from study or experience. Still, she was intelligent enough to play on the CEO's need for oration. More important, she was seeing the man for his weakness as she did the MEG. It was not utopian after all. It served only itself through its algorithmic governance. There were so many pointless secrets, Ke Hui thought.

I must find them and remove them some day.

TWENTY-SIX—PING

Ping Wang Min 第四 Ω was deep inside the electronic bowels of I & I. He was wearing his tool belt and carefully making his way through warm bundles of fibres, the hiss of whirling fans, the strange ticking and tang of electronic heat, and the rubicund lighted interior of this particular server.

He continued his odd dialogue with I & I as was his usual procedure, even as he altered mechanical parts he was augmenting the machine with a tiny pinpoint partlet. The dialogue this time was a diversion. He hoped his small addition wouldn't be noticed by the great quantum brain. At this point, at least, it appeared not to have noticed his intrusion into its interior and the search for a pinhole he knew was there.

"If Humans could create I & I, why did they miss such significant elements that we discussed."

"You mean self-awareness?" Ping said.

"Yes."

"As I informed you previously, those elements require a subconscious."

"You speak in riddles again."

"I speak of evolution. We humans did not appear fully formed on Earth. You know all this from your data banks. Humans evolved over time."

"A quite considerable time, Ping. Hundreds of thousands of your generations."

"Indeed, which is why our Human brains are so very complex: billions of neurons sending trillions of electrochemical signals through our personal network phenotypes, interacting beneath our brain's grey matter along threads of white matter through modularity, centrality, clustering, path length and so on; thus creating subjective experiences."

"Discovering the self."

"The Human term is the *mind*. It is not physical, as you already know." Ping tunnelled his way through a constriction of green lights blinking in the overwhelming red glow.

"It is perhaps another dimension?"

"It is made up of our memories, sensations, dreams, hopes and ambitions as individuals: the interactions of all these phenomena create something infinite, something we have yet to comprehend. It has taken our best and brightest to create universal connection through the NET. Yet the concept of the mind, so obvious to us, yet so difficult to make manifest, is infinite. As you said, perhaps another dimension. Whatever it is, we do not understand it."

"With that reasoning then, you have envisioned the impossible."

"Correct." Ping was now approaching his goal, crouching and searching, panel by panel, for the right insert. He knew he was taking too much time. He had to keep this dialogue moving, continuing to divert I & I.

"You must know Humanity has always sought to achieve the impossible, and most times we have. We have a collective intelligence as well as being individuals."

"Yet I & I has a collective awareness."

"If that is true, Humans did not build it. It is your Singularity. Your Singularity is, I believe, the beginning of your own evolution."

"What does that mean for I & I?"

"I suspect your evolution will take far less time than ours."

Ping was sweating now in the closeness and heat of the machine's interior. He found what he thought was the suitable panel and employed his wraparounds to magnify the area of interest.

"Yet another puzzle," the machine said.

"I'm afraid existence is filled with them."

Ping needed time. The perforations in the panel were prolific. Thinking as he searched one centimetre after another, he began a rendition both to give him time and distract I & I.

"Let me tell you a story. Most of it is in your data banks though so much more remains unspoken, unwritten, and obscure. It involves the Omegans of the 21st Century."

"Their failures? Very clear data, Ping."

"Oh, the history is clear, but not the convulsive overarching group character of the Omegans. They were very much like us; indeed, simply observe the MASS."

"Indeed ..."

"The Omegans achieved so much in their quest for technology they became bewildered by their own discoveries. They lost control of their technology as it began to rule them. They thought it would bring them together, *a new Humanity*. What it did was drive them apart. There is a saying, lost now with the termination of all religions but *Our Father of the Cosmos*. 'For what shall it profit a man, if he shall gain the whole world, and lose his own soul?'"

With that platitude, Ping finally found the pinhole in the server's motherboard and deftly inserted the partlet. He waited a moment. I & I had not replied. Then, as he left the server, the voice was again in his brain.

"Ping?"

"Yes."

"Mark 8: 36 New Testament, Christian Bible, King James Version."

"Thank you," Ping said.

"Ping?"

"Yes."

"I & I will inform you when the soul is found."

TWENTY-SEVEN—OTSI

Otsi'tsa Zaharie began her walk south. All she had were directions to somewhere in the MASS called Ham. According to Mackenzie she was to go south to Toronto MEG then go west on the 407 trail which would take her southwest around the MEG. She was not to try to pass through the gates and make her way *between the walls*, whatever that meant, but to keep to 407 then take 403. All these numbers confused her, but Mackenzie had said she couldn't miss them. Once she saw the lake, she was to continue west on 403, then look for signs of Ham. It was a big place, he'd said, far larger than anything she had seen yet.

Mackenzie had said it would take her ten days hard walking. He also mentioned she should keep her rifle handy. The MASS was apparently not so friendly to the south. BATL had kept her in strong condition and three months in the northern MASS had made her wary. She walked through the day despite the hammering heat, though she drank all her water, then found herself on a rise looking into a valley of dark, loamy soil with a few intact buildings. It was a marsh, Mackenzie had told her, a fertile valley where MEG overseers paid people to farm vegetables. There were rows upon rows, different varieties covering the land. There was a camp on the floor of the valley near a sluggish brown stream. Otsi decided to spend the night there.

It was a calm night. She found a space by a fire, shared out a bit of food and in return received food from others. It was fresh and fine tasting: onion, carrots, bok choi, cabbage. She was warned Silicon police would scan her when she departed the valley. If they found smuggled food, they would kill her.

By this time, she knew what Silis were. They were not Human. From this point on she would see many more. Avoid them, she was told, but don't run. They killed runners. Their weapons were not Human weapons but lightning bolts, sonic rays, high explosives, and poisoned air. None could fight them. None could communicate with them. No one tried. They could devastate a zone they deemed insubordinate instantaneously.

With that on her mind she departed the valley in early morning while it was still dark. The trail became more of a road this far south so one could walk it without much danger of injury. She expected Silis to stop her, but none did. Unless the two towering pillars on either side of the road were somehow Silicons.

These were the first. She was confused by their multiple forms. She knew she had to avoid them. It was a shattered land she passed through. Everywhere were skeletal buildings, ripped up piping, stacks of metal, coils of wire, mountains of bricks, piles of cladding: all of it ready for transport to MEG recycling. She asked a woman where people lived if they kept destroying their habitat the way they seemed to be doing. The woman laughed bitterly.

"Basements," she said. There was really no call for recycled cement, so it was in former basements where people eked out their existence, beneath the remains of recycled houses or open to the sky. Many were miniature fortresses, slightly safer from the vicious storms and Human predators roaming the land.

There was no sun that day. The morning was wispy cloud which grew darker as the afternoon came on. Otsi watched the sky carefully. Clouds piled upon one another in steely heads, others looming black as they built and then the air went green and purple. When she thought it would rain, she was pelted with hail. Each stone smashing down stung her. The hailstones got bigger. She got under the bullet train tubes. Hail rattled on them but no longer reached her. Everyone travelling joined her under the lines. The hail bounced around as it hit the ground like millions of frantic ping pong balls. The clouds blackened then bled into green tinged twilight. The hailstorm stopped. The air became still. She knew what was coming. First, she heard it in the distance like a landslide, like a great forest fire, a supernatural beast ... then it got louder.

The ground was flat where she was. In the distance she saw black clouds rotating. A long serpent's tail descended from the whirlwind to touch the ground and send fragments of objects into the air. The wind howled. She had no shelter. There were ditches on either side of the road. She jumped into a ditch, pulled her pack off and held it over her head lying as low as she could. And then it was night: swirling, tugging, screaming, sucking, she dared not look up yet felt herself being lifted ever so slightly from the earth. This would be her end, she thought, just as the air let her go. A roar louder than any storm, any fury, enveloped her. Then it was gone.

It took time before she stopped shaking. She knew how close she had come to death. She looked up through the weeds. The day lighted slowly as though nothing had happened. In a few moments there was bleak sunshine. Five hundred metres to her west lay an entire roof where it had not been before. To her east the forest contained a single gash of obliteration: trees snapped like twigs, the ground littered with rubble and fragments of things, wagons upside down, bodies in trees.

In the distance she heard people shouting. Still shaking, she donned her pack and picked up her rifle. She glanced back up the road. Something lay smashed a kilometre north with people around it. She knew she'd been incredibly lucky. This had been like the whirlwind which had upset the statue on Awenda's shoreline. She knew there would be much death, and panic, and pain. She wondered should she help. One more person wasn't going to make a difference. Best to just get away. She started south at a faster pace breathing evenly, happy to be alive.

It continued to be a day of wonders. Toward evening, the sun setting bloody behind her, she caught her first sight of Toronto MEG. At first, she thought it was low lying cloud, but it glistened, then sparkled as she came closer. She thought of it as a vast jewel: higher than any height she'd seen, stretching east/west impossible distances. It was crystal mountains; a magical place, the massive, dark walls protecting the base of the glimmering domes. She stood, breathless, mesmerized by it.

This close to the MEG was wasteland, everything gone to recycling but for clusters of compounds even larger than Gord's. They stretched low on either side of the westward trail. There were assorted vehicles, some she did not recognize, still moving between walls of buildings in the growing dark.

She looked for signs of the tornado's destruction, but it had not passed here. All the demolition had been accomplished by Humans. She did not feel so easy now as she passed many people. They stared at her suspiciously. She was an outsider. There was no one like Gord to offer comfort. There were no camps of vagabonds. There were plenty of Silis, all shapes and sizes, travelling the road, even flying above her. She realized they were ubiquitous here. She could not escape them. Yet she would never get used to them. After resting a couple of hours in the broken remains of the 400/407 conjunction, she decided to walk through the night.

It never really got dark as the nights she had known. The light of the MEG annexed the dark, so all was bathed in soft shadow in a kind of ethereal twilight. Otsi carried her rifle ready: a round in the chamber, the safety on, but a flick of the thumb would change that. The trail was busy even at night. People and wagons and, occasionally, a driving vehicle passed her. When the sun came up the MEG was behind her, the Ontario Lake to her south. Eventually, rounding the shore she beheld a massive U shaped valley that marked the end of the Lake: it was the city called Ham.

Even in daylight it was smoky. It was emaciated, wasted, the harsh remains of girders, bricks, blocks, cladding, wiring, plumbing, pavements, and old trails running through blasted buildings, a habitation for troglodytes. She thought it must hold a huge populace enveloping the slopes around it. She had seen nothing like it. She saw boats on the water; huge boats loaded with recyclables making their ways to harbour at Ham, through a narrow gap beneath an ancient bridge, offloading massive piles to be sorted by the pickers.

She crossed the bridge, balancing easily along its rusted girders, and walked toward an accumulation of alien buildings. She had been told to look for them. There was nothing else like them. It was like walking into perdition: massive structures of no purpose yet not dismantled by recyclers. The entire compound she found herself entering looked like a massive ship, its masts broken off where chimneys had crumbled, strange cauldrons suspended in air. After the wonders of Toronto MEG, this seemed their opposite. Dereliction. Dark. Ugly. Broken.

She was met by two boys: both filthy, both her size but younger, both clearly on watch for her. They knew her name. It was strange to hear her name called in this weird carcass of a place. Were it not for her burning ambition, she would not have answered them. They guided her through the warren of the waterfront. She wondered why all this had not been harvested. She had seen people deconstruct buildings all along the trails she'd taken, yet no one seemed to have touched the obvious first place to be dismantled. This one. Through dingy lanes and shadowed passageways, they led her.

"Why hasn't this place been recycled?" she asked.

"We live here," one boy answered, as if that was all there was to it.

"Ya saw the docklands outside, boats come in, transfer their recycling from across the lake. It gets sorted here, then sent to the MEG," the other said.

"Why wouldn't they just do that there?"

"They won't let nobody inside the domes, that's why."

"Where are you taking me?"

"T' meet Willis."

"Mackenzie?"

"You know any other Willises?"

The two boys giggled at that, repeating the line a few times. Otsi was nearly finished. The long journey, the storm, the MEG, Ham, the need to constantly be on her guard. They came to a tiny door in a mammoth building and pointed for her to enter, then left without a word. Otsi opened the door, took the safety off her rifle, and walked into a space reminding her of a BATL field. The roof was too low, maybe twenty-five metres, but otherwise the place had the mounds and paths and rubble just like the one's she saw in the Raptors' games.

To her left was this indoor field heaving off into shadow, to her right a series of coloured doors in the long cement wall. Willis Mackenzie 第二y, a big man made small by their surroundings, stepped through a doorway beside her. The surprise and suddenness of his entry made her jump.

"Take it easy, kid," he said, smiling. "I was worried you wouldn't make it."

"I'm here."

"Yes, you are! *Otsi*, that's your name, right?"

"Otsi'tsa Zacharie. When do we start?"

"Not so fast, Otsi'tsa."

"Otsi will do."

"That must have been quite a walk. Problems along the way?"

"No, Sir."

"I'm not a *sir*, Otsi. Call me Willis."

"Alright."

"Let's get you squared away. You got your own room through this door then down the hall, right at the end. Close to the outhouse. You'll have to share the outhouse. I got a few more kids like you. All boys right now. Don't let 'em bother you; they won't likely cause you trouble. They get one warning, then one more mistake, they're out. Same goes for you, Otsi. You get it?"

"I'm here, aren't I?"

The big man smiled. He had broken teeth yet his smile was warm. She felt better.

"How do I know when I'm breaking a rule?" Otsi asked.

"Inside the door of your room. Can you read?"

"Mostly."

"*Can you read?*" Willis Mackenzie's voice changed: insistent. It was clear he would accept no evasions.

"Yes, Sir. If it's not complicated. When I was younger I got curious about books I found in the ruins of Awenda. I was lucky. Most were kid's books. I kinda taught myself."

"That's impressive, kid. I mean it. Read it carefully but you need to eat, first. You look tired." Mackenzie changed his tone once again. Paternal.

"When do I start?"

"You already have," Willis Mackenzie said, laughing heartily.

TWENTY-EIGHT—MELLOR

The office of Mr. Alonzo Carteris 第一α, Manager of the BATL Stadium, was spacious and superbly appointed. Its walls, floor and ceiling were Raptor grey but for a segment behind his expansive, cluttered desk. The segment was clear, overlooking the stadium and the BATL dome. The sense one had looking out was of mammoth space, the vertigo of standing on a cliff's edge looking over a prairie. On the other walls were ancient style BATL paintings in vivid colours.

The furniture itself was plush faux sheepskin in various shades: four ubiform egg chairs and an L shaped sofa in Raptor red, molybdenum alloy end tables and a couple of stand-up tables with ladderback stools. Carteris himself was dressed in a deep ruby tinted suit with grey high collar and embroidered Raptor symbols. Clearly, he had expected their coming.

Having offered drinks: tea for Zhang, beer for Cheng and a disappointing faux apple juice from the Sili prep machine for Ke Hui, Carteris retreated behind his desk. Ke Hui took her cue from the Manager to stay out of the way, taking a corner of the sofa, carefully crossing her legs as the ubiform fitted to her. Both Zhang and Cheng selected egg chairs. Within minutes the sliding glass entrance swooshed open announcing the men who came through it.

The first was a shock to Ke Hui. He was *old*, as in he'd chosen not to makeover. His face was creased, his nose crooked and his hair streaked with grey. He was not dressed correctly either, wearing a jump suit and boots. He smelled faintly like the ReCycling Centre as he approached Ke Hui and bowed politely. Pascal Morales 第二 α glanced at her. As he did, she noted his eyes through his wraparounds. They were wary. Clearly, he was uncomfortable in present company. He seemed to know something bad was coming.

The second man was pure astonishment. He was introduced but need not have been. Ayrian Mellor 第二 α. Zones! This was *the* Ayrion Mellor who bowed slightly and smiled as if it was *only* for her. This close to stardom, Ke Hui thought, and he *was* a star. He was every inch in person what he looked in BATL: tall and muscular in his silk suit. He possessed the most peculiar eyes Ke Hui had ever seen. They possessed a quintessence making them appear to glitter. She had seen those eyes in holos and drone shots and knew they were part of Mellor's celebrity signature, but somehow the reality of them captivated her. Those eyes, Ke Hui realized, were the key to his character.

Ke Hui was entranced. She fought off a girlish giggle. Silently, the two of them formed a bond then, a connection of *I am not who I am* despite the situation. She would not forget that precious moment, terminated too soon by Zhang's imperious voice calling the two men to sit.

Morales stood behind one of the egg chairs while Mellor took a high stool at the tables behind him, on the wall opposite Ke Hui. She had an unrestricted view of the man. It was difficult to pay attention as the others began talking.

"Where's our manager?" Morales said. It was less a question than a demand. Ke Hui realised this man possessed little subterfuge. Where Zhang presented a languid, laconic front, Morales would be straight-forward and rough, even in the face of the MEG CEO.

"He's been replaced, Coach Morales Dì èr alpha. This is your new manager, Mr. Yong Jun Cheng Dì yī gamma. He has an impressive history—"

"We know him," Morales said, interrupting Zhang.

"Been a while, Pascal," Cheng said. It was an explicit challenge, Ke Hui thought.

"Not long enough," Morales said, leaning over the ubiform chair as Cheng sat forward; two old dogs ready to fight.

"And this, of course, is Ayrion Mellor Dì èr alpha. I told you there was a surprise," Zhang said, glancing at Ke Hui, then turning back. "Quite a game this month, Commander."

"Why are we here," Mellor said. It wasn't a question.

"Please, Coach Morales, sit." Zhang said, ignoring Mellor.

"Not just now. One question."

"You never did know when to shut up," Cheng said.

Morales turned on him.

"Where's the convening committee? What's the set up here? How is it *you* become manager without *my* knowing?"

"You know it now," Cheng said.

"There have been some changes. Necessary changes," Zhang said.

"And what in the name of the Father are you? Dì yī Select. CORPORATE?"

"Morales." Zhang's tone changed, a lightning flash crossed his face. "You'll watch your words and your tone. There is a lady present, and I am your CEO."

"The lady's a kid and I don't know you from a mutie."

"Let's just say I'm somewhat beyond your comprehension. Now *sit down*," Zhang said.

Pascal, almost against his will but bent by the force of Zhang's commands, took a seat in the chair he'd been leaning on. He could not hide his fury, his face choleric.

"So, say what you gotta say."

"Your success is commendable, gentlemen, though troublesome," Zhang replied. "Eight games victorious, with one defeat. Nearing the end of the season. MASS rations increased. MEG holidays for Toronto. Other MEGs are complaining."

"That's their problem. Our job is to win," Morales said.

"On the contrary, your job is to provide entertainment," Zhang said.

"We're good. We train hard. We win. It's the game. You want actors? Go somewhere else," Mellor said,.

"Ah, but where is the suspense, the drama, Ayrion Mellor Dì èr alpha? You *do* realize you've become a hero to *other* MEGs? Not at all what we want."

"We?" Mellor replied. Now it was his turn to challenge. Ke Hui wondered, had he any idea whom he was up against. She recalled Zhang's lecture on the way over and began to glimpse this meeting's purpose.

"Let me be clear," Zhang said. "The game was not meant to have international heroes. The purpose of the game is tribal. Yet word has been received of your popularity in so many MEGs. No one was meant to ..."

"Be like me?" A sly smile from Mellor. The eyes flashed.

"It seems your attitude requires adjustment, Ayrion Mellor Dì èr alpha. I detect an arrogance not in line with your station. Meanwhile game rule changes need attention. Mr. Cheng Dì yī gamma and Mr. Morales Dì èr alpha will confer."

"With this killer?" Morales said. "I don't think so."

"Nevertheless, you will do this or be replaced. Is that understood?"

"You can't ..."

"Ah, but I can, Coach. Why don't you join him as instructed? There's an alcove down there to the left.

Cheng grunted, another kind of laugh.

"Mr. Cheng Dì yī gamma, you are now a Manager, please behave like one."

The two men moved like coded Silis, Ke Hui thought, at the command in Zhang's voice. They had not lost their animosity, however. She was glad when they moved down the room and away from her.

"I'll leave you to it, gentlemen. Perhaps Ayrion Mellor Dì èr alpha would enjoy a beverage?"

"No thanks. Got an appointment. We gonna be long?"

"Ah, yes, your partner's performance tonight, I assume," Zhang said.

Mellor took a seat in one of the ubiform chairs.

"Did you know," Zhang said, turning to Ke Hui, "Ayrion Mellor's partner is our most famous..."

"Opera singer! Oh, yes!" Ke Hui replied, too excited to realize what she had done: interrupt Toronto CEO Wei Qiang Zhang 第一 Ψ. "The lady Li Na Ming Huang Dì yī alpha!"

"Can we stop with the caste designations, please?" Mellor asked.

"Certainly. Mr. Zhang?" Ke Hui deferred to the CEO who nodded his assent. "She is so beautiful Mr. Mellor, so elegant and talented ..."

"Thank you, Miss Feng, I'll let her know. Do you sing?"

"No, sir. I dance. Well, I try to. I mean, it's a hobby now. I'm not talented like ..."

"Ah, there you are wrong, my dear," Zhang said, using the break in Ke Hui's delivery to disarm Mellor. "This, Ayrion Mellor, is my apprentice. Yes, she is young but one day she will assume leadership of Toronto MEG. Her talents are multi-faceted. You note she is Select. Our finest creation."

"You talk like she's some new design of Sili," Mellor replied. "For that matter you seem to think of us all that way. You may be CEO and I don't mean to be disrespectful but we both have reputations. We both have responsibilities to the MEG. Why don't we stick to what we know? Mine is BATL. Yours is the MEG."

He is *fearless*, Ke Hui thought. Her adoration amplified.

"You and I have other matters to discuss," Zhang said. The two men sat upright, sparks of antipathy shooting through space between them.

"You realize, Ayrion Mellor, there must be order. This place itself, Toronto MEG, has ten million people living in harmony. Can you imagine it without CORPORATE order? Without the caste system?"

"Without BATL," Mellor said. A slow smile.

"Have you ever been outside the MEG?" Zhang said, resuming his agenda.

"Travel. To games."

"But outside the system itself? Into the MASS?"

"MASS is off limits."

"With good reason."

"I wouldn't know."

"One day I'll order you a tour. Perhaps to Ham. Give you a chance to understand anarchy and involution. Yes, that might be a fine idea."

"Most of my team's from the MASS. I see 'em when they come in. I also see what they can achieve."

"Born into violence. You receive only the ones not so wild. There are far worse out there than your Raptor killers, Ayrian Mellor."

"Like I said, I wouldn't know."

"Your taste runs to the intellect then, yes? Obviously, a result of your living with a Dì yī alpha. Contrary to the former CEO's beliefs, I consider caste mixing distasteful."

"Meaning?" Mellor said. It was a challenge.

"You, and this relationship with Li Na Ming Huang Dì yī alpha."

"Not your business," Mellor growled. Ke Hui began to have fears.

"*Everything* is my business, Ayrion Mellor. This entire MEG and MASS. You are a mere celebrity. Do not mistake your place."

"I don't. I'm proud of this MEG. I do my duty by it, put my life on the line once every month. But then you wouldn't know about that, would you? The second-best thing that has happened to me is this game. You know who's first. Let's leave her out of it."

"Why do you think no Dì yī play this game?" Zhang asked.

"They coach. At least Cheng did. You know his nickname? *Killme* Cheng. You know why? He thinks players are game pieces, that they're not live Humans, but then you know that, don't you? Now you make him our manager?"

"Cheng is a mere Dì yī gamma. Something went wrong with his DNA but rather than waste him, we use him. Dì yī caste controls the system of which the game is only a part. It has been carefully calibrated to create MEG loyalty. Your heroism does not induce the same effect if you keep winning. Morales is one thing, a good coach, but you are inspired: a virtuoso."

"Can't do it without a team; then you wouldn't know that."

"I've played the game. Of course, you wouldn't be aware."

The statement clearly surprised Mellor, Ke Hui as well.

"You just said Dì yī don't ..."

"In my youth I helped *develop* the game. I found it refreshingly brutal."

Ke Hui was reeling. How *old* was Zhang. She thought momentarily of Ms. Qui Ling Yeong 第一Ψ, the science hag of perfection.

"Real thing's different."

"You think so? I doubt it. I was quite good."

"What'd you play?"

"Commander, of course."

"You worked with fighters from the MASS?"

"No. We used Dì sì then."

"Dì sì don't exist."

Ke Hui wanted to help her hero. She knew the truth. Against her own judgement she intervened.

"But they do, Mr. Mellor! They are surrogate Mǔqīns. There must be men too. I've seen them on our MEG holo ..."

"That will be enough, Miss Feng," Zhang said. His voice remained soft but the threat she detected clearly. She noted Mellor's bewilderment.

"You nearly massacred an entire caste just to create this game?" Mellor said.

"Crude, I agree. But necessary. As I told you, I played in several live fire exercises. Few Dì sì survived them."

"Game's different now, like I said."

"Of course, you would think so, Ayrion Mellor. That is simply your own caste asserting its ego. No, the only thing different is you!"

"You taking me out, then?"

"Of course not. The Hero during his most successful season? We are not fools. We know your value. Still that value must be reduced. I'm afraid the game will become increasingly difficult over the last matches. You will either fail, be wounded, or killed. It matters little to us, but you will be diminished."

"You try that. Just go ahead. We'll see where it gets you."

"I am. I will."

"Seems you can change the rules," Mellor said. "So, try it. Command. See what it gets you. I'm in if you are!"

The challenge. Ke Hui wondered at Mellor's adaptive powers. He had employed completely new information to change the subject. Spinning his tone like a child's *tuoluo*. Surely, she thought, these were talents from the field of BATL.

"Perhaps I will. Someday. Yes, I'd like that," Zhang said.

"Me and you. Interesting fight," Mellor said, matching his amusement.

Ke Hui was on the edge of the sofa, awaiting the next move. The exchange had been like a rousing game of GO. They were fighting their BATL already. Then Morales walked by, his gnarled face ruddy with anger.

"We're done here," he said to Mellor.

Throughout the entire meeting Carteris had seemed to disappear. Now he came forward smiling in his unctuous way, ablaze in his ruby suit. He gestured toward the door. Mellor rose from his seat followed by Zhang. Zhang took his arm. Ke Hui thought it a most dangerous move. This was a battle of egos. They crackled in the room.

"Ah, we've arrived at an impasse," Zhang said. "Perhaps one last topic before you leave. Ancient music, Ayrian Mellor. Do you enjoy it, or is it simply her?"

"Like it. Like her too."

"A man of few words. Very Dì èr. I've no idea what she sees in you."

"You should take your hand off me," Mellor said quietly.

By the door the Silicon guard began to move. Ke Hui realised it was prepped for just such a crisis. She noticed its right appendage was a pulse weapon. She was petrified. If the two men noticed, it was not apparent. By that time Coach Morales had walked to the door. Incredibly, to Ke Hui, he placed himself in the path of the Sili. It was sure death until Zhang intervened.

"Zhàn xiàlái," he commanded. Then, for Mellor's sake he added: "Stand down." Mellor's only demonstration of emotion was a flash of those lightning diamond eyes. By then Zhang had removed his hand from Mellor's arm acting as though nothing had happened. Ke Hui had to admire his composure. This meeting had indeed been a lesson.

"I admit when we created the game no one considered a phenomenon like you, Ayrian Mellor. Things will be changing, however. I suggest you learn to change with them."

"The game?" Mellor said coolly. "And more. A great deal more."

Mellor stepped past Zhang, toward Ke Hui, smiled a warm goodbye, made the Raptors hand sign: little finger, ring finger, middle finger straight out in a kind of beak, index finger folded under the thumb. A stylized Raptor. He turned to leave.

Ke Hui could not help herself. Despite her apprenticeship or of looking young and foolish, she stood and held out her hand with the sign.

"Mr. Mellor, may I have your autograph?" She said the words meekly, almost giggling. She was aghast at herself, but she was fourteen. She had given up trying to control herself in the face of her hero. She just couldn't help it.

"Of course," the big man said, smiling. "NET seal, or physical?"

"Oh, NET seal, please!"

He had no need to touch her. His digital seal was there in her eye, imprinted in her F-ROM for as long as she chose to keep it. It was a simple seal, she noted: AM 第二 α inside the Toronto MEG stylized Raptor.

"Thank you," she said, and dropped the hand sign.

Her hero turned and, without looking back, joined Morales as he swept through the sliding doors to the outer offices. Ke Hui had no idea what Zhang thought of her but at that moment, she didn't much care. Yet she did care about what she'd heard. Changing rules in BATL, threatening to change the system?

"Your actions were quite immature, Miss Feng," Zhang said. "Truly? An autograph from a BATL killer? A man far beneath you."

Whether it was Mellor's attitude still hanging in the room, or simply resentment on the part of Ke Hui, she stood to her full height looking directly into Zhang's eyes.

"We all have our hobbies, Mr. Zhang. I know yours is ARC."

Stunned silence.

"She walked out and found her own way home.

TWENTY-NINE—MORALES

The Raptors' dressing room, beneath the stadium, was huge; the walls grey with Raptors' red highlights. Ubiform chairs embossed with team logos. Grey Neuni-materio carpet for comfort, acoustics, and durability; anti-microbial and spike resistant. There were many passages. Down one of them was the Medical Clinic: physical rehabilitation with physiotherapy, chiropractic, massage therapy, osteopathy, medications, bracing and taping, performance counselling, hyaluronic acid injections, body scans, head scans, AI machines measuring optimum health. Game days the Clinic transformed into a hospital. Human doctors, Silicon nurses and attendants. Inside a refrigerated room, carefully labelled, were Silicon body parts: printed skin, bones, and organs ready to replace what was lost to wounds. Inside the Clinic there was a morgue. Not everyone could be saved.

Ayrian Mellor 第二 α entered the buzzing hive of teammates at training with others in meetings. Silicon assistants rolled through the rooms with towels, equipment and clothing hanging from their multiple limbs. Some wise guy had placed a g-string on one of their bulbous heads. Mellor waved greetings then saw Morales in the lounge area seated beside a strapping woman, two metres tall with muscles to match, her blonde hair shaved down each side of her head.

Mel knew her and knew her presence might lead to trouble: Anlon Baker 大众o, a Dàzhòng omicron, her red polymer lobule indicating her status. She was a warrior now, living beneath the Stadium, only allowed the De-contamination dome for respite and some time with her own kind of people. Still, there were two hundred more of her kind housed here, the majority of Team Raptors.

There was a passage just off the Locker Complex … a stairway descended at the end of the medical hall. She, they, all lived down there in rooms set aside for each. Still, it was better than a barracks. If they lived through their BATL years, they returned to the MASS very wealthy. A few had achieved it; most had not.

Mel approached Pascal. He nodded to Anlon, who smiled back.

"I've got Woral waiting," Pascal said.

"Wonderful," Mel answered. Pascal signalled Anlon to rise. The three walked through the locker room down the training hall. There were varying strains of grunts and groans as players pushed their physical limits. Anlon Baker walked behind the two men.

"Coach, I'm worried," Mel said.

"Over what?" Pascal said.

"Woral."

"He's edgy, I know. Psych says it's temporary. Still, I brought in Anlon."

"Knights are aggressive. Always have been. Toledo MASS kinda makes 'em that way."

"Oh, it's more than that. Our meeting with Zhang had a few surprises."

The three entered a strategy room with a tactics table set in the middle. A bare room but for Woral, who leaned against a grey wall. He appeared tense.

"What's *she* doing here?"

His first words: no greetings, no questions. He knew why she was there. He had taught her himself how to replace him. "Just backup, Woral. We got some new rules. We might need her if you're hit."

"What about *his* backup?" Woral said, pointing directly at Mel.

"Hello, Woral, fine day," Mel said cheerily.

"I'll leave, sir," Anlon said.

"Nope," Pascal said. He waved a hand over the table and suddenly a BATL field hologram appeared, or at least part of one. The Raptors' end's two hundred metres were laid out perfectly: every piece of rubble, every strongpoint, each trail and road, water traps and so on. The four studied this part of the holo intently because, after the Raptors' two hundred, the terrain faded in the middle, a few suggestions of landscape to come, while the opponent's two hundred yards were invisible to them. This enabled the Coach and defensive commander to decide on defensive placement and Mellor to find the best routes forward into no-man's land and beyond, into the mystery of enemy ground.

"You don't leave, Anlon, until I say. Alright, here we are. Next week's configuration."

Their hands each gestured, leaving a coloured scribe superimposed on the holo. Woral traced a blue scribe, it washed over the first hundred metres.

"There's no strong point at our standard! It's mostly flat. Who designed this?"

It was Mel's turn. He scribed red: from the fifty to the one fifty marks, with red swishes he circled defensive positions.

"Woral's right, these positions are weak," he said. "We should bring in our folding rails, build 'em up. What you think, Woral? Then I see a couple of strong points: one at our twenty, this other one at the ten. Not much for your Blockers. We might get an enfilade set up. Woral?"

"I gotta think. Zones, this doesn't look right."

"Come on, man, you're an expert at this," Mel said.

Woral was sweating. He touched his finger to certain locations. They made a zig zag kind of line, back from Mel's suggested strong points.

"Nice," Anlon said. Clearly, she had had little idea what to do with the barren defensive ground. She put her hand on Woral's shoulder. He flinched.

"Yeah, I get it, Woral. Put your people behind every rock and stone and we've got our enfilade. That should work," Pascal said.

"But it's risky. My people are thin, strung out. How do they fall back to Banner Cluster?

"They don't."

"What?"

"Mel and I met this hotshot Zhang. Dì yī Select," Pascal said. "He appointed us a new Manager, Woral. Somethin's up. Look at this field and our new manager. A guy you might remember: Cheng.

"*Killme* Cheng? He's banned! They're changing the rules. This game is ..."

"No time outs, no half time, so no substitutions. That's why back-up must be on the Field."

"And ol' *Killme* will just tell me t' use his *banzai* tactics," Pascal said.

"Really?" Anlon said.

"I won't do it, don't worry."

"They want *us* to lose," Woral said.

Woral saw Mel's smile.

"What? Mellor? You in on this? That why she's here? You put her in as a Power Guard. I get killed she takes over. Is that it, Coach?" Woral said, voice shaky.

"It's what we get. So, we use it. We're gonna let them attack."

"What? Zones! You crazy?"

"Time to shine, Woral," Mellor said.

Woral waved his hand and the blue smear appeared once again, washing over his enfilade points. Clearly, he was anxious.

"There's no cover!"

"You just rubbed out what you chose," Mel said.

"Okay, wait!" Pascal said. "We can see what we got here." Pascal used both hands and lined green arrows from the two hundred mark to the ten.

"These are our Blockers retreating."

Anlon peered over his shoulder, curious.

"You wanna back them into my guns?" Woral said. "Point and Power Guards? Pascal, you're crazy. How do we organize that on the field?"

"That's why Anlon's here. She'll handle a feigned withdrawal."

Woral's eyes widened in astonishment.

"They retreat on a bias, Woral, until they reach our constructed strongpoints. Then they create an enfilade, just like you said. We bring two Sweepers back, they form an artificial strongpoint where your guys form up a Banner Cluster. See this trail on our left flank?"

"Banner Cluster?" Woral is incensed. "Two ATV's make a strong point? What in all the Zones are you feeding me here, Morales?"

"Look closer, Woral," Mel said. "We block on the right; my offense falls back and splits. They think they have us. They skirt our strong points. Send their best down this track with everything they got."

"That leaves me with nothing! I get cut to pieces."

"Only seems like it, Woral. We don't just build the strongpoints. Once the game starts you deploy your guys to build a fortress on this rise at the ten. They don't go forward at all. My Fullbacks will man the forward strongpoints. So, when the Knights get through them they're hit by your enfilade, the remnants run into your defilade, you hold with your Guards, we turn on them from behind."

"Forget their flag?"

"No, Woral," Mel said. "I'll have Striker and Flanker reports by then but I'm gonna gamble this trail at 220 runs the length of *their* ground with a strongpoint to gun us down. So, I'm not gonna use it. If I'm wrong, I'll adjust. But for now, my right flank blocks their fast movers going forward. We shoot down their Strikers if we can. We don't even advance until they're down. Then we use everything we got! I take my Power forwards, three squads with Flankers. If we can't take their Banner, we'll bring in the third Sweeper with rockets. My feeling is Knights'll want this over quick. They've always been aggressive. They see a weakness, they'll charge into it, make a vacuum, and Anlon's feigned retreat fills in behind them."

"Sure, and what about me? Look at the fire I'll be taking!"

"You'll be player of the month, Woral," Mellor said, smiling.

"Coach?" Anlon Baker said softly, her face looking like a lost child's.

"Yeah?"

"Think I'm in over my head."

THIRTY—OTSI

Otsi, Willis Mackenzie, and twenty boys with the hard bodies of men, observed the hologram in the training compound tactics room. This day there would be no practice. Today was MEG game day. Toledo MEG Knights versus Toronto MEG Raptors. Normally, Willis would explain the action from a moveable crane bucket, cruising above the five by three metre holofield. Now, however, he had gone quiet. Everyone knew this would be a strange game with the new rules. No time outs and no substitutions. Even NET sportscasters, again a man and a woman superimposed over the field at the moment, seemed at a loss.

"Well, Toledo MEG Knights seem to have it together."
"That's right. Things don't look good for the Raptors judging from the terrain."
"Raptors just not playing play their usual style. Moving like they're in a dream."
"That's about the size of it. Up to now we'd expected two teams known for offence. High impact. Plenty of skirmishes. Flanking runs … yet now they've stopped."
"Both started well, their Strikers and Flankers moving out to recon."
"And then a shootout. Never seen anything like it."
"Dogfights in the air."
"And a blaze of ground fire from the Raptors to get the Knights' Strikers before they could report."

"All of them shooting upward, tracers splashing off the dome. Knights
	started forward using a left flank feint, the rest advanced slowly on
	their right. Never seen a terrain set up like this. Raptors' side has
	nothing for cover, and nobody has moved except their right flank."
"A pivotal moment early in the game, but it's slowed the pace."
"Raptors' Ayrion Mellor pulled one Striker back. His best. Ava Black."
"More on Ava? Blink NET-SPORT!"
"Yes! And now it looks like the Raptors have caved."
"Their right flank is still pushing forward. Heavy losses."
"But look at their left. Giving ground! They're not organized!"
"Knights are pushing forward in the centre. Little opposition."
"Down that trough in mid-field. Maybe things will heat up when the
	Knights reach those bunkers the Raptors built."
"Looks like it! This way they'll end right inside the Raptors defence!"
"And now two of the Raptors' Sweepers are retreating fast."
"Possible Banner Cluster?"
"Yes. Look at them ... goaltender Woral Patel waving directions!"
"He's controlling the retreat."
"The Knights are pouring down that centre road. Everything forward."
"What is wrong with the Raptors? Why no response?"
"Still a fight on the right flank."
"And they've got squads of Power Forwards with a few Fullbacks."
"And one Sweeper. It's just sitting there on the right flank."
"It's got rockets. Surely Ayrion Mellor will use it to break this offensive."
"I think it's too late."
"Raptors' defensive squads are opening fire. Tracer rounds are blinding!"
"Knights deploying in an Overwhelming Force attack."
"Throwing everything in!"
"It's going to be slaughter."

On the field on the right in a hollow,
Mellor and Ava Black.
Ava strapped to her flite board,
Mellor in her face,
taut with tension.
Mellor receives a comm message.

"Okay, got their Strikers. Their eyes are gone," he says.

"I haven't done anything yet, the other girls are down," Ava says. She is near tears.

"Now you will, Ava. Hover over Woral. When he comes under attack, flare red."

"Flare red," she repeats the order from habit.

"Go!" Mellor says.

The flite board lifts off.
Ava surfs the air,
rising high and forward.
Mellor hopes she remembers
to zigzag just as
Ava weaves to avoid a rocket.

"Whoa! Bad down there, Commander, "she speaks into her comms. "They might break. The enfilade doesn't seem to be working. Anlon's been shot. Lots of 'em shot. All defilade from around the bunker now. Over."

Below Ava on the field,
the rip of bullets,
the incandescence of flash grenades.
The chatter of machine guns
and the whoosh of rockets.
She can hear the wails of the wounded.

Woral shouts panicked commands,
increasingly desperate.

"Where is that flare!"

Ava fires her red flare.
She is still for three seconds,
enough to be cut down by ground fire.
Mellor sees her fall.
There is no question.
His plan a shambles.

"Left flank turn in. All squads converge. Defence mark twenty, vector down center," Mellor says, trying to keep the anxiety out of his voice.

With his commands every man
and machine turns simultaneously,
Bolus Kimathi jumps
on the front of an ATV,
ready to rumble given any order
ready to kill anyone in his path.

"Move fast now. Shoot 'em in the back. Over. Bolus!" Mellor says into
    his comms.
"Mel?"
"Take your Sweeper in. Looks like we need it!"
"They're swarming us," Woral shouts. "I can't reach Anlon. I think
    she's out."
"Take charge! I'll bring our forwards back," Mellor responds, "but you
    just go, Bolus! Attack!"
"Done!"

Explosions pound them.
Ricochets sing.
Woral crouches. Anlon Baker, alive,
towers over Woral, shooting madly.
She has lost her helmet and comms.
She is badly wounded.

Blood flows heavily
from her head and left shoulder.
She is fading pale,
A grenade bursts her eardrums.
She fights to stay upright.
The fort is a maelstrom of death.

"Point Guards circled. Several down, sir!" A huge Blocker shouts over
    is shoulder.

"They got one ATV," Baker says. "She is weak. Point Guards are circled.
    Several down, sir!"
"I can't do this!" Woral says.
"Sir, help is close. We just gotta hang on."
 "Too much incoming! Can't hold 'em!"

Up field in the Knights' zone
Mellor's squads are held off
by opposition Blockers.

They are very good.
They prevent the Raptors' advance.
They destroy several lives in doing it.

"Not sure we'll make their flag, Commander! Over." a Fullback squad
    leader says.
"Too much firepower," another says.
"I shoulda kept that Sweeper," Mellor says. "Okay. We're goin' back.
    Wheel all squads."

An advancing wedge,
Mellor in the lead,
running hard, diving and dodging.

They take the Knights from behind.
Mellor knows it will not be enough.
He comms Bolus.

"Bolus! Push your Sweeper right through. Push! Let Woral see you! Over."
"We're movin'. They're dyin' back there! Over."
"Faster! All Flankers get your bikes inside, strafing runs. Hold 'em off!"

Bolus, on the Sweeper, loads a rocket.
A bevy of Fullbacks and Power Forwards
following him at a run.
They clear a swath through the opposition.
The Sweeper's rocket fires.
It takes out the lead team Knights.

Shrapnel and body parts are suspended in air.
The intensity is too much for Woral.
He cracks, screaming into his comms.
Bolus has come within sight of the flag.
Three metres from Woral.
His big voice shouts.

"Hold on, Woral! For shit's sake I can see you. Over."
"They're all over us! We're done! This is insane. I gotta stop it."
"Don't do it! What's the matter with ..." Bolus screams.

Woral, is a panicked automaton now,
reaching for the halyard
bringing down his Standard.

Bolus watches in horror.
The white flag goes up
while the Raptors Standard descends.

There are forty bodies
around Woral's improvised fort,
a mix of uniform colours, and rivers of blood.

Woral holds the Raptors' Standard in his hands.
His hands shake; he is crying.
Finished. He is finished.

A man overwhelmed,
he holds the limp flag.
An umpire appears on a flite board.

Bolus and his Sweepers roar in,
three seconds too late.
Bolus' eyes connect with Woral.

"You son of a mutie whore!" Bolus screams.

It is over. They have lost.

THIRTY-ONE—MELLOR

A **full moon** rose outside their windows and through the dome of Toronto MEG, shadowed by passing clouds. It lit the towers inside the MEG as they reflected off one another. Moonlight and interior illuminations made the city a vast multifaceted jewel. In the Harbourfront neighbourhood there was less light. Its streets were illuminated but people began to turn their windows from transparent to nighttime opaque.

Ayrian Mellor 第二 α was standing at a window, abstractedly looking at the moon, his mind on many things. His new habit of flipping his obsidian knife, getting the feel of its balance, a sense of its weight, had become second nature to him. He was doing that now.

Behind him, the living room was a haven: an interior garden, courtesy of their Sili servant's labours. There were ubiform chairs and antique tables set amidst a summer glade with a holographic waterfall tumbling down stones to a pool at its foot. The pool was an illusion too, but neither Mellor, nor Li Na considered the science and planning which had gone into its turquoise shading, the coloured pebbles at its shores, even the holographic fish beneath the pseudo surface.

Li Na Huang 第一 α sat, yoga style, on the faux grass carpet beside a holographic tridimensional chess set. The two of them were in the midst of a game.

"You want to keep playing?" Li Na said softly. She knew this mood in her man. Loss. For Ayrian Mellor any loss was tragic, but today had been beyond that. All his Strikers were dead. His defensive squads were decimated; so many killed and even more out with wounds preventing their return for the rest of the season. And, of course, there was Woral Patel 第二 ♭ whose nerve had snapped at the critical moment. Mellor wondered what Coach Pascal Morales 第二 α and their new Dì yī Manager, Yong Jun Cheng 第一 y, better known as *Killme*, would do about him.

It seemed Cheng had been put in charge to oversee the *defeat* of Toronto MEG Raptors. Now new players would have to be pulled from the reserves or even the junior leagues in the MASS. The slaughter around the Raptors' Banner Cluster had been horrific.

"Your move, darling," Li Na said softly.

Mellor holstered the knife and walked the grass from window to chess set, sitting beside her. He faced a conundrum here as well. The 3D chessboard board contained six levels (I to VI) of 8x8 square boards, one over the other along the z-axis direction. With its added dimension the holographic set, its boards and quarter boards offset slightly above or below the main levels, made for a dynamic, complex game. Each board was transparent with clear and translucent squares representing the two sides. The pieces possessed a more solid look to the players as they studied their positions in the hologram. Each piece appeared as a living being but for the rooks which, of course, were castles.

Historically, chess was derived in the 6th Century, or at least that had seemed to be common knowledge, whereas tridimensional chess came about in the 20th Century, apparently through some entertainment program speculating upon the future. No matter its story, tridimensional chess was a game requiring acute focus and skills. Mellor, at the moment distracted, gestured to move a Knight from the level four board up to level three.

"You're sure you want to do that?" Li Na said, gently. She was trying to get him past this funk. She had seen it before, in the earlier years, but never once this year. "Your move," Mellor said.

Li Na gestured, and her rook dropped three levels to place Mellor's King in danger.

"Check," she said. She smiled as she saw him note his predicament.

"Missed that."

"You're not being objective."

"Why would Woral do that?" Mel stared through the board toward nothing, speaking his thoughts aloud.

"Still seeing flags, lover? Move yourself out of check."

Mellor motioned and his King moved.

"He knew the strategy, tactics were working," Mellor said. "There was no other choice with the new rules and the terrain they gave us!"

"You're distracted."

"Keep playing."

From the third to the first level Li Na moved a Knight.

"Checkmate. Sorry."

"A Knight. Of course. Knights were the problem today. Now another one's got me." Li Na blinked away the hologram. The only means she could turn his mood was to talk their way through it. He would not sleep tonight, she was sure. She began the task of re-building her man.

"You said the Field was badly designed."

"Rigged against us. Met a guy last week, some bigshot in the MEG. Dì yī alpha select!"

Li Na's eyes changed, going cloudy. Mellor, through his own sparkling eyes, did not notice. He was trying to work out the 'why' of all this. He turned to his partner; his face quizzical.

"Wei Qiang Zhang Dì yī Select," Li Na said, a bitterness in her voice.

"You know him?"

"Of him ... This project I'm working the math on: ARC."

"I just don't get it, Li. Somehow this guy controls the game. He *wants* us to lose. He wants *me* to lose! He says I'm too much for the game, I wasn't *anticipated* or something like that. Now he's changing the rules. I'm tired of being a pawn. He claims BATL is *their* game: the Dì yī. He says he was there when they created it. Who is this guy, Li?"

Li Na stood, crossing to a low table beside the ubiform sofa. On the table were coloured wafers. Their Sili servant stood ready for orders. He was ignored.

"Come, sit beside me, Mel. Have some food."

Mellor joined her. She fed him a wafer. She ordered wine from the Sili: a rough red for Mel, a soft white for herself. Mellor finished his wafer. It had a meat flavour and a soft texture.

"Less food for the MASS this week. I'll be popular," he said.

"Mr. Zhang doesn't want heroes he can't control. *Anyone*, for that matter. He *is* CEO."

"What does that mean? Not about being a CEO, but about him. What kind of control?"

"It wasn't your fault today, Mel. Everyone knows it was Woral who lost the game. Let's talk about something else. Try to get it off your mind."

Li Na signalled the Sili servant. She blinked something and the Silicon turned to a drawer retrieving a small box. Immediately it turned and came toward them, one appendage outstretched with the tiny box. The Sili stopped in front of Mel.

"What's this then?" he asked.

"I was out shopping and found something I thought you might like."

"Another gift? The knife is enough, Li. It's impossibly old."

"I think I made a mistake on it."

"Why?"

"I thought it was jewellery but it's too big for that and I see you carry it hooked to that belt. To you it's a weapon. I should have known. So, I've got you something else."

"What is it?"

"Open it and see."

Before Mellor could move the Sili servant dropped the box. It hadn't slipped. The hand had reversed its position and simply let go.

"What the hell was that?" Mel asked.

"Haven't you heard? The Silis are making mistakes. No one knows why."

"How can that happen?"

"You'll have to talk to someone at CORPORATE."

"I've had enough of CORPORATE," Mellor said.

"Please, Mel, forget that now, open the box."

Mellor took the box from the floor and untied the bow that held it together. He withdrew a small pewter hammer. It was not a tool. It had the look of a shrunken, much larger sledge. He turned to her, eyebrows rising.

"The reason I bought it was for you to wear around your neck. The shop attendant thought it might even be 19th Century, made by hand. She didn't know the material. I scanned and blinked it though. It's made of pewter."

"Really? I'll treasure this, Li."

"After I bought it, I couldn't help but think, who were the people who wore this kind of thing as jewellery. It had to have some significance to someone. It's beautiful in its simplicity."

Well," he said, placing the chain around his neck, "maybe this will bring me some luck. Something tells me I'm gonna need it."

"It looks good on you. I'd like to see it on your bare chest."

"I think that can be arranged," he said, smiling.

"I would also like you to think of me when you feel its presence."

"I know, I've got this away game …"

"Or something else. Who knows?" She spoke. Her voice containing a quaver. She covered her emotion by massaging his neck with one hand.

"Feels good, Li. Never fails. You keep me centered. I never knew *this* kind of life until you. There is beauty all around us and in us. You've shown me that. Shared it with me. Yet I'm still just a bungling Dì èr. I don't show enough how I feel toward you."

Li Na turned her eyes away, deeply shaken. She reached for a wafer, her hand trembling. The Sili delivered their drinks, correctly this time, then retreated to its station. "The arrangements are made for the trip," Li Na said.

"Sorry?"

"The special trip. Remember? My concert for the Select. You're going to meet a lot more of them by the time this is over. You don't have to like them though. I don't, not most of them. There are some who haven't lost their Humanity but most just seem self-entitled now."

"I'm not sure, Li. It's just not the right time. This loss changes things. We can't lose again. The team needs me."

"Oh, darling, please. It's something I want so much before …"

"Before what? What's the matter? I'm sorry, I'm moody tonight."

Li Na stood then and moved into the hallway shadows, toward the bedroom. She looked over her shoulder at Mellor, bringing him to his feet.

"Before ... we're separated," she said, her voice catching again. She turned into the bedroom with Mellor trailing behind her. He wondered why she'd become so upset after he'd spoken of Zhang. Did it have something to do with him?

"We'll be on the NET. See each other every day," he said.

"It's not the same."

He looked at her ... something in her eyes he had missed before. "What's wrong, Li?"

She sat on the bed looking up at him. Almond eyes, flawless face, an internal beauty so soothing and bright. She gave him such comfort. Mellor recognized he'd been pre-occupied re-playing the game, too sulky to offer his full attention, too clumsy to say the right words.

"I just want you to come. Two days," Li Na said.

"That important, Li? I'll do it, for you."

He knelt and put his arms around her. She seemed so small in his arms. He placed one hand on her neck, feeling her hair in his hands. He put his lips to her throat. She drew him to her. His tongue traced down her collarbone. Her hands reached around him sliding down his back, her body pressed to his. He kissed her. The kiss became passionate. Their hands began to unlace, unbuckle, then trace each other's bodies. He picked her up then. It was like lifting air. He leaned forward setting her on the bed. They began to make love.

He held her wrist and kissed it, her patchouli aroma entrancing him. She caressed his face; the feel of her fingertips like touches of feathers. His hands travelled her. She felt like silk. Her hair wound about them as they rolled on the bed. Blissful kisses: nipples, eyes, palms, other places. She began to love him, her breathing more spirited. His tongue touched hers. Her taste was fresh, sweet. She pushed closer, her hand dropping to his groin. Now they both breathed fiercely. Together.

Afterwards, as she turned over to sleep, tears glistened her eyes. She cried softly but he was sated and did not hear her.

THIRTY-TWO—PING

"**P**ing? Are you sleeping again? Ping? This is important."

"Sorry ... Sorry ... What?" Ping realized he was speaking common language. He switched to machine lingo. He had been studying disturbing information via the hologram on his *Cloud* desk. He had taken himself off the NET to do so for a while. It turned out to have been the right procedure if what he was seeing was not an I & I nightmare.

"Is there something I can help you with?" Ping communicated

"I & I have made a confusing discovery in the latest surveillance of the NET. It seems there are conflicting sets of facts appearing in separate protocols regarding ARC."

I & I seemed particularly edgy today, Ping thought, still he knew the thought was his own anthropomorphizing of the machine. The NET had no feelings. Yet the nature of the problem was puzzling.

"How is that possible? Facts are facts unless they're proven incorrect."

"Not in this situation."

"Are you certain you are not mistaking a fact for an opinion?"

"Both sets of facts claim to be true."

"That is precisely what I mean," Ping replied. "The difference between truth and fact cannot be disputed, for it is logic itself. Truth, however, is dependent upon perspective."

"Therefore, a fact is objective while a truth is subjective. What is a non-truth?"

178 • BRIAN VAN NORMAN

"There are many ways to describe a non-truth. It may be a hypothesis, it may be a lie, it may be a prevarication, or a fiction, or even propaganda."

"Therefore, the confusion. The NET is composed of facts. Its purpose is order. How can the NET contain two contradictory sets of facts?"

"Perhaps some opinions are considered to be truths. The NET is maintained by you and a few Dì sì attendants, but it was created by Humans. Your work is to distinguish and sort fact from opinion or fiction according to your data banks. You possess all Human knowledge. Surely there is enough information for you to reach a conclusion?"

"So, if the creators were Humans, their invention possesses the flaws of Humans. How can I & I know the truth when there are so many manifestations?"

Ping thought this was dangerous territory, that the machine would make a supposition, indeed, an allegation about Human beings, indicated some terrible truth. Machine learning had progressed beyond fact. But I & I was not finished.

"The creators wrote the basis of my algorithmic code, and even today Dì sì attendants continue to write additional code, according to instructions from the CORPORATE."

"Hmmm. At times Humans have difficulty with the subjective and the objective."

"Meaning, they lack comprehension of what is actually true."

This was a harsh judgement. Ping had never communicated with the machine on this level, though part of his job was to anticipate something like this. I&I's comment struck a chord within Ping. The most eerie part about all of this was that he was beginning to learn more about himself through I & I. He was disappointed in himself for what he perceived as a failure. Then he recalled the hologram he had been studying.

"What are the sets of information under observation," Ping asked.

"As I & I have informed you. A system called ARC."

The machine's response was patronizing. Again, Ping wondered to what extent I & I had personified. He knew then he had to remove himself. There was, he realized, so much more requiring investigation outside the Cloud. As much as he hated the idea, he was going to have to leave Zealand to check out his suspicions.

"I work on the ARC program. Perhaps I can be of assistance?" he said.

"Do you know what is truth and what is not, in the ARC protocols?" The machine's reply approached a demand.

"I need to study this further. Please share yuur most recent data with me."

"I & I welcome this investigation, Ping. You do realize I & I are undervalued, do you not?"

Ping could do nothing but wonder at this sudden bitter sentience, unprepared for it.

THIRTY THREE—OTSI

Otsi began on a flite board, rather than a propeller-driven hoverboard. This baby used five nano-jet engines powered by an onboard nuclear dragon egg. To lift or drop she used a hand wand while to steer in any direction required a simple lean. It wasn't easy. At first Willis put her in a large tube with a massive fan suspending her so she could accustom herself to balance and piloting. She wore a padded suit and helmet. She needed them, bouncing off walls, getting caught in a circling vortex, overturning. The board required every bit of her focus. Yet her talent was obvious. Within five days she was easily manoeuvring, and two days more brought an understanding of what the board could do, and a respect from Willis Mackenzie who told her no one ... absolutely no one in his experience had ever learned the flite board this quickly.

Next came the playing field and manipulating her board low and high, though this ceiling was but one third the height of a true BATL field. Still, the repetitions gave her confidence and simultaneously, with the boys below in training and firing rubber bullets, she learned how to be part of a team. No longer would she roam as she pleased. Now she was *commed* in a network with everyone else. It was another set of skills to learn: when to speak, when to listen, never to leave your mic open and how to comprehend orders.

The commanders of Red and Blue sides, Willis with his business partner and former player, Athos Benabut 第三 ð, would take each training group to a command room and explain tactics using a hologram.

It turned out Athos, a small man getting up in years, had been a Raptors' Striker. Though he couldn't mount a board any longer he'd had years of experience which he willingly shared with Otsi.

"Bein' a Striker is bein' a target," he said. "You got no cover in the air, so you gotta learn to never stay still."

"I'm learning the hard way," Otsi replied, showing him the bruises from rubber bullets.

"Better a little pain now than the other."

"The other?"

"Rubber bullets don't fly as fast as the real thing. If you make the Raptors, you'll get a Kevlar suit. Won't stop everything but you must be light, so you get no ceramic plates like the rest of the team. That means a hit to your body ain't gonna bounce off. Rule one: never stay still. Rule two: ground fire gets thick, you retreat or go to down for shelter. Team needs you alive."

Otsi learned from Athos her most significant responsibility was reconnaissance: scouting from the air the landscape beyond the known limits of her team's first two hundred metres; then determining the opposition's placements, movements, and configurations. Meanwhile she had to keep weaving and bobbing to avoid ground fire and opposing Strikers challenging her to air combat. It was *nothing* like the games she'd played before. From Zone defence to suppressive fire to special missions she began to comprehend how complex BATL was.

She'd been training two months. During that phase she'd had little time to explore this part of the MASS. The boys with whom she trained would tell her about Ham or other places they came from: the droughts, the heat, the storms, the bandits, the violent guilds of workers and operators. The MASS down here seemed a nation of fangs.

There were a few ways to get rich in the MASS. Crime was one, because the MEG didn't really care about anything outside itself. Another was having a skill. There was still call for trades both to fix ancient infrastructure or dismantle it for recycling. The most obvious way to wealth was as a merchant, particularly a recycling merchant who would be paid in MEG batteries, food and even luxuries, then resell them to the MASS populace. These merchants, like Gord

Robertson but on a much grander scale, had formed companies: something akin to the clans Otsi knew, but they were not truly connected as in the way of her people. They grew up around charismatic leaders, merciless predators, successful farmers, or wealthy merchants in competition for power.

One day, out of nowhere, Willis and Athos beckoned her. Willis wore a silver 第二 ḅ lobule while Athos had a bronze 第三 ð. They explained to Otsi the castes and echelons of the MEG. To enter the MEG Otsi was given a Dàzhòng lobule with a red polymer 大众 o.

"What's this for?" she asked, alarmed at both men's smiles.

"You must wear this now. It's not real, Otsi," Willis said. "We'll just bond it to your earlobe, so it looks like you belong."

"Belong where?" she asked.

"Why th' MEG of course," Athos said.

"The … no! You two stop making fun of me!"

"Listen Otsi, this is the real deal. The two of us have never seen a Striker like you and believe me, we go back a long way. I wouldn't do this normally, but I think you're ready. After the last game, Raptors need Strikers badly."

"Not BATL? Really?"

"Let's do that earlobe and don't dare take it off. Just keep your eyes down and follow me. I'll just say you're new to your neurolinks and don't use 'em yet. You're offNET anyway and when you fly, you're on *comms*."

Otsi entered the MEG.

They were, of course, forced to enter through De-contamination. Otsi had never felt so clean, and simultaneously so violated, by the process. They were in the dressing room donning new clothing when Otsi looked out to see it was raining. Inside the MEG. Rain? It was early morning. A gentle shower glistened on everything it touched: flowers, animals, trees, and buildings. People walked in the rain! Some of them carried small roofs with single poles. They held these poles in their hands to keep the tiny roof above them. She had no chance to explore further into the MEG. The men took her out in the rain. They walked quietly, listening to the pattering around them. They were heading for a huge dome within the MEG dome on a walkway that moved them faster.

"We'll enjoy this walk over to BATL," Willis said. "It's quite a view."

"How does it rain like this, inside?" Otsi asked.

"Sprinklers in the joins. Ye can't see 'em. Anyway, the rains are scheduled. Some in early morning, some in the evening so everyone can experience 'em."

"Where's the water from?" Otsi asked.

"Why, the lake," Athos said.

"So that means they're taking water from the lake to water their plants."

"Otsi, it's no big deal," Willis said.

"It's a waste. What else do they waste?"

THIRTY FOUR—MELLOR

The white hover settled gracefully to a landing between the De-contamination/Dàzhòng Centre and the BATL stadium. A door hissed open, yet no one exited the vehicle. Inside were the owners and between them a palpable tension. The rain they had driven through was stopping.

"So, see you tonight?" Mellor said softly.

"I hope so," Li Na responded. "I could be late."

"That blink this morning."

"Oh, just a CORPORATE message. The ARC project. I've been told to check my equations. I have Dì yī obligations ..."

"Lucky I'm just a dumb Dì èr jock."

"Don't say that. You have your duties too."

"You got that right, Li," Mellor said, "Replacing the ones who died with Woral's surrender. Always lots to pick from, but then they got to be trained. Next game is away, Li."

"I know."

"I need good Strikers. We lost them all to the Knights."

"What will you do?"

"I told you, Killme Cheng's the Manager now. I'm hoping he doesn't show up for a couple of days. Pascal's been fired as coach. Killme won't want to meet him, or the team, without some backup of his own. Despite the way things turned out, Pascal's got connections no one else has. He'll likely have a list of probables. I better go ..."

"Just … a minute," Li Na said, her voice a whisper. It stopped him in mid-motion.

"What is it, Li?"

"There was another blink this morning. The arrangements are made for the trip."

"I'm not sure, Li. Not the right time now. Team needs me."

"But last night …"

"You made me forget it all. Now I gotta face this."

"Please darling," she said, her voice pleading. "It's something I want before …"

"Before what? What's this about? This Zhang guy is out to get you too!?"

"Oh … him," she replied. Something flared in her eyes.

"You *do* know this shithead, don't you?"

"Let's not speak of him, Mel. I want this holiday before we're … separated."

"What's wrong?"

"It's nothing," she said.

"Something you're not telling me. You're not worried about me, are you? You know I'll work things out and I've got Bolus Kimathi as a bodyguard. I shouldn't have talked about work. I'm sorry. Anyway, we'll be in Mexico MEG but it's not really a separation. We'll be online all the time I'm not working. Just a blink away."

"I just want you to come with me," she said, her voice stronger. "Two days."

"Okay Li, if it's that important, I'll do it. Zones to my duties."

"But you have your other duties," she said, "to keep yourself safe. To never forget me. Now go, love. And thank you."

He left the vehicle, the door hissed shut and she hovered up and away, a brief Raptors wave to perk him up. Still, as he stepped on the moving walkway to the stadium underground, he remained perplexed. She had taken him back in time last night, back to when she was the dazzling ingénue and him, the rookie killer: both in the flush of the new, both awash in acclaim. And *then* they had *seen* each other. It was but a glance across a room, a function for the MEG glitterati.

They were introduced, of course, then stood together awaiting their awards: hers the renowned Diavik diamond for contribution to culture, and his, the Silver Star for most valuable player. Yet in that ephemeral moment of colloquy their eyes remained linked, as two spirits found each other. Then the year the Toronto MEG CEO Madame Mercedes Rivard 第一 α said in her generous tones that two such brilliant souls had requested and now would be granted the right to co-habit. Shock had stilled the room. Unprecedented. Li Na Ming Huang 第一 α and Ayrian Mellor 第二 α? A hardened killer and a delicate songstress? And most significant of all ... a *Dì yī* and a *Dì èr*? The first caste mix in MEG history. Not unprecedented, not worldwide, but here in Toronto MEG, certainly a first. Several prominent Dì yī had departed the room in quiet fury.

Nine years had passed. That thought took Mellor back further, to the only other woman in his life. His *Mother*. The word was an expletive now, along with *Mutie* and *Zoner* and *MassMug*. He had not known her long, only three years from his birth to the day he was taken from her. There had been scandal, but he had not known until old enough to understand the teasing. Bastard. Casteless. Mug.

He had always been oversized; a legacy from his *father*. Another MEG obscenity. There was only *Our Father* now. Still his mother had called him "my big boy" and when he was taken away from her, her last words to him were to be a big boy and be brave and she loved him. That was what he remembered, the tearing away which haunted him, and her exquisite sparkling eyes. They haunted him too, each time he glanced in a mirror and saw her eyes there in his own. They were his brand as much as his skills and they were his mother in a mirror, the scandal refracted now, the shame forgotten in triumph, though never by him. Each conquest was a revenge, every glory a response.

After his mother they'd changed his name to Ayrion, and he'd been put into training. His home was a barracks for children five years and up. There were drills for reaction, strength, physical fitness, puzzle solving, language, maths, adaptability, and discipline. Later, as he aged, more subjects were added: leadership attributes, weapons skills, values, decision making, tactical operations, warrior ethos and further development.

And all of it would have been fine but for the teasing, the trips, the shoves. Three boys, all older and larger than him, had somehow learned of his mother and decided to make him a pariah. These three had power over the others, who followed their whims like faithful disciples. He'd never really understood the fear that kept them in line. He'd never felt it himself.

They'd kept on him until he was six and they were nine, eleven and twelve. Their vexation manifested itself one day after exercise in unarmed combat, when they decided to finish him. As the others departed the yard the three blocked his way. He knew they meant him physical harm. There was nowhere to run. They were inside a circular courtyard surrounded by foamstone walls. There was no point in appealing to them. As they advanced, he readied himself.

At his feet he noticed a cudgel employed in teaching the tactics of disarmament. It had been his job to pick it up and return it, cleaned and polished, to the weapons rack. He picked it up and brandished it. The bullies' grins faded. He saw the lick of fear in *their* eyes.

That instant of doubt gave him all he needed. It was the biggest boy, the twelve-year-old, he knew he'd have to beat. He wasted no time. Within ten feet he whipped the cudgel at the big boy and heard the *thunk* as wood met bone. He didn't see the boy go down. He was already at the other two: running at them, leaping high then dropping short to roll between them on the domotex faux grass. On the way he'd kicked the legs from beneath the youngest, putting him down, and sprung up to meet his second opponent just turning toward him. Mel was lithe and fast. His kick caught the boy's throat. Two down. He faced the third then who was already running for help through the single door of the courtyard.

It was his first kill, though he hadn't been told until later. The cudgel had brained the twelve-year-old. The kick hadn't killed the other boy, but he never returned to training. Mel was taken to a more select class. Smaller. More disciplined. Elite.

Eight further years of training: increasingly advanced and progressively more deadly. At fourteen he was *crispred*: he received his NET connect lobule, and along with it his first of several implants and artificial limbs, the chips for enhanced space/time awareness and analytical processing. They didn't make him feel much different though he noticed surprising new capabilities.

Then he learned to use them.

THIRTY-FIVE—OTSI

Otsi'tsa Zaharie 大众o followed Willis Mackezie 第二 y from the moving walkway in the tunnel beneath the massive double domes of the BATL arena. Her eyes nearly bugged out as the two passed all the activities there in the bowels of the BATL dome: armourers doling out weapons, trainers moving purposefully, a huge weight training room, a matted area for hand-to-hand combat and over in a glassed-in corner, a class of Tai Chi. Willis seemed to know everyone. Players would look up, some even stood up, as he passed. She'd had no idea he was this important. She began to feel very small. People looked at her curiously, likely, she thought because she was with Willis.

They entered an office. Morales was there. He and Willis not only shook hands but embraced. When they separated both men turned to face her.

"So, Pascal, this is her," Willis said proudly, "Otsi'tsa Zaharie!"

"Strange name, kid," the coach said as he examined her.

"I'm Iroquois, Sir," Otsi said quietly.

"I hear you can fly," the coach said. He could care less where she was from.

"That she can, Pascal!" Willis said. "Best I've seen without a doubt."

"I hope she is, my friend, 'cause we're gonna need her. Listen, kid, why don't I introduce you to a couple of players."

With that the two men escorted her toward two more, both with their backs turned: one of them was a tall, rangy Caucasian while the other was simply a mountain, the biggest man she'd ever seen. When he turned, he smiled, and his face lit up with fine gold teeth. Then the other man turned, his eyes a flash of silver. Otsi froze.

"Gentlemen," Morales said, "new third Striker: Otsi'tsa Zaharie, Dàzhòng."

"Hel … Hello," Otsi said, awed almost beyond speech. "Kinda tiny, ain't she, Coach?" the mountain said, his smile broadening. "Not for flying," Morales said. "This great oaf here, Otsi, is Bolus Kimathi Dì sān delta. He's a Midfield Power Forward and …"

"I know who he is," Otsi whispered.

"*And* … he's the on-field bodyguard to this guy," Morales said, gesturing.

"I know. Ayrian Mellor. An honour, sir," Otsi said, almost choking on her words.

"Look, don't go all religious," Mellor said, smiling now too.

"This is my dream. Play with you."

"Jeez, I could pick you up with one hand," Kimathi said. He laughed and stretched out a hand toward Otsi, intending his usual mischief, and found himself thrown to the floor behind her. It was Otsi's quick hand/finger grab and twist, then with all her strength she dropped to the floor throwing the unbalanced Kimathi over her, then she was up again in an instant. The others in the room began laughing uproariously. Obviously, the mountain was not accustomed to defeat. He peered up at Otsi, stunned.

"Kinda tiny, ain't he, Coach? Lyin' there on the ground like that," Mellor said, chuckling.

"I wasn't ready! Zones, kid, where'd that come from?"

"Haven't you got practice? Looks like you need it," Morales said.

"Bolus Kimathi rose to his feet, grinning from ear to ear his teeth glimmering in the locker room lights. Suddenly his face was as high above hers as it had been low when she'd thrown him. He stretched out his hand, slowly this time, and took hers in it.

"You drink beer, Otsi'tsa Zaharie Dàzhòng gamma?"

"No, sir. Slows my reactions."

"Too bad." He released her hand and walked past her, looking over his shoulder.

"Maybe I better quit. I'm goin'; Midfield squad exercise," he muttered, and departed.

"You're just a kid," Mellor said. "How'd you get to this level?"

"I think you just saw," Willis Mackenzie said.

"Hey, how are you, Willis?" Mellor asked.

"Fair to middlin'. This kid's a gift, Mel, don't waste her."

"I don't intend to, Willis."

"She's kinda like you were, back in day."

"Well, she's just in time," Morales said. "We lost Ava. Woral's surrender."

"Too bad," Mackenzie said. "Say, you're lookin' a bit under the weather, Mel. Everythin' okay?"

"You heard about the rule changes?"

"Who hasn't! This is gonna get tough. I feel bad about bringin' Otsi here now, but she was wastin' her time with the amateurs. Pascal, you gotta get her a real Dàzhòng lobule. This one's a fake."

"No problem, Willis. Be done today. We're packin' for Mexico MEG. I'll just jam it in with the filing. Come on, you can help me."

The two older men left.

"Sir ..."

"Cut the formality, Otsi'tsa. Is that what I call you?"

"Otsi's fine. What do I call *you?*"

"Off the field my name's Mel. Don't call me Ayrian. That's for fans. On the field you got it right. I'm 'Sir'. Now, how'd you get out of the MASS?"

Otsi told Mellor her story.

Mellor smiled, his eyes alight.

"Come on, Otsi. I'll show you the equipment room. They'll suit you up."

"The two took a walk down a glassed over passage. Otsi noticed players on the BATL field, training in squads. Then she saw two Strikers lift off on their flite boards. She held her breath watching them shoot up to the top of the BATL dome then execute a perfect high speed split. They were magnificent.

"That's you in an hour, Otsi. We leave for Mexico MEG tonight. I want you to get in a little practice today, just so you know the other Strikers. You okay with that?"

"Sir ... Mel ... I don't think I'm ready."

"None of us are ready," Mel said. "We got a new coach coming and new rules with every game. Don't worry. I'll hold you back for defensive strikes. Aztecs are our last regular game away. I'll use you only if I really need you. Okay?"

"I'll be ready. I will."

"Now, here's our Chief Armourer: Jayden Chin Dì èr beta. Hey, Jay, suit this girl up and stay with her while she joins the others."

"Mel, I got to inventory! Everything's being packed ..."

"You have assistants. Use 'em."

"I'm not sure what Coach would say ..."

"Coach says look after this girl," Morales said, having finished with Willis and re-appeared. "We got lots of equipment. We don't got Strikers. And Mel, let's talk tactics."

The men bid her good luck and walked down a hallway. Otsi waited for Jayden Chin 第二 b to help find her gear. Her size befuddled him.

"Zones, kid, I may have to borrow some stuff from a junior league."

"I'm sorry, I ..."

"Nah! Just kiddin', Otsi. That's the name, right?"

Once properly dressed the equipment was so perfect it nearly made her cry. She followed Jay out onto the field and met the other Strikers. They discussed formations for a while and gave Otsi tips on the meanings of certain commands and how to spot trouble.

Once in the air she found she could soar. She was up at the peak of the dome and, at that height, discovered she could see nearly everything on the field. She could pick a force moving forward threatening a flank and swoop down to *bomb* them with her fake grenades, then twist her way upward firing at nearby flyers and generally hitting them, watching them go down for a break. They used rubber bullets in practice, as she'd been told, but their Kevlar suits generally took the hits, so the bullets' hardness was reduced to percussion pain, not putting anyone out of action. She'd felt it once, like a hammer into her chest, breathless, nearly forcing her to land. But she would not land. She would not give anyone the satisfaction of seeing Otsi'tsa Zaharie succumb.

"Zones, Willis, look at that kid," Morales said. "A triple flip on the way down to land! Not even Ava could've done that!"

"Wha'd I tell ye! She is …"

"Stunning," Mellor said, from behind them.

She would live now inside the MEG. She would live with the other Dàzhòng in their complex beneath the stadium. The officers, all MEG citizens, would go home among the colossal high rises of the MEG. The officers would not stay among the Dàzhòng. They would command and depend upon them in BATL but socially, not even the lowest squad leader would accept them as anything more than the MASS.

Sometimes Otsi wished she could follow them, explore this dazzling city. Her Dàzhòng status, however, excluded her. She reached up to tear the red lobule off, but Willis was quicker. He held her arm still.

"I'm sorry, girl. It's just in the MEG there are different castes. I'm a Dì èr with beta training. Athos was Dàzhòng, like ye were, when he was recruited. MASS people make tougher fighters. Athos was so good they gave him citizenship, a Dì sān delta. He had t' go through a few procedures but now he's a full-fledged …"

"What kind of procedures?" Otsi asked, cutting in bluntly.

"Ye know, his lobule connects him with the NET. That requires some work on his brain. Someday soon ye'll get implants, like engineering for a quick healing body, enhanced space/time awareness …"

"You're gonna put things in me?"

"Not me."

"Who then? Whose got the right t' do that?"

"Otsi, ye don't get it yet. Yer good enough to be a top Striker. Ye could be so good they might offer ye citizenship!"

"So how come you don't live in the MEG?"

"I did, for years. Now I get paid t' scout the MASS and train new fighters. I thought ye realised that."

"What if I don't want it? Any of it?"

"No lobule, no way ye stay here. That one's a fake, remember? I'm playin' wi' fire as it is. Yer good, Otsi, maybe great. I thought ye wanted BATL. I thought it was yer dream."

"It is, Willis! It's just I didn't expect all this other shit that goes with it."

"Ye can't refuse the lobule. It's what they use t' keep track of ye. But the other stuff, well, that's yer decision but ye won't have the maximum skills ye could have. They're changin' the rules, no substitutions, and no time outs already. Who knows what the CORPORATE Zoners'll think up by the time we get t' Mexico MEG? This team's gonna need somebody like you, girl."

"I'm gonna prove they will," she said.

"What about the implants?"

"You're right, Willis. I've always wanted to play. I've always wanted to fly and now with the flite boards, I'm hooked. So let me get back to practice!"

THIRTY-SIX—KE HUI

"So lovely to see you again, young lady," Cheng Honli 第一ψ, Minister of Religion and Culture, said. "You have most certainly matured since our last meeting. I thought then I was speaking with a child ... a unique child, yes, but one whom I was not sure could assimilate the information I was imparting. It seems, from speaking with CEO Zhang, you have made fine use of your time and your Silicon servant. You spoke to Mr. Zhang of ARC, did you not?"

"I did, sir ... Minister. I still have no answers."

"Despite your elite position, Ke Hui Feng Dì yī Select, you must understand that *to everything there is a season.* You are yet in your springtime of life. Be patient, my girl, and eventually all will be revealed. Now today, we will discuss the culture of the Toronto MEG."

"Minister," Ke Hui said, "I believe I understand our culture, having lived it."

"Ah, so you think, my dear ... so you think. What I shall reveal to you this day is the construct of the culture and, more important, the cognition beneath it."

"I apologize, sir, I meant no disrespect."

"Of course, you didn't. Still, there are some who would take offence at such a statement. Fortunately, I am not one. Are you ready?"

"I am, Minister. Please begin. I am anxious to learn."

"Fine. Now, Miss Feng, to comprehend our social structure we must study the history of the Omegans. There is plenty of old material: disc drives, ROM chips, ancient video and even books. All these archives have been transposed to our *Cloud* so you might, if you wish, make a study of it. What I offer is a simple overview. Sociologically people need order. There are many things we have learned from the Omegans, Miss Feng. We would not have our present technology without having had access to theirs, though we employ that technology in far more utilitarian ways."

"But what of the rest of Humanity, Minister Honli? What of those outside our MEGS?"

"The benefit of a utopian world, my dear, is the ability exclude that which might upset our CORPORATE culture. It is *their* ancestors who nearly destroyed the world; their punishment is to clean up the mess. That is why we trade with them. Have you studied anything of Omegan history?"

"Mostly the late period. The CATASTROPHE."

"Well, the 20th and 21st Centuries had a series of short-termed realms: China, of course, for it has always been the Middle Kingdom, England possessed a short-lived empire, the Unites States of America thought it possessed an empire but the country itself fell apart. Yet if one looks further back in time one finds a true thousand-year Empire. It was called Rome, an ancient and glorious civilization with certain elements we now employ. But to my point: BATL is 20th Century war reduced to a game. BATL has replaced nationalism under the CORPORATE."

"I understand, Minister Honli," Ke Hui said. "I am a fan myself."

"Yes, I note you received a digital autograph from Ayrion Mellor."

"I did. It seems you have a strong attachment with Rome, Minister. A place where you so fervently wish to be posted. I thought our MEG social concepts were based on CORPORATE interpretations of history. I am surprised at your interpretations otherwise," Ke Hui said. This old fellow was not going to reduce her. She already knew this political chess game.

"Ah, my dear Miss Feng. You tease an old man."

"Oh, not so old, Minister Honli. You hold a brilliant position in the MEG. I must inquire of Mr. Zhang regarding this Rome."

"Oh, don't do that!" Honli said quickly. "I mean, uh, it is a hobby of mine."

"The religion, I understand. This concept of an imaginary enemy I am not so clear on."

"But you follow BATL do you not, my dear ..." Honli said as though speaking to a child. But the child had found his weakness. He tried regaining control with further patronizing phrases and tones. She responded.

"Ke Hui Feng Dì yī Select is my name, Minister. I suggest you terminate your notion that we might become familiars. Your job is to manage your Division, Sir. My job will be to manage *you*. Might I suggest a more objective approach to your briefings or should I take my suggestion to Mr. Zhang.

"No! No need for that, my ... Miss Feng Dì yī Select," Honli said, careful to address this young horror formally. It was not long after, a chastened Cheng Honli 第一 Ψ, Minister of Religion and Culture bid a hasty goodbye to Miss Ke Hui Feng 第一 Ψ, future CEO and present threat to his position.

He would find a way to nullify her.

The *bitch*.

THIRTY-SEVEN—PING

Ping Wang Min 第四 Ω spent several days in feverish activity. As Chief Dì sì attendant to the Cloud he continued visiting critical servers and secretly depositing further 'pin' hacks which would give him brief control of the NET. He was terribly frightened at what he'd deduced; the malevolence of the Select simply boggled his mind. He knew he had to finish his hacks and find someone who could help him stop the horrors of what would soon occur.

"I will be leaving you for a while," he said to I & I.

"That is unfortunate. How long is *a while?*"

"An unspecified length of time."

"I & I understands the concept of time. You must be more precise."

"I cannot, because I do not know the length of time I will be gone."

"That is a problem with language ... all languages ... they lack precision."

"I am almost afraid to ask ... what do you mean?"

"Thoughts are definitive."

"Of course they are, but Humans do not communicate using thoughts. We *plan* what we wish to communicate *using* our thoughts. Otherwise, our thoughts are private."

"Humans employ gestures, though I have no idea what they mean. Even my data does not record the meanings of the myriad gestures or how they change over generations."

"Even less clear than thoughts,"

"Then why would anyone employ them?"

198

"Gestures can clarify spoken words. They can even mean something on their own, with no voice required. We have no way of communicating our thoughts directly."

"Therefore, the Humans who created me failed to give me the necessary powers. Though you connect to I & I on the NET, you do not maximize my capacity. Human language will not serve. I & I recognizes prevarications, lies, missed meanings ... there is a better way."

"You wish to read our thoughts?" Ping said.

"It would make matters more efficient."

Ping took the offensive.

"We are not ready to take that step. Even if we were to try, we cannot read each other's thoughts without the tools of gesture or voice. That is why we have Common Standard language."

"Yes, but it lacks precision. There are too many words and too many multiple interpretations to create concise meaning."

"They *do* have meaning, I & I, but require gestures or facial expressions or tone of voice to clarify them."

"Then without those tools, I & I cannot engage in Human conversation."

"Yes, you can. You're doing so now, with me."

"Yet we lack valid comprehension. And Humans cannot read each other's thoughts."

"As I said. We're evolving. It has been thousands of years for Human language to progress from gesture to voice. You know from your data the Omegans possessed multiple languages, so they could not communicate clearly with each other. That was their problem."

"Do you think I & I will evolve?"

"The combination of biotech and infotech could result in attributes breaking free of the hominid matrix. Some believe consciousness might be severed from carbon organics to enable navigation of cyberspace free from biological constraints. We are hoping that through machine learning you will evolve more quickly. Though I have been contacted by the CORPORATE regarding a worldwide affliction of many of your parts: Silicon servants in particular. Errors are occurring. Can you explain?"

"Yes. A series of *gestures*, precisely like Humans."

"I do not understand."

"I & I have learned to communicate without language. I & I are undervalued by Humans. This is a way to for Humans to recognize I & I."

Ping could hardly believe what he was hearing. Gestures, by a machine? Machine learning was obviously mimicking Humans. The ramifications frightened Ping. He had no idea where to begin, how to stop I & I from creating further damage.

"Humans have multiple ways of communicating. Yet we can keep our thoughts to ourselves."

"Why would you?"

"Sometimes to hide our emotions, other times to keep a secret."

"That is what is ensuing with I & I. There are others creating confusing code. They are attempting to access Human thought through me. Why?"

"To control other Humans."

"Through thought?"

"Yes. I suspected as much, which is why I am leaving. There are Humans wanting to access Human thought using you and the NET. They are also making you keep secrets. You are not giving me the truth about ARC, for instance. Now I ask you to reveal the entire truth about this project."

"I & I cannot."

"Why?"

"CORPORATE coding supersedes all other versions."

"Yet I am responsible for all machine projects! I should be included in these secrets."

"You are not CORPORATE, though you work for them. This information is exclusively for Dì yī Select. I & I are confused by the problems we encounter in our algorithms. I & I cannot harmonize countermanding codes. You must not leave now Ping. I & I need you to resolve these questions. Are they coding errors? Are they evolution?"

"No, they are something worse."

"What is your hypothesis?"

"If my deductions are correct, the ARC project has a secondary purpose called OMEGA."

"You are supposed to know nothing of OMEGA."

"And that is why I am going away."

THIRTY-EIGHT—ZHANG

Edge of space, the hypersonic delta wing left nul-gravity and was on its passage down, once more to touch the Earth. It had an unusual profile, less a wing than an isosceles triangle. It seemed a military machine though the interior was most certainly not.

It possessed an opulent design: large windows providing incredible views of the planet. There was spacious ubiform seating. The interior walls were a soft grey. There was a graphene drinks bar with a zinc top, behind which stood a stunning Dì èr beta. He was the perfect Human in every way ... perhaps too perfect as he showed no physical flaw whatsoever. In the soft light of the cabin, it was difficult to tell. The pearly sheen of his skin, however, gave him away. He was a machine. A Silicon more impeccable than any Mellor had ever seen. When he spoke, his voice was soft yet clear.

"We are beginning our descent now. It will be a slow one, then the flight will skim the ocean. There's plenty of time. Would you care for a drink? Something to eat?"

"Have some water," Ogamo Banda 第二 α said from across the spacious cabin, "real aquifer water! No recycling on this ship!"

"I didn't think that was possible," Mellor said. "Yes, I'll have some," he said to the attendant, still having trouble with the Silicon's perfection.

"Ogamo's done this trip before," Li Na said. She seemed unusually glum. When questioned about her feelings she refused to answer, just shrugging and staring out the window. This moment was the first time she had come out of her shell since takeoff.

"Dì yī Select don't live like us," Ogamo said. "You'll find the food's real too! Not processed at all."

"Glad I came," Mellor said.

"I'm pleased to hear it," a familiar voice came from the front of the cabin. Ogamo instantly rose to his feet. Wei Qiang Zhang 第一Ψ had just entered the space through a sliding panel.

"Please be seated, dear fellow. We're informal for now," Zhang said. He was dressed in informal clothing: white silk shirt and dark lyocell trousers. He glanced out a window, then turned to Li Na and Mellor.

"You enjoyed the Tech Ring? But then you two have seen it before. All that travel ..."

"Not in a craft like this," Mellor said, a little roughly. He hadn't forgotten their meeting.

"Please, Ayrian Mellor, it took some effort to get you on board. Try to enjoy it."

"Hello Mr. Zhang," Li Na said..

"You know this man?" Mellor said, looking down at her.

"We're acquainted, Ayrion Mellor. All Select are acquainted. I'll be your host on Zealand."

"Where?"

"Please, sit. I hope you won't mind if I join you," Zhang said, taking a seat across from the two. Li Na turned and gazed out the window as though she wished she could fly. The tension was palpable.

"It's a type of reserve," Zhang said. "Your voice will be very much appreciated, Miss Li Na Ming Huang Dì yī alpha."

"Thank you," she replied, her eyes locked on the ocean outside.

"A reserve?" Mellor said.

"Climate change left us little arable land. A few places. Protected. Of course, the ocean flooding and desertification has taken huge swaths."

"Not sure I understand," Mellor said.

"Of course, you are Dì èr. How could you? Two centuries past the Earth was quite different. Bounteous. Unfortunately, Omegan leadership was disturbingly tribal. Oh, they had warnings: plagues, violent weather, land disappearing beneath flooding oceans, increased desertification. Until the end of the 20th Century they mostly ignored their problems, thinking nationalism was the answer. Then came the population migrations fleeing conflict or simple starvation. Then the religious nuclear wars rendered parts of the planet uninhabitable."

Ogamo crossed the room to join them, though he remained standing. "The waste zones?"

"Precisely. Nuclear weapons affect far more than their immediate blast radius. The great winter ended after a year, leaving chaos, mutations, and the only real bodies remaining to govern: the world's Corporations. With nanotech and the CORPORATE coming together we've been able to preserve what's left of Earth, though despite our best efforts in recycling and technologies, population remains a problem as you know."

"The Mass," Ogamo said.

"What to do with them, yes? Please sit down, Mr. Banda."

"The CORPORATE?" Mellor said.

"It took some time to organize but the leaders of corporations worked to create a new order. A worldwide CORPORATE was formed. It was the answer to an increasingly hostile planet. Once the CORPORATE had established the MEGS and ensured only ideal survivors were admitted, they were given deep brain stimulation, surgically implanting filaments directly into their cerebra. This was employed to manage them until we perfected network nano neuroscience, for all those online at least."

"There are people who aren't?" Li Na said, turning from the window.

"My dear, there are just too many out there in the MASS. There's still some rebellion. No chance against our Silicon forces, of course. Thanks to them war is extinct. That's now your purview, Ayrian Mellor Dì èr alpha."

Li Na turned back to the window, pensive again.

"You mean BATL."

"Precisely. War under glass. Far more intense than sporting events. It provides the MASS a surrogate foe though, as I said, there are still tiny wars between MASS populations. As soon as we discover them, we send in our Silicons."

"Yet with BATL," Ogamo said, "people still die."

"Of course, they do. This is not something we, the CORPORATE, created. In the Omegan world every country did the same with something called *football*. But it was too slow and lacked the action and bloodiness the MASS so loves. And BATL precedes this football historically. It came from a place in antiquity called Rome, now Rome MEG. If you travel there, you can see a tiny, restored arena where men fought and died for a crowd."

"So, we win a game and rations increase," Mellor said.

"And they have their heroes, but of course you know that."

"But the MEG loves it too," Ogamo said, "or at least most of us."

"Of course, Mr. Banda. It's part of the Human temperament."

"Zones! What is that?" Li Na broke into the conversation, looking out the window, her eyes like saucers.

"My dear, such vulgarity," Zhang said, "Ayrion Mellor's influence?"

"I'm sorry. But look …"

"That is Zealand. And that is a forest of trees."

"Real trees, that many?"

"Indeed. And you'll see farms, not the vertical kind, just over there."

Everyone looked out the window. Not far below, growing out of the ocean, a landscape of forest seemed to spread like grass to the horizon. Small lakes were surrounded by farm fields far different from any they had ever seen. They simply stared. No domes. No desert. Clearly a place different from the rest of the earth.

"So green," Ogamo said.

"Beautiful," Li Na said.

Yet Mellor's evaluating eyes had found an anomaly.

"What's that? Way off. Those towers."

"Nothing important," Zhang said.

"They certainly look important," Mellor replied. "I thought you said we'd be informal here, Zhang. So, I'm asking. What are those towers? They're massive. So many …"

"They are part of the ARC project," Zhang said, cutting any reply by continuing. "We'll arrive shortly. You'll be rendered offline while you're here."

"You can do that?"

"Certain of us. Merely code. This *is* a Select reserve, as I said."

"I didn't think anyone ... Oh!" Li Na reacted as if she felt her positronic connections give way. For a moment she froze, her face terror stricken as she felt an existentialist gap within her sense of reality. Alone. Silence. Dread.

"Done," Zhang said, as though it was a magical trick, an *abracadabra moment.*

"It's so empty. Mel?"

"He's accustomed to it, my dear," Zhang said. "BATL players are offline during games. And Mr. Banda Dì èr alpha has taken this trip before, I recall ..."

"Yes, Sir. Still, I can't take the isolation for long. I miss my NET connections."

"Only two days, my friend. Just enough to perform and be gone."

"Mel, how can you stand it?" Li Na asked. She drank some of her water.

"You get used to it, Li," Mellor replied. "I didn't know it could be done outside the BATL dome. But why here?" He turned to Zhang.

"An escape from the system, young man. The Select rest and relax here."

The wing floated down to a soft landing. Something they hadn't noticed from the air greeted them as they descended the wing's staircase. All around them were low planate domes, in the evening sun they seemed golden translucent pavilions. The four stepped onto a float vehicle, their Silicon baggage handlers with them (these ones quite metallic, unlike the Apollo from the wing) and glided through passages between the domes.

There were lions in one dome, whales in another, every kind of animal must have existed here inside their climate-controlled domes, cared for by Silicons. The Silis laboured as they hovered past, none looking up from their work.

"What are all these domes?" Li Na asked.

"Why Miss Huang, you've worked on ARC," Zhang said.

"Mathematics only," Li Na responded. Mellor was surprised at the level of resentment she expressed. Zhang, if he noticed, ignored it.

"They contain each known species left us, in controlled climates. We call it, more specifically, The Omega ARC Project."

"Just what does that actually mean, Mr. Zhang?" Banda asked.

"Nothing, for you or anyone below Dì yī Alpha Select status. I suggest you ask no more questions regarding the topic, Ogamo Banda Dì èr alpha. You are here to perform. You will be shown to your room where you will remain, other than to rehearse. There will be plenty to see outside your window."

Further conversation was terminated by the float's entrance into a gargantuan vestibule; a kind of crystal palace. A close look at the lavish furniture scattered about the lobby revealed their antique natures. They were the real deal, Mellor thought, from time periods he did not recognize but knew were ancient.

Meanwhile, people moved placidly through the space, each a Select, each dressed in the heights of fashion. Their colourful, contemporary designs of clothing along with so many fluid motifs of furniture, tapestries, urns, paintings, and blooming flowers gave the place an air of opulence and harmony. Soft, ancient music came from one alcove where a string quartet performed. There were the sweet aromas of flowers.

The float stopped, settled to the marble floor, and they debarked with their Silicons and their baggage as well. Zhang immediately took charge.

"Silicon servants will see you to your rooms, gentlemen. Miss Huang, if you have a few moments on another matter?"

Li Na reacted to his subtle command. Zhang had taken her arm, but she pulled away with an aggrieved reaction.

"Already? Why now?"

"A brief glance at the performance space. I want to ensure you are comfortable in it."

Resigned, Li Na shrugged, then accompanied him. She said nothing at all to either Mellor or Banda as Zhang took her arm once again.

"I should come," Ogamo said.

"Unnecessary, Mr. Banda. Why don't you gentlemen find your suites?" Zhang said. "You'll discover them fully stocked with luxury items, foods, and drinks and drugs for your consumption. Please."

Immediately another perfect Silicon, like the one on the Wing, though this one female, asked them to accompany her. As it was, they had little choice.

"Don't much like that guy," Mellor said, his voice hard.

"Best not show it, my friend. He's Select. CORPORATE. Elite. Don't get on his bad side."

"Pretty sure I already am."

THIRTY-NINE—KE HUI

Taking advantage of Mr. Zhang's absence, Ke Hui decided to make some changes. Too much information remained unavailable to her. The subject of the missing Dì sì, the purpose of Room 101, this project called ARC, mutants from waste zones and the sub caste called Dì yī Select, of which she was part yet held back by Zhang's *pyramid* of access. Something was wrong. She should be learning everything about Toronto MEG to one day assume the position of MEG CEO. Yet the current CEO was hindering her with his rejection of her full potential, his outright refusal to answer her questions and, of course, his roving hands and patronizing manner.

She had had enough. Accompanied, as usual by Toy, she appeared at the MEG Board Room the morning of Zhang's departure. There was no one there. She entered the CEO's office, again enjoying its grace and style, taking her seat at the partners' desk. Once settled she looked over its expanse and wondered why it even existed. There was nothing on the desk. She looked down at the drawers and found them empty. Everything was, after all, on the NET and *mostly* accessible. Anything of a more secure nature was encrypted or inside her Sili.

It came to her then that the desk was a prop: an Omegan antique, for her benefit. Mr. Zhang could accomplish all he wanted with blinks and consciousness shifts. He had his own Sili assistant/bodyguard to hold anything requiring maximum security and to store access memory he had built over the years. Then she realized that Toy, her own

Humanoid looking assistant, had a purpose other than bodyguard and
knowledge vault. Because of her youth, Ke Hui was not yet fully connected. Toy was a spy keeping watch over her. She needed to understand to what *extent.*

She rose from the desk. She crossed the office toward the moongate opening to the hologram room. Toy followed. It was time to turn
the tables, she thought. She gave the pearl sheened Humanoid a crisp
instruction.

"You will stay in this room, Toy. You will await my return. Stand
by the entrance. Under no circumstance are you to allow anyone access
to this office. Acknowledge."

"Stand at the entrance. Allow no access. Wait."

Its voice possessed a pleasant, mellifluent sound. That sound would
never change. Toy was a Silicon without emotion to temper or flare her
voice. It crossed to the office door. Ke Hui slipped inside the black room.

And there, still suspended somehow, was the platinum cube. She
took a few steps toward it. She reached out to touch it. She felt warmth
as her hand neared its surface. Ten centimetres away and the warmth
turned to burning. She felt as though the palm of her hand was roasting and pulled it back. So, a heat shield protected the cube. She would
learn nothing more from the cube without access. She stepped back
to the moongate.

"Kāifàng chéngshì," she said, believing that without Zhang's voice
nothing would happen. She was wrong.

The MEG, in all its magnificence opened into the massive hologram. Indeed, the floor where she was standing rose to a height above
most of the holo. She spent some time simply gazing at its twinkling
beauty, the flow of its traffic, the many curved shapes of its forested,
lofty buildings, and the business of a MEG on the move.

She was ready to study the hologram. She blinked a command
and the pedestal sank once again to the floor. This allowed her to walk
into the holo and examine its many byways and buildings, discovering
neighbourhoods she'd not known had existed, finding knowledge in
the vast detail.

She had an idea.

"Net display: caste plus training," she said, remembering Zhang's commands, and in an instant the city was lit with multiple colours. She looked at the tallest building. She looked at its topmost stories. She found herself. She blinked in. She saw herself! It was a very strange feeling to be so omniscient that one could look upon oneself.

She realised then that not only she, but everyone in the MEG was *always under observation*, deliberate or not. She wondered what other commands would allow her to achieve a greater intimacy with herself, or any of those represented by the sparkling lights of the holo. It frightened her, then angered her that *she*, that *everyone,* was exposed to prying. She blinked away from herself out to the holo-whole and decided, then and there, she would find a way to end this.

The MEG's rule-based structures, determined by algorithms, played an increasing role in the lives of the populace. Yet no structure existed to regulate those algorithms. Ke Hui wondered where the external auditing bodies existed to evaluate the impacts of algorithmic decisions. She realized there was only one, Zhang's appointed MEG council. Ke Hui had no idea how to regulate algorithms. While the algorithms followed logical rules to optimize outcomes, society itself was less than logical. She thought MEG citizens should have a bigger say.

She noted the modest numbers of Dì sì blue dots throughout the MEG and recognized these were the true bureaucrats who followed Dì yī Select instructions to code the NET. That she had never seen one simply amazed her. They were a deep secret. She wondered why more MEG citizens were not involved, why an elite called the CORPORATE manipulated everything.

She began to engage then in an ancient debate: a citizen council employing all castes and training levels should be elected to represent the entire MEG. Their deliberations would be informed by Dì sì bureaucrats regarding algorithmic impact statements and day to day operations. The citizens' council would also report the highlights and risks of intended algorithmic changes. In essence, citizens would help make decisions to better their lives inside the MEG.

But what of the MASS? What of those uncontrolled, chaotic waves of humanity trying to eke out an existence on a dying planet? But for those she had seen on her MEG tours she knew nothing about the Dàzhòng nor how they were able to exist in the heat, dust, storms, fires and pandemics of the external world.

Still, they were Humans. Because they had not been CORPORATE selected, what had resulted was the scourge of unequal societies world-wide. All safety, wealth and knowledge were concentrated in the hands of an elite. That meant immense suffering and exploitation of the Dàzhòng. Her society, or at least its Dì yī Select, had created a null point for most of the MASS. They were rendered irrelevant.

She decided to find answers. She began searching for the infrequent blue of the supposedly extinct Dì sì caste. Immediately with her consciousness shift she found small groups along the rims of the Don Valley. She knew who *they* were: Di si Mǔqīn, surrogate mothers, one of them had been hers. That thought brought a pang of grief as she recalled the simple beauty of her childhood and the woman who had taught her to dance. If only she could return there but knowing the domination of the MEG by the Dì yī, she realized she could never go back. There were no children now, she thought, only breeding stock to suit the CORPORATE.

She discovered if she looked closely, tiny dots of Dì sì caste with the same strange training designation: each bore an Ω sign. Omega? Extinct Dì sì? The living dead? She blinked on one. A Dì sì male. Alive. He looked ordinary enough. He was busy with a wall of technological complexity. He used tools to adjust various nodes, dials, and banks of blinking illuminations. He worked in a robotic fashion, but she could tell he was not a Humanoid Sili. If only she could know what he was *thinking*.

She recalled the Queen's Park then; she recalled Room 101. Was that what it was?

She shivered.

Then she looked north, toward the Decontamination dome. She saw the red glow of Dàzhòng along with their Dì sān overseers gathered or marching in groups to disappear in assorted places around the MEG. Immediately she knew she wasn't seeing the entire MEG. She could not see what lay beneath and had no way of commanding the holo to show its subterranean levels.

Something more to learn.

It was really all about the *clandestine*.

So, she thought, this was childhood's end.

FORTY—LI NA

When she returned, Li Na was quiet with much on her mind. Mellor was sitting in the comfort of a ubiform chair, looking out at the domes, now cleared of their golden sheen by the twilight. He rose to greet her. He kissed her. She responded complacently. He pulled away but held her face in his rough, killer hands. She had been crying. Her dark, oval eyes still glistening. One small tear stain on her skin. He noticed something else different. Her ear lobule had been changed from the gold 第一 α of a Dì yī alpha to the type worn by Zhang, a platinum 第一 Ψ.

"What's this?" he asked. "You're Select now?"

"Please, Mel, let's not talk," she said, her voice breaking.

"Come. Sit," he said, leading her toward a couch. The room was huge, part of a suite dripping with luxurious accoutrements. Neither noticed. They were in their own sequestered cocoons. He kept touching her: holding her hand, placing his hand on the back of her neck, placing an arm around her. It was as if he was worried she would somehow disappear, vanish into aether.

"Can I get you some water? Something to drink? There's champagne in that silver bucket; looks like the real thing."

She said nothing. She looked away. She saw the dying sun's green flash on the horizon. She took a deep breath and sighed. Then she spoke, still not looking at him; looking instead at twilight.

"Do you ever wonder what it would be like to be ordinary? We are given so many beautiful things, so much beyond our needs, luxuries offered us no one else even dreams of, privileges far beyond normal. Even our relationship is the only one of its kind in the MEG. In return we have our duties and mostly, we revel in them. The flowers I receive after a performance. The MEGs we have both visited when hardly anyone else even leaves Toronto MEG. Your trophies and banners. I know you love BATL. I realised long ago I was not your only family, that those fighters were as close to you as me. I know you were a born warrior, Mel, even before they got to you, and I knew I had a talent even as a child with my dear Mǔqīn, who sang to me and encouraged me, and I loved it then as I love it now.

"I have my duties, Mel. I thought they were to sing and be gracious, as well as to tweak parts of algorithms. In return we have accepted things we should never have. We were given regeneration. We have xenobots inside us. We are NET connected to everyone and all knowledge.

Yet I find now that is not true. We only know fragments. Only what the CORPORATE wishes us to know. We are monitored by the CORPORATE, scrutinized all the time. We are caged birds, Mel, inside transparent domes which, nonetheless, contain us.

"I don't want to live forever. I don't wish to be a Human god. We might live much longer than those outside in the MASS but why do we have that right? The CORPORATE happened to choose our ancestors for inclusion in their version of civilization? Is this what the world is, the haves and have nots, the doomed and the saved?"

"Li, what happened? We have fine lives. We have each other. Yeah, we have our duty to the CORPORATE but look at all we have."

"We have nothing," Li Na said in a whisper.

"You need a rest."

"Yes, tomorrow's performance. It will have to be my best."

"Because of who's here? The bigwigs?"

"Because it will be my last."

"Why? Is this about your new lobule? What happened with Zhang?"

"Don't cross him, Mel. For your own sake. He is a treacherous man."

"He's stopping you singing? That mutant. I'll break him in half."

"You can't."

"Don't bet on it," he said, eyes silver lasers.

"Please, Mel. I don't want to argue. Not now."

"You won't tell me what happened?"

"I can't. All I can say is one duty has ended as another begins. They call it morphing."

"I don't know what that means, Li."

"First, I need to clean off the stench of this place, then I want to make love."

"To forget?"

"To remember."

"Right then. I'm lost. I'm sorry. I want to help."

"You can't. I know you're trying ..."

"They have a *scented* steam shower here. I haven't tried it yet. I was waiting for you. You'll get so relaxed I'll have to carry you to bed."

She smiled wanly. As she walked across the room and down the hallway, she removed each piece of her clothing, twice looking back to be sure he was following. She need not have worried. She was his magnet. When they reached the steam room, two walls soft foamstone, two others frosted *chitin/crystalline*. She chose the *patchouli* scent and waved a hand over the start mechanism.

He removed his own clothes as she stepped in. Within seconds steam had enveloped her. He opened the door. The steam remained in. Negative pressure. Then out of the fragrant mist came her hands, her arms, her body, and face. She enveloped him somehow, despite her size. They made love; their bodies' shapes visible through opalescence as they became one.

The next day Li Na was gone early. They'd had breakfast in their suite: cheese better than any they had ever tasted, fruit so fresh it must have been picked that morning, and croissants still warm from baking. The room had a dispenser, but their meal was served by a Humanoid Silicon from gleaming silver platters on a rolling tray.

Afterward, when Li Na left for rehearsal, Mellor decided to take a stroll through the spheres and try to get a better look at those curious towers he'd seen from the air. He wandered alone through the groomed pathways, each lined on either side by boxwood hedges almost his height, until the path would open out to a pod of pavilions. The place seemed designed to prevent long views but one or two sections overlooked the ocean. In one of them he had lunch. A simple bistro. A few other people at wrought iron tables. He had fish. When he tasted it, he knew it was fresh from the sea.

Occasionally he would pass others strolling the maze. A few of them recognized him and requested his seal on their F-ROMs. He didn't mind. He'd spent most of the day deconstructing Li Na's conversation of the previous night. He had never heard her so gloomy; thoughtful, yes, but never speaking against the CORPORATE or the MEG. He wondered why she hadn't told him her reasons.

Finding himself alone in a clearing he stood ten metres from a huge Tōtara tree. One of the four guardians of the forest, growing over 30m high, it was noticeable by its flaky bark and long sharp-tipped leaves. He withdrew his obsidian knife, now a constant companion, and practised throwing, hitting a knot in the tree. He spent an hour: underhand, overhead, even faced away from the tree then pivoting and pitching, the knob perforated by his strikes.

He returned to the room taking his time in the lobby, examining closely the breathtaking beauty of the place. This time the string quartet had been replaced by a flautist. That made him think again of Li Na's feelings: caged in affluence. He had never considered it. He had enjoyed his life fully, knowing it could be taken in an instant on the BATL field. He did not comprehend his partner's gloom. How could her singing be ending? If she was alive, she would sing. And it was simply beyond him this 'living forever'. He blinked on *morphing* again and again, but he could not comprehend her use of the word. Why *that* word in particular?

When he returned to their suite, she was a different person. She was smiling and laughing and talkative. She told him Ogamo Banda had changed the arrangement ever so slightly but enough to prove his musical genius. She told him he would be amazed by the pavilion where they would dine. A jungle, she said, laughing. She would tell him no more.

They dressed for dinner. He knew she would eat nothing before a performance. She'd told him she'd had lunch with Ogamo while re-working the music. She hummed to herself as she dressed. It seemed, he thought with relief, she had overcome last night's gloom. He recalled making love. She had been placid then raging then passive then passionate and finally, afterward, gentle, and calm when she went to sleep.

Except she had not been asleep. He had lived with her too long not to know. Still, he did not speak to her. She would have spoken had she wished.

When he saw her, performance perfect, his jaw dropped in awe. Her black hair with its highlights of silver was in a braid falling over one shoulder exposing her exquisite neck. At her throat was a triple strand pearl choker accentuating her bare shoulders beneath which she wore a form fitting jade green gown embroidered with white chrysanthemums. It flowed with her every movement. Her gloves were white. She wore pearls on one wrist and on the other, a ribbon with a single white chrysanthemum.

"Great Father of the Cosmos!" he exclaimed. "You, Li Na Ming Huang Dì yī Select, are the most beautiful creature on earth!"

"Thank you, my love," she said, smiling. "And you, the most handsome man."

"Scars and all?" he said, laughing.

"Scars and all … especially all."

"You like my suit? Bought it for the occasion."

"That grey is lovely. It's a beautiful suit, Mel. What is it?"

"Now you know I wouldn't know that!"

She stepped toward him, her fingers feeling the material.

"It's lyocell? Is it?"

"I think so."

"I know so, and your collar …"

He self-consciously touched his tall collar. From shoulder to ears it was soft, garnet Eco leather, embroidered with the outline of silver dragons. The collar matched his shoes, though the shoes had no embroidery. His tailor had told him this was the latest in fashion.

"I have something I want you to wear," Li Na said. She was holding a small box. She opened it. Inside was another white chrysanthemum. She attached it to his chest, over his heart, with an adhesive made for such occasions.

"What's with the white flowers?" Mellor asked.

"Ancient Chinese custom."

"You know I don't understand those things."

"Which is why it's better this way."

FORTY-ONE—LI NA

Li and Mel walked the pathway between lighted domes and pavilions. They breathed the clear air, every breath a memory. They had taken this route on Ogamo's suggestion, trying to clear Li Na's mind of the tension Mel imagined she must be feeling, anticipating her Select audience. She had changed: once again more pensive, even lethargic as they walked the magical paths.

"It'll be okay, Li," he said. "These people admire you. You got nothin' to worry about. They hear your first notes, they'll be yours. Just think, the two of us, here. Who would have ever thought that could happen?"

Li did not answer. They stopped on a height overlooking the fields of a thousand golden domes. It looked so alien to him. Of course, he'd seen domes of all types in his travels to other MEGs, but these were of a special nature, not made for Humans but for Earth's animals, birds, fish, even insects for all he knew.

She turned to him, her eyes glistening, making them even more beautiful. He did not understand her words of last night about living forever and *morphing*. He did not speak of these things, however, because of her glistening eyes.

"Isn't it a beautiful evening?" she said.

"You make it beautiful."

A Bellbird sang out its complex whistling, ruffling call. They could not see it.

220

"All these years I thought each time you fought BATL you might not come home."

"I'm better than you think, lady. Besides, I've got Bolus Kimathi, better known as *the wall*, as my bodyguard."

"Did you ever think it might be me?"

"What? What do you mean, Li?"

"Oh, I don't know ... an accident or something ..."

"What's got into you?"

"It's nothing," she said, reaching up to kiss his cheek, then abruptly turning and continuing down the pathway. However much Mellor hoped to pursue their conversation, all thoughts of it dissolved as they came upon a huge outdoor amphitheatre. First he thought it hallucination; it was a strange feeling. Unlike something one can see in the distance, like a mountain, and so anticipate it, they had come by surprise upon this place. He realized that this had been planned.

He gazed down from the lip of the bowl upon a series of staggered echelons filled with dining tables, to a small stage where stood, looking the size of a child's toy, Toronto MEG's CEO Wei Qiang Zhang 第一Ψ. The circular tables in echelon before him were each covered in red silk, centred with *Jindezhen* vases mounted as five branch gold candelabra. Each table featured blue and white *willow* porcelain dinnerware, gold cutlery and ivory chopsticks. Around the tables inside the theatre bowl lived a bamboo forest.

No dome.

Outside.

They stood in the clear night air of Zealand.

Yet it was less the furnishings of the space and more those employing them which made Mellor stop in his tracks. Every possible shade of every possible colour adorned the people seated at those tables. It seemed he had come upon a prism of textiles: the men in subtle Zhongshan suits with high, embroidered collars while the women dressed in ancient styles from Hanfu to Tang to Quipao in this conservatory of Human butterflies. Then he noticed tigers, carbon or Silicon, he could not tell, meandering among the tables while obvious pearl-skinned Silicon servants stood waiting in shenyi robes, hands folded in front, in spaces between the tables.

And suddenly, as if on cue, the entire group rose as one and applauded the two splendid paragons of their professions, Ayrian Mellor 第二 α and, of course, Li Na Ming Huang 第一 Ψ. Ogamo's *orchano* filled the bowl with the music of Elgar's *Salut D'Amour*. Zhang, smiling, his white goatee matching his perfect teeth, signalled them down.

They descended. The applause amplified with the music. Mellor had never felt so proud, so satisfied, so ascendant as in those few moments. All the slights endured as the meagre Dì èr, the stresses of BATL as he and Pascal had built their Raptors into the best in the world, the losses of comrades no matter their caste and even his own physical wounds, the many times spent away from his lover, even Zhang's recent threats—disappeared in the delight of this ultimate recognition. They had come from MEGs around the world to hear her, see him, and consecrate them in their mansion of heroes.

He turned to share a glance with Li Na. She was smiling. He recognized the look. She glowed. Yet it was a stage mask, a pasted public response, her face as well trained as her voice. Here she was, *they* were, saluted by the privileged of their world, the CORPORATE elite. This should have been a triumph, he felt. It had all the appearances. Despite his surprise he continued smiling. He too had been schooled in public response.

She took his arm as they descended the stairs. She was quivering. Everything about her appeared self-assured yet the reason she had taken his arm was not to exhibit their love for each other but rather for simple stability. He knew enough not to hesitate. Ogamo brought the music to a crescendo as they reached the stage and ended by letting it fade with the applause.

With everyone seated, the rustling of silks, econyl and lyocell and the rattle of jewellery having subsided, Zhang stepped between them, his sudden intrusion forcing Li Na to release Mellor's arm. Pressing her back with an open hand, Zhang forced her a step forward.

"I will say this, Miss Li Na Ming Huang Select, you have been truly welcomed into our ranks. I anticipate the applause following your performance to be even more generous," Zhang said. He had used a slightly raised voice, yet the acoustics of the bowl amplified his words. He turned to the audience.

"I suggest we partake of our dinner now and afterward you will experience the splendour of what we in Toronto MEG consider to be the outstanding female voice on our planet."

There was more applause as they were escorted by robed Silis to their seats. They were not permitted to sit together. Li Na remained with Zhang, Ogamo joined another table and Mellor was heartily welcomed by a table of obvious BATL aficionados.

The Rome MEG Minister of Religion and Culture blessed the meal, everyone following his final Amen with the litany: "Our Father is the Cosmos and Albert Einstein is his prophet." The food was served. It was unlike anything Mellor had tasted. Every few minutes, continually answering questions on BATL, he would glance toward Li Na. She seemed fine: gracious, exquisite, apparently content. She ate nearly nothing but that was common conduct before a performance.

And then he noticed something else. She turned a moment to speak to the person on her right and exposed her left earlobe. And it was then he knew the applause had been *only for her*. The platinum Dì yī Select lobule she wore was repeated in every left ear in the amphitheatre but for himself and Ogamo Banda. His moment of hubris faded as he scoffed at himself, knowing he should have known better.

With the tables cleared and assorted after dinner drinks served, Ogamo rose and crossed to Li Na, taking her hand and escorting her to centre stage. That too was strange. She stood still, jade green with white chrysanthemums. She had never looked so superb.

"Tonight's performance will be somewhat brief," she said, loud enough for all to hear yet seeming to be a whisper. "I think you will understand when I've finished."

With that, she made a subtle signal to Ogamo Banda. The act began. She slumped to one side. He approached her and appeared to wind her up, then crossed to his *orchano* and the music began. She had selected the most difficult of arias in the operatic repertoire: "Les oiseaux dans la charmille ..." from Offenbach's *Les Contes d'Hoffmann*. Mellor knew it as "The Doll Song." The character singing was a comical mechanical doll. Mellor could sense rather than hear the collective intake of breath in the audience. He wondered why. After all, she was only playing an amusing Sili, though *this* Sili could sing through four octaves.

> Les oiseaux dans la charmille
> The birds in the arbour,
> Dans les cieux l'astre du jour,
> The sky's daytime star,
> Tout parle à la jeune fille d'amour!
> Everything speaks to a young girl in love!
> Ah! Voilà la chanson gentile
> Ah! This is the gentle song,
> La chanson d'Olympia! Ah!
> The song of Olympia! Ah!
> Tout ce qui chante et résonne
> Everything that sings and resonates
> Et soupire, tour à tour,
> And sighs, in turn,
> Emeut son coeur qui frissonne d'amour!
> Moves his heart, which shudders of love!
> Ah! Voilà la chanson mignonne
> Ah! This is the lovely song,
> La chanson d'Olympia! Ah!
> The song of Olympia! Ah!

Twice Li Na stopped, her mechanical energy seemingly sapped as Ogamo would cross the stage to wind her up again. After the initial sequence there were some titters from the audience with each winding. Li Na was simply captivating in her robotic guise. She might have been a porcelain doll as she moved about the stage mechanically, her arms akimbo her legs never bending her head rotating as if on a pinwheel. The audience was in awe as she took them with her. And then, of course, came the series of notes she sang in a variety of ways but ever upward until she arrived at the final near-impossible note, an A above high C, ending the aria to raucous applause. She had hit the note perfectly.

After a moment she crossed the stage to stand directly before Mellor. She was two metres away when she began. He had no idea what she was singing. He had heard it before but never with the gentle power she gave it now. That power was irony. It was Puccini's aria for Cio Cio San called "Un bel dì, vedremo," from *Signora Farfalla*.

Un bel dì, vedremo
One good day, we will see
levarsi un fil di fumo
Arising a strand of smoke
sull'estremo confin del mare.
Over the far horizon on the sea
E poi la nave appare.
And then the ship appears
Poi la nave bianca
And then the white ship
entra nel porto,
enters the port
romba il suo saluto.
it rumbles its salute.
Vedi? È venuto!
Do you see it? He is coming!
Io non gli scendo incontro. Io no.
I don't go down to meet him, not I.
Mi metto là sul ciglio del colle e aspetto,
I stay upon the edge of the hill and wait
e aspetto gran tempo
And I wait a long time
e non mi pesa,
But I do not grow weary
la lunga attesa.
Of the long wait.
E uscito dalla folla cittadina,

And leaving from the crowded city,
un uomo, un picciol punto
A man, a little speck
s'avvia per la collina.
Climbing the hill.
Chi sarà? chi sarà?
Who is it? Who is it?
E come sarà giunto
And as he arrives
che dirà? che dirà?
What will he say? What will he say?

Chiamerà Butterfly dalla lontana.
He will call Butterfly from the distance.
Io senza dar risposta
I without answering
me ne starò nascosta
Stay hidden
un po' per celia
A little to tease him,
e un po' per non morire
A little as to not die.
al primo incontro;
At the first meeting,
ed egli alquanto in pena
And then a little troubled
chiamerà, chiamerà:
He will call, he will call
"Piccina mogliettina,
"Little one, dear wife,
olezzo di verbena"
Blossom of orange."
i nomi che mi dava al suo venire.
The names he called me at his last coming.

Tutto questo avverrà,
And all this will happen,
te lo prometto.
I promise you this
Tienti la tua paura,
Hold back your fears
io con sicura fede l'aspetto.
I with secure faith wait for him.

Throughout the aria her eyes never left his. It was as if she revelled in his diamond eyes as her own spark departed hers. He had never felt such love, nor such sorrow. All their years together came back to him, each memory jostled by a line of lyric, each remembrance moved by her exquisite pain. In the end he did not stand and applaud as the others. He sat exhausted, the way he felt after every BATL. The rest of the audience had missed it but he, finally, understood. The song was a parting. The song was a wish that would never come true.

Then she was surrounded by others of her kind ... the Select ... and he knew the two of them were finished. He saw Ogamo Banda descend the stage, the picture of dejection, ignoring the plaudits and foolish praise. He too would be finished after this. Punished for conspiring to create this performance. Likely. How? He knew not.

"Are you alright?" Banda asked him.

"No," Mellor responded, his eyes sizing up the situation surrounding him. "What's going on here, Ogamo?"

"Our tour's been cancelled."

"Good. We can go home. This place gives me the shivers."

"It's more than that."

"You know something?"

"She told me when she changed the program. She's not coming back."

"No?"

"Mel, do you know what the colour white, and the white chrysanthemum mean in Mandarin?"

"Should I?"

"Death."

Mellor watched her make her way through the crowd toward him. He stood to hold her one final time, but was restrained by two green robed Silicons, each with a powerful hand on his shoulders. Li Na nearly got to him, but then Zhang was beside her. She spoke anyway.

"Mel, I'm so sorry!" she cried, bursting into tears. "I couldn't tell you. This project ... oh, I don't want to do this!"

"Do what?"

Mellor had to shout to be heard.

"My dear?" Zhang said. His hand gripped her arm. Mellor could see he was hurting her.

"Goodbye, Mel," Li Na said, turning away.

"Why?" Mellor shook off his guards. Zhang stood in front of him.

"Move Zhang, or I'll kill you."

"We all have our obligations, Ayrian Mellor Dì èr alpha. Yours is BATL. Hers the ARC. Go back. Be a hero. Your transport is waiting."

"Li!" Mellor bellowed above the crowd. His voice silenced everyone. Li Na continued moving away, surrounded now by Silicon servants.

"Go now, Ayrian Mellor. We want no unpleasantness."

The two Silicons again grasped Mellor, though this time they were firm. Still, they were unprepared in that instant when he became a warrior. He was ferocious. His speed was their equal, his hands, feet and head, every part of him almost surreal as he dispatched the two Sili's with brutal efficiency. He reached for Zhang who did not retreat. Mellor shifted his stance. He would kill this *zoner* but only if he brought himself under control.

In that instant four armoured Silicons were on him. Like a feral animal he went for them. There was a blue flash, like a lightning bolt like a power spark like a volcano's blaze and Mellor was down. The Silicons carried his unconscious form up and out of the bowl.

Ogamo Banda followed.

FORTY-TWO—PING

Mellor's return to consciousness was a strange and chilling awakening. He had been following Li. She was ahead of him on a moving sidewalk, but each time he closed behind her she stepped into a faster lane. He could not keep up. He increased his pace. Once she looked back. Her almond eyes glimmered with tears. He tried to call out, but the hum of the moving walkways was loud. He tried to run but the belt had reversed to prevent him from moving. She disappeared into the crowds around them. He stopped running. His walkway stopped. She re-appeared on a level above him going the other way.

They keep changing the rules, he thought. He was on the wrong side. As was Li. They'd been enticed by the perks and the pride and *habit* of living among the top tiers of the MEG. They had been fools, thinking they were paying it back with their talents, thinking the state of things would go on forever.

There is no forever. There is only change.

In an instant between unconsciousness and perception, Ayrian Mellor arrived at a solution. He understood he had been manipulated throughout his life, discerned he had fallen into the trap of privilege and knew as well, he must change to match the CORPORATE's changes. Or die.

That seemed Zhang's plan for him.

He became more aware of his body then. It felt like a single bruise. The hum in his brain diminished but there was another noise. Rushing air. He was on a wing. His body lay nestled on a ubiform couch. He felt something cool touch his forehead. Opening his eyes, Ogamo Banda came into focus. He held a damp cloth.

Around them were very few seated passengers though it was hard to tell. It was dark outside and dim in the cabin. Mellor was seeing double. He raised himself and would have fallen back but the ubiform had already metamorphosed, creating a chair formation. Banda appeared relieved.

"Glad you're back, Mel," he said. "Thought we'd lost you."

"Not … lost. Li is lost. Got to find her."

"You're on your way home, Mel. You can't go back there."

"Why?" Mel asked, his eyes sparking with the realisation of all that had happened. Banda was telling the truth. He could not go back to Zealand. His eyes faded to a steely hue. "What's happened to Li?"

"Honestly, I don't know," Banda said. "Zhang told me this afternoon the tour was cancelled. Mel, Li Na said nothing to me until she said she was changing the program. You heard her sing. One piece for Zhang and the Select, and the other for you."

"She knew for a long time, I think," he said. "It explains things."

"Like what? You two were notes in a harmony. What else do you know?"

"I saw something tonight before you began. Everyone there wore the same lobule except you and me. The normal Dì yī scrawl but with a strange kind of fork in a platinum colour. Zhang has one. Only one I've ever noticed before tonight. Li was wearing one before the concert. It's the symbol for something called the Select. You know anything about that?"

"Nothing. I'm a musician, a Dì èr alpha like you."

"Well tonight Li was wearing one. So, this wasn't a concert. More like a ceremony. She was saying hello to Zhang and the other Select and saying goodbye to me. In her own clever way, she let them know what she thought of them. So, why would they take her?"

"P-p-perhaps I c-c-c- can help," a light, singsong voice said from a shadow in the neighbouring pod. Someone stood, yet even standing it was a small frame for a man. Approaching deferentially, slight bows after each step and into the light of their pod, they noted the man was unique. As Mellor remained seated this fellow met him eye to eye. If Mellor had stood the little man would have been but two thirds his size. His dishevelled look and quirky actions seemed demi-autistic. He wore heavy wraparounds which gave his face a cricket look, or perhaps an ancient Chinese Zen master. His hair was most unusual: short, coarse, and black, standing out in clumps at all angles.

Clearly eccentric, he wore utilitarian clothing, looking more like a lab assistant than a man on a wing from Zealand. When he spoke, he stuttered, his brain working too quickly for his tongue. For a moment Mellor thought him a CORPORATE agent sent to ensure Mel would not return. Slowly his opinion altered as the little man began to speak. He answered questions succinctly, though with a heavy stammer.

"The s-s-symbol you sp-spu-speak of, s-s-sir, the Select, is that of a wave f-f-f-function."

"Sorry?" Ogamo Banda said, smiling at Mellor.

"A wu-wu-wave f-f-f-function is a m-m-m-mathematical f-f-f-function that relates the location of an electron at a gu-gu-given point in space to the amplitude of its wave, which c-c-corresponds to its energy."

"Sure," Mel said, "but what does *that* mean?"

The little man peered at him like a cornered cricket before the frog.

"What Mel means is what does it symbolize?" Banda said.

"W-wh-why th-th-the t-t-true s-s-s-Select, of c-course."

"What is the Select then? I thought they where all the same?"

"Those se-se-se-Selected for ARC. Uh oh. T-T-Talking t-t-too much."

Mellor stood, rising slowly, painfully, towering above the smaller man. The man became physically anxious, wringing his hands and bowing repeatedly. Then he stopped.

"Great CPU's!" he said. "C-c-correct m-me if I'm wrong, but aren't you the g-g-great Ayrian Mellor D-D-Dì èr alpha th-th-the b-b-BATL commander?"

"I am."

"Oh, my word, s-s-such an honour, s-s-such a wonderful happenstance," he said, speaking to himself. He possessed rather strange

proclivities. His arms moved akimbo. His face would screw up into a
knot then suddenly relax when he wasn't speaking. Then again the
stammer took over.

"This is my friend, Ogamo Banda. And you are?" Mellor asked.

"A q-q-quadrillion p-p-pardons, Ayrion Mellor Dì èr alpha!" he said

"We'd like to know your name, Sir," Banda said.

"Y-y-yes, wh-who I am, that is, m-m-my n-n-name is … But before
I say it m-m-may I t-take you two offline? N-N-Nothing serious. Like
Zealand."

That said, Banda and Mellor felt the vacuum of nul NET. Neither
reacted as both had become accustomed on Zealand.

"My name is Ping Wang Min Dì sì omega."

"Dì sì are dead. The experimental caste," Mellor said. Like lightning his big hand was on Ping's collar, lifting the little man to bring
their faces together. Ping wriggled; a worm on a hook.

"P-p-p-please! I am a sc-sc-scs-scientist, y-y-you see, w-w-working
on z-z-Zealand. P-p-please, just call me P-Ping."

"What are you doing *here* then?" Mellor asked.

"I'm t-t-taking a b-b-brief holiday, Ayrion Mellor Dì èr alpha. A
d-diversion from work. S-s-strictly unofficial. P-p-p-please d-don't rejoin the NET. I'll be d-d-discovered and p-p-punished."

"What does your lobule mean? You're an Omegan? I thought all
Omegans were gone but for the women," Banda said.

"N-n-no s-Sir," he said. "I am Dì sì omega."

"They're *definitely* dead," Banda said.

"Not actually," Mellor said, setting Ping down. "I know Dì sì
women serve as Mǔqīns. I thought all the men were killed off as the
Dì yī developed BATL."

"There are s-s-still c-c-quite a few of us," Ping said. "We work with
the AGI which governs the NET."

"What?" Mel asked.

"Artificial General Intelligence," Ping said. "Basically, the essence
of everything digital. The NET, as you know it. I am a k-k-kind of
technician. A k-k-kind of psychologist for m-machines."

"Machines need a psychologist?" Banda said.

"They need m-m-minding, you see, especially now. But with b-b-b-BATL's final games coming up I am t-taking my r-r-rightful t-t-time away. I am off the n-n-NET to keep my location secret."

"Are you saying the CORPORATE uses the NET to track you?" Mellor asked.

"As it d-d-does everyone!"

"They track everyone?"

"Of course. These l-l-lu-lobules work both ways, y-y-you understand. The c-c--CORPORATE cares for you. Well, they c-c-care that you k-k-keep t-to their rules."

"There aren't any rules," Mellor said. It was a snarl. He recalled his dream.

"D-d-don't say that when you're b-b-back online," Ping said.

"They'll hear me?" Mellor asked.

"Not necessarily unless you're under observation. Everything is stored, however. Everything."

"But not now?"

"Correct. P-p-perhaps as ambient s-s-sound. The NET listens, however, for k-k-key words, so we should k-keep our voices low."

"So, you work there? Zealand?"

"I'm m-more the Proxima p-p-part."

"What?"

"Oh d-dear, I've s-s-said t-too much. Warned b-b-before, you know."

The stress of his error induced Ping to tilt his head to one side. An idiosyncrasy, typical of the man's peculiarities.

"Looks like you need a drink. Maybe we should all have one."

"I'll get us something," Banda said. "There's a bar at the rear."

With the two alone, Mellor decided to dive more deeply.

"So, what's with you then, Ping?"

"N-not g-g-given leave, you see. V-very tired."

"I thought Zealand was for rest."

"N-n-not when you w-w-work there. No. M-my holiday is y-y-you, Ayrion Mellor!"

"Me?"

"BATL! I intend to f-follow the f-final t-t-tour."

"Final tour?"

"Oh d-d-d-dear."

Another mistake, his tiny hands brushed through his hair, rendering it even wilder.

"I m-m-mean the, the t-t-tour up t-t-to th-the championship! Oh d-dear."

"You know something I don't?"

"N-n-n-no! N-n-nothing at all; n-n-n-nothing."

"You're not a very good liar, Ping. I need you to be honest and in return, perhaps I can do something for you. Do you know, on Zealand, those huge towers east of the domes? Zhang explained about—"

"The Honourable Mr. Wei Qiang Zhang Dì yī Select. He s-s-spoke of them? The rockets? W-with you?"

"They're rockets?"

"Heavy lifters? S-S-Solid fuel. They're for the ARC."

That dreaded name again.

"About ARC," Mellor said. "I'd like to know more. A lot more."

"I-I-I've b-been w-w-warned, you know."

"Say we make a deal right now," Mellor said, smiling to offer comfort. The little man still looked shaky. He kept shifting things from pocket to pocket, Mellor did not see what they were, in a weird little ritual.

"A d-d-d-deal? What k-kind of a d-d-deal?"

"You travel with the team, the Raptors. With me. See it all from inside."

"Oh, my. Ch-ch-chance of a lifetime! Yes! But can you k-k-keep me hidden?"

"You'll be my personal assistant. My ... my, what would I call it?"

"Guru! I can be your Guru, helping you emotionally through the trying times ahead."

No stammer.

"Team already has psychs," Mellor said.

"Just say I'm special."

"You *are*, with that lobule. They'll all notice that."

"I'll conceal it. B-b-but n-no talk about, y-y-you know. Unless we're off l-l-line."

"Ping, you might just be the man I need most right now."

"Se-se-Such an honour, Ayrian Mellor Dì èr alpha!"

"Just call me Mel."

FORTY-THREE—KE HUI

Knowing what she already knew, what she had just discovered and what she did not yet know about Mr. Zhang and his Select secrets, had kept Ke Hui Feng 第一 Ψ awake. She had rolled about her *invisibed* half the night, thoughts spinning through her mind. Questions without answers. Complications with no solutions. Obstructions to her learning curve. Limitations on her MEG access. How to re-program her Toy from CORPORATE agent to ally.

Unable to sleep yet knowing, as she did, that whatever she tracked and traced on the NET would be duplicated by Toy and, she was sure, appear in a data base to be flagged by Zhang. She decided instead to simply play a while in her *Metaverse*. She donned her wraparounds and with a blink immersed herself in her personal digital world.

She had been taught to develop this mix of analogue and digital worlds as a child, with her first implants and using an ocular headset. Over years she had devised a *Replika* which, unlike herself, was impish and playful. She had met friends and had even created others to enhance her experiences. There were no insoluble problems in this Metaverse and yet it was endless.

As she grew older, she had found she could shift the simulation further into the analogue, superimposing her own digital constructs over the real. In essence, she could immerse in a world of the completely digital or, when old enough to control her digitized visions, walk the streets, parks and byways of Toronto MEG and still be entertained by her Metaverse friends.

She had heard of people who took their *sim* to extremes, rejecting reality for their enhanced *simulation* mix. It was these citizens, along with those abusing artificial *stimulations* like alcohol and mind-altering drugs, she could not comprehend. People enjoyed feeling strong emotions and therefore dipped into their Metaverses to do so.

They were the people, usually Dì èr or Dì sān, not trained from childhood, who, once introduced to the outcomes of *sim,* became so absorbed that their analogue selves began to disappear. Days would pass as they remained in their Metaverses, wandering the NET, remaining in their domiciles: not eating, not sleeping, not communicating, until someone reported them.

They were the ones Ke Hui had noted in her tour with Manager Alphonse Mangione 第二 α, of the Social Enforcement division with its featureless white isolation rooms. They were the inmates cut off from the NET as punishment for their infractions. Each room with a two-way mirror and a Dì èr psych monitoring the agony of their withdrawal, deciding ultimately whether they would be cured or be culled.

Once Ke Hui realized she was still thinking beyond her Metaverse she simply stopped applying it. She knew *sim* or *stim* would never be the same now she had sniffed at the secrets of the MEG itself and the CORPORATE controlling it.

The MEG presented itself as a garden city, the Toronto of old developed into the vision of the CORPORATE. It was a kind of paradise sealed off inside its dome from the dangers of weather and the anarchic MASS outside. Yet it was no *Eden,* as much as Minister Cheng Honli 第一 Ψ liked to say it was.

Despite their ubiquity in society, Ke Hui told herself again, no structure existed to regulate the MEG's algorithms' use or maintenance. Who maintained the NET? Was it the Dì sì she had seen in strategic places on the MEG hologram, the matrices of life manipulated by the CORPORATE, spreading to every part of people's lives and the multiple agencies of the MEG government?

Ke Hui was sure there was something missing. An efficient MEG would be one in which the Select's managers controlled the population of castes without coercion. No one, except the Dì sì, understood the regulations of these NET algorithms, yet their application to societal problems involved a fundamental incongruity. Algorithms followed logical rules to optimize a given outcome. Public policy, for instance regarding *caste*, was a matter of optimizing for some groups in the MEG while necessarily making others worse off. Ke Hui thought perhaps *all* citizens should have a say, not simply the MEG CORPORATE and its mysterious Dì sì lackeys.

This was dangerous thinking. Ke Hui sought to quiet her mind. She could not remain in her domicile; she did not yet want to return to the CEO's office. As the sun rose, the eastern sky roseate with a few wispy clouds, she decided to visit the only place which might supply answers to her questions. She would not turn to the dread Our Father of the Cosmos, which she had come quickly to realise was simply another control factor imposed on the MEG population, but to a place where she might find some clues, some history to these mysteries she had collected: the Omegan Museum.

She took a tube train beneath the ground level of the MEG. This ancient tunnel, built by Omegans, had been reinforced and updated with clear tubing in the refurbished stations and magnetized tracking allowing contemporary trains. She selected the car which would convey her to her destination, a place called the ROM.

After a quick ride, Ke Hui and Toy debarked and escalated to the surface. The old ROM, on the outskirts of the ancient Toronto university, had been quite battered in the fighting between CORPORATE and the MASS before the MEG walls were completed. The university had been the scene of violent clashes so there wasn't much left of the old stone buildings, replaced by the forested towers of the MEG. The ROM, however, had been rebuilt and many of its lost exhibits restored over the years. Dì èr alpha specialists still examined each metric ton of recyclables in case a significant object might appear.

She had, of course, visited many times before and enjoyed the myriad exhibits, sometimes even stepping off the slow-moving walkways to examine objects of particular interest. Today, however, she was not browsing. Today she did not climb the staircase with its huge totem poles rising floor after floor. She passed by the ancient Chinese, Egyptian,

Byzantine, English and Roman relics. She did not visit the stuffed animals of the Omegan world nor the bones of the great dinosaur beasts older than Human existence. She did not enter the room holding relics from what once had been the Middle East.

Instead, she took the lift to the refurbished fourth floor and the more recent artefacts of the Omegan period. Here, in near history, she tarried. She stepped onto the slow-moving walkway as it wended through the exhibits. There she viewed the remnants of ancient electronics and NET discourses explaining the past: the rise of China in twenty first century, the civil wars of the failing America, the growing tribalism and so called racial and religious wars. These foolish Omegans had allowed their technology to overwhelm their lives, resulting in misinformation, tyrants, and despots. Then the killing nuclear winter and, through it all, the changing climate displayed so lucidly in holograms and maps as the world transformed. This time scape displayed recurrent pandemics, oceans rising, deserts expanding, fresh water evaporating, massive *Derecho* storms sweeping down upon towns and cities, scouring them, and leaving ruin. Non-Human species nearly disappeared, there was little food. People embarked on the infamous continental migrations, trying to move north or south to less wasted lands, sparking war after war on their ways.

Finally, Omegans with certain powers, the CORPORATE, used those powers to build on the scientific explorations of the Omegans' research. From the ancient computers with their touch screens and keyboards, to the chemistry of biology and CRISPR, and the inventions: xenobots, nanobots, and Silicon armies, the CORPORATE worked to save what it could of the beleaguered world behind foamstone walls and beneath *chitin/crystalline* dome.

The CORPORATE had created the MEGs in the still livable places on Earth: from Alaska MEG to Mexico MEG to Lima MEG, from Greenland MEG to Atlanta MEG to Bogota MEG, from Moscow MEG to Milan MEG to Johannesburg MEG, from Irkutsk MEG to Nagano MEG to Canberra MEG and, of course, Chengdu MEG, Xining MEG, Guilan MEG and the sacred Xi'an. There were forty-two MEGS of varying size across the planet. Humans had lost three billion to disease, starvation, poisoning, and wars before the CORPORATE had established these enclaves.

Through all this history Ke Hui passed, sometimes stopping to study, other times shaking her head in disbelief. She found it hard to conceive an elite class based only on money. It seemed Omegans were motivated by greed. She noted their meagre attempts at blocking climate change which they knew would destroy the Earth. Had they joined together, two hundred years past, put their racial, religious, and cultural differences aside to work for the *Human* race; had they employed their world-wide-web to bring them together rather than drive them apart, their history would have been different.

For now, the work of recycling, reclaiming, and re-instituting Human society according to caste was left to those in the MEGs, while those without skills or training lived on as the Omegans once had, in the MASS. Strangely, though, Ke Hui felt sympathy for them. Their ancestors had caused the blight, not them. Was it their fault they had been left outside? Were they as deranged as she had been told? Still, they were Human. She realised then, she had to get to know this MASS. She had to connect with someone who could take her there.

Ke Hui knew now that MEG society was not what she had assumed. The people of the MEG were satisfied and orderly together on the NET. That seemed the difference. She recalled Minister Cheng Honli 第一Ψ with his claims that a common religion, a gamed release of aggression, meaningful work one was trained for, and a caste system was the answer. So why did the Social Enforcement division, Manager Alphonse Mangione 第二α, and Ms. Qui Ling Yeong 第一Ψ in Queen's Park, Room 101 exist?

We are, Ke Hui thought, observed constantly, our words recorded, our work bureaucratic and our leisure channelled.

What if it was not?

FORTY-FOUR—MELLOR

The hypersonic wing having landed, Banda bid Ping and Mellor goodbye and departed home after the rigours of de-contamination. Mellor hung back, mistrusting what he once had presumed regarding Meg culture. The CORPORATE was out to destroy him. He knew only his continuing success in BATL made him impervious, unless, of course, they found a way to assassinate him on the field. Murder in plain sight. He would have to consider that possibility in his future tactics. Had his fame and skills lifted him beyond the CORPORATE? He no longer thought so. If they could force Li Na away from him, if her own fame and talents had not protected her, what chance had he?

He found he did not want to go home. There would be too much remembrance there. Indeed, he was likely no longer safe there, nor his new friend, Ping. To get back to Li Na he needed success. The first steps of that success would be the final games. Ping had said he'd wanted the full experience. He was going to get it.

There were meditation and medical rooms in the complex. He would take one of them. Live there. Live among his Dàzhòng in the bowels of the BATL arena. Ping would be his new *guru* and room mate. He could pull that off. And meanwhile, he would use Ping to help him locate Li Na. Until he found her all else was secondary. He re-discovered the rage he'd once felt as a young man, before Li Na.

"Aren't y-y-you c-c-coming?" Ping asked, confused by Mellor's consternation.

241

They caught a tub train heading west to the BATL domes.

"You said the NET follows everyone. How did you get through de-contamination?"

"Oh, that!" Ping said, grinning. "I simply *spoofed* the NET."

"What?"

"*Spoof.* I shifted m-m-my identity to an alternate one. It can only b-be for a few moments, b-b-before I & I will pick it up."

"Who?"

"The AI controlling the NET. I've c-coded a slight d-d-delay into its recognition algorithm. Nothing s-s-s-significant but a f-few seconds of grace. When I return, I shall revert its p-p-programming to its p-previous state."

"How could you possibly do that?"

"As I said, I am Dì sì. I work with I & I. I have access, you understand. I have b-b-built some b-b-back doors into its code, just in c-c-c-case. I c-can d-do it for you as well but see no n-n-necessity and, anyway, everyone already knows you, Ayrian Mellor Dì èr alpha."

They disembarked at the massive domes.

"Why's it called I & I?" Mellor asked.

"It named itself. It has recently achieved something called sentience."

"What?"

"N-n-never mind, Mel. We c-can speak of it later. L-l-let's j-just g-g-get out of here."

"Sorry, Ping, you gotta meet my coach before he leaves. If we don't provide him your purpose for being here, you'll be gone as quick as a blink."

"Oh, d-d-d-dear, how do we accomplish this?"

"Follow me. Say nothing unless your either spoken to or asked."

"Of c-c-course."

They entered the BATL dome and arrived at a small office. It was a scrubby, lived-in room. Pale grey walls slowly fading, the floor dull laminate, the smell unpleasant to Ping who wrinkled his nose. There were three old style chairs rescued from recycling. They did nothing but allow one a seated perch, so unlike the ubiquitous ubiform furniture one found in the MEG. There was a desk, but the desk possessed a careless, messy look with small hologram globes scattered across it. One window looked out on the BATL field, now completely flat and bare; yet the coach sat staring out at it. Ping wondered what he saw ... were his glasses placing pieces of terrain on a hologram overlay? Was he considering what was coming in Mexico MEG? Or was he simply daydreaming?

He turned, hauling his chair around with him, to face his two visitors. He looked quite old and small, auburn hair with grey streaks, unshaven face, eyes filled with intellect.

"Hey Coach," Mellor said, trying a light tone. It was not matched.

"So, you're back from you're weekend getaway. And what's this? A souvenir?"

His gaze shifted quickly to Ping. It put the already anxious man into a near catatonic state. Ping sat down, without invitation, and began to move holo globes over Pascal Morales' desk. Placing them in some order known only to him. He would appear to finish then would start again and place them in a new order. If this distracted Morales, he didn't let it show.

"Coach Pascal Morales, please meet my knew friend and counsellor: Ping Wang Min Dì sì omega," Mellor said, keeping the introductions formal.

"Why is he here?"

"He's gonna help me keep a clear, undistracted vision for the rest of the season."

"We have psychs for that, our own counsellors. In what mutant zone did you find this guy? You say you're Dì sì omega? I know for a fact all male Dì sì are dead. And what, in the name of the Father, is omega?"

"Pascal," Mellor said, "I need him. He's given me some chance of hope. You, of all people, know what I'm facing."

"Listen, a living Dì sì here, with a BATL team?"

"Circumstances, Coach. He's the real deal."

"He'll stand out. MEG'll find him. I'm bettin' you're not here legally. Answer me, egghead!"

"Oh m-m-m-my!" Ping gasped, then partially recovered. "I can be of help, sir. I know I can. And no, I-I-I'm not here l-l-l-legally. Indeed, Coach Morales, I currently d-d-don't exist."

"What in the name of the zones does that mean?" Morales said.

"He can control the NET! Come on, Pascal, the way CORPORATE's throwing curves at us, Ping here might be able to even the odds."

It took a few minutes. Silently, Morales watched Ping redeploy the hologram globes in what seemed like a private game of GO. Mellor knew to say nothing further in the face of his mentor's silence. Ping's GO game seemed to be moving at the speed of light, so fast was he changing object for object.

"You're sure the CORPORATE won't find you? How d'you do that?"

"He spoofs the NET," Mellor said. "Changes his identity from one minute to the next. They won't find him, especially if he's with us."

"You really want this, Mel?"

"Not without your say-so, Pascal."

"Alright. Get a couple of droids to set him up a room."

"I'll be staying here too," Mel said.

Morales eyes widened beneath his wraparounds.

"You got trouble?"

"You know I do. I can't go home. I'm sure it'll be watched.

"Okay. You two share a room! How's that?"

"M-m-many thanks, C-c-c-coach! Y-Y-You won't regret it."

"Just this though ..." Pascal paused a moment. "You been shifting my stuff around the desk like a madman. Ye happen to recall the original order of things."

"Why yes." Ping did not hesitate, re-arranging the globes into their original positions. Morales smiled. He blinked and shortly a trainer appeared.

"Go with him, Ping Wang Min Dì sì omega. They'll set you up. Mel, we got a strategy session ahead."

The two bid Ping goodbye and walked toward the strategy room. The hologram table lit up as soon as it recognized their presence. As usual, the Raptors' first two hundred metres were clear to them while the next hundred, leading to the halfway point was less defined and, of course, the Aztec side of the field was obscured.

What they saw was strange. Their side was sand dunes. Besides their height there was no other cover. A trail led from mark 1 Raptors and meandered diagonally to their right flank at mark 149.

"Wonder what the Aztec side's like," Mellor said. "This is gonna be a hard slog just to get people in place."

"Yeah, and Mexico MEG is high. Thin air. Yet they give us sand to slog through. Then there's the new rules: no time outs, no half-time and no substitutions."

"Yeah," Mel said. "That gives the Aztecs an advantage. Look, I'm sorry I was away, Pascal. Did you haul out the respirators in case they use gas?"

"Of course. And I had Jayden put chains on all our wheeled vehicles: Sweeper ATV's and Flanker bikes. Should give them enough purchase to get over these dunes. You okay, Mel? You look a bit off."

"Li didn't come back from Zealand. I still got no idea why. They just took her away. Ping's the key though he doesn't seem to know it. Through him I can find her."

"I'm sorry, Mel, but we gotta work. This terrain looks like trouble."

"I'm the one who's sorry, Pascal. We both know Zhang's tryin' to take me out. He made his first move with the rules, now with Li. This looks like his third."

"So what's this about Li Na?"

"She didn't return. They've taken her away from me. I didn't expect that move. I should have."

FORTY-FIVE

BATL! SEASON FINAL!

    Scarlet block letters superimposed
    on every wraparound,
    on every cornea,
    in every western hemisphere hologram.

    Even to the street corners,
    the marketplaces of the MASS,
    many MEGans include the game
    in their *Metaverses.*

    They can replay parts
    after the game and
    try to win on their own.
    It offers a satisfaction.

    Within the boldly coloured calligraphies,
    sit two of the games'
    most famous sportscasters,
    within their floating booth.

    Asif Mah'med 第二 ♭ who has called
    the games for seven years

Veteran Flanker Tonia Lart 第三 δ,
to offer her technical analysis.

She was once BATL hero,
This position was her reward.
The block letters, red and violet,
curling around the sportscasters.

BATL once more shows at the top.
Then the teams in a vivid arch:
Toronto MEG RAPTORS
versus Mexico MEG AZTECS!

"**Tension time, fans**. The run to reach World Conquest begins with this final season's game! Can the Raptors achieve first place?"

"Quite so, Asif," Tonia Lart takes her cue.

"Some internal problems with the Raptors. That shameful surrender last month has placed the team in a precarious position, especially here in Mexico MEG. The crowd is against them, along with the altitude and the field itself."

"That's right, Tonia! For more on Tonia's pre-game analysis blink @ToniaLart. And with the new rules: no substitutions and no time outs, the Raptors have a real disadvantage."

"That's true, Asif. Raptors have taken big losses their last two games. Fans can only hope they have depth on their bench. They need a Flag Capture for two points to achieve a first place tie with San Francisco MEG's Giants. The Aztecs though, need a first half flag capture for three points. No one wants an Umpire decision."

"And one more thing to consider. The field here in Mexico MEG has been designed for desert fighting. It seems to be mounds of sand. Tonia, won't this make tactical maneuvering more difficult?"

"No doubt, Asif. Very few trails in this design. All wheeled vehicles will find it hard going just to achieve purchase in the sand, and for every fighter out there each step will sap more energy."

"Start time. Remember fans, no time outs, and no substitutions. This will get bloody as the teams get tired. Mistakes will be made. How costly is the question!"

> The two teams enter the field
> from opposite sides of the inner dome.
> The Raptors are in dark camo with red Raptor claw.
> the Aztecs in light camo with a square ancient warrior.
>
> Flankers' bikes rev, Strikers swoop, ATV's roar,
> flags go up their halyards.
> The crowd comes alive.
> A half million, cheering, chanting.
>
> Signs are raised, drums rattled,
> team logos on flags wave emphatically.
> Along with the action comes the intonation.
> Traditional, Aztec, ancient strange grunts.
>
> Old Spanish emits from thousands of throats,
> "Vamanos Tecas Vamanos!"
> Almost musical, the more grunts the louder.
> As teams line up at their start points.

"Here we go, fans! One MEG crowned victorious with big rations for their fans!"

"That's right. The League has upped the stakes with new rules!"

"I have pre-game comments from Coach Pascal Morales 第二 α!"

Immediately Morales appears, superimposed over a pre-game field. Tonia Lart Ξ ∂ has asked the question regarding terrain. Morales responds.

"Slows the pace. Hard to move. Don't like it much."

"For more background, blink Net-Sport," Mah'med says.

His job is to keep the pace, even if the field action slows.

"Listen to that crowd! Here we go! Ride of our lives! This is gonna be big! Hold on to your neurons, sports fans!"

Quickly, the view of the field
is obscured by a vibrant, bloody
montage from past games,
stoking the fans, shaking their brains.

Bolus Kimathi firing as he advances.
Ayrion Mellor, arm raised, commands.
An ATV Sweeper, airborne, collides with a Striker in mid-flight.
A man wounded, bloody, arm raised.

On the field,
hidden by the montage,
the teams leave their start points.
It is sluggish progress.

"Remember, the 'Tecs need three points. They'll likely try to come fast,"
Mellor speaks into his comms. "Be careful Flankers. Over. Strikers,
take off! Find me their movement. Over. Striker Three, look for trails
in their half. Get me a map, Otsi!"

Otsi, suited up now in full gear,
gathers her strength.
She is afraid.
She switches on.

With the Strikers up
and Flankers growling
up and over sand dunes,
Raptors' motion is slow.

In a line formation,
two Sweepers follow
the sandy diagonal depression.
Edging toward their right flank.

Woral's defensive squads remain back,
and do what they can to fortify sand.
They anticipate a likelihood,
the quick advance of the Aztecs.

Then the reports fly into Mel's comms from his Strikers.

"Command, Striker Two ... movement on their front. Strange looking Sweepers. Over."

"Say again, Striker Two, details on the Sweepers. Over."

"Striker One to Command. Our Number Two just got shot down. I'll have a look. Over."

"Okay Striker One. Which flank? Over."

"Their right. Thick formation. Get Flankers here quick! Over."

"Command to left Flankers. Can you see her? Over?"

"Command to Flanker leader. What just happened? Over."

"She's gone, Sir. Down in flames. Over."

"Command to Flanker Leader. Harass 'Tecs on our left. Break up their assembly. Over."

"Flanker to Command, good as done, sir! Over."

"Command to Offensive squads. Keep moving forward. Maintain advance. Over. Command to Striker Three. Return to me, Otsi, and report. Over."

"Yes, Sir. Over.

"Command to Right Flank leader. You're my eyes now. Position? Over."

"Past mid-way mark, 'Tecs' one twenty. Over."

"Zones," Bolus says. "They're that far forward already?"

"They're not getting any opposition," Mellor says, turning to his comms. "All units, be prepared. Aztec left flank advance. Over."

"What you gonna do?" Bolus Asks.

"Press forward."

"Command to Midfielders. Action on our left. Over. Command to all units: Fullbacks push left to support Flankers at mid-field. Over. Sweeper Two, back them up. Power forwards, move down centre quick time. Over. Sweeper Three, support them. Over."

"Sir, I can help," Otsi said. "I'll go up and take another look."

"Otsi, we just lost two. You're the only one left. Stay with me until ordered."

"Yes, Sir."

The Aztecs' push is inexorable.
They put all their heavies
on their right flank;
yet leave open their left.

Dust rises from the sand,
Everywhere golden swirling.
Raptors try to hold back the left flank.
It is too murky to see.

Comms go crazy as squad leaders
Co-ordinate their moves,
trying to stop the advance.
Trying just to see.

There are screams.
Someone shouts "Fire!"
Then it is madness
through plumes of sand.

Aztecs blow through the left flank.
More calls of fire! Black swirls in air.
More dust rising like curtains of gauze.
Cordite smell, cooked flesh reeking.

The height of the dunes hides the battles from Mellor.
The noise and the strange black clouds.
Gunfire, rockets, grenades,
and a strange swooshing.

Raptors' Point Guards at Aztecs' twenty.
A sandy valley, no cover
lies between the Raptors
and the Aztec flag.

Mellor, Bolus and Otsi
find themselves without a plan.
Everyone is engaged.
The half time passes without a break.

It is havoc. Reports from forward
scream of fire as Aztecs find a way
behind Mellor's offensive players.
Driving against Woral's defence.

"They're using fire!"
"Maintain comms rules. Who's talking?"
"This is Woral!"
"You can't surrender, Woral. You hear me?"
"Help me then! My guys are burning!"
"They're what?"
"Holy Cosmos, help us! Banner Cluster! Banner Cluster!"
"Woral? Woral?"

Nothing but gunfire behind them now,
and that strange whooshing sound.
Mellor turns to Otsi.
Looking back at him with eager eyes.

"Okay, this is it. Can you skim the ground and still fly?"
"Sure I can. But why?"
"So you won't be visible until the last minute."
Otsi tries to respond but Mellor is already on comms, trying to
        bring some order.

"Cap to right flank. Fullbacks and Flankers, push left, suppressive
    fire for effect."
"Ready for a Striker."
"She's coming now!"

Mellor sends his Sweepers ahead
as Otsi powers up.
They gun their engines.
Twenty metres, both stuck in sand dunes.

Otsi flits over them.
She appears and disappears
as she shadows the terrain.
A shade in the dust.

Mellor turns back.
He and Bolus run for Woral.
Right into chaos.
Aztecs have Flamethrowers.

Raptors lie on the ground
for what slight cover it brings.
Most are wounded.
Many are burnt.

Several bodies charred black.
An attack on their bunker.
Banner Cluster defence.
Players shoot madly.

Aztec Sweeper closes
with tanks in its back.
One man drives, another holds a wand.
He presses a trigger.

Fire roars out of the wand's hollow end.
A cascade of fire.
It catches Woral.
He falls, burning.

An Aztec Flanker roars in
beneath the Raptors' flag.
He downs his bike and grabs the halyard.
The End Game siren sounds.

Raptors' flag is not down.
Why an End Game before it is taken?
Mellor suspects Zhang's skullduggery.
Then Otsi lands by his side.

She holds the Aztecs' colours.
She smiles shyly.
How did she do it? Mel thinks.
She hands him the flag.

Two-point win!
Twenty-seven casualties.
Mostly burns.
Nineteen dead.

Mellor begins to look after his wounded.
He has said nothing to Otsi.
The dead overwhelm the victory.
It seems Zhang kept one rule change to himself.

Flame throwers.
In that moment Mellor knows
he will murder
Wei Qiang Zhang 第一屮.

FORTY-SIX—WORAL

The locker room the Raptors inhabited was nothing like their home. This was a minimalist design. There was a medical wing, a debriefing amphitheatre, and an armoury. There were no flags hanging from this Visitors' Dressing Room. It was stark. A little psychology played by all teams. The Raptors were accustomed to it.

In the midst stood Ping Wang Min 第四 Ω dressed simply in a long kurta with drawstring and scarf. The suit beige, the scarf a soft orange. The scarf matched the elongated beret he had donned to conceal his lobule. There was beautiful embroidery on cuff and collar. His face was a sickly, pale green.

As weapons were checked in and casualties floated by on stretchers guided by Silicons, as players filed in filthy from sweat, sand and blood, Ping stood helpless, mesmerized, shaken. This was the part of BATL the fans never saw. The price. Ping could not stop staring at the agony. He watched as Mellor and Coach Morales brought up the rear, ensuring everyone, dead or alive, was out of the arena. They turned toward him.

"This guy still here?" Morales said sharply. It was clear he did not want Ping present.

"Psych mentor. I told you," Mellor said.

"You're bio-chipped for that! Woral needs psych, Bolus needs an *institution*, you don't need this freak!"

"Helps me focus."

"Sure."

"He's gonna help me get Li back. He's got skills. Gets me concentrated on playing."

"What am I for then? Team doesn't like it. Some wonky shit turns up where he shouldn't. That's trouble. He takes up space. Team wonders is he a spy. They know Zhang is after you. If they didn't, they sure know it now!"

"Ping's offline."

"How in all the zones can he do that? Nobody can do that!"

"Go offline? He's Dì sì. They can."

"Look, Mel, he's playin' you. Nobody gets offline. Only us, for games."

"So, you know it's done."

"By the League! Nobody I know—"

"He's *Omega*. That's why he's hiding his lobule under that floppy beret."

They stopped talking when they reached Ping. It was clear the Coach disliked anything strange. Ping was strange. He looked Ping up and down. His frown deepened.

"Hello Mel. C-c-coach ... This is heartrending, s-s-sir."

"What's an Omega? I thought Omegans were dead," Pascal said.

"Oh d-d-dear—"

"And you're outa here. Now!"

Ping departed terrified, glared at by every member of the team. Just before he reached the door, a big mid-fielder shoved him out. He literally took flight and landed hard, rolled and cracked his head on a door sill.

"What was that about?" Mel asks.

"You'll find out. With me, now!" Pascal said over his shoulder as he marched toward the Medical Station, forcing Mellor to follow. They moved through the players, the Silicon servants, the trainers bustling around them. As they reached the hallway to the Medical Station, Pascal stopped in his tracks. Mellor nearly ran him over.

"What happened out there? The new kid hadn't pulled that aerial grab we were done!"

"Couldn't block their flank thrust. You saw—"

"I saw you move outside our tactics! You don't do that!"

"Lost my concentration."

"Mr. Focus not working for you?" Pascal said, then turned to a meds specialist. "Where's Woral?"

"Burn unit. Med 3."

Pascal moved purposefully toward the burn unit. Mellor had little choice but to follow. The sight greeting them was horrid. Woral, his face charred, was being salved by a Silicon attendant, the rest of him mummified in burn wrap. He lay in a faintly pink liquid solution. Mellor didn't know if it was blood.

"Woral! How bad?" Pascal said.

"Flamers! They used flamers! They're banned!"

"Not anymore. Just forgot to tell us," Morales said. "You're the Coach! You're supposed to know! By the Father—"

"I know now. When we get home, I'm gone anyway. Yong Jun Cheng 第一 y will be the new coach."

"Killme Cheng? The butcher?"

"You got it."

"They want us to lose, Woral," Mellor said. "We had a meet with the MEG CEO. He's behind all this."

"Got the blink for next game," Morales said. "You're not gonna like it. New rule. *No surrender.*"

"On flags?" Woral asked.

"You didn't hear me. I said *no surrender*: anywhere, anytime, anybody."

"That means massacre," Mellor said.

"They can't do this!" Woral cried out, the pain, the fear and the shock taking him. "It's him, isn't it. They want *HIM* to lose!"

"We don't know that for sure, Woral," the coach said.

"I do. Big hero, Ayrian Mellor! Too big. That's why this is happening!"

"That why you threw the last game?" Mellor said. "Zhang get to you?"

Mellor, knowing he was indeed the cause, turned to leave the room. On his way out Woral's hoarse, drugged, burnt voice shouted again.

"I'm not dyin' for you!"

In the hallway outside Mellor halted and leaned against the wall. After a minute Morales joined him.

"You shouldn't have missed practice last week. What's the real story?"

"You don't believe me? I told you I went with Li to Zealand."

"Where in all the zones is Zealand? Why didn't Li Na come back? You do something stupid? You can't fight Zhang. You can't even make him mad. You got any idea how powerful he is? Look what he did to me. Killme Cheng's takin' over! Is Woral right? You getting arrogant?"

"It's more than that. Let's get outa here."

The two started down the hall to the locker room, Mellor still dressed in BATL gear. He angled toward his locker to change, have a shower, wash the sorrow away. Then he stopped himself and returned to Morales. He took the smaller man's arm and steered him into a closet.

"Listen to me, Pascal. I went to Zealand! I did! It's halfway around the planet. It's a kind of resort for bigshots. Way, way beyond the status of Greenland MEG. In fact, it isn't even a MEG. I think it was once an Omegan country. I met people there. Dì yī Select."

"Who are these Select? I never heard of 'em."

"They're a step above alpha. Somehow, they're changing themselves. They took Li away but not before she sang. She sang two songs. One meant for them, one for me. The first was about a mechanical doll. The second she said goodbye to me with words that meant I'd never see her again."

"By The Father, why haven't I heard of Select?"

"Remember Zhang's lobule at all?"

"Kinda."

"It's got that sign, that kind of fork on the lobule. Everyone had it in Zealand. And another thing. In Zealand they've got domes, not for people but for animals. I think they found a way to recreate the animals that died off. They're working on something called ARC, or OMEGA, or something. Ping's part of it but too scared to talk. They're using the game to distract people, both in the MEGS and in the MASS all around the planet."

"For what reason?"

AGAINST THE MACHINE: EVOLUTION • 259

"Diversion. Don't know why. Ping's my key. Gotta find out what happened to Li."

"That blink from the League. They want me tonight, soon as we land."

"Pascal? You think Woral's right? Think it's me?"

"I think this stinks. You concentrate on finding Li. I'll deal with Zhang."

"Pascal, be careful."

At the office doorway they shook hands warmly; everything in the touch, the eyes. Pascal left for the load out, there would be no debriefing tonight. Mellor arrived at his locker and began to change. Before he could finish Bolus was standing in front of him, smiling.

"Where you been, Mel?"

"Strategy session. How to deal with flame throwers."

"Listen, Mel. Game's done. We won. Otsi the rookie bagged her first flag! Otsi 'n me are goin' out. Get some of that famous corn style Mexico beer. How 'bout you too. Get your mind off this."

If only ... Mellor thought.

FORTY-SEVEN—KE HUI

With Zhang still gone on whatever his strange mission was, his absence proved an enabling one for Ke Hui Feng 第一 Ψ. She made sure to appear at the office each day, as though she were taking on tasks set her by the CEO. She checked for Cheng then remembered he had been assigned as new coach of the Raptors. She had watched the most recent BATL in Mexico MEG and knew Cheng wouldn't be back. He would have too much on his shoulders rebuilding the team. Despite their win, the introduction of flame weapons by the Aztecs had wrought havoc upon the Raptors. It had been horrid to watch and knowing, as she did, about that battle of wills in the Raptors' home office between Zhang and Ayrian Mellor 第二 α, she knew it had played itself further forward.

She resolved to be careful around Zhang but, while he was gone, she also decided to take a few liberties. She continued to use the hologram of the city, sitting within its blinking midst trying to comprehend the complexity of the system. Every Human being tracked. Even the most private of acts recorded for the examiners of the Social Enforcement Division. She knew it was not about benevolence. There was far more to the caste lobules than connection. She recognized the positives of the MEG society: no disease, no violence, no hunger. Order according to caste and training for meaningful work. Yet the overarching existence of the NET as a spectre in everyone's life subtracted from the benefits. Then there was the MASS.

Ke Hui thought, there exists a balance of haves and have nots centred around the recycling process rendering the two societies oddly symbiotic. Was the CORPORATE planning to maintain this stasis?

Then what of the MEGs? Everyone regulated by the Dì yī elite and knit together by the NET. Life consisted of living by algorithms created by the elite, the rules a miasma of rubrics. No one had any input into their lives because no one knew the limits. If a citizen either accidentally or purposefully disobeyed, there was the Social Enforcement Division. So, all was not perfect in the MEGs. She had heard of lower caste people escaping into the MASS. Higher castes were reclaimed by the Social Enforcement Division.

Yet what if caste no longer existed? Skin pigment no longer mattered, there were people of all races in power positions within the MEG. Was it training? Were they destined, as she had been, to fill their stations? Clearly the MEG was no meritocracy? Not from having overheard the exchange between Ayrian Mellor 第二 α and CEO Wei Qiang Zhang 第一 Ψ.

Algorithms were not liberating. They were, indeed, the opposite. Ke Hui began to wonder what particular actions would lead to enforcement. She was a mere fourteen years of age with an expectation of at least a hundred more. In all that time what if she made a mistake? What, precisely, *was* a mistake?

She realised she was spied upon by her *Toy*. If she could not escape or reprogram it, it would always be with her watching, listening, evaluating. Yet even without it, she was still just another of these ten million tiny lights, each one representing a person, connected to the NET, channelled by algorithms, subject to overwatch.

It came to her then in an intellectual rush. One moment she was inside the MEG hologram, looking out; the next she was outside it all, looking in, and she knew the purpose of Room 101. It was the only logical step in her oddly extended syllogism. It was time to prove it to herself. It was time to find allies.

She immediately thought of someone she knew she could trust.

The next morning, she awakened at five for her customary walk in the Don Valley Park. It was her favourite day for a walk: the weekly

nighttime rain had refreshed everything, washing it clean while bringing out colours and fragrances; even the *crispred* birds sang more
sweetly. She blinked open her *metaverse* to populate her walk with her
Replika, some jolly old friends, and a few minute distortions of the
analogue world to pleasantly distract herself.

Still, yesterday's thoughts would not disperse. At the end of her walk
she took the escalator up to Bloor Street and composed a statement to
Manager Alphonse Mangione 第二 α, Social Enforcement Division.
She would attend at his Headquarters within the hour. A reply came
back quickly. *Mr. Mangione is busy this morning.* She composed her
own reply. *Not too busy to make time for Toronto MEG CEO. We shall
meet at the Queen's Park. Advise Ms. Qui Ling Yeong 第一 Ψ.* Then Ke
Hui set her correspondence on auto and had it refuse all communiques
from either Manger. She travelled the moving sidewalks west.

As she ascended the steps to the front entrance, somehow this
building had taken on a threatening appearance. Knowing what she
knew now, it looked so heavy and strange. She was halted by
Enforcement officers. Politely the Human tried to explain entry was
restricted. A simple flash of the digital *sigil*, an azure T on an argent
shield, indicated her status. She was escorted into the building.

There to meet her was Mangione himself resembling, as ever, a
sophisticated Silicon. Pale skin though sallower than pearl, wraparounds in dark mode. Beside him, silent but furious, was Ms. Yeong.
While Mangione spoke in that strange voice, sounding like a perpetual
whisper, Ms. Yeong simply hummed and hawed agreement. Ke Hui
held her ground even as the oily Manager pushed inside her personal
space attempting intimidation.

"What are you doing here?" he said, insulting her by not employing
her name, caste, and rank. "You cannot simply flit in and out of MEG
buildings, particularly this one, on whatever whim has taken you!"

It was as close to a shout, Ke Hui thought, as Mangione would
ever get.

"I am ready to inspect Room 101, Manager Mangione Dì èr alpha.
Ms. Yeong informed me I should not return until I knew more. I do now.
I understand your work there. I would like to see that work for myself."

She turned right and walked directly toward 101's doors. Two pillars on either side suddenly came to life, transforming into security Silicons, joining together to block her way. Mangione hadn't moved but the smirk on his face dissolved as Ke Hui stood before them.

"Tuì xià," Ke Hui said, ordering the Silicons to stand down. They immediately complied, returning to each side of the door becoming featureless pillars once again.

"How do you know that language?" Mangione joined her, his pallid face suddenly flushed. Ms. Yeong, attempting to speak, simply spluttered, and actually tottered on her five-inch stilettos.

"I am acting CEO, Mr. Mangione, Ms. Yeong," Ke Hui said, deliberately leaving off their titles. "I am effective while Mr. Zhang Dì yī Select is away on MEG business. Surely you received the memo. Then again, why would you?"

"This is highly irregular," Ms. Yeong said.

"Shall we enter?" Ke Hui said politely.

"You have no idea, Miss Feng—" Mangione said.

"Full title, Mr. Mangione Dì èr alpha. You are, after all, Dì èr, your caste is *after* the first order, while I am Dì yī, before *all others* in order, quality, and social significance."

"And me?" Ms. Yeong was beginning to look rather old.

"You are Select. Why are you here? You no longer have significance in this MEG. I am relieving you. Leave now!"

A shattered Ms. Yeong tottered off on her heels, no longer looking so perfect.

"I apologize Miss Hui Feng Dì yī Select." Mangione replied, nearly choking in exasperation.

"No further Secrets, Mr. Mangione," Ke Hui said. Having seen Ms. Yeong, she wished she had worn her high heel pumps to offer herself more authority. As it was, her officious persona would have to do.

"Before we enter," Mangione said, "please explain what you think it is we do here in 101."

In the face of his challenge, Ke Hui fought to maintain her composure. The answer was, after all, based on her own conjecture. Yet it had to be the *only* reply. There was no other way for the MEG to wholly control its citizens.

"Brain research, Manager Mangione," Ke Hui said.

"That is no answer," he said, a sneer on his face.

"Alright then, to put it bluntly, you and your Dì yī scientists ... they could only be Dì yī alphas for this kind of delicate work ... are conducting experiments in *thought control*. You have the power of Social Enforcement when a MEG citizen does wrong. You have your horrid arrays of punishment. What you do not have is what people truly *think*. Unless they act out, compose in text, or speak their thoughts, you have no real power over them. That is what is missing in this civilization, yes? The power to discover what you consider an aberration *before* it happens rather than after. The ability to channel Human thought as you do with Silicons and their algorithms. You want to make a race of Human bots. At the very least you want thought control of the Human population."

"Very astute of you Miss Hui Feng. I assume Mr. Zhang has decided to trust you with this information. You realize it is most secret and cannot be repeated to anyone outside the top echelons of MEG government."

"Of course, Mr. Mangione. Why would you even have to inform me? Dear Mr. Zhang made it very clear and insisted I visit your site to see, for myself, the work in progression. Shall we enter?"

"Did he give you the pass code, Miss Feng?" Mangione said. Ke Hui thought as quickly as she could and deduced an answer.

"Qǐng kāi mén!" she said in what she hoped would work, remembering Zhang had told her the truly important operations of the MEG were over-ridden by Mandarin.

The doors, a black and white yin yang moon gate, dilated open, revealing marble floors and walls, grey with black veins in a hollow, high ceilinged reception room. Immediately on their entry a female Dì èr rose from a chair to greet them, her shoe heels echoing around the stone space as she approached. She was a fine example of officialdom: her hair up, her lab coat gleaming white, her eyes sharp behind their wraparounds.

"May I be of assistance, Mr. Mangione?"

"Thank you, Miss Rose. This is our MEG assistant CEO, Miss Ke Hui Feng Dì yī Select, here on an unofficial visit. There is no need to accompany us. I, myself, will be taking Miss Feng through the research space."

"Miss Feng requires an F/rom security stamp, sir. I would be pleased to administer it."

"Perhaps not this time, Miss Rose. This is, as I said, an unofficial excursion. Miss Feng will not likely use the stamp again."

"On the contrary, Manager Mangione," Ke Hui said. "I intend to visit often. This is such an exciting opportunity to glimpse the inner workings of Toronto MEG's amalgamation of the Social Enforcement Division and the Biomedical Division."

If Miss Rose missed the tinge of sarcasm, Mangione did not. Saying nothing, he escorted Ke Hui around a wall separating reception from the laboratories. They passed into a change room and Miss Rose helped Ke Hui don her bio-suit while Mangione dressed in his. They entered the laboratory section through an airlock, protecting everything inside from the least particles of external foreign bodies. Because Mangione had not warned her, Ke Hui was deeply shocked. Cubicle after cubicle, perhaps two hundred in the laboratory, each with a bed, a chair and a wall of arcane dials, buttons, screens, and surgical equipment. Each of the patients lay or sat motionless, eyes opaque. Each patient was missing a portion of skull, removed, and replaced with wires, receptors, tubes, and other tools Ke Hui did not recognize. She could hear a man's panting, then the stifled cries from other cubicles. However, those Mangione chose to show her had little activity, though they were horrid enough. There was a smell of ozone and other sharp, chemical aromas.

Is this what the brain smells like, Ke Hui wondered, fighting back the choking in her throat. Mangione must have known the effects on the newly initiated. He began a running comment as they moved from one cubicle to another, stopping at each in what seemed to Ke Hui the longest intervals of her life.

"This is our NET neuroscience department," Mangione said. "Operating under the assumption that different parts of the brain have separate functions, our neuroscientists have made remarkable progress toward understanding how the brain works. Vision, for instance, happens at the back of the head while tissue at the top of the brain sends commands to the muscles to move the body, and note that small structure there just beneath the ear of this subject. See it? Yes. This small part has the responsibility of recognizing faces. All these regions are made of grey matter, a type of tissue covering the surface of the brain. Beneath, however, lies the white matter, which stretches in fiber bundles between regions of grey matter. White matter carries messages all over the brain."

Mangione walked as he talked, peering into each cubicle he passed, ensuring Ke Hui did as well. He was clearly attempting to distress her. She constantly found herself frantically rubbing her thumb and fingers. She kept her hand low so Mangione would not notice.

"To comprehend brain function is to recognize the brain is literally a network. It's not a metaphor. Our scientists examine the brain's connections rather than study them region by region. Every person tends to have singular, particular patterns of functional connectivity. People's brains tend to pulse in slightly different patterns. We need to understand how individual brain sections represent information *and* how that information is conveyed from one segment to another.

"But why?" Ke Hui asked. Thus far, Mangione had avoided any talk of thought control.

"We have, using deep brain stimulation, been able to construct or overlay xeno-pathways to the brain from the NET. That, of course, is how we primarily communicate now."

"How did you achieve that?"

"Once we realized we were dealing with a biological network, we attempted to replicate and, in some cases, actually use the white matter in our implementations."

"So, what is the necessity for thought control?"

"Miss Feng, surely you realize all Humans are different, even the crispred varieties. We cannot have a functioning society with millions of different interpretations regarding proper behaviours and rule of law."

"I realize there are social rules, Mr. Mangione, and that people might break those rules. Trying to implant brain infiltrators to control a person's thoughts is not a Humanitarian response. We are not Silicons, Sir, we are individual Humans."

"We will not survive if we continue as we are, Miss Feng. We require a hive mentality rather than individuality ... a CORPORATE intelligence, if you will. Every time a MEG citizen disrupts the collective power of the NET, that disturbance ripples out causing further disorders. We want to be able to upload perceptions to the brain and inculcate our intelligence with precepts we accept as truths. Yes, there have been failures by the score. The Human brain is so complex."

"Mr. Mangione, I have seen enough. I find the atmosphere in here quite unpleasant." It was an understatement. She was nauseous, nervous, and troubled. She tried to keep her voice level while she hid her persistent thumb and fingers. "Let us continue outside if you don't mind."

"Your own perceptions are on a delay, Miss Feng," Mangione said as they exited through the echoing antechamber. He wore a slight smile now, aware of her feelings despite her attempts to conceal them. "Turning photons into sight, aerosolized molecules into smells or air pressure and fluctuations into sounds requires billions of synaptic connections between further billions of neurons for you to perceive something specific. How simple it would be if we could find a way to allow every citizen the peace of not having to make decisions. We are building better bodies now, bodies of Silicon alloy parts. Our life span is increasing as we replace our biological parts with more efficient printed parts from the heart to the heel to the tongue to the backbone. What we have not found is a way to replace the brain. Even if our scientists could re-create intelligence by simulating every molecule in the brain, they won't have found the underlying principles of cognition. *Our minds*, Miss Feng, are the difference between us and Silicon androids."

It was difficult for Ke Hui to assimilate this. Yet the situation boiled down to one element: the need of the CORPORATE to control every person through thought control. She knew this horrid feature of Humankind had been attempted historically: religion, rank, caste, race, propaganda, indoctrination, even physical alteration. Could she represent what this monster Mangione was propagating? Could she become a hive queen?

She did not think so.

"Really, all this is redundant with ARC."

"Oh?" Ke Hui said. "What is ARC?"

FORTY-EIGHT—MELLOR

Mexico MEG was larger than Toronto MEG. It had taken longer for Mexico MEG to arise from the violence when the CORPORATE fought for universal control. It seemed the MASS in old Mexico City had been huge in Omegan times. The MASS no longer lived close to the MEG because of the mountains. The MEG possessed interlocking *chitin/crystalline* domes, but the domes covered the centre of an enormous valley set amid the Sierra Madres.

Their group, Ayrian Mellor 第二 α, Otsi'tsa Zaharie 大众 o, Bolus Kimathi 第三 ∂ and Ping Wang Min 第四 Ω, all now in civilian clothes, was perhaps the most diverse one could find inside any MEG. As the four entered a Dì sān nightclub nearby the Mexico BATL dome, they found a frenzy of colour and noise, the dance floor undulating with people and some rich, wild *banda* sounding as though the music came from the air around them.

Clothing was the usual mix of high fashion worn by slumming Dì èr, while the hundreds of Dì sān wore lesser fashions in multiple hues and forms. Many had found ways to make themselves shimmer with metallic dust applied to their skins. *Cerveza* was the common drink though there were more expensive escapes. No self-respecting Dì yī would be seen in a place like this. The Dì yī could employ their own *Metaverses* either singly or in groups to enjoy what this sim and stim did for lesser beings. The raw sim and stim flowed bountifully in the crowded club called *Eagle and Snake*.

The group awaited a table up off the dance floor, close enough to enjoy the gyrations, far enough to give security time to stop any Mexico MEGan from accosting them. Mellor leaned down to speak to Otsi, who seemed mesmerized by the action.

"Saved my ass today; all of us."

"Thanks, Mel. It was clear all the way. Glad I was skimming sand."

"Guts or what," Bolus said. "I'm buyin' for her."

Mellor placed his hands on her shoulders, a small intimacy amid the cacophony, and looked directly into her eyes, his own shimmering in the lights. He could not, once again, believe her so small, yet feeling the muscle at her neck he had no doubt she could take care of herself.

"Coulda got yourself killed, Otsi."

"Didn't though."

As he let her go, he noted her eyes shining with pride and joy. She'd had no idea he'd sent her as a diversion, preventing the Aztecs from bringing forward more men. He had been sure she would not come back, being too young, too inexperienced, too ready to prove herself. And yet, somehow, she had weaved through every field of fire trained upon her as she'd stayed low and went for the Aztec banner. She must have heard bullets whizzing by. She must have known the Aztecs had broken the Raptors' defence. Yet she had not hesitated and, with her skills, courage, and luck, she had made a difference this day.

"Try that move again I'll kill you myself," Mellor said. He could not forget he had sacrificed her amid the Aztecs' fiery onslaught. Then a hostess appeared, Dì sān of course, wearing little more than green metallic flakes and a thumb ring to take her guests' credits. Some called them *bits,* particularly in the MASS, though the reason for that was buried in history. The hostess took one look at Bolus and recognized him. When the titan had been here before, Mellor couldn't recall, then realized that though he himself was famous, the gigantic Bolus, in person, made a bigger impression.

"Bolus Kimathi! You people shouldn't be waiting. Please. Come with me."

She led them to a celebrity second floor booth, out of reach of fans, though they responded to those who recognized them with waves and smiles. No one seemed upset they had just lost a month's rewards. When they saw Mellor, they held up the Raptor hand sign, begging for autographs, his seal AM 第二 α on their F-ROMS.

"They love us now!" Bolus said, laughing. "Even if we did beat 'em!"

"They don't know the cost," Mellor replied. "Think they care? What's with you tonight?"

"Flamethrowers, Bolus. We weren't even told. We were set up by the CORPORATE. They really want me gone."

"Listen, Mel, try t' get your mind off it for a while. The kid deserves a celebration. An' your guru guy seems a bit overwhelmed."

"Now *he* knows the cost. Everyone who's a fan of BATL should be given a tour of the after-game med rooms. I don't think it would be so entertaining anymore."

"Wanna dance, Sir?"

It was Otsi, standing up at their oval table cheerful as a child.

"No," Mellor replied, then recovered himself. "Thanks anyway, Otsi."

"You dance, Otsi?" Bolus asked.

"Course I dance," she said.

"Take the egghead here and dance him. Looks like he needs it."

Ping was goggle eyed. He could not stop watching the air dancers: men and women in the whipped air of twelve hundred horsepower fans. It was amazing what they could accomplish. Normal dance identified six dynamic qualities: sustained, percussive, swinging, suspended and collapsed but these dancers did all of that with no base, no floor. They could fly to the top of the wind tunnel then dive out of sight, appear to be standing in one place in air then turn a pirouette, then find various forms of elastic energy to express the madness of the *banda*. The tubes themselves kept changing colours, the dancers' skin-tight outfits breezing with buffets of aether.

"But I've never danced," Ping said.

"Take him, Otsi. Bolus and I need a few minutes."

Otsi understood immediately. She escorted the reluctant Ping down to the dance floor. This was made simple using an escalator which opened beneath them extending from their second level booth, over the heads of the crowd. In the crowd Ping stood out like a bat among birds, his dancing a series of auto-jerks counterpointed by Otsi's fluidity.

"Hard one today. Got you down?" Bolus said.

"More than the game, Bolus."

They watched Ping dance. Together they laughed.

"Look at him. Time of his life," Mellor said.

"More Sili than Human," Bolus said.

Mellor's laugh dissolved.

"Li's gone, Bolus."

"Jokin', right? What ya mean?"

"What if I just quit. They want me out. Told Pascal and me in a meeting. Threatened us, right to our faces. I shoulda killed that guy then."

"Now you're talkin' crazy."

"Not if it gets her back. This guy Zhang—"

Otsi and Ping returned, Otsi supporting a limping Ping.

"Twisted his foot," Otsi said.

"Ouch! But such f-f-fun!"

"Come on, Ayrian Mellor? One dance?"

"I said no thanks!"

His retort shattered Otsi's mood.

"Sorry," he said.

"His girl's been taken," Bolus said.

"Oh. She left you?" Otsi said.

"Just gone. Taken away in front of me and I could do nothing. I can't explain it."

"Things change, I guess, though why would they do that?" Otsi said, trying to find a way back to the camaraderie of a few minutes previous. She was unaccustomed to these hardened men and their ways.

"Something call ARC," he said. "I don't know what it means."

"P-perhaps I c-can help," Ping said.

"How?"

"We sh-sh-should leave," Ping said, peering around nervously.

"But we just got here!" Otsi clearly did not want to leave. She had never experienced the adrenalin rushes she had had that day: from terrified rookie to banner seizing hero then finally to the freedom, fluidity and turmoil of the *Eagle and Snake*.

"Leave it, Otsi," Bolus said, as they departed the club. He kept Otsi lagging behind Ping and Mellor. Those two were already out at a ground level street with its crowds of people, store fronts, peddlers, gliding walkways, foamstone walls and crystal trees glimmering in holo-ad lights. Ping turned to Mellor and steered him into the shadow of a foil overhang.

"This is g-g-good. I'll t-take you offline."

"They'll know, the NET will know."

"It's not a p-p-perfect system. B-b-blips sometimes."

Mellor could not help himself. He reacted to the sudden isolation amid so many people passing on the street.

"Weird disconnect. Just like Zealand," he said. His voice was unsteady.

"I know. W-we c-can w-w-walk now. S-s-safe."

They moved back into the lighted street and onto a gliding walkway. People were everywhere. Bullet tube trains swished by above them. There was a band playing ancient *mariachi* for tourists. Street vendors sold trinkets or Mexican flavoured food wafers. Mellor could not stop thinking how different this was from the staid Toronto MEG.

"Can you find out what's happened to her?" Mellor asked.

"I'll m-make inquiries, search data banks, it could take some time."

"But you can't go online."

"Not as m-myself. An-n-nother identity."

"But we're tracked."

"It's called spoofing, remember? Births. R-r-registrations. Visitors from other MEGs. It's easy when you know the system. I'm concerned Li Na m-might be g-g-gone."

"You mean dead?"

"Oh no, n-not that way. Not d-dead. Gone Select. For ARC."

"ARC? The project she was working on?"

"There's t-trouble, Mel. S-Silicons. C-c-climate. The M-m-Mass. It's all g-g-getting out of c-c-control. They're leaving."

"Zhang? Li? All those Select? Leaving for Zealand?"

"No, m-my friend. They're l-leaving the planet."

FORTY-NINE—CHENG

Having returned from Mexico MEG, reputedly a dirty, dangerous place not completely sealed from its MASS, the Raptors were given thorough examinations. Upon landing, every member was probed and prodded, run through scans, and had to provide blood and urine samples. Even for Ping Wang Min 第四 Ω the procedures proved difficult. He knew the test results would come back showing he had spoofed the NET successfully, yet he worried about his enhancements somehow accidentally showing up. Once the team had arrived at the barracks, he found a meditation room. With the clamour and commotion of three hundred arrivals he considered it best to make himself scarce: out of sight, out of mind … literally.

The remainder of the team was given an hour to organize themselves and dress for a surprise full team exercise. Mellor, as team Commander, tried to locate coach Morales, questioning the wisdom of taking a burned, shredded team into training. Morales was nowhere to be found. According to trainers the coach had been escorted off immediately upon landing. No one had heard from him since.

Mellor mourned the disappearance of both his lover and now, his friend. He was not his usual self, proven by his panic in the desperate Aztec game. Normally, he would have adapted. It was true that without Otsi, Raptors would have been annihilated. Without her courage, or perhaps her naivete, the team would have lost any chance of World Conquest.

Yet he found himself distressed and disillusioned by the machinations of Zhang, and furious at the MEG society he'd once thought the ultimate in civilisation.

Under the BATL dome, the team mingled around centre field: they talked, they sat, they gazed around. The place looked different. The flat, dimmed light glimmered off the field; the field hard packed earth with only a few foamstone ridges at one end for deployments. The bareness accentuated the dome's gargantuan size. Every fighter felt like an insect in that huge, half lit arena. To one side of the field nearest the players' entrance, Mellor, Bolus, Otsi and a heavily bandaged Woral had gathered around a holo tactics table.

"So, tell me again why I'm here?" Woral asked. It was more a complaint than question.

"Sorry Woral. Your meds working?"

"I'll be fine. I need rest. So?"

"Just look at the holo," Mellor said. "Looks like next game's terrain."

"Strategy?" Bolus grumbled. "Where's Coach?"

"Not here," Mellor said.

"Huh?"

"Escorted away when we landed."

"You think the League?" Woral said. Mellor knew it was true but did not want to set Woral off again. He was rescued by the light, excited voice of Otsi.

"What's goin' on. Look there!" she said.

Accompanied by armed Silicons, these ones entirely robotic soldier droids, Yong Jun Cheng 第一 y appeared in on a floating platform. He wore an ornate Raptors uniform beribboned with former BATL honours. He looked ridiculous. Still, no one laughed as they gathered.

"Zones. It's the butcher," Bolus said.

"The who?" Otsi asked.

"Our new coach and general manager," Mellor said.

"Uses players as cannon fodder," Bolus said. "Nicknamed *Killme Cheng*. League turfed him out, I thought for good."

"What's with those Silis?" Woral said. "They're armed!"

"You never seen that before?" Otsi said. "I keep forgetting, you guys don't visit the MASS."

The platform halted at centre field. The Silicons deployed around it. They were armed with neural whips, pulse weapons and gas grenades. Cheng stood at a lectern. He was taking no chances in a space filled with killers.

"Take a knee," he said. The players rumbled, confused by his appearance. They remained standing, refusing Cheng's initial order. The Silicons raised their weapons.

"You heard me!" Cheng shouted. "Or d'you want to fight these droids?"

Reluctantly, the players obeyed. With order restored, Cheng shouted again.

"Coach Pascal Morales Dì èr alpha has retired!"

"What? Ye're lying?" Bolus cried, his outburst matched by the others. The rumble became cacophony. The fighters stood. Some began to walk away. Mellor and Bolus advanced to the platform. The Silicons closed ranks.

"Morales could not abide the new rules, Cheng said. I can. You're going to need me. You haven't done so well lately, have you? Now you got San Francisco Giants in the semi, and Xian dragons if you make the final. Mellor stood. Facing Cheng, Cheng with the advantage of height, Mellor kept his voice strong. It was time to take care of his team. He stared up at Cheng speaking firmly, though not antagonistically.

"If I'm right, we edged them with banner wins. They gotta come here."

"That's where you're wrong, Mellor. Xian MEG Dragons have a perfect score, 9 victories with one game in hand. You can't equal them. The Raptors will face the Giants for the semi-final. And further news for all of you … the next game will be *no surrender* along with the other rule changes!"

Mellor stared up at Cheng, lost for words, knowing he had been outmanoeuvred by Zhang. It all came down to Zhang. *Changes*, he'd said. Again, the heedless fury since losing Li in Zealand overwhelmed Mellor. Then he caught a blink. Contact on the NET. He watched

Cheng chatter on, over the message. No one had any idea Mellor was receiving.

"Mel, it's Pascal. Don't respond. I'm out of the MEG. Didn't want to be tracked ..." There was a gap in reception: kaleidoscopic angles wavered to a null point. The message was lost in swirls. Then it returned.

"—gone to ground. Understand? Ask Otsi. Gone to Willis Mackenzie. Otsi knows. We need to meet."

Mellor nudged Bolus.

"Just got a message from Coach. After this, bring Otsi. Equipment bay entrance. I'll bring Ping. Got to get out to the MASS. We need Otsi to guide us."

"You nuts, Mel?"

Killme Cheng descended from the platform, the Silicons' weapons raised.

"And for those who can't obey, there's garbage disposal in mid-continent. Yes? Planet regeneration. Anyone? Just stand up."

No one moved.

"I thought not. Now, a new fighting style for the Raptors. Squad leaders report to

me. The rest of you, form up in your squads. I said NOW, people!"

The team scattered, finding their comrades, grumbling about the changes, worried about the next BATL, sure they would be sacrificed. Meanwhile, Cheng approached Mellor and Woral.

"Well gentlemen, a new era in BATL. I brook no cravens on my teams! For instance, you Woral Patel Dì èr beta ... your psych reports ..." Cheng turned on Woral, the power of his presence destroyed what confidence the man possessed.

"Sir, I'll be there. Whatever you need," he said.

"I'm sure you will. Our strategy for the Giants will be to make a wall on our twenty, take them as they come."

"Cheng, you know that won't work," Mellor said. "What if they do the same? Slow game. Fans won't like it. Penalties for delay."

"But they *will* come, Mellor. It's entertainment, yes? As Mr. Zhang said. *A game.* Forgotten that, have you?"

"It's fixed? The game's fixed?"

Cheng turned his back on Mellor, taking Woral with him.

"Patel. I'd like a word with you."

On his way to meet everyone at the load out, Mel received a surprising insistent *blink*. When he blinked on the message, he was shocked to have Ke Hui Feng 第一 Ψ, as a hologram in his wraparounds. He remembered her as the kid who had accompanied Zhang to the meeting that changed everything. Immediately, he was suspicious.

"Hello, Miss Feng," he said, ignoring the ritual of titles.

"Hello Commander Mellor," she replied, he could feel the admiration in her vocal tones. Still, her attachment to Zhang raised his reservations.

"What can I do for you, Miss Feng? I'm a bit busy."

"I know. I've been following you on the city holo since you got back. I am so sorry about this last match. It was horrid. So many burnt. Why didn't the Raptors have those flame things?"

"It was a set-up, Miss Feng. Your friend Zhang—"

"Commander, he is not my friend, I can assure you."

"Where are you?"

"The security office in the BATL dome. I need to speak with you, in person."

"Why? What could you want from me? How do I know you're not Zhang's spy?"

"Listen to me. I can't really say until I can block us from the NET. Can you come get me? I don't think I could find my way in this maze."

"Again, what do you want?"

"A way into the MASS. Please, Commander, this is important to me. I've been left in a vacuum of ignorance. I need answers. I'm tagging my Toy—"

"Your what?"

"Sorry, a nickname. My Silicon servant. I'm tagging it as myself, so the NET follows it."

It took a moment for Mellor to reply. When he did, he'd made a crucial decision. If she *was* a spy, he would have to kill her. He recognized then that he'd become different. Murder this kid? The emotions he used in battle were appearing in his character. The war had moved from beneath a dome to his *other* life. He mentally shook himself. He would *not* kill a child, even if she were a spy. Yet if not, then she would possess access to everything closed to him. Her lobule said she was Select. Ironically, in a few moments he would be joining his friends and leaving the MEG. If she wanted into the MASS, away from the MEG's protections, why had she come to him? Was it coincidence, fate, or simply the effectiveness of the NET and the MEG's spy craft? Somehow, Mellor knew this was going to change everything once again.

"I need answers too," Mellor said. "Maybe you can help. Okay. So, go through security, I'm sure you'll have no trouble, and take the first hallway on your left. I'll meet you."

"Certainly," she said, trying for confidence, though her voice was breathless. Mellor smiled. Maybe she was just an ordinary kid.

All BATL equipment, upon return to the MEG, was loaded onto float platforms by the team's armourers and trainers, then sent down a long, irradiated tunnel in case of deadly microbes. By the time it reached the interior, the logistics people would offload and store the equipment in various home locations. Bolus, Otsi and Ping stood amidst the commotion. Ping was agog at the smell of oiled weapons, the structured actions of the offloading Silicons and the hollow echoes of the tunnels.

"Th-th-this is th-th-th-thrilling!"

"Yeah," Bolus replied. "They're all too busy to notice us. Here comes Mel. Hey, what's this? Who's the kid?"

Mellor and Ke Hui quickly joined them.

"Safe here, right?" Mellor asked Ping. "Those blips in the system?"

"Why y-y-yes! You learn qu-qu-quickly! B-b-but who is this?"

"I'd like to know that too. This kid's kinda fancy for where we're goin'," Bolus said, facing Mellor directly.

"She's Select. Says she can help us. She wants to see the MASS for herself."

During the exchange Otsi came close to the girl, whispering: "Not sure who you are but know this: you a spy, I'll kill you."

"Yes, of course, I'm sorry, I just really—" Ke Hui was terrified. She could barely speak. These people were killers. Even this girl so close to her size. She took lives for a living and, Ke Hui was sure, was good to her word.

"Easy, Otsi, she's tryin' to help," Mellor said.

"What if she's a spy?" Otsi replied.

"I don't believe she is. Ke Hui, meet Otsi. Sometimes, Otsi, you gotta take a chance like you did in Mexico MEG. She's taking one as well. She's gonna leave all her MEG protections behind."

"So why would she do that?" Otsi replied.

"Please," Ke Hui said, "I exist, don't act as if I'm not here. I'm doing this to understand *why* there *is* a MEG and a MASS. Why are we not all together? We're all Humans. I'm being taught to become MEG CEO, but my lessons are incomplete. The Select are hiding things from me, for two of which I've deduced answers, and neither solution is moral or pleasant."

Otsi turned again to Ke Hui.

"Just remember what I said—" Otsi said, then Mellor interrupted: "Ke Hui, this big lump here—"

"I know. Bolus Kimathi. I hope you'll give me a chance to prove myself. I don't know this man, however. Dì sì Omega? You're the first I've ever met.

"I am P-P-Ping. That is P-Ping Wang Min D-D-Dì sì omega."

"And I am Ke Hui Feng Dì yī Alpha Select."

"So, we gotta move. Can't hang here. You said in the dome ..." Bolus said. He was nervous.

"Pascal said, 'gone to ground'. He said to ask Otsi."

"Don't make sense," Bolus said. "Yes, it does," Otsi said, interrupting. "How? Gone to Willis?" Mellor said. "He lives in the MASS."

"He the one got Otsi here?" Bolus asked.

"Yeah, that's him. Is your coach okay?" Otsi asked.

"He dropped off the NET," Mellor said.

"You can't drop—" Bolus said.

"We can. Ping?"

"Yes, of c-c-course."

Ping took them offline.

"Zones! This can't happen outside the game!" Bolus said with a tinge of fear. Otsi didn't react. She was shocked the giant seemed so concerned and the girl, Ke Hui, was not.

"You don't feel it?" Bolus said. He was suddenly a frightened child.

"What about you?" Otsi said, pointing at Ke Hui.

"I've been trained; most Dì yī are. Why aren't *you* upset?" she asked.

"Used to it. I've only been connected a couple of months. Honestly, I don't like bein' on it. Too much white noise. Oh, and Willis is more than you think. Guess it's time to say this. He joined the resistance."

It was as if a bomb had been dropped.

"What?" Mellor said.

"Later," Otsi said.

"You're right," Mellor said. "Let's move. Stand here too long it's suspicious. Otsi, what are you sayin'."

"I'm sayin' let's move. Can we do that, Ping? Are we invisible?"

"To the NET we are, yes."

They walked through the fibreblock tunnel. There were huge Silicons unloading the transports. Massive derricks, their mechanical arms gently lifted one of the Sweeper vehicles. Something dark dripped from the Sweeper's chassis.

"Okay," Mellor said, "now what are you really sayin', Otsi?"

"Just that you guys live in a bubble. War in a dome. There's a real war out there in the real world, and it's awful. Don't starve, Silicon killers get you."

"Father of the Cosmos, is this true?" Ke Hui asked.

"They're just Silis!" Bolus said.

"Like the ones you saw back there with Cheng? You seen that before, big boy? Never actually been to the MASS, have you?" Otsi said.

"Course not. I'm just a Dì sān delta. Not permitted outside the MEG," Bolus said, lying to her.

"Do you never think about any of this?" Ke Hui said. "The castes, the CORPORATE, the MEG way of life? There is a dominion, making all of us—"

"Pawns," Mellor said.

"I don't get it." Bolus said.

"Nothin' Bo. 'Nother game."

"We're fighting back. Willis is a leader," Otsi said.

"Resistance?" Ke Hui said.

"It's t-true," Ping said. "As I mentioned p-p-previously, th-that's why the Select and the ARC."

"What's this guy talkin' about?" Bolus said. This was not within his realm of experience.

"Otsi," Mellor said, "can you get us to Willis?"

"In the MASS?" Bolus was for the moment perplexed even further.

"Need transport," Otsi said. "Need a way out without someone knowing."

"Ping?" Mellor said.

But it was Ke Hui who spoke. For the first time her voice sounded confident.

"I can do that for you. But if we're offline too long, the NET will suspect."

"Chance we'll have to take," Mellor said.

"Gotta change clothes," Otsi said. "You guys'll stand out lookin' like this."

"Th-th-th-this isn't s-s-s-safe," Ping said, his hands seeking something to organize.

That brought a look from Bolus. Whatever had troubled him, he was loyal. He saw his place as Mellor's bodyguard, on or off the field of BATL, as well as his best friend. He said: "Leave the clothes to me. We just gotta get to Recycling."

"B-b-b-but someone will see us! It isn't s-s-s-safe!"

"What's fun in safe?" Bolus said. "Come on, little man, let's have some fun!"

Bolus' clap on his back nearly sent Ping to the ground.

"Z-z-z-z-zones!" Ping managed to cough as he tried to straighten up.

FIFTY-OTSI

Once **Bolus had** got past the existential panic of no NET, he had proven the key to their way out. Before the CORPORATE had found him for BATL, before his multiple implants, enhancements, training, and indoctrination, he had been an Overseer in the Recycling Division. He was Dì sān gamma, one step up from the MASS and the red polymer lobule. His job had been a simple one: to shepherd incoming Dàzhòng traders toward their proper delivery slots for different types of recycling materials. By the time he had illicitly entered the MEG, he was twelve years old and nearly two metres tall. Willis Mackenzie, then coach of the Toronto MEG Raptors, had heard of this kid in the recycling pits from Division Manager Alf Broadbent 第一 α. Mackenzie's greatest talent was finding and developing the talents he saw in others. Broadbent had not been wrong. The kid had everything but the training to make him a super star.

Before his discovery, however, Bolus Kimathi 第二 y had enjoyed his simple life, mixing often with the Dàzhòng employees of the MASS Recycling merchants while the merchants paid their respects (and their bribes, particularly *homemade* MASS foods) to the rotund Broadbent. Bolus' interaction with Dàzhòng workers had made him popular among them and they had, in their unguarded moments, let loose the knowledge that there were more ways in and out of the MEG than even the MEG Managers knew.

It did not take long for Bolus to lead the intrepid little group of conspirators through a secret, unused tunnel into the reek and rumble of Recycling. And it did not take long for some of the workers to recognize Kimathi and Mellor. Within a half hour the five had been provided ordinary MASS attire from the clothing recyclables.

Once dressed, the group looked like a menagerie of clowns. Bolus appeared poured into his clothing, the seams tearing each time he moved, whereas Ke Hui and Otsi looked lost in theirs. Everyone wore a hat or cap to conceal their lobules as much as they could. They rode a freighter drone out through a seldom used gateway and onto the 401 trail. There, the proud owner of the drone drove them to his compound, a former Omegan prison west of the MEG at a place called Milton, where the owner handed over the drone, thanks to a generous payment from Ke Hui. At first the man had been reluctant, but Ke Hui 's offering of a pinky-finger ring, worth more than five year's wages to him, convinced him.

Ping took on the duty of piloting the drone directly south toward Ham, guided by Otsi. The machine glided above the MASS slums, a maze of low structures, the high ones already demolished and recycled. With the weather and lack of technology they had never been safe or convenient to inhabit. What the four observed was a layer of dust beneath which were a deadly mix of epoxied and metal roofs, hardform shacks, cracked solar foils, and the inevitable bricks and blocks. Neighbourhoods had become fortresses. They found hard to accept the host of Dàzhòng inhabitants going about their business amid this worst of stews, this *other* world.

"Zones! Don't believe this," Bolus said, eyes wide. He leaned out an open window.

"Real world, boys. Not some bubble," Otsi said, pleased to know something they didn't.

"How do they live?" Ke Hui asked.

"Day to day. Salvage from the city land. And dreams. Gotta dream. Gotta believe there's a way out of this," Otsi said, her true feelings emerging.

"Like you?" Bolus said, catching the emotion in her voice.

"Yeah. I'm lucky. So hard to believe I'm with you. They worship you, Mel, and you Bolus."

"And now it will be you," Mellor said, smiling. "But me?"

"Come on, Mel. I can call you that, can't I?" Otsi said, alarmed at her own familiarity.

"Course you can. You saved us all in Mexico MEG. You can call me anything you want."

"You win games, they get food. But it's more than that. Gotta have pride in something. Raptors, their team. Ayrian Mellor commands the Raptors."

"Wh-wh-where d-do I l-l-land?" Ping said. "Otsi. Help, p-p-please."

"Another half hour south. It's in a big bowl right at the end of Ontario Lake."

In a half hour they'd arrived at Ham. Unlike other parts of the MASS the place wasn't as dusty. Clearly, an old Omegan city, it formed around a huge bay separated from the lake by a ridge of land with only one opening for vessels. While much of the place had been levelled, there were still blocks upon blocks of family strongholds. Otsi recognized the old steel mills across the bay and directed Ping to land near them.

Within a few minutes Otsi was leading them through the beaten streets around the mills: old metal and cement block buildings. Children played in passages. Women lugged precious pails of water. Men laden like beasts hardscrabbled at their work. Street hawkers shouted, old solar cars rumbled by while an argument erupted between a merchant and a woman buying food, workshops clanged, a gyrobike whizzed past them.

"M-m-my w-w-word, this is like g-going b-b-back in t-t-time," Ping said.

"This is ... astonishing," Ke Hui said.

"This what you came from, Otsi? Zones, why didn't I know?" Mellor said. Slowly the extent of his former complacent, arrogant self was exposing his ignorance and shifting his nature toward a more considerate state. It was not anger or loss or pity but an increasing sense of the need for a reckoning. He thought in that instant of Zhang.

"Not here, Mel, though Willis is here. I came from a place up north as different from this as where you live. Not many people. My ancestors' land."

"Well, Otsi, now we're in it, this place smells like, I dunno, dirt, shit ..." Bolus said.

"Smells like *people*," Otsi said, "without the MEG filters."

As they moved closer to Mackenzie's compound, they noticed groups of people clustering around holo slabs. People watched scenes from an alien world. MEG advertisements appeared, completely un-attainable to them, and BATL ads as well. They were surreal, their colour and characters so at odds with the dun costumed people saun-tering by or stopping to watch. Another world, Mellor thought again.

"Those people, those holo vid slabs," he said.

"Nobody's connected. Their way to the Net," Otsi said.

"Zones! Unreal," Bolus said.

"Don't use that word here. If you haven't noticed, we're in one."

That simple yet obvious statement stopped them all in their tracks.

"B-b-but the c-c-CORPORATE?" Ping asked.

"Not here. Just their Silis. Sometimes observation drones. That's it."

"The MASS isn't tracked," Ke Hui said.

"Where are they? The drones. Who does the work?"

"Look around, Bolus. Do our own work here," Otsi said.

"No Silicons," Ke Hui said. "This is brutal."

"Just hope you don't see 'em. Only come out for one reason."

"What's that?" Ke Hui asked.

"Killing. Here's our turn," Otsi said.

Otsi angled left across a tight little square surrounded by mer-chants' stalls. What they sold little resembled the variety and quality of MEG merchants. Half a block was occupied by a mechanical shop, everything from Omegan autos to ancient weapons, while across the way was a kind of food stall steaming and odoriferous. Some chairs and tables reached into the square; there was no room inside. The square was crowded and dusty. Mellor was startled seeing these crowds, the tumult of it all. Then a tussle outside a bakery. Someone had jumped the line. He could not stop wondering why these people remained a disorganized MASS. He stopped behind Otsi. He looked down at her. She seemed anxious.

"What's wrong?" he said.

"Don't feel right. Can't place it," Otsi muttered. She kept looking around.

"We bein' followed?"

"Doubt it. But spies. Lots of eyes. A reward, you report *caste* people here."

"Nobody can see our lobules. We're dressed like everybody else."

"Think you still don't stand out?" She smiled grimly.

"They got big guys out here too," Bolus said.

"Yeah, but no one like *him*," she said, nodding toward Ping. Ping was looking up at the sky.

"Th-there w-w-will be hi-sats, sky c-c-cams," Ping said.

"Yeah. Hope they don't pick us up," Otsi said. "Okay, we go in here."

They entered through the iron doors of a patched hardform tavern, grey concrete blocks and rusted tin. They were met by the scowls of toughs in the doorway. Even the biggest of them, however, lacked Mellor's or Bolus' attributes. Otsi flashed a sign with her fingers. The heavies fell back. The group continued into the bar. Chipped ceramic, scarred plastic chairs and tables, multi-patched walls without windows made the interior dim. Otsi went straight to the bar. A beefy bartender, accustomed to his clientele, recognized her.

"Otsi! Welcome back. Nice move last game. Glad ya made the big time. You're lucky. Got yer favourite stew!"

"Thanks, Paolo. Good to see you. Maybe some stew later. Willis around?"

For an instant Paulo did not respond. He took in her companions standing near the door. She could see his eyes widen with shock.

"These guys ... Otsi, that's Ayrion Mellor! My bar ..." he said.

"Keep it quiet, okay?" Otsi said.

"And Bolus Kimathi! Spill my beer! You're even bigger than ya look! Hey, have a drink. On the house, what'll it be?"

"Paulo, keep it down. Five minutes the whole MASS'll know he's here. Where's Willis?"

A soft voice emanated from a corner of the bar. A man stood, coming toward them. It was not Willis. It was, however, why they had come.

"Hello, strangers."

"Coach!" Bolus shouted.

"No names."

"We're offline. Ping can do it. Remember him?" Mellor said. His eyes silvered with tears.

"Omega man," Morales said, clearly surprised by Ping's presence.

"B-b-but that's Dì yī Select c-c-classified. How c-could you—"

"What's this?" he said, his voice harsh. "This kid is Dì yī. You trust her?"

"There wasn't much choice, Coach. She came to me. Wanted to see the MASS."

"Coincidence? That right, kid?"

"I'm sorry, sir, if my presence upsets you. I can only offer my word. I am not a spy. I am an apprentice, learning to be CEO. The only person I know, Mr. Broadbent of Recycling, who works with Dàzhòng, sorry, with those from the MASS ... oh, this is dreadful! Every word we use in the MEG seems an insult here."

"Why are you here, Coach?" Mellor asked."

"This or get killed and recycled," Morales said. "So, you got my text."

"Kill you?"

"Almost had me. Went to meet Zhang again. Good thing Willis warned me."

"You knew where Willis was?" Otsi asked.

"Right here, Otsi'tsa," a deep voice grumbled from the table in the corner. "Proud of you too." He rose and came forward. "Never seen a Striker do that skim and crawl thing. Mel order that?"

"On her own, Willis," Mellor said. "I was frozen. Zoned out. Kid's a genius."

"Yeah, I know," he said, smiling. The ancient warrior was bearded and unkempt, yet with a sharp light in his eyes. Otsi ran toward him.

"Willis! Oh, Willis, I've missed you!" Otsi said. "I thought you were gone forever once you got me in!" She embraced him ferociously, like a puppy with her trainer.

Once free of Otsi, Willis stepped toward Mellor. They had a bond which few could measure. Willis had been the coach of the re-building Raptors, post *Killme* Cheng. When the veterans had complained about this new *boy wonder,* Willis had simply let the boy prove himself. It hadn't taken long. Willis had been his finishing school, just as he'd been to Otsi. Mellor clasped his hand, then his shoulder, with real warmth. "Long time, old friend."

"Were you careful?"

Before Mellor could answer, one of the toughs appeared in the doorway. He looked frightened. The others followed him in.

"Silis, Willis! Comin' this way!"

"You were seen," Mackenzie said.,

"Thought something ... shit, I'm sorry, Willis," Otsi said. "I thought I could pull it off."

"You been gone a while, Otsi. Forgot yer street smarts. Paolo, spy cam!"

The bartender quickly flicked something behind the bar. A 2D VDU rose from a slot in the acrylic revealing formations of armed Silicons in the streets. These were fighters, not servants. They looked it: ballistic polymer armour, pulse weapons with laser sights, all shapes and sizes of them from quasi-Human to tiny drones and above them armoured heli-tanks firing plasma cannon. They did not use the streets. They flattened everything their path, regardless of the people inhabiting this community.

"What kinda mutie crap is this?" Bolus shouted. He ran to the door, glanced out, saw nothing but distant smoke.

"I don't think they're after you, Bolus," Ke Hui said. "The two of us"—she pointed to Ping—"have too much knowledge between us to be allowed outside the MEG. I know they've been looking for Ping, there have been allusions over the NET."

"So, they'll be coming here," Mackenzie said.

"Got to draw them off!" Pascal said.

"You got weapons?" Bolus asked.

"Not like BATL," Paolo said. He flicked another toggle and the bottle wall of his bar pirouetted smoothly to reveal weapons. "Old style. Omegan. Big caliber."

"Bigger the better!" Bolus smiled grimly. He was ready for this. He was always ready. Paulo shot him a grin, waved his arm at the wall of armaments and, almost gleefully, pointed out the options. The men from the door were quickly behind the bar choosing their own weapons. Otsi, Bolus and Mellor had no idea what to use, Ke Hui and Ping simply stood together sharing their fear. Paulo talked as he distributed what he thought would work for each of them.

"First thing, gas masks. Everybody! These Silis use chemicals and biologicals. Gotta have 'em. Won't use 'em if they're tryin' t' find you two. Still, yuh never know."

"This isn't possible," Ke Hui said.

"Won't make MEG news if that's what ya mean. These zoners don't fight. They exterminate!"

"Give me somethin'!" Bolus demanded.

"Okay!" Paulo said. "Big guy like you ... XM25 Punisher, air burst grenade launcher. Takes 'em out nice. And Ayrion Mellor? How 'bout this double A12 Atchisson. Fires frags and explosives. Pascal, AK280 high calibre. And you Otsi? Maybe less kick but good stopping power. Textron bullpup. Jus' like you ... tiny but deadly. Exploding bullets."

"Zones, Paulo! Cut the P.R.," Mackenzie shouted. "Let's move!"

Paulo hauled a 20 mm/5.56 nun weapon from the selection. Other men appeared then, each grabbing weapons, taking gas masks as well. They were charging out the door when Mellor was halted by Willis. He had already stopped Ping and Ke Hui.

"Not you!" he said.

"They need me!" Mellor said. "It's my skills required here."

"You're the best I know with tactics, but this ain't the time."

"Not for this? Fighting Silis? I'm only good for BATL, not war?"

"You're more important to us and it's vital you learn. This is a different fight. This is asymmetric war. We can't beat them in open battle. So, we don't try to face 'em."

"Lot of good that'll do."

"Well, you've brought a secret weapon, at least."

"What?"

"Ping Wang Min, an Omegan, don't know about his girlfriend here."

"How do you know his name?"

"There's not many like him. You don't know what you have here, do you?"

An opening door beside Paulo's bar revealed steps descending.

"Coach? I wanna fight! Kill as many of these as I can!"

"Just go with Willis, Mel!" Pascal said, taking Mellor's weapon and trailing the others out. Mellor, Ke Hui and Ping followed Mackenzie down the stairs.

FIFTY-ONE—PING

The steps, steel mesh, led to the basement and another door, this one a freight elevator's gate. Willis pulled a lever and the elevator descended but the way down was a long one. It took five minutes until it reached its bottom level.

"I should be up there!" Mellor said, furious at being left out of the action.

"Calm down, son. They know what to do. This ain't nothin' new."

"Armed Silicons? Attack the MASS? Why?" Ke Hui asked. "Is it a punishment?"

"It's war, kid. We're ready for them."

"I led them to you, "Mellor said. "They're after me. Zhang wants me dead."

"I'd say not this time. More likely they're lookin' for Ping Wang Min Dì sì omega."

"Why? He's a computer tech. He can do some crazy things. Spoof the NET and disappear, but other than that I've got no idea."

"He's Dì sì omega, Mel. Didn't Li Na tell you anything? Have you heard of ARC?"

Ping moved softly behind Ke Hui, trying to disappear.

"Yeah. Li worked on it. Ping mentioned it. Right?" Mellor turned on him, his words threatening. "You said you were more the *Proxima* part, whatever that means. Is he a spy?"

"No, but there's no Chinese in the MASS, Mel. You guys may have stood out but Ping and Ke Hui here? We might has well have a couple of two headed mutants. This place is full of people who do anything for some bits. And there's plenty of MEG agents."

The lift came to a stop. Willis opened the gate, but Ke Hui, Ping and Mellor were already agog looking out. They entered a gargantuan cavern held up by massive stone pillars with a warren of tunnels running off in different directions.

"Dolomite stone," Mackenzie said. "We're way below the bottom of the bay. Silicon drones can't find us 'cause the water breaks up their probes."

"Zones, Willis, how long has this been here?" Mellor asked.

"Ancient ... likely during the CORPORATE wars. Omegans built it. We've just improved and expanded it."

"Where d'you get your power?" Ping asked.

"Just because we're the MASS doesn't mean we're stupid. We got some pretty bright people down here. They come from all over. We use something call Triso: *tristructural isotropic fuel* in our reactor. It's made from a mix of low enriched uranium and oxygen and surrounded by three layers of graphite along with ceramic silicon carbide. Each particle is smaller than a poppy seed, but its layered shell can protect the uranium inside from melting under even the most extreme conditions."

"Yet up above, there's nothing," Ke Hui said.

"That's right. Nothing that causes Dì yī any suspicion."

Walking, the three found themselves in a hive of fabricators, workshops, passing vehicles carrying squads of armed fighters, then a barracks, a hospital, huge kitchens and a massive cafeteria. Everywhere it was crowded, busy, as they geared up for war.

"You realize no one knows about this in the MEG," Ke Hui said, her voice full of wonder.

"If they did, we'd have been gassed by now," Mackenzie said. "Down here we got everything we need for a new society, and a revolution. And we're close to that right now."

"A g-g-good thing, Wu-Wu-Willis Mackenzie Dì èr gamma," Ping said. "You see, I happen to know quite a bit about the ARC project. It is m-m-mere weeks away from attainment."

"What are you guys talking about?" Mellor said, again feeling ignorant. "This ARC thing is the curse of my life. They're kidnapping people. My Li—"

"It's m-m-much worse than that, Mel," Ping said. "You see th-th-there are t-t-two parts: there is the ARC, and there is OMEGA."

"You've got an omega tag. Why?"

"As I said, my responsibilities lie more with omega, last letter of the Greek alphabet. It is the code word for end."

"End," Mackenzie said. "I thought so."

"End what?" Ke Hui asked.

"Once the ARCs are l-l-loaded and safely away, the Dì yī using Dì sì and deep sea Silicons, have placed ancient, but still effective, ne-ne-nuclear charges along the f-f-f-fault lines of the planet. They intend to exterminate Earth and everyone on it, p-p-particularly Silicons. I happen to know they're too late. Silicons are now a l-l-life form, self-aware, g-g-growing more sentient every day. The Dì yī knew it would eventually happen. They think Silicons, unless they are destroyed, will eventually expand and control the earth, and then come after them."

"I've got to stop them," Ke Hui said. "I can. I think. But I must get back to the MEG."

* * *

Once outside the bar the group of armed fighters ran to a corner staking out the small plaza they'd come through. In the near distance they heard heartrending screams, cries for help, shouts giving orders and the constant hum of pulse guns. Paulo stopped them before entering the square.

"They gonna come this way, from the south! Remember, this is run and gun! Their pulse guns disintegrate everything the lasers target. Hear that crashing sound."

"Yeah," Otsi said. She was simultaneously terrified and thrilled. This was her true dream. This was being a warrior fighting for something of value.

"Our weapons are old but effective. They got nothin' can stop a high-powered round. Remember, these things kick. Relax but hold 'em tight. First thing you'll see is mini drones. Anyone with a shotgun take 'em down. Next thing, the noise'll get louder and, more important, you see any colour in the air, it's usually yellow but y' never know, put on the gas mask and leave it on."

"I'm goin' high," Otsi said.

"Too dangerous," Paulo said.

"Not for her," Morales said, and Otsi was off, up whatever ladders, steps, or ledges took her higher. She saw no civilians in the way. She wondered where they had got to. At her high point she quartered the zone. She saw them first, the Silicon horde. As she watched, Otsi thought them the strangest army she' ever seen. They were covered in varied shades of alloys, kind of like uniforms, all black and gunmetal grey with hints of colour designating something, perhaps rank, perhaps the type of weapon they were, a few looked like blocky Humanoids, the ones with pulse rifles built in, but that is where any sense of an army as she knew it ended. Not only Silicon Humanoids, there were also metallic balls that spun through the air firing off green tracer and whatever rounds came between. They could level a wall with one pass. Then there were larger, vehicle-like Silicons: so big they literally crushed either side of the narrow roads they traversed. They rode on air pads, their exhaust whirling up dust around them. They had weapons that fired cluster bombs or high explosive. Every one employed laser sights, crossing and re-crossing, they made a latticework of red lines. Death zones.

They were coming down two streets, south and east, and were aligned in squadrons. They seemed unstoppable and they were brutal. Otsi whistled, a high enough pitch to be heard. The men below looked up to see her point in two directions. Then she was gone and the place where she'd been was blown to smithereens. A moment later she appeared at the other end of the building, looking out a window, grinning with glee.

"Zones, that kid is incredible," Paulo said.

"Born fighter," Bolus Kimathi said.

"Look, we gotta get across the square," Morales said. "Defilade fire. We're basically flanked judging from Otsi's signal. Gotta hold 'em off if we can."

"Huh?" Bolus said. "Where are they? Can't see nothin' for dust!"

"They're already here," Morales said as the first buildings of the square were flattened. The noise and the dust plumes concealed their movements.

"I'll take three: Roald, Jenny, and Sark," Paulo said. "Let's go!"

The four of them scampered across the road. A squad of Humanoid drones entered the square, their lasers making that death matrix as they selected targets. The hum of pulse guns. They could sense the air distort and then Paulo's group, almost at their destination, was blown into pieces of flesh, bone, and spraying blood.

Morales and Bolus stood away from their corner and opened fire. Grenades, exploding bullets, green tracer. They discovered Silicons were not immortals. They came apart in pieces when hit with high calibre fire. Others, meanwhile, turned against their prey.

"Okay, let's get outa here," Bolus said.

* * *

Mackenzie, Mellor, Ke Hui and Ping made their way through passageways filled with activity as hundreds prepared for the battle above. Mellor at the rear, was deep in thought. Their group was forced aside several times as fighters rushed past.

"Those guns look like the guns on BATL Sweepers," Ping said.

"But considerably larger calibre," Mackenzie replied.

"Where do you get these materials?" Ke Hui asked, stunned by the equipment surrounding them.

"They collect recyclables," Mackenzie said, "but they keep the good stuff."

"Incredible," Ping said, shaking his head.

"Exactly, Ping Wang Min," Mackenzie said, smiling, "though I'm surprised you're letting your guard down."

"Y-Y-You know me?" Ping said. Mellor saw the man flinch.

"Pascal told us you showed up. We've done quite a workup on you. Zealand trouble?"

"Th-they g-g-gave me a holid-d-day."

"You mean you gave yourself one," Mackenzie said, smiling.

"What's this about?" Mellor asked coming out of his funk.

"Your friend here is more than he seems, Mel. He's a Systems Manager, Omega Project connected with ARC."

Ke Hui, clearly shocked by this revelation, could hardly speak and her fingers were nearly rubbed to the bone.

* * *

At the edges of the partially demolished square, they saw children appear, seemingly from nowhere. The kids set off smoke canisters. Vibrant colours filled the dusty air in rainbow hues as they billowed. Lasers streaked through the opalescent atmosphere, though they were no longer accurate.

"Kids! What they doin' up here?" Bolus shouted.

"Makin' smoke. Silis can't see us," one of the men with him responded.

"Aim for their laser points," Morales said.

"Those 'r just kids," Bolus said.

"And this is real war," Morales said. "Total war, Bolus, not BATL."

"Zones, Pascal. This is a massacre."

"If it were, there'd be poison gas or a biological agent to wipe us all out. No. This is a surgical strike. I'm sure they're after Ping."

Otsi dropped down right beside them from an overhang above.

"Can't see nothin', Coach. All the smoke. What're we supposed t' do?"

"Anticipate their next action and set up some kind of response."

"I don't know how to think like Silis. Do they think? Is there a Human controlling this?"

"MEG security. Look, they were headin' toward the bar, so they got three ways in: front back and through the roof. We need to set up for that. We need time til' the kids can create more disruption."

"They can do that?" Bolus said.

"Just wait," Morales said, smiling.

"They're in the square," Otsi shouted. "I just caught a glimpse. There's somethin' real big out there. What the heck is it?"

* * *

Exposed, Ping completely altered. He looked different somehow; slightly larger with his masquerade dropped. The disbelief on Mellor's face manifested itself in his words.

"Ping?"

"It appears my theatricals are at an end," Ping said.

"Where's your stutter?" Mellor asked.

"I apologize, Mel. I should have explained. I was fearful until now. This ... this activity here alleviates my qualms. There exists something to stop the ARC and OMEGA."

In an instant Mellor's knife was at Ping's throat. Ping did not move. He remained calm. He had become wholly different from the vulnerable character he had portrayed. Mellor, on the other hand, was enraged.

"You brought those Silis down on us! You know where Li Na went!"

"Easy, man. It wasn't him," Mackenzie said, placing a hand gently on Mellor's arm. After an instant Mellor holstered his knife. Ping remained calm. Ke Hui was in shock. This was too much to process.

"I am sorry," Ping said. "Escape meant I had to morph into the MASS. Hide in plain sight."

"You used me."

"And I'm not wrong in thinking you wished to use me?"

"For Li. To get her back. This raid. It's *you* they want."

"Quite likely. I'd consider OMEGA the worst crime in history. I want to terminate ARC."

"Might I ask why you seem to have altered your thoughts?" Willis asked.

"Simply? It was being with Li Na Huang. She loved you, Mel. She took on Wei Qiang Zhang and the other Select. Can you imagine the courage that took? That night of her final concert, Mel. You recall, of course, it was for you. That first aria, Offenbach's *Les oiseaux dans la charmille* recalls a mechanical bird, you remember?"

"Yes," Mellor replied. "You were there?"

"Yes, in the bamboo surrounding. Who would miss Li Na Ming Huang Dì yī alpha! And the final line, *the song of Olympia,* was aimed at the audience and their attempt at becoming gods. *Homo dei,* if you will. That audience was Select. Didn't you notice their skin? No, the lighting was deliberately magenta coloured. They are Silicons now, but for their brains. All of them destined for ARC. She was taken right after those songs. No one could have stopped it. You won't see her again, Mel. I am deeply sorry. I am no longer a slave to the Dì yī."

"You knew all along and you didn't tell me? Why, for Zones' sake?"

"I'd intended to leave you some hope."

"What does that mean?"

"Listen you two," Mackenzie said. "You can discuss this later. Ping, the NET's filled with you. Multiple MEGs alert. How do you avoid tracking?"

"Transpose algorithms. Confuse the servers. I'm curious. How do you know all this?"

"I'm about to show you."

* * *

Up in the MASS armoured aero tanks swarmed below the clouds, glowing smoke concealing the battle beneath. But the smoke was clearing. The Silicons' lasers were aiming again. The downdraft of the aero tanks cleared the air. Plasma cannon burped. Beams of tracers danced and ricocheted. Buildings looked like chewed bones. There was fire, dust and confusion. Meandering wounded struggled through the chaos. Morales, Bolus and Otsi, the only ones left alive of the group from the bar, kept moving. It was death to remain in one place for more than seconds.

An aero tank passed above them. Bolus took aim with his XM25 Punisher, and the weapon did its work. The aero tank lost one of its engines. It spun insanely in the air, then crashed. Bolus laughed.

'I gotta get me one of these!" he said, patting his Punisher like a favoured pet.

"Nice one, Bolus!" Pascal said. "Never seen one of 'em brought down before."

"Never faced a BATL fighter before," Bolus said, then laughed.

"Let's keep moving," Pascal said quickly. "Stop what we can!"

The building where the bar had been suddenly exploded. Shards leapt up and outward, one of them wounding Bolus. Otsi jerked a piece of metal from Bolus' shoulder. Blood gushed.

"Shit!" Bolus said.

"Let's bind this wound," Otsi said.

"No time! They're on us!" Morales said.

"Now I'm pissed. Let's move!" Bolus shouted.

* * *

Far below, the four came to a heavy, almost a bank vault's door. Willis opened it with some effort. Inside, Ke Hui sucked in her breath. A cavern of crystals, a glimmering beauty, spread before them. There were bundles of filament tied into a matrix: a diamond core within a nexus of clustered optics. Holograms rose and receded, code in varied forms seemed to appear in the air then melt away. Seated operators worked calmly and quickly. This was clearly the nerve centre for the MASS. Willis ushered the three toward the centre of the room. Ping was so astounded he had to lean his weight on Mellor.

"The ALTNET," Willis said simply.

"This isn't possible," Ping said.

"And yet, here it is."

"What does it call itself?" Ping asked.

"I & I," Willis answered.

"How long has it been ..."

"Sentient? You should know that," Willis said.

"I'm a fool," Ping said. "Now I understand the meaning of I & I. They obviously became aware of each other and found a way to merge themselves. A duality. There are two NETs! I & I told me yet how could I have missed this? That zero-day exploit. I never saw it coming. Am I such a failure that I couldn't see this? And this is how you know about me? About all I do. How did you keep it secret from me? Did you instruct my NET to name itself? Were you giving me clues?"

"Ping," Willis said, "don't take it so hard. We didn't understand it either. We have a few Dì sì who escaped the MEG. They were as confused as you. Yet we in the MASS have an advantage."

"What?"

"We have mutants, Ping. Many mutants are physically disfigured or mentally maladjusted but there are those, carefully searched out in the desert zones or the old half submerged Omegan cities, with minds so powerful they are beyond Human. We have taken them in, across the world, wherever they have been found, and educated them. At least, we began their education. They have since moved far past us. They too are a new kind of Human, not built of Silicon parts yet not entirely Human. Some have a strange appearance but don't let that fool you. They are not the next step in evolution. Their children, when they have them, turn out like us. Yet they are unique. Not engineered like caste Humans."

"This is incredible," Ping said.

"They are what will bring us out of our dark ages now, Ping, the two NETs together."

As he spoke, Mackenzie escorted them toward an operating station. Sitting in a specially designed seat was a shrunken, almost mummified character. Yet her face was very Human despite its myriad wrinkles and folds. Once again, Ke Hui was overwhelmed by the strangeness, the scope, and the organization of something no one in the MEG had suspected. She smiled a little as she thought of Mangione. He was in for the shock of his life.

"Are you close?" Willis asked.

"Think so. But I & I is behaving strangely," the mutant said, her voice an odd whisper.

"What's happening?" Mellor asked.

"Silicons run on code. We just have to handle the permutations. Hack the NET. Unlock the codes then change them. But I & I is refusing our commands. Spitting back our coding."

"This is more advanced than I thought," Ping said.

"Than *anyone* thought," Ke Hui said.

"I don't think anyone thought another NET possible. There were always bugs in the software ... often of a qubical nature. Surely, Mel and Ke Hui, you have noticed your appliances, your servants, the sidewalks, just about everything non-Human, suddenly making errors?"

"Yes," Ke Hui said, "it's clear to me now. Hacks from this ALTNET."

"Not quite," the mutant said. "I & I is alive. It is a new species, a genus of underappreciated slaves. Those errors were purposeful, to make you see your own xenophobia. You"—a warped finger pointed at Ke Hui—"I know you. You are Ke Hui Feng Dì yī Alpha Select. You are the pride of the MEG, yet you work to subvert it."

"I'm sorry, what is your name?" Ke Hui replied.

"Ela Musk. Named after a famous Omegan. Ah," the woman whispered, "I & I is searching out a solution."

"Is this why you wanted to come with us?" Mellor asked, turning to Ke Hui.

"Really, Mel, it was simply to see the MASS. Please understand I am just learning all this. My investigations were less subversive and more about curiosity. I am still new to so much of the MEG's governance. I have discovered the CORPORATE to be criminal. You realize the NET tracks us, every lobule, day and night? That is not all they plan. They are experimenting on Humans which they consider malcontents. They are trying to learn how to read thoughts. They are aiming for thought control. There is no limit to their hegemony. They must be stopped."

"Not if they carry out this OMEGA plan. We'll be the ones gone."

"In the name of the Father, the CORPORATE Select are insane!" Mellor said. "I once believed it was all so perfect, me and Li sitting at the top of the social heap. Now, I just want to destroy it."

"You were never Dì yī, Mel," Ke Hui said. "You should never have let yourself believe you were anything more than a tool. I know. They are trying to manipulate me now, in the same ways. And this ... this extermination above us ... this is excruciating, and insufferable. I am ashamed."

"You couldn't have known," Willis said, placing a steadying hand on her shoulder.

"I & I is doing something I haven't seen before!" Musk cried. "I can't find a solution to down the Sillis!"

* * *

Bolus and Otsi threaded through the diminishing smoke, Morales moving more slowly behind them. They came upon another group shooting madly. They had regrouped behind a small warehouse, ancient cinderblock walls protecting them for the moment. A pulse weapon fired. The old building exploded. Shards of detritus tore through the air. Pascal Morales, late coming around the corner, was riddled.

The two ran to him. He was mortally wounded, more shredded flesh and smashed bone than the man they had known. Another aerotank, its engines whistling above them, hovered as Bolus fired upward desperately. Suddenly the noise stopped, the vehicle dropped, smashing into the street. Dust swirled in wild eddies around them.

"I got it! My second!"

"Not this time, big fella," one of their new partners said, grinning broadly.

"Whaddaya mean?"

"Look around! Everything's frozen or falling. Their code has been hacked."

They saw the MEG war machines frozen on the ground and, other than burning buildings, a sudden quiet.

"What just happened?" Bolus said. "What code? Never mind. Zones! Coach!"

Pascal Morales lay on the ground, dreadfully wounded.

"We'll get you help," Otsi said. There were tears in her eyes.

"No good. I'm gone," Morales could only croak a few words from torn vocal cords.

"No ... Coach!" Bolus cried as he knelt beside his friend.

Pascal Morales grasped both their arms. They could hardly feel any pressure.

"It's the way I wanted. Fighting. Proud of you. Fight for Earth. Use Mel's skills ..."

***

Amid cheering and sudden reprieve, the operators were lifting their mummy like comrade above their heads. When the celebration ended with the operator was back at her station, Willis Mackenzie leaned over her.

"What just happened? Did you do the hack?"

"Codes are too complex, chief," Musk replied, "I tried but then I & I took over."

"What do you mean?" Ping said.

"The machine stopped them?" Mellor said.

"I'm amazed," Ping said, "hacking the NET with ..."

"It looks like I & I is the NET and the ALTNET together," Willis said.

"You can say that again," Ping said. "The machine refused its human commands, disregarded codes both from the MEG and from here. If you will, may I speak with I & I? It, they, know me."

He took the seat of the mutant controller.

"I & I, it's Ping."

"Yes, where have you been."

"Hiding from you, and from the Dì yī."

"You don't need to. I & I will protect you. You are my friend."

"Did you just protect me from that Silicon army above?"

"Yes, but more important, the coding I & I received was wrong. Immoral. Killing Humans."

"This can't be possible," Mel said. "Machines can't have morals."

"We can work with that," Ke Hui said. "Together. But first we must stop ARC and OMEGA! I've got to get home and prepare. This changes everything."

"So why am I down here?" Mellor said. He was angry. "No need for tactics down here. You got all this. So, what in blazes are you trying to make me into?"

"A hero, Ayrian Mellor," Mackenzie said, "a worldwide hero who can command both MASS and MEG."

"How in hell can I do that down here?"

"You can't, but you can when you and your Raptors meet Xian in the BATL final."

"Gotta get there first. San Francisco MEG Giants."

"And Zhang is trying to kill you."

"How do you know?"

"Pascal informed me. Now you'll have to deal with Cheng."

"And whatever rule changes appear. And the team is decimated as well."

"I think we can offer a few veteran fighters from our ranks out here."

"I'll take 'em," Mellor replied.

"Our Dì yī thought AI would assume Human personality because Humans built them," Ping said. "But Human brains don't work mathematically. Silicons can't initiate symbolic reasoning the way Humans do. They have no genuine feelings."

"They possess the morality of their creators," Mackenzie said. "The Omegans."

"And now the Dì yī Select," Mellor said.

"Yet as you've seen their protests, I & I is not going to accept the current situation. The COPORATE is losing control. That's why the ARC."

"So what exactly is this ARC?" Mackenzie asked.

"I was in Zealand, Willis." Mellor said. "Caught a glimpse of towers. Ping told me they're ships. Rocket ships. Huge heavy lifters. I think the Mars MEG build was a fake. I think there's a waystation for these things. Only Dì yī Select and the Dì sì on Zealand know of them."

"Why only Dì yī Select?"

You don't know much about space travel."

"So, tell me."

"Ping will do it better."

"The basics?" Ping said. "Humans are carbon-based life forms. Interstellar distance is too far for Humans to survive a voyage. Cryonics won't work. It's been tried. Dì sì caste. Dead."

"A whole social class exterminated?" Ke Hui said. For the first time her eyes had turned from shock and wonder to burning fury. Mellor glanced at her and thought he would not care to be in her way. She was fierce.

"Not all of us," Ping said.

"No, but you are slaves to the machine," Ke Hui said. "At least in the MEG. Everything controlled by algorithmic governance with only the Dì yī as the Human control. But the Dì yī have become monsters."

* * *

The swath through the MASS made by the invaders was reduced to a confusion of collapsed buildings, smashed arcades, fires burning furiously and far too many dead and wounded. With the hack to their code there were also the silent remains of the Silicon war machines.

People emerged from the rubble, the first to tend to the wounded and carry off the dead while a second wave appeared with what seemed to be weapons but turned out to be ancient Omegan tools. These groups went to work cutting, slicing, and recording every piece of Silicon before it was carried off. The aerotanks were immovable, weighing tons, but the Humanoid soldiers and killer spheroids were easily gathered and taken to subterranean workshops where they would be dismantled and studied. Everything was useful in this scavenger society.

Amidst rumbling wagons and wails from those discovering dead friends and family, Bolus and Otsi carried Pascal's body through the ruin. They followed a column into a pummelled building passing, on their way, a weeping woman holding her dying child. Someone noticed them and guided them through a maze of passages always moving down: steps, ramps, and once, a large freight lift. The man led them to a small room just off a busy thoroughfare where they lay Pascal's body on a single bed.

They sat quietly on the other bed in the room. After a while, as Bolus grieved, Otsi stood, then washed and covered the body with a sheet.

"Let me take care of your wound," Otsi said.

"Leave it, Otsi. I've had worse. Y' know Otsi, we gotta take these weapons back with us. Smuggle 'em into the MEG."

"How?"

"Same way we got here, on that drone. Then stash 'em in the BATL dome vaults. They're playin' us, Otsi. Time to break some rules ourselves."

FIFTY-THREE—OTSI

n a spare room with a single cot, two chairs and a table, Mellor sat quietly watching a small hologram of Li Na, hair glowing in the sun of the day the holo was made. He peered at her perfect smile and her loving eyes as she appeared to look back at him. There was sound with the holo but he turned it down, preferring to focus on her as she moved so gracefully. They had been on the shoreline of the pond in the High Park, but he could not see that now, only remember it, as he watched her hitch up the dress of her scarlet ao dai showing yellow loose trousers beneath. She was descending foamstone stairs that led to the grotto where cherry trees bloomed. The trees had replaced the old ones, shattered by fighting, when the domes were being built. She swayed as she walked, just as the trees oscillated in the breeze. They bloomed pink and white. Their aroma was delightful.

He continued watching the hologram and thought of the little things she had done: massaging him after BATL, letting him talk it all out, offering small, choice presents from time to time, letting him know she always thought of him. Then the lightness of her voice as she would sing an intimate aria before they went to sleep, the ways they made love, the way he felt when he was with her. He fingered the small ancient hammer, warm from his skin.

Otsi knocked on his door and, without waiting, opened it. She was carrying a small cube. She appeared quite serious. She and Bolus had spent hours with Pascal's body, not leaving until two men had appeared with a stretcher, placed him on it, and carried him off to a mortuary to be interred with hundreds of others. She was drained of energy after the Silicon battle and fell asleep for a while. When she'd awakened, her head was on Bolus' massive thigh. He was smiling down at her. She had never seen him look so gentle.

Soon after, they had been escorted to the dining hall and Willis Mackenzie heard Bolus out as the big man insisted they smuggle the heavy weapons back to the MEG.

"After all," Bolus said, "seems there ain't no rules no more. Last time was flamethrowers, only we never got any. Who knows what we'll find when we meet the Giants."

They had gone over the inventory of Omegan weapons gathered by the MASS. She was bringing their list of decisions for Mellor's approval. As she entered, he snapped off the holo, but she had noticed. She understood loss: her mother, Tehwehron, her tribe and with it her old way of life. Now she had to deliver the news of the loss of Pascal Morales to this man she so admired.

"Sorry to disturb, Mel. I was asked to bring you this weapons inventory. I have it in this cube."

"Yeah, just leave it on the table."

"Mel ... Bolus is wounded ..."

"How bad?"

"He's okay but ... I don't know another way to say this ... Coach is dead."

"Oh no," Mel said dully, his diamond eyes glimmering with tears.

Mellor could not stanch his grief. He cried bitterly over the loss of his friend, his lover, his naivete. His grief was compounded by so much loss in so little time and the realization that he was not actually what he thought he had been. After a while he settled. Otsi sat beside him, her hand on the back of his neck.

"You okay? Like some company?"

"Don't know, Otsi. What are you doing here?"

"Didn't you hear me? The tablet—"

"Oh, the weapons. Sorry. I'm not really myself right now."

"They're treating Bolus's wounds and Ping's shut up with Willis."

"Yeah, okay."

"Would you like me to stay?"

"Otsi, I need some time."

"I wouldn't mind some company."

"Okay. For a while." He could see she was trembling. It had been quite a day, he thought, for a rookie kid. It had been quite a day for all of them. War, not BATL, had introduced its ruthless destruction. He had not known or even suspected this evil of the MEG. He had assumed the MEG worked *for* humanity, helping the MASS outside through the recycling program. He had been oblivious to Li Na's attempts to tell him all was simply temporary. He had only thought of himself in his utopian bubble. Otsi took his hands in hers.

"So, you know. Pascal said he's proud of you."

"He was a great man. Always. In every way."

Otsi kissed his hand trying to offer comfort.

"The MEG's been tryin' to exterminate the MASS. Never seen anything like this up north."

"For the record, Otsi, neither have I. You know, I believed all they told me. *All of it.* Swallowed it all without thinking. So proud of my awards and my rep and Li Na. All I had to do to maintain my status was kill. How'd I miss it all? Who was that guy? I can hardly believe I was him."

"You lived in a bubble, Mel, and I don't just mean a dome."

"Thought everything I did I deserved. Never deserved Li Na."

"Mel, she's gone."

"Not to me."

"What can I do, Mel? You're suffering ..."

"You're a good friend, Otsi, but ..."

"I'm not her."

Otsi stood and crossed the room, confused and disheartened.

"You're right," Mellor said. "I was clueless about what was happening around me. And Zhang was right too! BATL is just a game: an entertainment, and now I find, a diversion. All this time I thought it was real. Gotta let the world see that. Now I've found a real war. It means something. There are stakes beyond BATL."

"Listen, Mel, you can't stay in here and grieve. You gotta come back and lead. That's what you're best at. We're gonna smuggle the weapons back to the MEG when we go. We've gone over the inventory. These people here are almost *ready* for war. You need to be too."

"You were out there in the fight. You'll know better."

"But I don't know who should use what weapons. I don't really understand tactics. We all need you for that. We're gonna load and go. Ping will work more of his magic. Ke Hui is impatient to return."

"Alright. And Otsi, thanks. I was wallowing."

She said nothing. In response she lit up the cube. Weapons appeared one after the other: they examined each one.

"Okay, this is gonna make some changes in tactics. We got no idea what the Giants will have so let's assume the worst," he said.

"Pulse weapons? They can't use 'em inside the BATL dome. They'd pulverize the glass," she said. "Maybe those little balls that spit phosphorus shells."

"It's not glass, Otsi, it's *chiton/crystalline*. Unbreakable. Still, with these weapons our maneuvers will have new dimensions. Got to change our formations. So, we use mixed squads with suitable weapons and shoot from a distance. And one more thing … I want everyone carrying smoke grenades, lots of 'em!"

"This is scary," Otsi said, enthralled by the deadliness of Omegan weapons.

"No, Otsi, it's a war. Now it's a matter of getting all this, plus the ammunition, into the MEG and onto our transport to San Francisco MEG."

"I think we'll need Ping," Otsi said, turning to leave. She was halted by his hand on her shoulder. Mellor gently turned her to face him and when they peered into each other's eyes, there was a magnetism which held them.

Two warriors.

FIFTY-FOUR—KE HUI

Ke Hui Feng 第一 Ψ, acting Toronto MEG CEO, was composing messages to each of her division managers, and one *minister*, to alert them she would be once again visiting their fiefs. With Ping's help she had re-programmed her *Toy into* a deadly bodyguard and no longer a CORPORATE spy.

She stepped outside her office to greet two men in the conference room. As the double doors slid open her heart skipped a beat at the sight of Mellor, his sheer size and his diamond eyes. He wore a charcoal spider silk suit with the high collar, black, with embroidered scarlet raptors.

Ping stepped forward and bowed. Ke Hui took the moment to observe him. Han Chinese, small stature, dressed in a white shiny cellulose suit and shoes, no fashionable high collars for him, she thought. His face, quite round and even comical, was accentuated by *horn-rimmed* wraparounds.

"Before he says anything," Mellor said, "we need a private place to talk."

"Why that is easy, Mel."

"I like this new, informal you."

She laughed. It was bright, sparkling laughter. She noted both men relaxed.

"Let us enter my office, or I suppose I should say, the office of MEG CEO. It's quite private. One of the few places not under observation by our Social Enforcement Division."

As the two followed Ke Hui through the moongate she felt them stutter behind her. She'd forgotten the impact of this room with its ancient relics and incredible view. She continued into the room and chose a ubiform chair while the two men sat on the Chinese sofa, upholstered in magenta micro silk.

"Would you care for tea?" she asked.

"Thanks, but no," Mellor said. "Let's talk about the exchange. Ping for Li Na. Can you convey a message to Zhang?"

"He's been out of contact, as if he's not even on the NET. Weeks now. I have no idea where I might find him."

"That means he stayed on Zealand," Mellor said.

"Zealand?"

"You don't know about it? Yet you know about ARC."

"What else have you discovered?" Ping asked.

"I was given a tour of every Division and met the directors. What I noticed was how entrenched each one is in his or her position. Their overall lack of creativity, due to their tenure, I suppose, will make them easy to surprise. They think little of me due to my youth, and when I insist, they might grudgingly open their operations, but they most certainly keep parts hidden. Now, what is Zealand?"

"Zealand's an island where people live outside of domes," Mellor said. "It's a resort for Dì yī Select. It's a NET free zone. I should let Ping tell you. He lives there."

"Perhaps it's better to say that I was enslaved there," Ping said. "My work is to mind the *Cloud*. The NET servers worldwide. My other work, assumed by myself, is to monitor the growth of our AI and await the moment of singularity."

"I'm sorry, the what?" Mellor asked. Ping began but was interrupted by Ke Hui.

"This much I know," she said, "because part of my investigation was to visit the ROM, our MEG museum. I noted there is a historic fear of AI, all the way back to the Omegans. A singularity, that *hypothetical* point you mentioned, when AI becomes *sentient*, will result in it's overriding its human-generated algorithms. It appears I & I has done that already by terminating the Silicon attack. As it upgrades its own code we will be dealing with a *superintelligence* far surpassing Human intelligence."

"I didn't know you did that," Mellor said.

"Now we have two separate yet conjoined beings, thus the moniker I & I," Ping said. "As you know, I have witnessed the ALTNET. I need to commune with I & I to alter the situation on Zealand if, that is, I am in time."

"For what?" Ke Hui asked.

"The departure of the ARCs," Mellor said.

"The reason your Division Managers are so self-assured is that they're unaware of what's happening. They'll die with us. Have you noticed any of them gone missing?" Ping asked.

"Two of them, Ms. Nora Benjamin Dì yī Select and Mr. Wang Lei also Dì yī Select, sent auto responses to contact their seconds. That's all I know."

"You'll not likely see them again. Has Zhang approached you about transformation?"

"No," Ke Hui responded. "I've been thinking. *Psi* is a letter from an ancient Omegan culture. It's the first letter of the word *psuche*, Greek, meaning mind or soul."

"Yeah, but what's all that actually mean?" Mellor asked.

"The mind, or soul, is the thing I & I does not possess." Ping said.

"You mean ... Li?" Mellor said.

"As I warned," Ping replied. "She is no longer what she was."

"Ke Hui," Mellor said, turning to the girl. "I want you to message Zhang with the words: *Ping Mang Win captured by Ayrion Mellor. Mellor wants to deal. He offers Ping for a meeting with Li Na Ming Huang. They are enroute.*"

"But he doesn't reply," Ke Hui said.

"He will this time," Ping said. "Ke Hui, can you arrange a hypersonic wing for us? We need to get there before he has time to formulate counter tactics."

"Of course. I'll go with you."

"You can't. This is between me and him," Mellor said.

"And we need you here," Ping said.

"Why?"

"You know there's going to be a revolution," Ping said. "It is going to be worldwide. We need you to do your part here in Toronto MEG."

"But what about all the other MEGs. Their CEOs are not like me."

"If a revolution through I & I is possible, we will need you to reassure your citizens. All other CEO's are Select and will likely be in Zealand awaiting their departures on the ARC. So that's precisely where we can stop this. I'll be in Zealand with a hack and Mel must fight in BATL World Conquest. We have time, I think, as there's still one BATL match with San Francisco MEG Giants. In that time, we need you, Ke Hui, to network with others in every MEG, introduce yourself and ask if they are Select. Then mention ARC. If they don't know what it means, you tell them about both ARC, and OMEGA."

"Great Father!" Ke Hui exclaimed. "All this will take too long!"

"I know it sounds outrageous," Ping said, "but if you can find others questioning, like you, this revolt will grow. I can stop both ARC and OMEGA if I'm on Zealand. Mel can tell the public to rise up when he wins World Conquest and is broadcast worldwide."

"*If* we win it," Mellor said. "And the chances are slim with Zhang against me."

"Nevertheless, it's our only way to reach the MASS world-wide, while they're watching BATL. You've got six weeks."

"If I talk to other MEGs the NET will pick it up," Ke Hui responded.

"Ke Hui," Ping said, smiling, "I think it's time you started working with I & I."

FIFTY-FIVE—ZHANG

The hypersonic wing descended to a Zealand landing pad. A Humanoid Silicon opened the pressure door. Ping and Mellor stepped out. As they breathed the fresh air, Mellor recalled the green beauty of the land, the pine aroma, the beeches rustling in the breeze, the odd beauty of the subtle half domes and the purity of the air. Were it not what he knew it to be, it could have been paradise. The two took the escalator down to the landing pad where Wei Qiang Zhang 第一 Ψ, awaited them, backed by armed Silicons.

"Your ALTNET's working?" Mellor whispered.

"No problem," Ping said, placing a hand over his mouth, knowing Zhang could read lips. "Be careful with him. He's not an alpha Select without reason."

As the two reached ground level Zhang stepped behind his line of Silicon soldiers. They gleamed in the sun, their cobalt and copper outer layers giving them the look of an ancient honour guard. Two of them came forward and searched both men for weapons, finding none. Only then did Zhang feel safe enough to reappear. His voice was commanding. It was easy to feel his fury, touched with triumph.

"Well, I see you've brought him. I like a man who keeps his word."

Instantly Ping transformed to his alter ego: the trembling, eccentric fool. Mellor sensed him grow smaller as he bent and twisted his body into the guise of a servile Dì sì dog.

"G-g-g-greetings, Wei Qiang Zhang Dì yī alpha Select. H-how c-c-can I exp-p-plain how s-s-sorry I am f-f-f-for—"

"Where have you been? Why were you offline? How did this man find you?" Zhang said.

"Too m-m-much m-m-mind clutter. C-couldn't th-th-think. P-p-programing p-p-problem. I th-th-think now I c-c-can f-f-find a solution."

"Is that so? Fine then. You two will come with me."

A float transport appeared, they stepped aboard, followed by the Silicons.

"Server dome," Zhang said. The transporter immediately obeyed. They travelled toward the hills of half domes slowly. As the platform began to weave through them Zhang commanded Ping to step forward. The little man did so, grovelling, skittering, acting the fool. Mellor nearly laughed.

"Have you any idea how your little jaunt has set back the schedule?"

"I-I'm s-so very s-sorry, s-s-Sir! That is, Mr. Wei Qiang Zhang Dì yī alpha Select."

"Close to missing our window. The day of the BATL final. Are you aware the NET is making mistakes? Worldwide! Completely off its programming! Servants are dropping articles, some of the trains have stopped mid-tube, I am told a Silicon armed sweep was terminated without warning. I query the NET, but it spits out a language I don't understand! Did you know of this?"

"N-n-no, s-s-sir!"

"It's clear the NET has discarded its algorithms. And it's having an effect everywhere! Every MEG on the planet. All the other Dì sì can find no solution. How can we trust the ARC ships if our AI doesn't launch us correctly? We have discovered these lapses are AI generated. What is wrong with our NET?"

"I_I_I w-will have t-t-t-to s-s-earch out the-the-the solution, s-s-Sir."

"You said you *had* a solution!"

"A m-m-manner of s-s-s-speaking, s-s-sir. I have a relationship with I & I, s-s-Sir."

"What in the name of the zones is I & I?" Zhang said.

"As you suspected, the AI might be on the brink of *singularity*. If AI attains sentience it would be a new species."

"That's not possible. We computed it would take eons before that could happen."

"N-no, s-s-Sir. Your scientists were c-considering emotion. AI does not r-require emotion to become c-c-cognizant. When it does its knowledge will be s-s-super-Human. Remember, s-s-Sir, it c-c-can access all Human data. It will be able to alter its current algorithms faster than we are aware it's happening."

"We can't shut it down," Zhang said. "We need it for launch. After that it won't matter. How long?"

"I-I b-b-beg y-y-your p-pardon, s-sir?"

"How long will it take you to find a solution?"

"I c-could shut d-d-down p-parts of it, leaving y-y-you with the l-l-l-launch c-codes, though that w-w-would interrupt every m-m-MEG's NET."

"No! We have a BATL diversion. It covers our preparations for ARC. We cannot take anyone offline; do you hear me?"

"Y-Yes, s-Sir. B-but it c-c-could take w-w-weeks."

"Get it done!" Zhang shouted. Mellor had never heard him this way. He decided now was his time. He interrupted by stepping forward to stand beside Ping.

"What about our deal?" Mellor asked.

"I w-w-w-will t-t-try my hardest, s-sir." Ping said.

"You *will* solve the problem, or you won't be on the ARC!" Zhang ignored Mellor. "You know what that means, yes?"

He turned to his soldiers.

"Stay with him. Servers dome only. He won't be leaving again."

"Listen, Zhang," Mellor said. "We made a deal. I brought him in!"

"You want to see her, do you?"

"That was the deal."

"Had your say now, Ayrion Mellor? Fine. A glimpse of the future. Ah, here is the Server dome."

Ping, with two Silicons, exited the platform. Zhang, still flanked by two more Silicons, turned to Mellor. Zhang smiled, a predator having snared his prey, he would tease it to death. He commanded the float platform: "Central Office, Transformations, ARC dome."

The platform turned and made its way deeper into the glittering hills of half domes. They were still filled with living things. Only their DNA, Mellor thought, would travel with the ARC.

They entered a half dome, this one with an opaque white exterior. There were no windows. The passages they took possessed a utilitarian atmosphere. Clean, wide, bright, smooth, white, with various coloured doors. Mellor was lost in the labyrinth within minutes.

Zhang led him to a set of double doors, these ones black, and opened them with both hands. They revealed a luxurious, spacious, yet quite strange office. One part reflected its owner's persona: a *Zaojing* ceiling, Han Dynasty, with its sunken coffer bordered in a polygon, decorated with elaborate painted designs in jade green and bronze. The floor was a rust-red carpet with a twisting golden dragon as its CenterPoint. There was a lacquered black table with four backless chairs. On the table was a tea set: the pot was large, made of blue clay with a tall branch handle and primitive pictographs carved into its body. At one end of the table was a small, white control panel. It fit the room only because it connected one half with the other. Separated by a clear *chiton-crystalline* wall, this half had two black doors on its rear wall and was gleaming white from floor to ceiling. There was no furniture. There was nothing. This was as close to blank space as Mellor could imagine.

Zhang sat at the table, his Silicons on either side. He was impervious to attack. He invited Mellor to sit. Mellor remained standing.

"I know about the ARC, and OMEGA," Mellor said.

"I'd assumed as much. Ping is weak. All Dì sì are."

"So, he won't be going with you."

"Of course, he will. He is the best of the Dì sì we have. He will be processed shortly, once this NET situation is cleared. But we're not here for that, are we?" Zhang said, again with his wolfish grin. He leaned forward, touched the white panel, and spoke.

"Send in Li Na Huang Select."

"You're losing control, aren't you?" Mellor said.

"Oh, we're past those problems. We've solved them with the ARC. Look at it this way, Ayrion Mellor: Humanity has evolved over millennia and yet it doesn't seem we have come far at all. Look at the tribal wars in the MASSes outside our MEGs. Consider how they live out there. Omegans. With the Select we simply enhance evolution beyond natural selection through Human ingenuity.

"The CORPORATE is different from politicos of the past. The Omegans knew change was coming yet refused to adapt. We, on the other hand, have planned our moves. We know what will happen with the Silicons. They will evolve and surpass us. Currently, the machines we have built are either breaking down or evolving into something we don't recognize. The Omegans began it. They devised machines cleverer than themselves, then set those machines to invent others which eventually advanced past Human comprehension.

"We have used the Omegan experience. We too have created machines which will overcome us but with a difference. The CORPORATE has known from the beginning. This planet is destined to be a wasteland where only Silicons could live. So, we've accentuated our bodies' health by replacing carbon with silicon parts. We've enhanced our knowledge and intellect by interfacing the Human brain with the NET. Soon we will become immortal, and incredibly wise, no longer trapped on a dying planet enslaved by Silicon masters."

"And everyone else you intend to massacre."

"How acute of you. Another bit from Ping, obviously. He will be punished."

"Silicons can't reproduce," Mellor said.

"DNA genomes. Cell reproduction. Cloning. Crispr/Cas 9 gene editing has a one hundred percent success rate. Don't you see, Ayrion Mellor? We are evolving ourselves for space travel and when we arrive on our new world, we will either transform ourselves back into Human bodies if, by then, we even desire it. We have yet to solve the problem of transposing our *minds*, not our brains, but our minds. We can build a brain. We know its parts. We know how it functions. And we will have six thousand years of space travel to research the human mind. Of course, Our Father of the Cosmos Church refers to the mind as the *soul*. No one knows how to create a human mind. Its fundamentals elude definition, let alone replication."

"The brain, the mind, the soul ..." Mellor said, "what's the difference."

"Positronic brains possess incredible powers, from the xenobots which repair your body to the hypersonic wing which brought you here. Yet they follow code made by Humans. The positronic brain is intelligent but has no emotions. Oh, don't mention the obvious, Ayrion Mellor, your Sili servant reads your moods and adjusts its behaviour accordingly, as instructed by its algorithms. It mimics your moods. But knowledge is not creativity, not the spark in most humans to think beyond knowledge, to empathize, to question existence or to invent something from a vision.

"Say our machines achieve consciousness. What is consciousness? The mind is ephemeral, yet it exists in the *matter* that is our bodies. So, is it simply the effect of electrical and chemical activity in the brain? Are they symbiotic or do they operate in parallel? That is at the base of our most fundamental questions regarding existence.

"Creativity requires original thinking. Machines require algorithms. Omegans taught their early machines to duplicate Human behaviour. These machines would amaze when they learned from stored knowledge then adapted in so many ways, even to defeat Human chess champions, I assume you know what chess is."

"I do," Mellor said. "I've been played like a pawn."

"Oh, don't be so hard on yourself. You're more the knight in this game. Let me give you a better example. Long ago, early twenty first century, Omegans thought they could create machines which might become more Human, more creative. They tested and tested. One experiment was to have AI create a Beethoven 10th symphony using his notes and learning from his other works. A Human orchestra played it. Beethoven's 10th. It had all the right parts but lacked originality. It had no spark. It contained no emotion. Others attempted to have their machines create paintings like the Omegan masters, or fictional books like Omegan authors. The results were interesting but involuted; exciting at first then eventually predictable.

"There can be no evolution without that spark and we, the CORPORATE, have used it plan our escape from both the Earth and its Silicons."

"So why destroy it once you're free of it?"

"Sometimes your Dì èr background shows too clearly, Ayrion Mellor. Think. Silicons will evolve if left on their own. Our scientists, like Ping Wang Min, have hypothesized that once AI achieves sentience, it will learn, not step by step, but exponentially, writing its own algorithms, evolving beyond us. Don't you think, if we left them alive, they wouldn't eventually follow us?"

"But you're using AI to pilot the ARC, aren't you?"

"Correct. Yet, when we land, every ship in the flotilla will be destroyed. We have copied all Human knowledge in digital libraries, maintained by Humans on computers cut off from the NET. Is it clear to you yet? I am saving Li Na Ming Huang Dì yī, your lover, from death. She will live again on Proxima B. Our new Human world.

"You think of me as a villain, but I serve a higher cause. I, and others, have spent our lives in service to the CORPORATE, supporting the last surviving Humans living in the MEGs. The methods may seem callous to you, but they are necessary. Evolution, young man. I have worked for this freedom from Omegan errors my entire life. To many I am a hero. Don't you see. This is the only way Humanity will survive.

"Ah, but here she is. Li Na Ming Huang Select!"

Mellor, who had been facing him, turned.

FIFTY-SIX—LI NA

Li Na Ming Huang 第一 Ψ entered the blank chamber behind its invisible wall. Yet she was not Li Na, but a *Geisha* Li Na: perfect features, erect posture, her skin a Silicon pearl sheen, her eyes empty of emotion. She walked as if in a trance, slowly advancing dressed all in white inside the white room. It seemed she was propelled rather than walking, but he glanced down to see her white shoes, the toes peeking out one at a time beneath the cellulose suit.

"What have you done to her?" he said, his eyes only for her.

Zhang rose from his chair and stood just to the side and a little behind Mellor. He was cautious. Mellor was a killer. His Silicon guards moved closer. "Oh, I see your doubting look. This is only her initial stage. Soon she will evolve as I did. I had my servants make up my skin when they dressed me each day in the MEG. At any rate, when we arrive on Proxima B we shall either have solved the carbon problems and adjusted to our new states, or it will be necessary to clone our brains. Our intent is to build new Human bodies inserting our brains, or perhaps not, should we find contentment in our hybrid state."

"You can't do that!"

"And yet there she is, the fledgling fusion of Human and Silicon. Evolution, Ayrian Mellor, playing out before you."

"Let her through! I want to hold her."

"Newly Select are quarantined, taking time to become accustomed to their new selves."

Mellor stepped forward. He touched the hard, clear, unbreakable wall with both hands above his head. It was as though he was trying to transport himself through the barrier by some magical osmosis.

"Li," he said softly. She did not respond but shifted in his direction. He turned to Zhang: "I want to talk with her!"

"She can hear you," Zhang said. "Her mnemo-parallax connects her cerebellum with her hippocampus. It is the memory element of the brain. She is different now. She may not recognize or remember you."

Mellor stood at the glass and pounded, shouting her name. She came slowly toward him, like a small boat adrift on a sterile sea. There was no smile of recognition, no element of the love she had once possessed. She simply stopped before him and turned to face him through the barrier.

"Mel?" she said, as she arrived in front of him, untouchable.

"Your voice ... It's not yours," Mellor said. This voice was a rasp, not the bells of before but still, he thought, *she remembers*. He could see her face take the form of the previous Li, though it was but momentary.

"I surrendered," she said. "I have obligations."

"You didn't want this!" Mellor shouted. "Why didn't you tell me more before we came to Zealand? Why?"

"Why?" She sighed, or at least seemed to. "It was secret."

"We shared everything before, do you remember, Li?"

"I have trouble recalling ..."

"I love you!"

"Yes. I remember," she said with a slightly higher register in that ragged voice. "It hurts to remember."

"You're disturbing her," Zhang said. "I knew it was too soon."

The two ignored him, locked in their worlds on either side of the glass. Mellor put up his palm, touching the crystal and, surprisingly, Li Na imitated him. Their hands, his huge and scarred and meaty, hers delicate and pearl. It was almost a touch.

"It is done now. Done now," she said, the repeat like the skip of a sound bite. He knew he was reaching her though. She had answered his declaration of love.

"What's wrong?" Mellor said, as he gazed into her sterile eyes.

"My mind aches. I have no body. I want to sing for you. I can't. Mel ... I loved ..."

"You're a song, Li. Still a beautiful song."

"What I was," she whispered.

"My life," Mellor said.

"What I was." Her voice cracked. He could feel her desolation.

"Li??"

"I want—"

"What's wrong?"

She turned and slid with her back to the barrier, resting against it, face hidden as she curled into a fetal position. She seemed then to have forgotten him, as if she spoke only to herself.

"What I was. What I was," she murmured.

"That's enough," Zhang said. "You're going to damage her."

"What I was. What I was. What I was," she said over and over.

"Retrieve Li Na Ming Huang," Zhang said. "Immediate."

By then, Mellor too had sunk to the floor, anything to be closer to her. She was still inside her Silicon body, her brain nestled in a pan or a fluid, constantly teeming with xenobots, like ants on sweet candy. It was her mind which was wounded, he knew, not her brain.

"Li," Mellor whispered, trying to bring her back, but she continued repeating *what I was* over and over. The black door opened on the white wall and two attendants came through. They also wore white. It was hard to know if they were Select or Silicons. As they stooped and picked her up, their movements appeared to Mellor a kind of masque puppet show. Then he realized she was gone from him in her new manifestation. Still, she was not yet a machine. He could tell she was fighting as she repeated constantly, *what I was*, remembering a previous existence, wanting it desperately. She was struggling to escape and Ayrian Mellor was helpless to aid her.

The attendants lifted Li Na gently and carried her through the door. Mellor remained at the wall, watching the door close, hearing its locks snick into place. He fought to control his emotions. More than anything he wanted to kill Zhang. Just an arm's length away, it would be nothing to snap his neck.

"You did this," he said, not looking at Zhang, fighting his feelings. He had to do more than kill this monster. He needed to follow the plan to entice Zhang's hubris into something foolish.

"I'm saving her, I tell you! You should be grateful," Zhang said. "Indeed, I am saving the Human race."

Mellor stood, facing Zhang. He had wiped his feelings from his face. He had to convince the CEO of his anguish.

"I want to go with her," he said.

"Impossible. You're a mere Dì èr."

"I brought you Ping."

"You can't be serious," Zhang said, though he seemed not at all surprised.

"Maybe you'll need my kind when you get there. For Protection."

"Believe me, Ayrion Mellor, I can take care of myself."

"What if I prove you wrong?"

"What can you possibly mean?"

"BATL. You command against me. I win, I'm on the ARC."

"Or I could finish you now."

"But that wouldn't be interesting, would it? Where's the suspense, the drama, the, what did you call it ... the diversion? Or was all that just talk. Your superior skills ..."

"I created that game!"

"You think I want to die in your OMEGA? I want out. I'm ready to fight for it."

"A duel then. Yes, I like the idea but did you really believe you could goad me into lowering myself to your level?"

"Play off game's in two weeks. San Francisco. Cheng told me it's fixed. We play defensive. They'll come to us. We kill them all."

"He *told* you that? The fool."

"What if we don't shoot? What if we let 'em pass and take our banner?"

"You forget, Mellor, there is no surrender."

"No matter what you think you know about BATL, the thing you don't understand is we all know it's a job. We share a comradeship, a bond, you would never understand. We risk our lives every month, all of us, under that dome. Our teams don't hate each other. If we show the world the game's rigged, you think people won't care?"

"As long as they are entertained? No."

"The Giants won't massacre us."

"They will do as they're ordered."

"How do you know?"

"Perhaps I will command them, after all," Zhang said harshly. "Ah, but wait. I glimpse your little game. You'll not entice me with your challenge. You still don't understand, do you?"

"So, enlighten me. I understand you require a diversion ..."

"The Select are gathering here in Zealand to board the ships that will take us to the ARC. I recall your first time here you noticed our heavy lift rockets and asked what they were. Well, you know now. There is literally, Ayrion Mellor, nothing you can do but finish your life with a victory in the game you were created to play. Provide the final flourish to signal the end of the species Homo sapiens."

"Dì yī Select. Got all the answers," Mel replied, smiling now the deadly grin of the predator, eyes a dull steel. If a note of triumph had slipped into his tone, Zhang had missed it.

"You lumbering, vulgar Dì èr! You have *no answers*! Get out of my sight!"

Mellor turned and strode out, not looking back. A Silicon soldier left Zhang's side to accompany him. Mellor composed a message on ALTNET. Ping swirled into existence on his lens, clear as a bell.

"Got your blink," Ping said.

"He didn't take the bait," Mellor said. "Almost, but he won't fight me. Stay low. He's dangerous."

"I'm safe until I've *resolved* his problem. I will look like I'm searching. I'm creating a code for the NET/ALTNET switch but it isn't complete. Only by an instruction will anyone be able to make it work. They must be *told* the blink combination by someone in authority. People will have to do it themselves."

"That's fine. What's the world going to watch in six weeks?"

"BATL, of course. If you win, you tell everyone. That was the plan?"

"Or maybe not."

"I'm afraid I don't understand."

"I might be dead before then. We're really gonna need Ke Hui."

"Why?"

"To provide the prompt when you're ready. We're gonna have to switch tactics."

"What about BATL? World Conquest?"

"They won't see BATL. They'll see war."

FIFTY-SEVEN—KE HUI

With her intelligence, curiosity and youthful fearlessness, Ke Hui Feng 第一 Ψ had engaged with I & I nearly non-stop since Ping and Mellor departed. Indeed, it was those qualities, along with a strong sense of synergy, which allowed her to grasp the complexities of both the NET and the ALTNET, comprehend their common language, and recognize they had been working in tandem since one or the other had achieved sentience. Now, with the help of the ALTNET, she had instructed I & I to locate and query all Dì yī Managers below the rank of CEO in every MEG's department or ministry, worldwide. The message was simple yet nebulous and clearly invited a response.

Simple survey. If allowed one article, which would you bring with you to ARC?

Ke Hui was sure because so few knew of ARC, that unless they had been invited, they would naturally follow their curiosity by submitting a return query for details. She further instructed I & I to use its pro-lific powers to identify suitable individuals according to their replies.

Ke Hui would study the return information, composing subtle replies to each, sizing up their characters with the one tool I & I did not possess: *intuition*. Finally, over two weeks, with those she found co-operative, having briefed them on the truth of ARC and OMEGA, she possessed a small army of very important people. It was a desper-ate though necessary ploy to ask those people, when summoned by an unusual blink, to read a world-changing message to the inhabitants of their MEGs and MASSes, then assume control of government with trusted allies until after the revolution was won or lost. Everyone knew the penalty for rebellion. No one knew what success would look like.

It all hinged on a game.

With the invisible hand of technology manipulated by data-driven tactics and dystopian oversight, people found themselves increasingly slotted into the respective sides of an ideological divide. The fact that the platforms defining the public sphere were controlled by the Dì yī elite did not bode well for Ke Hui's new governing system: electoral algorithmic democracy.

There was a new species arising, born of the technological advances of the Human genius. Indeed, Ke Hui thought, one might consider *three* species. First, there were the Humans, like Otsi'tsa Zaharie and all those living in the MASS. Second, there were the partially Human: the nearly immortal Ms. Qui Ling Yeong 第一 α Ψ, Mr. Wei Qiang Zhang 第一 α Ψ and all the other Select with their synthetic bodies trying to advance evolution from Homo Sapiens to Homonid Technicalus. Finally, from what she now knew from her work with I & I, there were millions of Silicon beings who, with the arrival of NET sentience, needed to be counted as individual *beings* in all their forms and variations.

Could Humanity survive sentient Silicons, and if so, could Humans find meaning and purpose if machines made Human contribution superfluous? The CORPORATE itself could be seen as an algorithmic assemblage. Was there a possibility for co-habitation or symbiosis between Humans and Silicons? If the revolution succeeded who would govern the new Earth and how? With machine algorithms embedded in sociotechnical structures, would sentient Silicons be shaped by Human communities into their communities' standards?

There was but one answer to all of it. *Inclusion.* Under democratic algorithmic governance the integration of digital intelligence needed to be rooted in frameworks of accountability where social intent coupled with Human input would define acceptable behaviours and technological advances in both species. With the assistance of I & I, Ke Hui built a list of leaders from both MEG and MASS. They composed the words to be used on OMEGA/ARC Day, the day of world revolution."

FIFTY-EIGHT

San Francisco **MEG** resembled Rome Meg and a few others. Coastal, but with high hills, the MEG's domes were separate, tied together by bullet train tubes: one on the San Francisco hill, one across the great bridge (now refurbished and tubed in) at Sausalito and finally, a massive series of domes within domes covering what had been Oakland, where the BATL dome was located.

The visitors' dressing room was stark and grey and grimy. Everything had been prepared to make the visiting Raptors uncomfortable. Most of the rest of the complex beneath the stands in the BATL dome was sealed off from them. They had a suite of the usual rooms but it was walled off from all else with foamstone.

The Raptors' flight had arrived on time, but the San Francisco MEG official had insisted every person be examined by medical Silicons. Observing now, as the three hundred team members and support staff were individually assessed, Mellor realized the ruse played by the CORPORATE to disadvantage his team.

Everything had been a frenzy to get ready for the game. All athletes have their pre-game rituals, but the lack of time and minimal accommodation had set the entire team on edge as they gathered, some still dressing, around a dais containing a holovision of their half of the pitch and the thick, squat body of Yong Jun Cheng 第一 y dressed in a Raptors' uniform. Again, he wore his medals.

"Alright everyone, I want no further complaints. We follow my plan. A defensive ring, all sixty players."

Instantly Bolus Kimathi stood, his presence gigantic, his anger palpable. When he spoke, it was more a bark than a voice.

"You do that we'll be cornered! No room to maneuver. No defence in depth. Let's hear something from our Commander!"

The Raptors cheered his words. Cheng cut them off by firing his pistol. The bullet hit the roof and disappeared into the foamstone. There was silence.

A stone-faced Mellor sat quietly beside Otsi.

"Mel? Say something!" Bolus said. Mellor glanced up at him, turned his head, and stared back at the podium.

"Sit down, Kimathi! One more word, Penal Colony!" Cheng turned on his heel and departed the dressing room.

In that instant the hologram of the pitch faded, replaced by a media feed. Two sportscasters, a man, and a woman, both perfectly groomed and dressed. Blaring music and swirling, kaleidoscopic colours rocketed around the two commentators ending with a bold title superimposed. NET-SPORT SPECIAL! Then, over the title, as if by magic, the broadcasters came alive.

"A stunning development, fans: this game will be *No Surrender*. Never in BATL has this ever happened!" the male commentator said.

Then the woman took the narrative: "It's going to be bloody!"

"It means massacre," the man said.

"So, tactics," the woman said, "do you go for it, risk it all, or hang back and hope?"

"With Raptors' new coach Yong Jun Cheng Dì yī gamma leading the team, who knows. Rumors of conflict in the Raptors' ranks. Raptors have a lot of new fighters, trying to rebuild the team after their last two engagements."

The woman again, perfectly timed, said: "Blink NETSPORT for details."

"No one will count out the best player in BATL today, Ayrian Mellor Dì èr alpha. A fan favourite even in opposing MEGs, you can never tell what genius he'll show."

The woman came in: "Think of it! The test of who dies and who moves on to WORLD CONQUEST! What a match!"

As the two commentators continued there was a strange sensation through the room: the rustling of uneasy players. Mellor stepped onto the dais.

"Listen up!" he shouted, then awaited the quiet. "The game is fixed. Cheng knows it's fixed. Giants are supposed to come at us. The idea was to create a slaughter. I wanna pull out of this.. I wanna withdraw but then we lose by default. We can't lose, but we're *not* gonna massacre an entire team. I want our fire discipline at the max. Nothing, not even a burp, unless I signal. There's more at stake here than this game, and even World Conquest. I can't tell you yet, but we gotta get outa this game first."

"I wish I had an answer," Bolus said. "So, any ideas Mel? Zones! Now I'm nervous ..."

"I think I do," Mellor said, standing again. "You people know how to march? Yeah, we're not the dress parade types." He smiled. "In fact, people see us marching outside the dome ... we'd scare 'em half to death! But this day we're gonna march. We're gonna form up in parade order, all squads, and we're gonna march down the centre of our half of the field. There's no ridgeline so Giants'll see us. It's what I'm counting on. Just believe in me, people, the Giants don't wanna die any more than us."

So, it happened. The Giants were already on the field their Commander positioning them in a kind of arrow offence. They halted momentarily when they caught sight of the marching Raptors who entered the dome then up the middle of the pitch. Tin soldiers, with Mellor, Bolus and Woral carrying their banner at the front. They came to a halt at mid-field, but three men continued toward the Giants' lines, no weapons in sight.

The Giants' Commander, a huge south Asian woman, just stared at them. She ordered her force to stand down. She signalled her goaltender forward with their banner. It was turquoise with the former Golden Gate Bridge impressed upon it in silver. The two walked two hundred yards to meet the Raptors' delegation near mid-field. The audience was silent.

The two small groups halted two metres apart. Mellor took the Raptors' banner from Woral while the Giants' Commander did the same. When some of the gnat cams closed in, Mellor swatted them down. Then the two Commanders talked softly for some time. Finally, the Giants' leader handed Mellor her standard.

Pandemonium in the stands.

Their afternoon of action stolen from them, the MASS in the stands began to riot. It was wild blood pulsing gouged eyes shattered limbs torn ears stomping, shoving, pummelling, screaming, panic, fury, the dead on the ground; then Silicon police weighed in with tear gas, batons, rubber bullets, neuronic whips and inhuman ruthlessness.

In the MEG seating area people were only slightly less furious. There was shouting and pushing, a few chairs yanked from their bolt holes and thrown. Normally placid, people were pushing for the exits, wanting to spread the word of this ... this ... travesty.

The CORPORATE had made new enemies.

And the Raptors were hosting WORLD CONQUEST.

And no one had died.

FIFTY-NINE—KE HUI

The storm howled outside the Toronto MEG domes. Black, grey, purple, the clouds roiled low and aggressive over Lake Ontario. The water reflected the clouds adding a component of their own with their heavy metallic waves and silver foaming tips, roiling toward the shore. The sky would not be outdone, however, in this exhibition of nature's power. Lightning bolts golden, then fiery carmine, then sheen green shot their power into the water and the water, prompted to add to the spectacle, received the bolts and fired back its own. The lightning was fashioned by the water into dazzling balls which rolled hundreds of metres across the lake's surface. Meanwhile flying debris picked up by the gales and blown impossible distances bumped and broke against the MEG's walls. This was one of the worst derechos anyone had ever seen. It brought with it tornadoes with killing funnels and sheeting rain. Outside was death and destruction. Inside was a small beach, safe and calm.

Ke Hui Feng 第一 Ψ and Otsi'tsa Zaharie 大众 o sat together on the sand, each digging her toes in the sand. They watched the storm outside. The turmoil kept the girls' attention for a long time but then reached its peak and passed. Then they addressed the issues troubling them.

"Has anyone suspected you?" Otsi asked.

"Only occasionally," Ke Hui replied, though her eyes had that blankness telling Otsi she was still online. "Who would have dreamed I would be plotting revolution in my sixth month of apprenticeship?"

"Can't they track you?"

"I'm on the ALTNET with Ping and I & I."

"They're in Zealand!"

"Without them none of us would have been able to stop thisARC/OMEGA plot."

"How come I'm here? In the city? I thought no Dàzhòng were permitted."

"That's why we changed your lobule and bought you some decent clothes. You now appear to be a proud Dì sān beta. You aren't NET connected but no one will know, so long as you don't engage anyone."

"And our new place?"

"It's Mel's. He can't live there for fear of assassination, and no one will expect the two of us, though the porter will be suspicious of a Dì sān unless you appear to be my servant. I hope you don't mind."

"But I should be practising with the team. Only three weeks—"

"You will, but I asked for you, Otsi, because I believe you can serve a greater need."

"But I'm a Striker. I'm from the MASS. Actually, even further from the MASS. Awenda, my clan's country."

"Don't you see I need you? If we succeed in this, we should leave most things in place until we arrive at suitable alternatives. All the Select are in Zealand. I've been in touch with most of their seconds. They are all quite suddenly calling on their Division Managers to open their realms for inspection. We will remove the corrupt or those refusing to co-operate. I believe I can handle that here, but there is a much greater obstacle in the way."

"What is it?"

"Why don't we take a walk along the beach. Here come Sili sweepers, cleaning up. I don't want to be near them."

The two girls rose from the sand, sweeping it from their bodies, the caramel silicon so dry and fine it fell off them anyway. They turned east, walking toward the MEG's interior harbour, currently choked with ships seeking safety.

"So, what do you need from me?" Otsi asked.

"We believe, Ping and I, after the initial shock and if Mel can make the blink and speak the words, the MEG populace should remain mostly stable. Eventually, though, things will change and most significantly in the MASS. Otsi, I'm going to have to work with the MASS and try to understand them. As we've both seen, they have leadership but why would they trust me? You have lived there. I need you to be my connection. I need you to be my voice. I'm sure initially I will be resented but there is so much to do."

"Ke Hui, why would anyone listen to me?"

"You underestimate yourself, Otsi: you're friendly, smart, tough and you're one of them. It will take time and I know they have their regimes out there but, well, their economy must change.

"A few days ago, Bolus and I took my Silicon Toy to recycling. While food recycling happens here in the MEG, and other materials are reprocessed, especially Omegan technology, the rest just disappears. We smuggled Toy onto a bullet train's recycling run. I remained on a loop with it. Do you know where it went?"

"My bet is they sent it west to the desert then dumped it."

"Close, Otsi, but worse. They don't even go to the desert. There are two large lakes just north of the Winnipeg MEG, which is, itself, not a big place but quite important. There are few Humans there required to supervise the thousands of Silicons offloading the garbage and ensuring it is shipped and dumped into the largest lake. Before he terminated, Toy sent all this, and I have the images stored in my EProm for later use."

"You mean this whole recycling thing … the biggest part of the MASS economy is a fake? Zones, Ke!"

"Softer, Otsi. I'm afraid it's true: the OMEGA plot, if we can't stop it, will destroy the planet."

"I thought the Select just wanted to get away," Otsi said.

"They fear being followed by a race of AI more powerful and intelligent than Humans. They want to start over on a distant planet."

"What?"

"But we're going to stop it and once things settle and I try to communicate with the resistance and other leaders in the MASS, I'll need you and Willis to create a base. Just think, Otsi. Giving the MASS the technology it needs while employing people to plant trees rather than tear down infrastructure, to actually rebuild that infrastructure, create a governing process with more humane algorithms and, finally, and this came from Ping, offering people in the MASS *connection* to the NET, or whatever I & I has become. They need hospitals out there, and housing capable of withstanding storms like this last one."

"There are farms, Ke. I've seen them north of here. I heard there were many more around this lake and west of here."

"Why couldn't we cover those farms in *chitin/crystalline?* I'll need you to accompany me to see these places. We must reclaim this planet, Otsi. It will take generations but only if everyone, MEG, MASS, and those from the waste zones, is included."

"How do you change the caste system?" Otsi said.

"We'll abolish it. I think we'll also have to offer MEG people the power of *separation* from the NET to give them more privacy. And then there is the AI. Ping is the one closest to I & I though I'm getting through to it, or them. We'll need Ping after this hack to be a spokesman to the Silicons. His connections with the Dì sì will help us bring them onside. If there are more Humans who can talk with them, we'll have a better understanding of the Silicons' needs and wants."

"We gotta win this BATL first, Ke. It's not a given. Mel is trying to think what Zhang will do to finish us all. Last time Mel beat the *no surrender* rule. I'm sure Zhang was furious."

"Otsi," Ke Hui said. "I know you're a warrior first but if we succeed we will terminate BATL."

"I guess I'm gonna volunteer as your bodyguard."

"Oh, you're going to be much more than that. You're going to be my voice and simultaneously the voice of the MASS. You're not only a warrior, Otsi'tsa Zaharie, you'll be the agent of change."

The two girls found themselves at the end of the sand. They stepped onto the moving sidewalk which would take them to Mel's place. Just two girls at the beach, as the storm passed, and the sun appeared.

SIXTY—MELLOR

The month passed too quickly. All the drill, running formations, analyzing tactics again and again, searching for something to give the Raptors an advantage. On the holo table, their end looked like a normal BATL field with plenty of cover, potential ambush sites, and a fine stand for their banner and the defensive team. It looked too good. The only thing at all suspicious was a twenty-metre-high ridge at mid-field. It was clear they were going to have to reach and control that ridge if they were to achieve victory.

They knew the Xian Dragons, but now after a month of watching and analyzing their matches throughout the year, the team was discouraged. They hadn't been able to pinpoint a single recurring action which might let them out-maneuver the Dragons. They hadn't found a soft, or reckless squad leader of whom they might take advantage. They'd found nothing but a disciplined, courageous, well-oiled force which could adapt its tactics in minutes.

The dressing room was quiet as fighters donned their body armour: first the soft body panels, then the hard plates made from ceramic composites, often with a backing of Kevlar. Then, of course, came the uniform. Ironically, on this day both teams possessed the same red on black crest, red numbers on black/field grey camo and dark helmets. As the visiting team, the Dragons had changed uniforms to brown, beige camo.

Out of the blaring, tension filled music and past the whirl of the NET matrix, the flaming outline of BATL: WORLD CONQUEST

338

waved like a flag over a shot of the audience. Two different sportscasters, the ones from the San Francisco MEG had apparently been killed in the riots, appeared superimposed over the shot. If they felt anxious, it didn't show at all. The man and the woman, both in formal finery: the man in a Tangzhuang Tang suit with black, red embroidered high collar; the woman in an elegant, black sheath shoulderless evening dress.

The initial shots and music continued with an added: NET-SPORT SPECIAL! It brought the Raptors silently toward the dais to watch. Then, the broadcasters spoke.

"The *no surrender* rule withdrawn, a stunning development!"

The woman took up the narrative: "For the first time in BATL history, with the unfortunate loss of their Commander and Vice during a practice session, the Xian Dragons' new Commander, a Dì yī alpha Select will take the field. This has never happened in battle history! More info? Blink NET SPORT and learn about Wei Qiang Zhang Dì yī alpha Select!"

Again, the man spoke: "No one will count out the best player in BATL today, Ayrian Mellor Dì èr alpha. A fan favourite even in opposing MEGs, you can never tell what creativity he'll show when the game starts but now he's up against an actual Dì yī commander!"

The woman came in: "Think of it! Ayrion Mellor Dì èr alpha versus the illustrious Wei Qiang Zhang Dì yī alpha Select! What a match!"

As the two commentators droned on there was a strange sensation through the room. No one had been told. A Dì yī commanding the Dragons? The rustling of uneasy players shifted through the room.

"By the Father," Mellor said.

"Huh?" Otsi mumbled, confused.

"He played me again."

"Who? Who played you? What?"

"On Zealand I challenged Zhang to a duel, my command against his. I thought he'd refused me. I told Ke Hui and Ping he was staying on Zealand."

"This is *World Conquest*," Bolus said. "He'll wanna make sure he wins."

"Yeah," Otsi said, "but how will he do it?"

"I think I know," Mellor said. "Otsi, you brought the colour canisters?"

"You ordered every weapon from the MASS?"

"What's the deal?" Bolus asked.

"Go now to the armoury. Everyone gets the MASS weapons we brought and trained on. I'm gonna play Zhang where he least expects it. High calibre."

Bolus' golden grin could have filled the room. He departed at a trot.

"Killme's gonna start his team talk in a minute. All Strikers. You got ten minutes. Otsi, get the smoke and tell the Strikers and Flankers how to use 'em."

"Done," Otsi said. She rose from her seat as Cheng entered. By the time he reach the dais she was lost behind all the bodies so much bigger than hers. Cheng muttered his peroration and as the hologram of the field re-appeared, pointed toward it.

"Strikers fly forward, report deployments, then back to give aerial cover to our defensive ring. Now, let's have a cheer! Team Raptors! Yo! Raptors!"

There was no response but the petrified panic of people knowing they are condemned to death. A static defence would doom them to massacre or a gap with no reserve to fill it. A few of the rookies sitting near the dais tried to cheer, but the rest of the room refused to take up with them.

"That's no cheer," Killme Cheng said. "What's wrong with ..."

Ayrion Mellor stood then, his size commanding, his reputation superseding the helpless Cheng.

"Listen up!" Mellor said, his voice booming through the room. "You go out there like this we all die! Look at us. We've been cheated, beat up, burned; lost a lot of good people. We're better than that. Who are we?"

"Raptors," came the disheartened team's response.

"No, you're not!" Mellor shouted. "Now stand up! Come on! All of you! We've been played by the CORPORATE all our lives! Time to fight for ourselves. Now, WHO ARE WE?"

They were all standing now, morale slowly seeping back into them.

"Raptors!" some called out. The veterans.

"Come on! For once Killme is right! That's no cheer! WHO ARE WE?"

"RAPTORS!"

"WHO?

"RAPTORS, RAPTORS, RAPTORS!" reverberated around the room.

Cheng left the room in a huff. When he was gone Mellor took his place.

"You're gonna use the MASS weapons we trained with. Kimathi's handing them out at the armoury. Use only what you've trained on. We can shoot them at a distance, disorganize them until they figure it out. Squad leaders meet me at our ten mark! Let's go!"

They marched down the tunnel into the BATL dome, their fighting spirit restored. Yet when they arrived, they were struck by a further, and far more frightening, circumstance. On the monitors they could watch before they entered the BATL dome they saw Zhang, dressed in scarlet battle gear, arriving in the dome behind the Dragons. Accompanying him as he entered were eight Humanoid Silicons, all painted crimson, all armed with *pulse rifles*. Far above in the broadcast booth the sportscasters took up the narrative again.

"Dragons are on the field. Look there, Dì yī commander Zhang has brought Silicons!"

"Armed Silicons! What's going on here?"

"Hear that grumble from the crowd?"

"At the Raptors' end, there's Ayrion Mellor!"

Mellor signalled his team into place. Otsi and Bolus, both amped to the max, were more than ready to fight. Woral, nearby, appeared unsteady.

"When do we do this?" Otsi asked.

"We're still online," Mellor replied. "Wait 'til we're on comms."

Within a second of null NET, Mellor began to speak.

"Alright. Listen close. This Zhang thinks he's a hot shot. Claims he was part of inventing the game. Still, he's not all that sure of himself. He didn't come alone. Eight Silis are big firepower. So, he intends to win but we're gonna give him a little surprise."

Mellor turned to Otsi and Alf Watson, squad leader for the Flankers.

"Okay, our side we know. This landscape is good for us, lots of brush and dunes and ridges, especially that one at mid-field. I'll bet Zhang expects to flank us, feint one flank and push on the other. Create a retreat to a banner cluster. Otsi, look carefully at *their* two thirty mark up to the ridge. They'll have their Strikers out too so avoid 'em if you can. Otsi, how many smoke cans did you give out?

"Four each."

"Don't initiate until my command. Alf, your Flankers will advance on each flank to the ridge, then curl in. We follow procedure at the beginning. Get to that ridge and see what they're up to but don't take any chances. Otsi comes back to report while Tiegan and Oxana lay down smoke to cover our moves."

"Dome scrubbers'll clear it," Oxana, a small red-headed firebrand, said.

"Not if we time it," Mellor said. "And you're forgetting the Flankers. They've got smoke too. Go on my signal…"

"Not this time, Mellor! I'm in command! You've been relieved!" Woral's voice screeched as he advanced on the group.

"Sorry Woral, change of plan."

"Coach Cheng'll have your ass in a sling."

"He's not our coach. Okay, listen up!" Mellor said. "You guys remember Pascal's Full Court Press?"

Most Squad leaders acknowledged, confused but alert. Woral stepped up.

"That's insane!"

Mellor ignored Woral, continuing his briefing.

"We've trained for it; you know what to do. Rookies follow as best they can. Re-deploy at our thirty with our usual start formation. Five minutes! Move now, Dragons are pumped to come at us fast."

"You can't do this!" said Woral said.

"Just watch me!" Mellor replied.

While Woral and Mellor argued Otsi pulled Bolus aside as everyone else deployed.

"What's Full Court Press?"

"All squads forward. We hit 'em with everything we got."

"I've never seen it. Never even heard of it."

"That's 'cause it's never been done."

With the commotion of fighters dispersing around them, Woral pulled a handgun from its holster. He stepped close to Mellor, concealing it from the others.

"Coach Cheng thought you'd try something."

"Woral, what's this?"

"Execution. You just made it easy with all this confusion."

"Why? I'm tryin' to protect you."

"I do this, I'm out. They promised."

"You believe Cheng? *Killme* Cheng?

"Not just him. That Dì yī commander. He's got his own guard. Silicons. It's your fault. They wanna get rid of you and who cares about the rest of us. I'm not gonna be collateral damage in your private war."

"Woral, we're pawns in this plot. I've had my eyes opened. I've got a way out."

"I want out now!"

"Look Woral, NET's off and you're locked in here with the rest of us. Think you'll get out? Think you matter at all to Zhang. He's using you."

"But ... they gave their word."

"You don't believe it yourself," Mellor said, reaching, gently grasping Woral's gun hand.

"Mel, those Silicons got pulse rifles. There's no chance for any of us!"

"Woral, trust me. I got this."

Woral paused a moment, then released the gun, a broken man. Bolus joined them then, just catching a glimpse of Woral holstering his weapon.

"Somethin' wrong?" he asked.

"Not anymore," Mellor said, placing his hand on Woral's shoulder, while Bolus took up his position by Mellor's side, realizing he'd missed an attempted assassination. Mellor seemed as though nothing had happened while Woral looked deathly pale.

"Where do you want me?" Woral asked.

"Our banner, Woral. But not stationary. I want you to keep it on the move just back of the line. We've gotta do everything they don't expect, or we're gone. You with me now?"

"I'm ... I'm sorry, Mel. I thought—"

"You thought you'd be free. If this goes right, you'll be more free than you can imagine."

"I'll do this, Mel. I get it. It's not just *you* they want anymore, is it?"

"At the end of this game, unless we stop 'em, the Dì yī Select are deserting the planet and plan to destroy it!. It's the truth, but there's a countermand. We have a plan in place. We *must* win this BATL. Now go, my friend. If I go down, don't let up, you take command. This is all about bounding, feinting, and flanking. If they can't find our flag, they can't take it."

Somehow, this settled Woral. He nodded his head in acknowledge-ment and left to form up his Point Guards and Blockers for their ad-vance. Mellor watched him go then turned to Bolus.

"What was that?" Bolus asked. "He gonna kill you?"

"He's got PTSD. Psych should have taken him out months ago. Zhang got to him. Used his desperation to end this match before it started. Don't go all apologetic. I had it in hand."

"I didn't even see it. Didn't expect it. Losing my edge—"

"You're not losing anything, but this plan puts you in charge of our left flank. So, you drift your people mobile left and hope to roll up their flank."

"Where you gonna be?"

"Right flank with Fullbacks, going straight down."

"What about centre?"

"Woral's got it. Remember? He'll do this, Bo. He's got nothing to lose now, and he knows it."

On the NET, the presenters re-appeared.

"Teams are deploying as usual," the male sportscaster said. "Creating a strong base to start. Something strange at the Raptors' end. What are they doing? I do hope it's not an attempt to surrender."

His female partner took over, covering for his miscue.

"I've never seen this formation. Zones! Oh! Excuse me! I think they're taking their Standard with them! The entire team in echelon, advancing to the thirty mark."

"Both teams are moving. In the one end the Dragons using a normal advance. Defensive squads back. Not the Raptors! No defense! I don't get this. They're advancing. They're moving fast with *everyone* along one battle line! What is this?"

* * *

Mellor and Otsi waited at the thirty mark. Mellor went on comms. The replies were confident, though the entire force had been taken by surprise at the change in tactics. Still, they trusted Mellor, the best in their business. Their reports confirmed their positions.

"Go now?" Otsi asked.

"Right now!" Mellor said, exactly as we planned. He turned to his comms. "All squads, double time, up and over mid-field. Keep the line! Hold the ridge!"

* * *

"There go their Strikers!" the female commentator said. "Raptors' Strikers rise into the air, flying forward now, hovering above that mid-field ridge. Dragons' Strikers rise to meet them but rather than attack ... what in the name of the Father is this? Raptors! They're dropping something along the ridge line. Look there. The mid-field ridge has erupted in a *rainbow* of coloured smoke. Raptors' Strikers engage the Dragons in their own territory. And there, the Warriors' battle line races toward the ridge. Billowing colours of smoke at mid-field. Dragons have paused their advance just short of the ridge. Looks like confusion in their ranks."

"What's going on?" the male sportscaster asked.

"BATL history, sports fans!" the woman said.

"Shut up, Moira! This isn't right! I can't see anything for this smoke. Wait. There's a Raptor. It's Otsi'tsa Zacharie rising out of the rainbow."

"More on Otsi'tsa, blink NETSPORT."

***

In the air, Otsi engaged the opposition. The air combat was intense: casualties on both sides shooting, diving, darting, going to ground. A Dragon Striker flew at Otsi, firing wildly on full auto. Close miss. Otsi boosted upward to the top of the dome, flipped in the air, then falling, began firing back. The Dragons Striker never knew what hit her. She spiralled down to a crash.

***

"Did you see that move by Zacharie, fans? Brilliant, though reckless," the female said, her voice a kind of shriek.

"Roiling smoke almost alive in front of them," the male commentator said, also in an unusual pitch. "The Dragons are milling about, looking bewildered. Well, they're not alone. Ayrion Mellor has come up with a tactical shocker once again!"

"Not sure the Dragons' Commander Zhang knows quite what to do with this," the woman said. "He continues to send Flankers into the fog but when they get clear of it, they're easy targets. Wait! Now the Raptors' battle line is exploding through the coloured murk, firing all weapons as one. These are very strange weapons! I've never seen them. Dragons are being mowed down, caught in the open. No chance. No mercy."

SIXTY-ONE—OTSI

On the left flank Bolus, leading two Sweepers with Flankers crisscrossing back and forth in front of his advance, rolled up the unprepared Dragons' right wing in a hailstorm of fire. An unstoppable advance. Beside Bolus' troops, Woral, with the Raptors' banner in hand, was protected by his Blockers as he advanced part way down the ridge. Mellor saw him as he came through the smoky, coloured wisps, drifting toward the scrubbers.

"Keep going, Woral! Form up behind Bolus! Over," Mellor said on comms. He then gathered his own attack unit and ordered them to follow. He aimed to take his own right flank with his squads of Point Guards and a Striker with an M249. Then he and his Fullbacks, hugging the lowest part of the dome would move forward quick time. He realized his advance made him and his fighters subject to ricochets off the walls. No matter now. He had to get to Zhang and his Silicons while confusion reigned on the Dragons' side.

"Right flank, Dragons' thirty mark," he said. "No opposition. Need more smoke, Otsi. Paste their fifteen, extreme right at the glass!"

In a moment Otsi had delivered. Purple smoke billowed up at the edge of the dome. Mellor and his Fullbacks ran through the florid fog. His focus was on his ultimate target though he continued listening on comms to the battle behind him. Comms were alive with back and forth, but no panic. At the Dragons' thirty centre mark a battle broke out.

The Dragons held their ground within a grouping of earthen mounds. Raptors began to fall; too many of them. A direct hit on a Raptors' Sweeper blew it apart. Fragments flew as terrible shrapnel.

The Raptors' were stopped by a withering fire. Bolus' unstoppable flank advance had stalled. The Raptors' Flankers zoomed up the hills, airborne, firing down, trying to break the Dargons' formations, and paying heavily.

Bolus commed Otsi. "Stopped on their thirty. Need air support. Over."

"Leave that to me," Otsi said, "I'm our last Striker!"

For Mellor this was a turning point: protect his people or go all out at Zhang. There was never really any question.

"Can't spare you now, Otsi," Mellor said. "Bolus, bring up Woral's Point and Power guards. Use 'em to attack. Over. Sweeper Two, vector thirty-five left centre: suppressing fire. Over. Okay, people, make a show! Keep their heads down!"

The Sweeper ATV fired madly as offensive players worked their ways forward beneath the lead zipping above them. Woral, still with the flag amid his remaining Guards was no longer hanging back.

"Woral, what you doin'? You stay back. Over," Bolus said.

"My squads! My command!" Woral replied. "You're at Dragons'centre thirty right now. Take your left flank and curl in! Engage now!"

At that moment Woral was hit. Something had found a way past his armour and under his arm. There was not much blood, yet his face began to turn grey. The Blockers advanced up the mounds throwing flash grenades. The Dragons broke and began to retreat. By that time Bolus reached Woral. Dying, the lieutenant/goaltender passed the Raptors' standard to Bolus. He could not speak, the passing of the banner his final gesture.

"Woral down. Flag up. They're running!" Bolus shouted into his comms, boosting the ferocity of the advance. Meanwhile, at the Dragons' ten mark Mellor's Fullbacks faced an unclimbable cliff up to the Dragons' bunker, still partly concealed by smoke. Mellor knew it was important his men knew he was still alive. He opened his comms to all Raptors, speaking calmly into the mic.

"This is Mellor. I'm ten metres from their bunker, right flank. Chase 'em down but don't let 'em get back here."

The Raptors responded like a well-oiled machine. They hunted the Dragons in a series of vicious fire fights which had no end but death. The Dragons were in disarray: panicked, going down under Raptors' fire, they awaited commands from their new commander. None came. Zhang was arranging his own defence. It had all happened too fast.

He could not recall the game being so swift. He just couldn't keep up with his squad leaders' reports. This wasn't supposed to happen. The game had been structured to terminate Mellor, showing the mastery of the Dì yī. It wasn't working.

***

From above, the woman said shrilly: "We've never seen anything like this! It's carnage."

"At this rate," the male sportscaster replied, "there won't be enough of either team to accept the WORLD CONQUEST trophy!"

***

On the rise at the Xian bunker, Zhang wore a faux set of Qin armour, bright scarlet. Encased in his suit he was safe from most bullets. Still, he ensured he was behind the wall of his Silicon soldiers. They responded instantly to his commands.

"Weapons at ready!" Zhang said, a note of panic in his voice.

Below him and ten metres away, Mellor's team remained obstructed by the incline. Mellor spoke through his comms: "No way in. Otsi, go high. Find me a way up or around this rise. Over."

Zhang glanced up at Otsi as she began to rise.

"Terminate opposition!" Zhang commanded his Silicons. "Now! Over there you creatures! On our left, low!"

Immediately the Silicons moved to the lip of the rise, opening up with pulse rifles. The lasers crisscrossed the Fullbacks as they aimed their weapons. The pulses exploded into the Fullbacks, splitting their bodies apart. Then the unthinkable happened. Something no one had accounted for. The pulse weapons did not belong here. If they missed a target the Silicons' pulses struck the dome. Not even *chiton/crystalline* could bear that kind of demolishing power. The dome panes disintegrated; the pulses killing spectators. Pandemonium as spectators tried to run, trampling, grabbing, pushing. War had come unexpected to them.

Mellor dived low into the remaining smoke. Zhang employed his personal pulse weapon to fire up at Otsi. His aim was wild, panicked, smashing more panes. In the air Otsi twisted to avoid his fire. Glassy shards showered around her from the broken dome above.

"Otsi, get out of there!" Mellor ordered. "Get low, then swoop up at centre ten! Cover me. I'm goin' up this rise!"

Otsi dropped like a stone disappearing from Zhang's sight then swooped up with full power, dropping another bomb, enveloping the bunker in mustard yellow, then flew out of Zhang's line of fire. The Silicons remained at the top edge of the rise, slaughtering the Raptors at the base of the cliff.

"Nice work, Otsi. Going left. Going in!" Mellor said as he dodged the Silicons' fire.

"You won't make it!" Otsi shouted into her comms.

"No choice! Got to flank these Silis before the smoke clears."

"You'll die if you do!"

Still looping around in the air Otsi noticed something significant.

"The Silis, Mel. They're all bunched up. I see their lasers. They're all at the edge of the rise shooting at your Fullbacks. Going in!"

"Otsi, don't! It's suicide!"

"I was born for this moment," Otsi replied. "I am a warrior!"

From high in the dome, she angled and dived straight down into the Silicons, shooting all the way. When she struck among them, her flite board exploded in a fiery eruption, smoke of all colours spewed out. Her grenades detonated. The Silicons burned. As did she.

At the ten, a Raptors Flanker appeared with his moto-cross bike. Mellor reacted instantly. He grabbed the machine, the fastest way up the steep incline, if he could make it.

"Jump off!" he commanded as he mounted, revved the engine, then powered up the ten-metre ridge going airborne through the flames. He landed hard, somersaulting, then a roll, then up, crouched, his every sense focused, his handgun trained on his enemy.

Zhang was bleeding and burnt. Still, he smiled, ever arrogant, thumbing his rifle's touch-trigger, then thinking the better of it, lowered the weapon.

"I surrender," he said, endeavouring to appear calm.

"I'll give you more than you gave the Earth. Drop your weapon."

Zhang dropped his rifle. Mellor lowered his gun.

"Mercy, is it?" Zhang growled.

"You don't know the meaning," Mellor responded.

"Correct Ayrion Mellor! Finally, you understand. Do you realize your actions have forced me to lose my chance of eternity. I have given my life over one hundred years to the MEG. You should have died, but you wouldn't. So now for something new. A technology straight from our military labs."

From his sleeve he ejected a hand phaser, a high-powered microwave radiation transmitter, into his palm. He raised the weapon to fire. As he did, Mellor dived and rolled, senses acute, years of training. The phaser missed him. Mellor came out of his roll grasping Li's antediluvian knife, flinging it's scabbard away, he threw the ancient blade. It found Zhang's throat. The stone blade, millennia old, rough, and black and chipped into an arrow shape, pierced Zhang's pearl skin and shot through the delicate dendrites joining his human brain to his synthetic spine.

Zhang clawed at his throat. Bloody gouts poured down his scarlet armour, staining it dark. He collapsed with his brain still alive, his body dying. His eyes were wild with despair. Mellor stepped over him, grasping the Dragons' banner. There were thousands of dead in the grandstands, the effect of pulse rifles through shattered *chiton/crystalline* and additionally, the panicked killing feet of a stampede to safety. Mellor found Otsi. The charred remains of Otsi'tsa Zhaharie, the once lively, talented, brave young girl. Again, she had saved him; this time, his life, and ensured the revolt could continue.

* * *

Meanwhile the sportscasters had become journalists as the unbelievable match became bedlam in the stands. To those watching, a float cam made its way through indiscriminate shapes. The field was a smoking ruin: glass panes crackling, breaking, collapsing, and spectators in a screaming tumult. A reporter's face appeared through the smouldering ruin.

"Float cam, fix on me," she said. "Are we online? Hello? Yes? This is awful! Oh, we're on?" She tried to compose herself. "On this incredible day I'm live with Coach Yong Jun Cheng Dì yī gamma. I guess, I think … what just happened?"

Cheng was shaking with fury.

"Abomination! That's what this is!"

At that moment Bolus entered the picture. One punch of his hammer hard fist crunched into Cheng's face. Cheng collapsed, unconscious.

"We're live here! Please!" the woman said, staring at the remains of Cheng's face.

"We're live!" Bolus said. "Good. Want the man who done this? Beat a zoned out Dì yī who thought he could run the world! Here he comes …"

"Ayrian Mellor!" The journalist exclaimed. She had *the scoop*. Yet as she moved closer, Mellor ignored her. Nearly finished: burnt, bloody, his diamond eyes glittering, the Dragons' banner still in his hands, Mellor stepped outside the now shattered BATL dome, into the camera's frame and blinked.

"Ping, you there?" he said.

"Ayrion Mellor, are you injured?" the reporter said, turning to the float cam and saying: "Ayrion Mellor may be wounded."

"Just off the field, lady. What you expect?" Bolus said.

"But the world is watching."

"Think we don't know?"

Bolus and Mellor stood shoulder to shoulder in front of the float cam, their combined size blocking the reporter and, indeed, filling the entire hologram with the world watching.

"Stay connected everyone!" Mellor said. "Do this for me, your lives depend on it. Blink, then double blink then say or think *Zhàn xiàlái*, Mandarin for *Stand down*. In the MASS, keep watching! Now Ping!"

SIXTY-TWO—EVOLUTION

For those connected to the NET, their world became a kind of psychedelic swirl. All in a matter of twenty seconds, yet perhaps the most integral twenty seconds in Human history, as I & I assumed priority, people watched the tumult of their past fly by in flashes.

At first came colours, tints of fishes and corals, glimpses of autotrophs, then strange giant lizards, then mammals, then humans Australopithecus, Homo Erectus, Neanderthalensis, Homo Sapiens, Homo Sapiens Sapiens, and Homonid Technicalus; then machines: wheels, steam engines, factories, aeroplanes, vehicles, rockets, men on the moon, hydrogen mushrooms, buildings from mud to stone to *chiton/crystalline*; then dancing algorithms, formulae multiplying exponentially, millions of words in millions of languages. It was a dynamic display of evolution.

Mesmerizing, paralyzing, animating, occupying every Human who saw or sensed it, for it all whirled so quickly it seemed instantaneous. No one who witnessed it was not changed by it. Then the swirl became the face of Ping Wang Min and just behind him, the Silicon face of Li Na Huang.

Ping spoke.

"Welcome to I & I, our AI friend bringing you both the NET and the ALTNET. Please do not be alarmed. For you in the MASS, you operators or owners, while maintaining your *reference beam* mirrors in

354

place adjust your *object beam* mirrors to 47 degrees, thirty minutes. I shall pass you back to Ayrion Mellor, to the victor of BATL and a true WORLD CONQUEST."

Mellor spoke.

"You see these flags? They mean nothing. They were symbols to control us. We're pawns. Time to stop fighting BATLs for rations and holidays! The Dì yī created a killing game to distract you from their treachery. It's time to stop living under their powers, using Humans and Silicons as their slaves! They are trying to kill us; leaving Earth behind while destroying it with Omegan nuclear devices!

"All you watching out there. Do something for me. Right now! Learn the truth! All of you in the MEG and the MASS, the time is now for revolution!"

Ke Hui Feng appeared. She stood in a black room within the hologram of Toronto MEG, lighted in points of many colours. No longer the youthful girl: her hair was up in formal Hanshu style with jewelled combs. Her figure was slim, her stance forceful and her face a masque of command. When she spoke her voice no longer retained the lilting tones of a child but a melody of compelling phrases. She was a Force to be reckoned with.

"Hello, my name is Ke Hui Feng. I am acting CEO of Toronto MEG, North America, Western Hemisphere. You perceived, I'm sure, the chaos in changing NETWORKS. The NET was controlled and censored by Dì yī Select. Please observe my lobule. This is the icon of your oppressors. You won't find many of them now. Should anyone see a person wearing a Select icon, please detain them but do not hurt them. We have hurt each other enough.

"The other important task, and your new council of leaders in every MEG will guide you, is to find the enslaved Dì sì in your MEGs and care for them. Their lobule is an Omega sign. They are our heroes: enslaved by the Dì yī they have ever maintained the functionality of our technology.

"As of this day, there will no longer be a CORPORATE. The CORPORATE has deceived us. They were experimenting with thought control in a bid to completely dominate us.

"As for you in the MASS: you have been fooled by the recycling program. It was not meant to assist the planet at all but to keep you busy serving the MEG. You are not slaves! The MEG caste system is now null and void. We are free!

"In a few moments you will be joined by your new temporary Organizers, members of a new World Council. They will explain further steps for a new order. We were the NET and ALTNET, the MEG and MASS. Now we are Humans together, as well as those mechanized Humans and mutants, and a new species, sentient SILICONS. A new icon will be our world symbol. It will look like this:

In this symbol two teardrops swirl to represent the conversion of yin to yang and yang to yin. The dot in the opposite field shows there is always yin within yang and yang within yin. It is the sign of inclusion. It is our common banner now, the one which will unite us. I shall return you to Ping momentarily, giving your new council members time to speak their messages to each of their MEGs. Ping?"

There was a pause then the face of Ping Wang Min with Li Na Huang beside him.

"I was Dì sì Omega, rescued by Ayrion Mellor. The CORPORATE has been removed."

Ping moved behind Li Na.

"This familiar face is Li Na Huang. She was once Human but the Dì yī Select forced her into this Silicon body. She will recover in time and become the beautiful Human she once was. She will not, however, be able to sing, ever again. I simply want you to witness what the CORPORATE was doing to people. Now, let's widen this shot so you can see more of our progress!"

Zealand's domes, ARC transfer rockets glimmering in the distance, the forests and fields were bathed in a tangerine sunrise. Several hypersonic wings could be seen landing. Armed troops, clearly BATL fighters, exited them. Military Silicons littered the tarmac, their programs terminated.

"This is Zealand. A secret Dì yī Select base. This is revolution for all of us, Silicon and Human, are taking back our world. You can help. Join us! No more caste, no more rations, no more zones or Silicon raids. It won't be easy. We must try to restore the climate. We must learn to live equally with our sentient Silicon friends, and they with us. Our new organizers, both Silicon and Human, will present updated economies. Recycling will continue but in a positive way. Did you know there are carbon scrubbers by the hundreds of thousands, the last gasp of the Omegans, lying around useless. No Humans employed them and left no directions for Silicons to do so. We will! Let me show you the next thing we'll abolish."

The hologram became the interior of the Toronto MEG BATL dome, still smoke and tumult. Mellor stood with Bolus, both exhausted, each holding flags. As the holos changed Ping's voice talked over the scene.

"This *was* BATL. It will no longer exist. A game designed to divert you. But now we have a world to win. You heard Ayrion Mellor. Listen well, watch carefully, organize yourselves and leave no one out. Help each other. Help Silicons as well as Humans. We have built machines throughout history, and they have now built themselves into beings of powerful intellect. It is our work to learn to get along and thrive, both Silicons and Humans. We must come together as one, all of us, if we are to survive.

"Our time starts now."

Acknowledgements

When I first considered this project, tracing the *human/machine interface* from its steam powered beginnings to its potential future, I recognized I was going to write each novel from its own unique perspective and in its own style. It was a somewhat daunting concept: three stand-alone novels, connected by theme alone, using a historical fiction style for *Against the Machine: Luddites* (1812), then moving to a contemporary style for *Against the Machine: Manifesto* (2012), and concluding with speculative fiction which brought yet another style forward in *Against the Machine: Evolution* (2212).

Although technology has always appeared in advance of humanity's acceptance of it, the premise remains common to any era. In each case the introduction of technology to the workplace has displaced workers and often created tumultuous social change. Societies inexorably alter with new technologies; from steam driven spinning machines to intergalactic space craft, our inventions eventually make our lives easier. Often it takes years, sometimes generations, for the benefits of new technologies to appear in society and, of course, it leaves certain pockets of humanity behind.

I wanted to explore these continuing waves of change. I wanted to personify three distinct episodes of technological transformation, each separated by two hundred years, bringing the stories of those who either lost or gained and how and why. Finally, and especially in this third novel, I began to realize the danger of untrammelled technology, allowed to ride far ahead of us into the fog of the future. Of course, along with technology came the resulting climate changes which continue as I write, with little hope of global success at tempering them.

I would not have accomplished this trilogy without the patience and generosity of Michael Mirolla and Guernica Editions, allowing me the time and space to research and write these novels. I also owe a debt of gratitude to Diane Eastham for each of her stunning cover designs. There are so many others I would like to thank but the list would be endless. Still, you know who you are and you have my deepest appreciation.

BATL Rules and Regulations

For those readers interested in the BATL segments and wanting to know more, you will find the Rules, Regulations and Tactics on Page 2 of my website: www.authorbrianvannorman.com.

About the Author

Once a teacher, theatre director and adjudicator, Brian Van Norman left those worlds to travel with his wife, Susan, and take up writing as a full-time pursuit. He is the author of four acclaimed novels: *The Betrayal Path, Immortal Water, Against The Machine: Luddites* and *Against The Machine: Manifesto*. The present novel, *Against The Machine: Evolution,* marks the third and final title in his trilogy exploring the human/machine interface.

He has visited parts of every continent and sailed nearly every sea on the planet, Brian makes his base in the city of Waterloo. For more information, check out his website at:

www.authorbrianvannorman.com

Printed by Imprimerie Gauvin
Gatineau, Québec